MURDER WILL OUT

MURDER WILL OUT

A Mystery

JENNIFER K. BREEDLOVE

MINOTAUR BOOKS
NEW YORK

This is a work of fiction. All of the names, characters, organizations, places, and events portrayed in this work are either products of the author's imagination or used fictitiously.

First published in the United States by Minotaur Books, an imprint of St. Martin's Publishing Group

EU Representative: Macmillan Publishers Ireland Ltd, 1st Floor, The Liffey Trust Centre, 117–126 Sheriff Street Upper, Dublin 1, D01 YC43

www.minotaurbooks.com

Designed by Meryl Sussman Levavi

The Library of Congress Cataloging-in-Publication Data is available upon request.

ISBN 978-1-250-38261-0 (hardcover)
ISBN 978-1-250-38262-7 (ebook)

First Edition: 2026

10 9 8 7 6 5 4 3 2

To Maria,
who always said I could

and to Oona, Carolyn, Janet, and Rivkah,
who walked with me while I did

Our dead are never dead to us,
until we have forgotten them.

—George Eliot

Though it abyde a yeer, or two, or thre,
mordre wol out.

—Geoffrey Chaucer

PROLOGUE: THE HOUSE

Cameron House and silence were old friends.

From its beginnings more than two centuries ago, a deep stillness had settled in the mansion's thick walls. It seeped into the floorboards and writhed lazily upward from the granite foundations; it twisted up through the grand stone chimneys and spiraled out with the smoke into the chill Maine nights. The house liked the quiet. Silence made it easier to listen.

On that chilly March afternoon, the silence in the massive old house was broken only by the quick thudding of the one living heartbeat still in the room.

Effie Cameron sat in her ancient rocking chair, facing out at the ever-changing waves as they hurled themselves upon the unyielding granite coast. Her veined hands, folded peacefully in her lap, rested on the afghan she had crocheted many years ago of soft wool dyed in the shifting variegated green-blue of the ocean in summer. For most of her ninety-nine years, Effie had started each day exactly like this: sitting in the front window of the once-opulent mansion her great-grandfather had built over two hundred years ago, counting the lobster boats as they passed, and waving to the islanders who walked the seaside path every morning.

The heartbeat was not hers. Today, her eyes, once bright and crackling with intelligence and humor, were empty; the body was devoid of life. Effie was gone.

The old woman's visitor stood motionless, brightly embroidered couch pillow still dangling from one slack hand, carefully looking anywhere but at the still form in the chair. Killing Effie had not been the plan. But the old woman had been stubborn, unwilling to listen. Unreasonable, shortsighted. And finally, most infuriatingly, so complacent and patronizing—shaking her head at every suggestion, refuting every argument, and at last announcing with icy politeness, "I'm afraid I cannot help you; now, if you don't mind, it's time for my nap. You may let yourself out. Thank you for your kind visit." At which point, she'd turned her head away and closed her sharp blue eyes.

Who did she think she was? *You want a nap? I'll give you a nap, you patronizing cow.*

It had been easier than expected. On some level, Effie's killer had to admit that killing Effie might have been the plan, after all. *No one will know. She was ninety-nine years old; she dozed off quietly in her rocker and never woke up. No one will suspect. It's a mercy, really.*

And now, the next, reasonable, hungry thought, *now it's almost done. Only one more obstacle . . .*

A whisper, faint but unmistakable, floated up from the dead woman in her rocking chair: *Murderer,* it breathed.

The pillow slipped from nerveless fingers to the floor. The visitor's focus jerked back to the body in the chair.

Effie was still dead.

Of course she's still dead, you idiot. You're imagining things.

But another whisper floated across from the other side of the room, out of the shadows near the old butler's pantry; then, another, from the alcove by the fireplace. *Murderer. Murderer.*

The visitor inched backward, heart pounding, toward the finely carved wooden archway leading to the foyer, eyes darting around the room as though looking for the source, catching fleeting glimpses of impossible others in the room: a tall man in a gray suit leaning against the mantel, a pair of elderly women in black bonnets, backs ramrod straight, on the divan. From the shadows behind the old spinet piano, a broad-shouldered fisherman's piercing glare . . . and others, vague blurry others, all whispering accusingly: *Murderer. You killed her. Murderer . . .*

The visitor backed away, lurching unsteadily toward the heavy front door, terrified to look away from the rage and contempt twisting these impossible flickering faces, so many, so very many people, there and yet not there . . . *Murderer*, they whispered, *murderer murderer murderer . . .*

The door would not open; it was stuck. Hands suddenly slick with sweat jiggled the bolt, jerked the handle back and forth, to no avail. The whispers grew into a crescendo of fury, pressing closer—*Murderer murderer you killed her murderer*, they said.

With a final panicked yank, the visitor felt the bolt give way, and the door swung open. No living person observed the terrified individual who slipped out and ran along the coastal path back to the village in the slanting light of the late-afternoon sun. But Cameron House saw, and those it sheltered.

Then the front door closed gently; an unseen hand turned the lock, and some invisible pocket claimed the key.

The bright decorative pillow lay on the floor beside the rocking chair, still bearing a depression on one side, about the size and shape of a face. The paramedics would shove it out of the way when they arrived, and the police would take no notice of it. Miss Effie was so very old; she had obviously died peacefully in her chair on this quiet March afternoon, and it would be a long while before anyone thought to ask questions.

The house could have answered all the questions, if not for its own silence.

But it would remember.

CHAPTER ONE

Somewhere between her third-floor walk-up and the lobby, Willow had spilled coffee on her sleeve. This was not unusual; most of her clothing had coffee or food spots somewhere, the result of too many backpacks and tote bags combined with the leaky travel mug she had never bothered to replace. She almost skipped her mailbox; everything of importance happened online, so the box rarely contained anything but junk. Still, Willow did a quick pivot to the little alcove with its battered square doors, fit her key, and retrieved the sheaf of envelopes and circulars.

She shivered in the chilly predawn as she hurried along the Chicago lakeshore toward the chapel, quickly shuffling through the stack as she walked. She managed to send another splash of coffee over a car dealer's coupon and a Thai carryout menu, narrowly missing the handwritten envelope beneath them. The envelope with no return address, bearing a postmark from Little North Island, Maine.

Her heart gave a twist; she stopped short, and the early-morning jogger nearly collided with her back. Willow barely noticed.

Slowly, mechanically, she tossed the junk mail into the

recycling bin outside the campus chapel. The envelope went into the voluminous pocket of her ancient Irish wool cardigan; she would look at it later.

She wasn't ready to open it now.

Brilliant rays from the orange sphere of the rising sun stretched across the lake waters, bathing Willow and the chapel and the whole campus in golden light. *It reminds me of the sea*, she thought. *But it isn't the sea.* People in Chicago had an annoying habit, she had found, of pretending Lake Michigan was no different from the ocean—of course, most of them had never visited coastal Maine. And on this particular May morning, all Willow could think of was how it was not the ocean.

She fit her key into the university chapel's back entry and wrestled the door open, shoving her backpack into the doorway so the door wouldn't fall closed again. Retrieving her coffee from its precarious spot on the step, she ducked inside and made her way through the sacristy, along the nave, and to the choir loft stairs. Another key, another stairway. By the time she moved through the last door into the organ loft itself, the sunlight was sifting through the stained glass windows down the nave; it scattered colored flecks of light through the rose window above her, framed by the facade of the chapel's grand pipe organ.

Willow dropped her backpack and cardigan next to the organ console, slid off her sneakers, and pulled on her battered and unfashionable black organ shoes. Their smooth soles were nearly worn through to her socks from years of treading the organ pedals, and the squared-off heels had gone lopsided, but they got the job done. She eased into her usual morning routine: scales and études, then a couple of intense hours on a new Duruflé fugue—attacking the same four bars twenty times, twenty different ways, before moving on to the next four. It was tedious work, granular work, but it gave her mind something to focus on, something that was not the envelope in her sweater pocket. Finally, she shifted into her last hour, when she gave herself permission to open up her scores and play the music she loved—Bach, Messiaen, Price—enjoying the instrument and the acoustic.

By now, people wandered the chapel below; Willow could see them moving in and out of the rearview mirror one could find on every organ loft console, put there so the musician could see the progress of the service. Students stopping in to pray that they would do well on their finals (Willow, in her on-again, off-again relationship with God, had a feeling studying might go further in that regard than prayer, but who was she to say?) shared the space with visitors and neighborhood locals. An older woman walked through, holding the hand of the little girl by her side. Willow watched them all in her peripheral vision as she played, feeling a little like the Lady of Shalott, as though her existence, too, depended on viewing the world from a little aside, a little above, and through a mirror. A witness. A watcher. Not quite a participant.

Willow reached into the backpack for one more score. Her hand hovered for a moment; she dropped the pack and picked up her sweater, retrieving the envelope with the Maine postmark. Her hands shook as she carefully slit it open with the nail file on her key chain and pulled out the sheet of stiff cream stationery inside. She immediately recognized the neat handwriting, though she had not seen it in fifteen years. She shifted position so the organ console's light shined on the letter, and started to read.

Dear Willow,

I have begun this note several times, but I find it impossible to say the things I need to; I have so much to tell you and so much I wish to know about you. You are an adult now; your choices are your own, and I hope you can choose forgiveness for the wrongs done to you. If not, perhaps curiosity—or a desire to tell me to my face what you think of me—will bring you back into my life.

But whether you forgive me or not, please come back to Little

North, if not for the wedding, then whenever you can. But please—and this is important—come soon. I know it has been a long time, but you are still part of this place, and it needs you.

The Willow I remember could never resist mystery or adventure. I hope life has not crushed that quality out of your spirit.

There is much more to say, but it will have to wait.

I miss you. Please come.

With love,
—Susan

With love. Sue had signed the letter, "With love." That in itself was enough to make the tears well up. *Sue still loved her. Sue wanted to see her. Sue wanted* her *forgiveness.* A weight Willow had carried for fifteen years lifted off her heart, one so old and familiar she could—sometimes—almost forget it was there.

Willow turned back to the letter, realizing some of its details didn't make sense. For one thing, it was dated March 8, more than two months ago, but the postmark on the envelope confirmed that it had been mailed from Little North just last week. Even more puzzling was the ornate letterhead at the top proclaiming the letter to be from "Dr. Susan Davis, Cameron House, Little North Island, Maine."

Aunt Sue was living in Cameron House? What, Willow wondered, had happened to the cabin, the little log home on the edge of the Cameron acreage, where Willow had stayed with her aunt—honorary aunt, she corrected herself mentally, though Sue had felt more like family than most of Willow's blood relatives—for most of her childhood summers?

Willow's godmother, Susan Davis, had been a close friend of her parents and one of the few adults who didn't find the peculiar little girl to be terribly peculiar. The arrangements had been perfect for everyone: Willow's adventurous mother and father could spend summers climbing Machu Picchu or kayaking the Alaskan fjords, while Willow got to wander the paths and hills of the sleepy Maine island or quietly rock on the porch swing with Sue on cool summer evenings.

Then it had ended—no more summers on the island, no more Aunt Sue in her life. Her parents refused to tell Willow what had happened or why, only announcing one day that she would no longer be spending summers on Little North. Willow never heard from Sue again, until today.

Willow retrieved her phone and typed "Cameron House, Little North Island, Maine" into the search bar. The list of results was flooded with sponsored posts from Gilded Age websites and "Haunted Houses of New England" travel pages, but they were all years old and listed Effie Cameron, whom Willow vaguely remembered from childhood, as the property owner. She next plugged Effie's name into the search engine—more information, but not the answers she was looking for: Effie Cameron had passed quietly in her home in March, of natural causes, at ninety-nine years of age. Survived by one nephew, Geralt Talbot, aged eighty-three. Active in the life of the village. Member of the North Islands Historical Society. No mention of Sue.

A little down the list of search results, Willow came upon a more recent Reddit post with screenshots from an article in the Island's tiny local newspaper: ECCENTRIC CAMERON HOUSE HEIR LEAVES ESTATE TO CARETAKER.

"Here we go," she murmured as she enlarged the images and skimmed the text.

A few minutes later, she sat back, her eyes wide. According to the news article, Sue and Effie had become close friends over the past decade, and Sue had cared for the property and helped Effie in her last years. When the old woman died, islanders were shocked to discover that the childless Effie had left Susan Davis her entire estate—a move that threw a shock wave across the community. Most had expected the elderly nephew would inherit the house and its land, but there was also talk of developers who had been pressing Effie to sell the property for decades. Then there were the preservationists who had been working with Effie to get the house onto the National Register of Historic Places. Overall, the islanders quoted in the article expressed their shock that a member of the oldest family on the island would leave her estate to a retired history professor from *Michigan* of all places. Between lines of text, Willow could all but hear the disapproving murmurs.

Willow next navigated to the home page of the little newspaper the Reddit post had come from, hoping for more recent information, but the site was behind a paywall; without a subscription, she could do nothing but scroll through recent headlines, one after another.

Until the one that made her heart lurch, tucked innocuously on the screen between a report about lobster fishing disputes and commentary on the new cell tower recently raised across the bay:

SUSAN DAVIS OF CAMERON HOUSE FALLS TO DEATH ON EVE OF WEDDING

Willow sat frozen on the organ bench, as though some part of her believed that if she remained immobile enough, she could make the world stop, could go back to a time before she had read the headline. As though she could wish it out of existence.

Glancing at the organ console mirror, blood pounding in her ears, Willow saw again the gray-haired woman and little girl, like a time-out-of-time vision of a younger Willow and her beloved Aunt Sue, moving through its hazy frame once again. On impulse, she turned away from the instrument to see them more clearly. The older woman grinned and swept the child up in her arms, holding her high and turning in a slow circle to take in the whole of the space. As she eased the girl back down into an enthusiastically returned hug, Willow caught a glimpse of both of their faces, radiant and full of love.

She turned back to the organ console. Silently, she began to sob.

CHAPTER TWO

The old man careened across the village green in his state-of-the-art luxury golf cart, taking a perverse pleasure in watching pedestrians scatter in panic before him. Stubbornly maintaining his speed, he thrust a bony arm out of the side of the cart and shook his glass-topped cane at them.

"Watch where you're going, you idiots! What in the hell is wrong with you?" he shouted as he slalomed around the large white pine in the center of the green and onto the bumpy gravel road heading out of town. For good measure, he let out two resounding blasts on the cart's air horn, though his potential victims were, by now, far behind.

Idiots, he thought, swerving the golf cart around a pair of middle-aged hikers who seemed to think the road belonged to them, letting the air horn rip one more time. The hikers scowled at him, and the woman flipped him the bird, which immediately made him feel better.

The cart lurched to a stop in front of the towering hulk that was Cameron House. Geralt Talbot swung his legs around to stand, but faltered as a wave of dizziness swept over him. Reaching under the seat, he pulled out a bottle of the lemon-flavored, nutrient-enriched water his staff made sure he was always supplied with. He cracked the seal, swigged half of it down, and grimaced; *if this horse piss ever came within spitting distance of a lemon*, he thought, *I doubt the lemon would bother to spit back.* He finished the bottle, tossing it into the back seat of the golf cart with the other empties, then climbed the porch stairs and let himself into the mansion with the key he'd swiped from Aunt Effie years ago, stepping into the grand entry hall of the once-opulent old home.

Susan Davis had done well by the house in the short time she'd been here. Effie had somehow kept the place fairly clean—God even knew how without outside help. But Susan's restoration work on the old mansion after Effie's death had been the talk of the village. She had replaced missing balusters along the second-floor landing and repaired cracked boards on the curving grand staircase; formerly drafty window frames now kept out all but the harshest Maine winds, and the old wraparound porch was more stable and level than it had been in decades. And she did it all with recycled and repurposed materials, the very same ones that would have been in use when Cameron House was first built—no plastic wood putty or vinyl framing would dare come near while Sue was working. Her care for the old mansion and its history had won her the respect of the village. Her willingness to call Geralt a jackass when she opined he was being a jackass had won her his.

He found himself wishing she were there to call him a jackass again, one more time. She surely would, if she knew what he had to do now.

This house was never meant to be hers, he thought wistfully, *but my God, what she could have done with it if she'd had more time.* Something twisted in his heart; he gritted his teeth against the feeling until it passed. If he were more familiar with the emotion, he might have recognized it as grief.

A calm voice spoke from the second-floor landing. "Good afternoon, Mr. Talbot."

The hair on the back of the old man's neck stood up to immediate attention, and an icy chill swept over him. Geralt whirled around at the sound, nearly losing his balance.

The man looking down at him was . . . utterly unremarkable. Thin, of average height, with dark hair beginning to gray at the temples and a neatly trimmed beard shot through with silver. "Who in God's almighty creation are you?" Geralt thundered when he regained his voice. "And what are you doing here?"

The man lightly descended the wide staircase, pausing on the bottom step, the grace of his movements making him seem younger than the gray-threaded beard would suggest. "I worked for Miss Effie Cameron for many decades, and for Miss Susan since March." One corner of his mouth lifted in a half smile. "You could say I come with the house."

Geralt's face hardened. "Well, they're dead, and I'm here, and Effie's will says the house comes to me. I don't need advice, so you"—he jabbed his cane at the man—"had best brush up your résumé and get out." He turned and stalked back to the door.

"Mr. Talbot," the man called after him, a hint of tension in his calm voice, "you must not sell Cameron House."

Geralt stopped short. *The unmitigated nerve*, he thought, and turned back. He drew breath to start shouting again, but hesitated. *This could be bad*, Geralt thought. *If someone's spilling the beans, this whole thing could blow up in my face.* "What makes you think I would sell the house?"

The man walked closer until he stood face-to-face with Geralt. "Because, Mr. Talbot, you are facing three lawsuits, four attempts at unionization to fight the low wages you pay your workers, and an Internal Revenue Service audit regarding decades of questionable tax practices. What property you do own is mortgaged to the hilt, and I am under the impression you have several balloon payments coming due. Without a strong influx of capital, your entire financial empire will collapse within a matter of months. Perhaps weeks."

Geralt froze, his face chalk white.

The man smiled gently. "Miss Effie, contrary to what you may believe, was not senile. She paid attention, up to the end."

Geralt sagged against the doorframe, his bravado gone. "It won't make a fart in the wind's worth of difference. At least if I sell before the world knows everything's falling apart, my wife will be taken care of, and I'll have a little comfort in whatever time I have left. If I wait too long, I could lose . . . everything."

The man gave him a speculative look. "That is all you want? Comfort and care?"

"Do you have any idea what decent care costs these days? I'll off myself before I wind up in some god-awful piss-stinking Medicaid nursing home." Geralt shuddered.

"What if I could offer you a chance for something better?" the man asked.

Geralt's head jerked up and met the implacable dark eyes.

The strange man stepped back and pulled out a ring of keys. He moved to a pair of forbidding, glass-paned French doors opposite Effie's bright sitting room, a locked doorway in a locked house on an island where few ever locked anything. A brass plate to the right of the doors read THE NORTH ISLANDS HISTORICAL SOCIETY.

The man turned the key and walked into the dimly lit library, gesturing for Geralt to enter after him.

Geralt followed.

Half an hour later, the two men stepped out of the library again. Keys reappeared; the door was locked. They looked at one another speculatively. The man in the dark suit stepped back, gave Geralt another deferential nod, retreated up the steps, and disappeared down the hall.

Geralt's gait was unsteady as he made his way to the front door of the mansion. But his face bore an expression of something like hope.

With a hand on the heavy doorknob, he turned back to look over the foyer one more time. The dark-haired man had gone about his day, but now there was someone else here, standing in the shadows beyond the staircase—a young man, tall and almost impossibly handsome, wearing a gray pin-striped suit and matching fedora.

Geralt's heart clenched, and his teeth bared in a snarl. "No," he rasped, "not you. Go away."

The man did not move or speak.

"Go away!" Geralt cried, lurching forward, cane in hand. "Not you. I don't believe in you. You aren't here. Get out. *Get out!*" His voice rose to a shriek, and he realized he was shaking. He closed his eyes, breathed in and out. Opened them again.

There was no one there.

CHAPTER THREE

There was no question in Willow's mind; she would return to Little North. The semester was ending anyway, so she touched base with her thesis advisor, graded the last of her undergrads' papers, booked herself a place to stay, and got on the road, praying she could make it in time for Sue's memorial service.

Willow had feared the sights and smells of the Maine coast might have faded into the haziness of childhood memory, but the rush of familiarity swept over her with an almost painful clarity. From her seat in the stern of the passenger ferry, she inhaled the sea air, taking in the distinct flavor and scent it shared with no other place in the world. Bright lobster buoys bounced up and down in the rolling swells, each painted with a distinctive color palette showing which lobsterman it belonged to. Hoarse cries from a flock of hungry seagulls carried to Willow across the sea as a pair of porpoises swam past the stern of the boat; a little farther off, a cormorant flapped its waterlogged wings in a desperate attempt to go airborne. Willow silently rooted for the bird to break free of the water and take flight.

As the boat passed the first marker and turned out of its

sheltered bay into the ocean, the temperature of the air plummeted about fifteen degrees in the space of a few seconds. Some passengers moved into the sheltered indoor part of the boat, but Willow stayed where she was, tugging her music conservatory sweatshirt over her head and pulling up the hood. She watched as Little North Island rose out of a strip of morning mist: There was the town dock, and there was the Dockside restaurant, with the best lobster roll on any of the islands. There was the Congregational church, its white clapboard bell tower rising from the hill by the main village. There were the granite-topped hills she used to hike up every summer and pretend she was queen of all she could see, and the rolling woods of spruce and pines that carpeted the valleys between them.

And there, a little west of the village, was Cameron House, the rambling old mansion where Little North's founding family had always lived. It had begun its existence more than two centuries ago as a modest stone farmhouse, and as the Camerons' wealth had grown, so had their home. Its present-day version sprawled out over the property as though grown directly from the granite foundations of the island, crowned by turrets and dormers that rose to varying heights along the asymmetrical roof; atop it all, a widow's walk perched like an inevitable afterthought.

As the ferry rounded the last marker into the harbor of Little North, the air warmed, and in an instant the salt-sweet smell of the sea blended with that of the old fish the lobstermen used for bait, diesel fumes from their boats, and food from the restaurant. The captain pulled up to the float; the mate tightened bow and stern lines to the cleats and plopped down ancient wooden step stools, automatically extending a gnarled and seaworn hand to help passengers off the boat.

Willow checked the email from the vacation rental site again; it instructed her to pick up the key to the cabin at the Pottery Shop, the last business on the town dock before the restrooms. Seeing Sue's cozy log home listed on the holiday rental website as some anonymous getaway for strangers had been a slap to the face, but shock had soon given way to resolve. She couldn't really afford it, but she'd booked the cabin for herself without hesitation. She would do this last thing, for herself and for Sue. Even if it was too late.

Cautiously, Willow stepped inside the Pottery Shop. It was warm and golden and welcoming, and Willow immediately loved it. The honeyed wood of the walls and shelves displayed handmade ceramic pieces by the shop's different artists, from large platters to mugs to little dishes molded in the shape of mussel shells; there was even a rack of delicate ceramic jewelry. A wide counter separated the shop from the workspace. To the rear of the store, a small, round woman sat bent over a pottery wheel; a few tendrils had escaped her silver-threaded black braid and sprang into tight curls at her temples.

"I'll be right with you," the woman said, eyes focused on the clay in front of her. A batik tunic in swirls of greens and purples and oranges flowed over loose black pants and fisherman sandals; the sturdy apron she had thrown over her clothes was smeared with clay and paint. Willow watched as the woman cupped the lump of clay with firm hands, slipping her thumbs into the center and effortlessly guiding the lump into a curved shape, broadening and lifting it until it bloomed into a vase.

The woman's eyes flicked up, locking with Willow's; only for a split second, but it was enough to send an infinitesimal jitter down to a hand, throwing the emerging piece off-balance and twisting it into a misshapen version of itself. The woman sighed and cupped her hands again around the clay, compressing it back into the wet mass it had been when she'd started. She shut off the wheel. Her jaw clenched a little as she said stiffly, "It's you. Willow, is it?" The woman crossed the shop and began scrubbing the clay from her hands and nails in the utility sink against the back wall.

It seemed like forever before the potter dried her hands and returned to the counter. Her expression was neutral, but her lips pressed together, her gaze a little averted; the woman's warm olive skin carried a layer of pallor beneath it as though she had not slept well—or enough—recently.

"Nice to meet you," the woman said, without the smallest pretense of a smile; Willow did not believe the woman thought meeting her was nice at all. "I'm Rina Montalto; this is my shop, and I also run the inn and cabin rentals. I'm glad you made it." She reached under the counter and pulled out a key ring in the shape of a log cabin, with two keys hanging on it. "Here you go; here are the keys. Not that anyone locks things up much around here. It's a pretty safe place."

Willow nodded shyly. "Thank you for reaching out when you saw my reservation. I didn't know who to call or . . ." Her voice trailed off.

Rina Montalto's jaw tightened again, as though biting back something she knew she shouldn't say aloud. With obvious effort, she smoothed her face again into a neutral expression. "I saw your name on the B&B rental and knew it had to be you. I'm glad you're able to be here for her service. The pastor said you'll play the organ; Sue would like that."

"Thank you. I'm glad too," Willow said. Her voice was hesitant as she continued, "Do you own the cabin now? I was surprised to see it on the vacation site; did Sue sell it?" The thought of the cabin belonging to someone else made Willow's heart hurt; Sue had always promised Willow the cabin would be hers one day.

Rina shook her head. "No, she still owned it; we took care of the properties together. The big blue farmhouse B&B outside the village is mine, and we have several small cottages and cabins we manage—managed—" Rina's voice broke a little.

"I understand," Willow said awkwardly. She did not, in fact, understand, but she did not know what else to say. Nor did she know why this stranger was giving off a vibe of barely contained hostility toward her.

A voice, harsh and abrasive, interrupted them from the shop door. "Got a good deal on it, I expect—even this harridan knows you get what you pay for, and God knows you won't get much." Willow turned and saw an old man leaning insolently in the doorway, tall and gangly with a windblown shock of white hair and eyebrows to match. He wore a cream-colored, half-zip sweater and plaid pants and was waving his ornately glass-topped cane at Rina from the doorway, glaring at her.

The woman's face darkened with anger. "It's none of your business what I charge, old man," she bit back, "but for your information, our rates are perfectly consistent with the costs for accommodation anywhere around here."

The man sneered. "That's because *you* own ninety percent of the accommodation on this island, undercutting anyone else for miles around and screwing up the economy by making Little North a place no one with actual money to spend would touch with a ten-foot pole. And you think you and your little preservationist friends are going to get Cameron House now—well, you can forget about *that*! My lawyers—"

"You can shout and threaten legal action all you want, Geralt Talbot, but when Miss Effie left the house to Sue, she was *absolutely* clear she wanted it to stay as it was, preserved and still housing the historical society—"

"Hah! You know what else my dear departed Aunt Effie said she wanted? She wanted a surviving Cameron to inherit the house if Susan died. So once my bloodsucking lawyers do their jobs, *that*"—he jabbed his cane in the direction of the Cameron mansion, narrowly missing a row of brightly colored mugs—"will officially be *my house*! You and your historical society be damned!"

Rina's face was livid, with high circles of red at the top of her cheeks. "It's not just *your* house, it's your *family's* house, with generations of history! Of all the pigheaded, self-centered, solipsistic, close-minded—"

"Generations, my octogenarian backside!" he snorted, shaking the cane for dramatic effect. "You're just steamed that if she'd died one day later, it could have all been yours."

Rina looked ready to lunge at the man—or start throwing beautifully glazed bowls and platters priced far out of Willow's range—as the silence in the little shop grew taut and Talbot waited for her to respond. Willow watched as the other woman fiercely held control, then released a shaking breath and shook her head. "I can't. I just can't." She turned to Willow; her voice was flat, cold. "You know where the cabin is, you have the key, let me know if you need anything." She turned and walked to the rear of the shop and opened the back door, pausing to offer her parting words to the sneering old man. "And you," she said harshly, "I don't know if Hell will even take you when you die, you shriveled old fossil, but I look forward to the day when they have the opportunity to decide."

Rina slammed the door behind her.

CHAPTER FOUR

Geralt Talbot's face broadened into a self-congratulatory smile; he'd gotten Rina Montalto's goat, which had of course been his aim all along. *Artsy-fartsy hippie shrew*, he thought with grim satisfaction. Sue Davis had deserved better than people like that in her circle.

He regarded the girl who stood gaping after the Montalto woman's exit, pale and nondescript with her tousle of dark hair and rumpled black dress and tights. It wasn't that she was particularly thin, he mused; no, the girl was *narrow*, compressed, as though she were trying to take up as little space in the world as possible—to be unseen, unnoticed.

And yet. Something in the eyes . . .

He jabbed his cane in Willow's direction. "And who in the hell are you?"

Willow tensed. "I'm Willow Stone; Aunt Sue—honorary aunt, no real relation—was my godmother. I saw in a newspaper article that she'd passed, and I'm here for her memorial."

Geralt regarded her, one enormous eyebrow raised. "So, you're the one. Sue's girl from way back. Heard about you." He looked at his ostentatiously expensive watch. "Cutting it a little close, aren't you? Service starts in a couple of hours."

"You heard about me?" Willow asked. "From whom?"

"From Sue. Believe it or not, we got on very well together." He paused. "She spoke of you often. Never stopped hoping you'd come back one day. And here you are." He gave her a sidelong glance. "A little late, but at least you got here."

The girl's mouth trembled; in another few seconds, the tears would overflow. Geralt rolled his eyes. "Oh, good God," the old man said. "You're going to cry now. I can't abide crying women; I'd rather they just shout at me."

"Yeah, I noticed," she shot back without missing a beat. She sniffled. "I'll work on it."

Oh, I like this one, he thought.

With a cynical grin and a small, ironic bow, he said, "See you at the service. There's a reception afterward, thrown by that antiques dealer who fancies herself a pastry chef. Health inspector's paradise." He tossed his cane up and caught it in the middle. "It'll be a hellscape. See you there, Sue's girl." He exited the shop and started back up toward where he had left his state-of-the-art, luxury golf cart parked haphazardly between the bandstand and a tall pine tree.

Willow impulsively followed, calling after the old man. "Mr. Talbot, can I ask—"

He turned back to her, the same sardonic glint in his eye as before, waiting.

Willow said, "A newspaper article I saw said Aunt Sue was getting married, but not anything about who the groom is—was—" She cleared her throat awkwardly. "I feel like I should meet her fiancé, pay my respects . . ." She trailed off as Geralt Talbot began to chuckle. Within seconds, he had burst into cackling laughter, ignoring nervous looks from passing tourists.

He reined himself in, dabbing the corners of his eyes. "You want to meet the fiancé, you say? A little late for that, Sue's girl; you already have."

At Willow's confused look, he smirked and gestured to the back of the shop. "Her. That foul-mouthed Italian shrew somehow persuaded your normally sensible godmother to marry her, God knows why." He cackled again. "Welcome to Little North Island. Enjoy your stay." He turned away and resumed walking.

Willow followed and called after him again. "Mr. Talbot?"

He called back over his shoulder, still walking, "What is it now, Sue's girl? I have things to do."

She took a deep breath and asked the question she had been holding inside since she saw the clipping, the question no website had answered. "How did Sue die?"

Talbot stopped abruptly; then he sagged a little and looked down at his feet. He said flatly, "She fell. Doing repairs or something. Must have lost her balance."

Willow frowned. "Yes, that's what the newspaper said; I only wondered if—"

"Well, if you read it in the newspaper, it must be true," he interrupted, and he began to walk again. Then he turned back to Willow. "Come over to my mansion this afternoon after the reception. Beautiful view from the widow's walk. We can have another little chat."

The corner of Willow's mouth twitched. "*Your* mansion, sir?"

Another wicked grin; he turned and leaped behind the wheel of the golf cart with a spryness that belied his need of a cane and, with one more blast of the air horn, took off down the road from the village.

Rina retreated down to the sandy strip of beach below the tide line. She left her shoes at the trailhead and walked along the water's edge, letting the wet sand squish between her toes. When she came to the stone jetty where she and Sue used to watch the sun set over Bald Hill, she brushed the sand off one of the great rocks and sat.

So that was Willow, she thought. The girl wasn't Sue's real niece, yet something in Willow's eyes reminded her so much of Susan that it felt like a fist squeezing her heart.

Since Sue's death, Rina had often come to this rock, imagining Sue sitting with her, perched on the boulder, arms around raised knees. Rina listened to the lapping water and the familiar *clunk-clunk* of round cobblestones shifting against each other in the water, picturing Sue listening too—just the two of them, comfortable in each other's presence. Sue had been Rina's calm, her stillness; with the image of Sue here with her, Rina felt the knot in the center of her gut begin to release a little.

You were unkind, you know. That's not like you.

It was very like Sue, Rina thought, even the Sue of her imagination, to wait till she was starting to relax and only then come at her with whatever was really on her mind.

"But—what is she doing here?" Rina retorted as Sue-in-her-mind picked up a flat stone and skipped it across the placid water. "She has no claim on you, no right to decide, now of all times, that she suddenly wants to be family again."

That's not the point, and you know it. Or maybe it is the point.

Imaginary Sue managed seven skips; real Sue had rarely gotten more than four, or maybe five on a good day. But if Rina was bringing Sue back in memory, she could have the flat piece of basalt skip as many times as she wanted.

But she couldn't seem to stop the words she knew Sue would say to her if she were here. *You lied to me. That's not like you either.*

"She has no right to you, no right to your affection or forgiveness, no right to *anything* of our lives here on the island. God, Sue, it's been fifteen years—she had plenty of time to come back if she wanted to."

She came as soon as she could.

"Not quickly enough, was it?" Rina's voice was hard.

And whose fault was that? Not hers, I think.

Rina's breath caught, the guilt threatening to swamp her; now the tears came. "Jesus, Sue, how can you welcome her back? How could you even think of writing to her, asking her to come, after what she and her parents did to you?"

And what did she do?

"They broke your heart!"

Imaginary Sue turned her face to Rina and smiled, that rich, full, vulnerable smile so few people had ever seen. *And you made it whole again. But that's not what this is about.*

Rina wiped snot from her nose and crossed her arms over her chest; she had never been a woman who could weep attractively and had long since stopped caring. But she wasn't ready to let go of this. "Why would you have reached out now? Invited her—them—to a day that was supposed to have belonged to us? Why can't you be happy with the new life you have—had—" She heard the past-tense verb from her own lips, and the tears ran harder. "Dammit, Sue, weren't we—wasn't I—enough?"

Sue gave her the Look, the one she remembered, the one that halted every argument in its tracks. Rina called it Sue's *cut-the-crap* look. *Stop it. Just stop. She was a child when all this happened. And now she's an adult. She came, she's here. And you were cruel and hurtful to her.*

Rina drew breath to retort, then dropped her head. "Okay. Yes. You're right. Do you ever get tired of being right?"

The corner of Sue's mouth twisted in a familiar half grin that made Rina's heart ache. *Evidently not.*

Rina gave a watery chuckle. "Okay. Okay, I'll try to—well, to not be horrible to her. It was—oh my God, that bastard Geralt—"

Sue was looking out at the sea again. *Rina, please. You know I don't like that word.*

Rina leaped up from her rock, clenching her fists in a sudden burst of anger. "Come back from the dead and tell me to my face, and maybe I'll—"

But Sue was gone.

And one day, Rina would have to accept that no amount of imagination or memory would bring her back.

CHAPTER FIVE

The church's pastor had been uncomfortably vague in his emails about Willow playing the organ for Susan's memorial service, and she had no idea when she was expected. She made a quick stop by the cabin to drop her things off, taking a few minutes to wash up and tame her hair into a short ponytail at her nape. Then, operating under her accustomed musician timetable of "early is on time, and on time is late," she grabbed the pack with her scores and beat-up organ shoes and hurried to the church, arriving forty-five minutes before the service was to start.

Willow was surprised, despite Rina's earlier comment, to find not only the church but the organ loft unlocked. She flicked the organ's toggle switch to the on position, her soul sighing contentedly as the familiar *whoosh* of air filled the reservoir, ready to push through the pipes as she played. Tentatively, she pulled out a couple of stops—an eight-foot flute coupled to its four-foot partner on the swell—and moved into one of Bach's simpler fugues, exploring the colors and sounds of the unexpectedly lovely instrument and listening as the imitative voices gently overlapped one another.

Pipe organs, Willow reflected, might be as varied as people, but they were a lot more consistent once you got to know them.

Willow was halfway through her favorite Pachelbel ricercar when she became aware of the petite woman in lavender standing in the doorway of the choir loft watching her. Willow finished the phrase she was playing, managing to come to a cadence in the music within a few bars, and lifted her hands from the keyboard. She looked up at the woman.

The woman was not just watching, she was glaring daggers.

Oh no, Willow thought. *What have I done now?*

Mrs. Patricia MacFarlane Ramsey checked the delicate gold watch on her left wrist, the one her husband, Hank, had gifted her eleven years ago the first time she caught him with another woman.

As head organist of the historic Little North Congregational Church, Patricia would of course play for this morning's memorial. She had allowed herself sufficient minutes to walk calmly to the church without untoward exertion—visible perspiration would not be acceptable. She had a certain station to uphold in this village, and appearances were important. Her makeup was smooth and natural, her hair had precisely the right amount of lift but not too much, and her lavender designer suit was appropriately smart and well fitting from all angles.

Patricia MacFarlane Ramsey would not perspire today, but someone would.

She approached the organ console, lips pursing as the unfamiliar young woman awkwardly extricated herself from the high bench, accidentally bumping one of the pedals as she did so, wincing as the misstep sent a blaring sixteen-foot principal tone down the quiet church.

"Good morning," Patricia said with a frosty smile. "I see you are enjoying our lovely historical pipe organ. You may not know it is on Maine's historical organ register, and musicians from all over New England travel here to play it, provided they apply in advance and are given permission to do so." The girl did not have to know that "all over New England" was approximately three people from Boston and one from New Hampshire over the last ten years. "I am Mrs. Patricia MacFarlane Ramsey, and I am on the Board of Regents as well as being choirmaster and organist here at North Island Congregational. I do not believe we have met?" She extended her hand to the terrified young woman.

The interloper briefly clasped Patricia's slim, dry hand with her own clammy one, swallowed visibly, and replied, "I'm Willow Stone. It's . . . nice to meet you."

The girl was afraid of her. Good. Patricia asked pointedly, "And where might you come from? Is it a place where it is considered acceptable to step into unfamiliar churches and play their instruments without invitation or permission?"

Oh no, Willow thought, understanding immediately. The pastor may have invited Willow to play for Sue's memorial service, but she would bet her organ shoes that he had not bothered to inform the regular organist. And the organist, rightly, was annoyed in the extreme.

"Mrs. Ramsey, I am so sorry for the misunderstanding," Willow managed to stammer. "I'm Susan Davis's goddaughter; I've been emailing with Reverend Barton about Aunt Sue's memorial, but it never once occurred to me he would have invited me to play without the knowledge of the church's regular organist. Please accept my deepest apologies for trespassing here." She knew she was groveling; she didn't suppose it would help much, but she couldn't think what else to do.

Patricia sniffed, clearly unmoved. "Miss Stone, can you appreciate how dismaying it is for me to walk in this morning, preparing to offer my own ministry as a musician to this woman who was such a pillar of our community, and find a stranger seated here, playing the organ as if it were her own?"

Thanking God the black knit dress hid the droplets of perspiration now coursing down her back, Willow could only stammer, "I can, and I'm so sorry; again, please know I would never have done so had the pastor not explicitly—"

"Well then," the woman interrupted, "I will need to have a word with the pastor, won't I?" She turned on her heel and left the loft, her heels clicking smartly on each step as she descended, returning a few minutes later with the wary-looking pastor.

In the end, despite Reverend Barton's obvious terror of his organist, Mrs. Ramsey was persuaded to a compromise: Willow would play quiet music as people entered the church and again at the end as they left, and Patricia would play the full service itself as she had planned. The pastor made a brief attempt to push for more, but Willow knew better than to let herself get nudged one inch further into Patricia's territory. Besides, Willow reflected as she eased into a transcription of her favorite Fauré motet, fifteen minutes of prelude music before the service would conveniently free her of any obligation to perform awkward social niceties with strangers.

At precisely one minute before the service was to start, Patricia Ramsey pointedly cleared her throat. Willow quickly gathered her music from the rack, slipping off the bench so the woman could take the spot she clearly deemed to be hers by divine right. Willow didn't mind; she was happy to spend most of the service in the corner of the loft, as far out of Mrs. Ramsey's peripheral vision as was possible in the limited space.

At the pastor's cue, Patricia launched into the opening hymn. Divine right or not, Mrs. Ramsey was not a good organist, Willow realized. No wonder Reverend Barton had been so solicitous.

Willow gazed down over the loft railing at the gathered people below, whose clothing ranged from floral dresses and Big Church Hats to the plaid chamois shirts and heavy work boots of thc island fishermen. A few others wore simple clothing that looked somewhat old-fashioned; Willow noticed the pair of elderly women quietly knitting at the far end of the pew together, wearing long black dresses and matching bonnets. She half remembered them from the Quaker meetinghouse Sue used to attend on the north side of the island—Sue had taken Willow with her a few times, and there were usually a few differently dressed Quakers scattered among the majority of modern-dress-wearing worshipers; these two particularly stuck in her memory.

She recognized Rina Montalto, sitting in the front pew with several other women—the "family" pew, Willow thought with a pang. Geralt Talbot was there as well; an elegant young blond woman—his daughter? Willow wondered—leaned her head on his shoulder in an affectionate gesture she would not have expected the cantankerous old man to tolerate.

"Welcome, brothers and sisters, as we gather to bid farewell to our sister Susan," the pastor intoned as the service began.

The church was nearly full; Sue had obviously been well-liked on the island. Near the rear of the church, a melancholy-eyed young man in a gray pin-striped suit sat next to an elderly woman, holding his hat awkwardly in his lap; she wore a yellow-flowered housedress and purple cardigan over mismatched knee socks and L.L.Bean boots, and her hair was pinned up in a braided coronet.

Readings, responses, remembrances. *To everything there is a season. The Lord is my shepherd. I am the resurrection and the life.* Willow wondered why, with a whole Bible to choose from, people tended to choose the exact same readings for every single memorial service.

At one point, Willow realized she and Patricia were not alone in the organ loft; a man in an unadorned and unfashionable black suit had slipped upstairs unnoticed and taken a seat in the opposite corner of the loft. His well-groomed beard was peppered with silver, and his dark hair was neatly slicked back; his eyes, dark and sharp, roved the room as restlessly as Willow's. He caught her looking at him—of course he did, she thought, given her utter lack of social skills and subtlety—and gave her a courteous nod before focusing again on the service. Embarrassed, she turned back to face the front of the church and attempted to do the same.

Finally, Reverend Barton made his closing remarks, inviting everyone to a casual reception that afternoon at Diana's Café and Antiques—presumably named for the pastry chef and antiques dealer Geralt had referred to earlier. Patricia lurched through the final hymn and, with a false smile and glance full of venom, slipped off the organ bench for Willow to take the postlude.

Willow took her seat and set the stops for her favorite Bach work. She poised her hands and feet over the keyboards and began to play.

The church's organ was far too small to render Bach's massive passacaglia and fugue in anything like its proper glory, but Willow didn't care; she doubted any organ scholars were present to criticize her repertoire choices. Once the music had died out, Willow quietly packed up; she shoved her musical scores and battered shoes back into her backpack, closed the swell box and powered down the organ, and slid off the bench. Most of the church had emptied out by now, and both Patricia and the unfamiliar man had departed.

She debated hiding in the organ loft till everyone was gone, but the thought of Mrs. Patricia Ramsey coming up to chase her out was enough to stop that plan in its tracks. She quietly made her way down the choir loft steps—but halted before stepping out into the open church foyer. Two men's voices were engaged in hushed argument.

"We had an agreement, Talbot. The old lady's gone and the lesbian's out of the way, so for God's sake, get on with it!"

Willow's breath seized in her chest, like someone had punched her hard in the gut. She stood motionless, pressed tightly against the wall.

"The deal's off," she heard Geralt Talbot say bluntly. "I've had a better offer. You're out."

Silence hung in the air; then the second man spoke, his voice soft but threatening. "Think carefully about this, old man."

"You say *I'm* the one who needs to be careful?" Geralt growled back. "I suggest you remember who you are dealing with. *I* call the shots on this island. If I decide you're not a man I choose to do business with, what are you going to do? Sue me for breach of contract? You're the one conspiring to commit felonies here, so I wouldn't—"

"Prove it," the other voice challenged. "And before you even try, remember how many skeletons are in *your* closet, old man. It takes two to conspire. Be very careful before you think about crossing me."

"I don't need to," Talbot scoffed. "You're deluded if you believe you hold any power over me. Now get out; what are you thinking bringing this to me today? Show a little respect."

The other man murmured, his voice so low Willow had to strain to hear, "Oh, I'll show respect. I'll show it at your funeral too, old man. After all, when someone with one foot already in the grave kicks the bucket, how hard are they going to look for a cause of death?"

The stage-whispered words hung in the air ominously.

Geralt's voice dropped even lower, as though he had moved closer to the other man. "I would suggest you mind your tone, you sniveling lowlife. There are no more Camerons; I'm *literally* the end of the line. And you need me. You all need me. Do not ever—*ever*—threaten me again." He paused. "Now get out."

She heard heavy footsteps tromp their way out of the church foyer and outside. Willow waited motionlessly to make sure they were both gone; after a full minute of silence, she slipped down the final two stairs and stepped into the church's foyer.

And came face-to-face with Geralt Talbot.

CHAPTER SIX

"Eavesdropping on your elders, Sue's girl?" Geralt asked dryly. "Nasty little habit; you should work on it. Or get better at not getting caught."

They stood for a moment, regarding each other.

Willow broke the silence. "Who was that?"

Geralt waved his hand airily. "No one you need concern yourself with. Just a local buffoon." He glanced at her with an insouciant grin. "So, you actually do have some talent on that pipe organ thing. Sue said you did, but I figured she was blowing smoke up our collective behinds. Your playing is a sight better than that Ramsey woman's, anyway."

"You knew I was there, didn't you? And you didn't say anything." Willow frowned, puzzled, as she came to the next realization. "And you kept talking, knowing I was listening. You *wanted* me to hear."

As though she hadn't spoken, he continued breezily, "Everyone pretends she's worse since she drove her car into a tree however many years ago, but the truth is she was always terrible." Geralt jerked his head in the direction of the door. "Are we done here?"

"He said, 'The old lady's gone and the lesbian's out of the

way,'" Willow pressed, her impatience rising. "So I need to ask you again: How did Sue die?" Her voice was steady, but something inside her quivered violently as she spoke the words. "Did she fall? Or did someone push her?"

The old man's face darkened. He stepped closer, close enough for her to notice the deep shadows carved out beneath his eyes. "You need to watch your step, girl," he said quietly, the intensity of his voice belying his earlier careless tone. "This island is a sinkhole of secrets, a tangled mess you haven't got a prayer in heaven or earth of sorting out. And some of 'em don't want to be sorted out. Leave them be," he said, and stepped back as though to leave. "And be careful where you start asking questions. I would recommend keeping your curiosity under your vest."

Too late for that, she thought, a seed of anger twisting out of the mire of her grief. *This has gone way past curiosity.* She persisted. "Did that man kill Sue?"

Geralt gave a harsh chuckle. "Him? No, almost certainly not. That idiot doesn't have the balls God gave a vole—or the vision, for that matter."

"Was it you, then?" Willow cringed inwardly at her own words; *Oh God, did I say that out loud?* she thought.

Geralt barked out a single mirthless syllable of laughter. "I knew I liked you," he said almost proudly, "I liked Susan too; we were friends. And I don't have many of those."

There's a surprise, Willow thought, mentally rolling her eyes.

Geralt's face turned uncharacteristically wistful. "And no, I would never have hurt her. Not in a thousand years." He looked back at Willow, almost gently. "It's good you came back. Susan wasn't sure you would. But you did. Even if—" He stopped, didn't go on.

Willow nodded. "Of course I came." She paused. "Even if what?"

His expression unreadable, he replied, "Nothing. Just . . . be careful who you trust, that's all."

She almost smiled. "And should I trust you?"

"Absolutely not," he snorted, his face returning to its usual half smirk. "Time to go," he said breezily, stepping back. "You may love hanging about in churches, but I'm afraid if I stay much longer, lightning bolts will take me out, and the building along with me. Houses of God have little use for me, and the feeling is mutual." He winked again, resumed whistling, and strolled toward the door.

He seems to be an all-around terrible human being on a lot of levels, Willow thought, *and possibly a criminal as well, but God help me, I almost like him too. I'm not sure what that says about me as a person.*

He had also, she realized, glossed over one more significant part of the conversation she'd overheard. "And it doesn't bother you that your friend the vole basically threatened to kill you?" she called after him.

Another snort, a hand waved in dismissal, as he kept walking. She persisted, "Who was he, Mr. Talbot? At least tell me his name. Maybe I'm not the only one who should be careful, you know?" But he was gone.

Willow slowly moved across the village green toward Diana's Café and Antiques, turning the conversation over in her head. Had Sue's death been intentional? Surely if there was any suspicion of foul play, there would have been an investigation.

On the other hand, if it had been an accident, someone had clearly found it a very convenient one.

Convenient for whoever it was in the vestibule with Geralt Talbot, her mind whispered to her. *Come to think of it, it is pretty convenient for Geralt, the last of the Camerons too. Him and "his" mansion.*

Mackenzie Reyes ran a tattooed hand through the tousled rainbow of waves on the unshaved side of her head; she hurried back across the green to her mother's café, knowing her mom would be yelling for her any minute.

Food-laden tables had been set up inside and out; guests chatted and ate as they moved through the rooms. A sign on one of the patio tables invited guests to choose a handmade ceramic cup to drink from and take home as a remembrance from the day. Little knots of people gathered around, examining the variety and choosing their cup with care.

Mac's stride broke a little when she saw Willow Stone, standing a little apart, as though hesitant to approach the gathered guests.

Why did she have to come? Mac thought. Everything about Willow's presence on the island was awkward. Worse, it was likely to cause Rina more pain, and Rina had quite enough pain right now.

But . . . *Be kind*, her mother always said. *Everyone has their stories; most of them you will never know.* And Willow's sorrow and isolation were almost palpable. Mac walked over to her, gestured to the sea of ceramic cups, and said, "She made them. Rina. For the wedding." Scanning the table, Mac was pleased to notice a half dozen or so of the cups Rina had let her glaze. She sighed wistfully. "Now they'll be remembrances of Sue instead."

Willow hesitantly stepped forward and picked up a ceramic cup, light blue with darker teal swirls at its base, then put it down again, as though unsure what to do with it; Mac thought she might have been blinking back tears. After a moment, Willow turned back to the tattooed young woman. "I saw you at the funeral, sitting with Rina, right?"

Mac nodded. "Yeah. With my mom—Diana." She gestured to the combined café and antiques shop. "This is her place; we moved here about fourteen years ago, when I was little. We don't have any family to speak of off-island, and neither did Rina or Sue, so we kind of adopted each other." She mentally kicked herself when Willow winced at her words—Willow, who had been like family to Sue once.

There was an awkward pause. Willow didn't know how to ask what she needed to ask, but she forced the words out, anyway. "I never knew why she left, why my parents and she stopped speaking and I couldn't come to the island anymore. But now . . ." She shifted uneasily. "Did my parents cut her off because she's . . . ?" Willow trailed off.

Mac looked at her pointedly, her eyes narrowing a little. "You can say the word, you know. Gay. Lesbian. LGBTQ. And as far as I know, yes. She came out to them, they kicked her out of the house, told her she was going to hell and was unnatural and all the usual homophobic nonsense, and cut her off."

The air whooshed out of Willow's lungs. She didn't speak.

Mac said accusingly. "She wrote you letters. For months. Years. You never answered. Eventually, she gave up, assuming you and your parents were a united front."

Willow was slowly shaking her head, bewildered. "I never got any letters. Not until last week. Not a word. I thought—I thought she—"

A voice interrupted from inside the restaurant. "Mackenzie! Mac, come help, please!"

Mac called back, "Coming, Mom!" With a quick, doubtful glance at Willow, she slipped inside.

CHAPTER SEVEN

The thought of facing a roomful of strangers made Willow's spirit shrivel into a hard knot. She would stay forty-five minutes, she told herself as she entered Diana's Café and Antiques—an hour if she could handle it; enough to satisfy the social niceties. Surely forty-five minutes was doable.

A swirling sea of people talked and hugged and talked some more; the chaotic buzz of their rising and falling conversations, melded with the clinks of silverware and dishes, were almost comforting in the anonymity they afforded.

The anonymity was short-lived. It took mere seconds for Willow to feel a prickling at the back of her neck as eyes darted to her and quickly away, to perceive the shifting of heads and faint whispers behind hands. The prodigal. The awkward girl who left and never came back. And from some, the whispers stung enough to draw blood: The homophobic relative. The ungrateful goddaughter. The one who cut Sue off from family.

It's not fair, she whispered savagely to herself. She hadn't known. She was a kid when it all happened. And her parents . . .

How could they? I know they aren't the most open-minded people in the world, but to have done this? Without even an explanation?

But another little voice inside her whispered back, *You're not a child anymore. You could have reached out at any time. You just assumed she was the one who had left you. And now it's too late.*

Willow wanted nothing more than to run, to get back on the boat and never have to face any of these people again. But there was Sue's letter, written months ago, begging Willow to come back . . . *You are still part of this place,* she'd said. *It needs you.*

And then there was the conversation she had heard in the vestibule, the whispered threats. The unknown speaker had been at the service; surely he would be here at the reception as well. He had threatened Geralt, who had been Sue's friend; worse, he had implied that Sue's death had perhaps not been an accident, after all. And if *that* were true . . .

Willow had failed Sue, letting the years go by, not taking the steps to mend the rift between them. She couldn't run now. *And so help me,* she thought fiercely, *if someone* did *kill Sue, they are not going to get away with it.*

She would stay. She would listen.

Forty-five minutes.

Willow caught sight of Rina, sitting beside the window, a little knot of women surrounding her; Mac was there, and a young woman with red hair and round glasses. A tall woman in a wine-red suit—Diana, Willow guessed, the café owner—brought Rina a plate and a steaming cup and murmured in her ear; for a brief moment, a ghost of a smile crossed Rina's tear-tracked face. Rina's closest friends, and probably also Sue's, Willow realized—the family Sue had found, had made, for herself, in the years Willow had been gone.

Before Diana could move on to circle the room again, Mac stopped her and whispered urgently in her ear. The pair never so much as glanced Willow's way, but something about their body language made Willow sure they were talking about her. Rina, too, was pointedly looking past and through but never at Willow. Only the redhead briefly caught Willow's eye, with a quick look of sympathy.

It was more than she had expected.

A familiar gravelly voice sounded nearby. "I'm eighty-three damn years old; I'll do what I want and eat what I want. And I have no interest in listening to some moneygrubbing female who thinks she can boss me around." Willow turned to see Geralt Talbot approaching, still waving his cane. "Ahh, there she is! Sue's girl!" He sauntered over, the glamorous blonde she'd seen in church at his elbow. "I don't believe you've yet been introduced to my lovely *young* wife." His wicked grin dared her to let the slightest surprise show on her face.

The woman shot the old man the side-eye, snagged two glasses of red wine from a passing server, and pressed one into Willow's hand with a wink and a subtle waft of expensive-smelling jasmine and sandalwood. "Here. You'll need this to get through the afternoon. I'm Naomi. It's nice to meet you." She turned back to Geralt. "If I were a money-grubber, I'd stuff as much saturated fat and salt down you as you wanted; it would get you out of my hair faster. You know your blood pressure can't handle it. So how about you lay off the salty food and empanadas for today?"

"What my blood pressure can't handle," he growled back, "is being ordered around." His voice rose. "Now I'm going to get some goddamn ham!" He stalked off to the food table.

Naomi sighed. "He does like to listen to himself shout, doesn't he?" She grinned at Willow. "He's okay, though. And a good guy under all the noise. I mean, it's not moonlight and roses, but we like each other, which is more than a lot of married couples have after a few years. Tell me I'm wrong."

Willow thought of her parents, of the tense silences and cool politeness that filled her childhood home. Of her parents' betrayal, still stinging like the oozing wound of a scraped knee. "You're not wrong."

She realized she liked Naomi.

She also realized that if Geralt Talbot inherited Cameron House, Geralt's young wife would presumably inherit it as well; sooner or later, Geralt would die, and Naomi would get the mansion. But surely . . .

Naomi turned and gestured over a slim, dark-haired woman standing nearby. "Audra—Audra, this is Sue's goddaughter, Willow." She turned to Willow. "This is Audra DuBois. My personal assistant."

Willow guessed Audra was a little older than Naomi, maybe in her late thirties, attractive and professional-looking without being glamorous—the image of the cool and impersonal employee. But the smile she gave Willow was real. "Pleasure to meet you," she said in a clean British accent. "You played the organ, right?"

Willow nodded, and Naomi looked impressed. "That was you? You're fantastic."

Audra nodded. "You really are. It was lovely."

Willow blushed. "Um . . . thanks." She casually looked at her wrist; good God, had it only been ten minutes?

Breathe, she told herself. *Breathe and smile. Ask questions, look interested. Breathe.*

A paunchy man sporting the most unfortunate comb-over Willow had ever seen swaggered up to the trio, reeking of Old Spice and self-importance. "My goodness, if it isn't all the loveliest women on the island, gathered in one place. And you would be Miss Stone—" He pumped Willow's small hand with his giant one. "Welcome to Little North, my dear—the name is Henry D. Ramsey Jr., but everyone calls me Hank. So edifying to have our lady of honor's dear niece back on the island at last—"

Willow tried to interject that she was not Sue's niece exactly, but he pressed on, giving her no opening.

"I believe you've met my lovely bride, Patricia."

Willow glimpsed the sour-faced organist at his elbow and winced inwardly, wishing she could disappear.

Naomi rescued Willow from having to reply. "You're too kind, Mr. Ramsey," she said sweetly. "And we all know your lovely wife outshines us all." She shifted her false but brilliant smile to Patricia.

Patricia's eye twitched ever so slightly. "Mrs. Talbot," she said, "*such* a flattering dress. Wherever did you find it?" she asked, her voice dripping with syrup.

Willow shared a lightning-quick look with Audra, which confirmed as clearly as if the other woman had spoken: *Yes. They really do hate each other that much.* Willow was certain the temperature had precipitously dropped about ten degrees in their area of the room.

The beefy man did not appear to notice or care. He shifted his attention to Willow. "You know, of course, Miss Stone, how vitally important the hospitality industry is to the economy of the coastal islands, and I'm proud to be able to do my part—the resort hotel over on Great North is one of mine, and the long-term parking over the bay where you no doubt have sheltered your car is one of mine too, so we can keep Little North pristine and unpolluted and automobile-free . . ."

Willow watched helplessly as Naomi and Audra melted into the crowd, slipping away from Hank's monologue; Naomi mouthed a silent *sorry* in her direction as she slid away. Willow could hardly blame her for making good her escape.

Hank kept talking. His properties, how many, their price points. His collection of vintage cars. The write-up of his "hotel empire" in a midsize Boston paper. The stateroom upgrade he had finagled on the most recent of his and Patricia's annual cruises. Boredom soon transformed into annoyance, and annoyance to desperation, but Hank had Willow well and truly trapped; all she could do was smile and nod, vainly eyeing the crowd around for an opportunity to slip away. Willow sneaked a look at her watch—twenty-six minutes. Tuning Hank out, she surreptitiously surveyed the room and the other guests.

If she'd hoped for an inkling of who had argued with Geralt earlier in the church, she came up empty; she caught no obviously negative body language between Geralt and anyone else in the room, and Hank's bloviating baritone made it impossible to listen for the voice she'd heard in the church. There were a lot of flasks slipping out of coat pockets and sly winks as men doctored one another's lemonade. At least four different people slipped Geralt empanadas, which she was certain Naomi would have vetoed had she seen. She still felt the prickling of eyes on her in fleeting speculation, shifting guiltily away when she caught them at it, the sense of whispers being passed from one person to the next.

Another look at her wrist. Thirty-four minutes. Hank was still going and showed no sign of slowing down. "Here on Little North, you know," Hank explained, "any whiff of a plan to build a resort along our lovely coastline brings out the preservationists and historians in full force—it's a shame, really." He jerked his chin in the direction of the Cameron mansion. "When I think of that giant old eyesore of a house, falling to disrepair, on such a beautiful and valuable piece of land . . ."

Willow's ears pricked up, and she suddenly cursed herself for not paying closer attention.

Hank was interested in the Cameron family property? To tear it down and build a hotel?

Before Willow could ask Hank to elaborate, someone jostled her from the side. She turned, torn between a desire to hear more about his schemes for the old mansion and relief for any excuse to shift away from his endless, pointless pontification.

Diana, Mac's mother, had somehow materialized, carrying two large sheet pans. She said brightly, "Oh, Mr. Ramsey, we're bringing out the desserts now. I know tres leches cake is your favorite—oof!" She seemed to nearly lose balance for a second. "Here—Willow, is it?" She pressed one of the sheet pans into Willow's hands. "Help me out? I'm afraid I'm going to send one of these flying across the floor." Diana wove her way over to a table by the interior wall; Willow, frustrated but at a loss for what else to do, managed a look of feigned apology to Hank and Patricia and followed.

She put the dessert down on the table next to Diana's tray. "Thank you for rescuing me," she said a little shyly. Forty-one minutes; she was going to make it.

"That man will talk till the stars go cold, and keep talking," Diana said with a shake of her head. "I'm Diana Reyes, by the way. This is my place." She cut a square of the cake, moist and golden with a layer of fresh strawberries and cream atop the golden sponge, and put it onto a plate. She pressed it into Willow's hands and handed her a fork. "You look like you need a minute. Go sit outside; I'm told my grandmother's tres leches cake recipe is legendary, and who am I to argue? Then come back and talk to Rina. She's hurting, and she needs you."

"But—"

"She doesn't know she does, and you might not know it either, but it's true. More than that—you need each other. Best stop running away from it."

Before Willow could respond, Diana slipped away.

Willow exited the café and took a seat on one of the broad granite boulders outside. The village green was blessedly calm after the buzz and movement in the little shop; Willow had indeed needed this quiet moment and wondered how Diana had pegged her so perfectly. Willow took a bite of the cake, then closed her eyes for a moment, lost in creamy berry-laden bliss. Diana had not been kidding about her grandmother's recipe.

She was pulled out of her sugar trance by a little chuffing sound a few feet away. She opened her eyes to see a sturdy, loaf-shaped corgi, its brown-and-white coat splashed with patches of black and gray, sitting on the ground next to her. His pointed ears stood at full attention as he gazed up at her longingly; one eye was blue and the other brown, but both intently followed her fork from plate to mouth and back to the plate again, as though willing the utensil to tilt just enough on its journey to let the morsel slip off.

"Look," Willow said firmly. "You are super cute and undeniably appealing. But this is tres leches cake. This is Diana Reyes's grandmother's tres leches cake. I am told it is legendary—and having tasted it now, I can verify it deserves every bit of its status."

One drop of drool fell from the dog's white muzzle down to the grass. Either he lacked the grace to appear embarrassed at his social faux pas or he was concentrating too hard on the movement of the fork; the heterochromatic eyes followed her fork up and down, and Willow could have sworn the dog was deliberately sucking his cheeks in to give an impression of underfed emaciation.

As one-sided as the conversation was, Willow realized this was probably the most satisfying company she had found since arriving on the island. That was worth something, wasn't it?

At some point, a good-size dollop of cake, graced by a neat slice of strawberry, fell off the plate. It did not make it to the ground; the dog caught it halfway down.

They both pretended it was an accident.

CHAPTER EIGHT

Willow drew out her dessert for as long as she could. She hoped she could drop off her empty plate and sneak away, but Diana caught her eye the moment she slipped back into the restaurant, pointedly gesturing in the direction of the kitchen with her chin.

Willow gritted her teeth; once again, she was caught, and there was no escape. As she entered the kitchen, the women helping with the food passed around knowing looks. The word had gone around: *Diana says Rina and the girl from Sue's past need to have it out.* Within seconds, each found a tray for the restaurant or a bag of trash that needed carrying out.

Rina was silently arranging delicate cookies on a tray: a row of glazed butter cookies with rainbow sprinkles around the edge, next to another row of chocolate thumbprints with raspberry jam, for contrast.

The silence grew long, then longer; finally, Willow broke it. "I never knew," she said, all in a rush. "She disappeared from my life fifteen years ago, and I never heard a single word from her again. My parents told me she didn't want to be part of our lives—my life—anymore. I thought it was my fault, something I'd done, but I never knew why, and now . . ."

Her voice trailed off. Rina calmly continued arranging the tray as if she had not spoken, a row of bumpy golden pignoli cookies inside the chocolate row.

Finally, Willow said, "Anyway . . . I wanted to thank you. For being there for her. And to say how sorry I am for your loss."

More silence. Willow awkwardly turned for the door.

Rina spoke at last. "And you believed them? After all the years, all the love she gave you—you believed that load of crap?"

"I was thirteen. I thought everyone hated me," Willow answered. "Besides—what else was I supposed to think? She was just . . . gone."

Rina slammed the tray down; the cookies jostled, their carefully laid concentric circles threatening to dissolve into a wild jumble. "That's crap too. You ignored her, the one person in her whole intolerant past life she thought she could count on. You never answered her calls, you blocked her emails, you returned her letters unopened, you gave up on her."

Willow shook her head, still confused. "That's what Mac said—but I never got any letters. I never heard a single thing from her."

"Oh, *please*!" Rina exclaimed, banging her fist on the counter for emphasis; the cookies shifted again, a few of them breaking in half. "She told me all of it. Every week for months, until your parents threatened legal action for harassment if she didn't stop. And even then, every birthday, every Christmas, she *still* wrote. And every letter returned unopened—*every single one*. She *never* forgot you, and she never stopped trying! How *dare* you blame one bit of this on her!"

Willow felt lightheaded as the carefully ordered pattern of her memories moved from order to chaos, shifting and crumbling like the cookies on the tray.

Sue had written? To her?

She groped back through the past to the surly self-absorbed teenager she had been. Surely her parents wouldn't have—

In a painful flash, Willow realized they would. And they had. *I was a naive idiot*, she realized. *It never occurred to me to even suspect.*

Willow was starting to shake. "Rina—" she said, but all the words were gone. There was nothing to say, not a single sound or syllable in the universe that would undo the past.

Rina was done listening. She picked up the tray of cookies with a jerk, not caring that her careful rows were shifting dangerously or that she had not finished filling it; she needed to get away from the face of the girl whose big, wounded eyes threatened to suck the wind out of her righteous rage.

"It's too late. It's over. You lost your chance. She's dead. *She is dead.*" And in a single fluid movement, Rina swept through the swinging door and out of the kitchen.

Until, with a thud, she tripped over Geralt Talbot's cane, which he was waving around from where he stood behind the door. She fell, banging her left knee hard, sending cookies and crumbs skittering across the floor.

All sound in the room ceased. From her undignified position on the floor, knee throbbing and elbows planted in cookie fragments, Rina saw eyes opened in shock, frozen faces and open mouths.

When the silence broke, it was to the sound of Geralt Talbot cackling gleefully at her misfortune.

No, Rina realized, her rage still had *plenty* of wind behind it.

The room and everyone in it stood frozen in time, as though some child had created a life-size diorama and sprinkled cookie crumbs over it like glitter.

The stillness broke. Rina pulled herself up from the floor and lunged in Geralt Talbot's direction, her hands clawed as though to gouge his eyes out. Diana was able to snake an arm around Rina's torso, holding her back and out of scratching distance; at the same time, Naomi Talbot and her assistant moved forward as well, trying to pull Geralt away from the furious little woman.

Then the shouting began.

"You horrible, evil troll of a man, I will have you clapped in jail, I'll have you charged with assault, how dare you, how *dare* you—" Rina spit at him, struggling against Diana's arm.

"Assault, my ass!" Geralt spit back, still waving his glass-topped cane, "If you touch me, you unhinged shrew, I swear to God you will be out of business and off this island so fast—"

Willow could see spittle coming from Rina's mouth. "Unhinged? Go to hell, you disgusting misogynistic scumbag—"

Geralt was inching forward, shaking off his wife's arm. "And if you believe for one second that you can intimidate me into letting your woke lefty friends take over that house—"

Their voices were overlapping now as Rina continued her tirade. "I don't care how much money you have or how long you've been on this island or what property you *think* you're entitled to—"

"It's going to be my house, and when I tell you to get out, then *out you will go!*"

"*I'll see you dead first, old man!*"

Silence fell as Rina's last words rang out into the room—even Geralt stopped his stream of invective before her fury. Her face was livid, twisted with rage; Willow, standing in the kitchen doorway, understood in that instant what the expression *had murder in her eyes* looked like.

Into the thrumming silence, Geralt drew himself up to his considerable height, jaw clenched with anger. He curled his lip and growled menacingly, "Now you listen here, and listen good, you unhinged harpy, if you know what's—" And he stopped.

His complexion suddenly turned gray; the blood left his face, and he sagged onto his cane. Audra, ever the efficient assistant, quickly pulled over a chair, and Naomi helped Geralt ease down into it. She worriedly checked his pulse as he gasped for air, and she murmured, “Geralt, honey, we talked about this; you need to try to stay calm. This isn’t good for you.”

His face contorted as if he were trying to muster the strength to start shouting again. Instead, he sank back into the chair, defeated.

His left hand sagged toward the floor, still clutching one of Rina’s handmade cups. Audra slipped it out of his hand and said, tension radiating from her voice, “He needs water. Or juice, or—can someone please get him something to drink?” She held the cup out to no one in particular, her eyes darting around the room.

It was Rina who stepped forward. The fury had left her face, which was now numb and stunned and pale as unglazed ceramic. “I’ll get some lemonade,” she said as she took the cup from Audra. She brushed by Willow and into the kitchen.

The tableau remained, a circle of staring faces, all directed at the old man in the chair. Some of the onlooking gazes were sympathetic or worried; others had a satisfied air of self-righteous complacency—just deserts, reaping what he had sown, and so on—and a few looked nearly gleeful at the old man’s misfortune.

Willow slipped out of the kitchen to join a terrified Naomi by Geralt’s side. The old man glared up at her and muttered, “For God’s sake, Sue’s girl, no need to gaze down on me like I’m some sad, pathetic, weak old man. I’m fine. It’s probably that Mexican woman’s cooking making me sick; everyone else in here is next, I’ll be bound.” His voice slurred a little, and he let out a violent belch.

It was enough to break the spell; the tableau broke, and people shifted, returning—or pretending to return—to their own conversations. A few took their cue that the gathering was starting to dissolve and slipped out quietly; others followed.

Naomi murmured to Willow, “This has been happening over the past few weeks, a little at a time and getting worse—the tremors, the slurring, the stomach upset . . . And he keeps refusing to go see a doctor.”

"Christ Almighty, woman, I'm eighty-three years old, and all those doctors do is tell me to stop doing the few things I have left that make life vaguely enjoyable. I'm *fine*." But even as he said it, Willow noticed the quiver in the hand clutching his cane, the slight wobble of his head.

Naomi shook her head. "You're *not* fine, and you know it," she retorted, trying to keep her voice low. "Your kidneys are shot, you're early-stage diabetic, your heart is doing things it shouldn't, your liver isn't doing what it should, and your blood pressure is through the roof. You're a mess."

"And you're a meddling witch, and it's none of your business."

"I'm your *wife*, for God's sake, and I have enough of a medical background to know this is *not* plain-old aging. Something's—"

Geralt shushed her with a quelling glare as Rina came back into the room with the cup; without looking at him, she held it out. He snatched it from her hands, downed it in two gulps, and held it back out to her. "What's the matter? Too cheap to make reasonably sized cups for the party? Clay too expensive for you?"

Seeing the rage begin to build in Rina's face again, Diana swiftly moved in with a lemonade pitcher from one of the tables, took the cup from Rina, and refilled it for him. He gulped down the second cup, and a third. Diana eased Rina away, her arm around the trembling woman's shoulders.

Naomi shook her head. "For God's sake, Geralt, once or twice in the course of a day, you *could* simply decide not to say the most awful thing you can think of in a given moment."

"Humph." Geralt pried himself out of the chair into a standing position, irritably waving Naomi away as she tried to help him. "Oh, piss off, woman. I'm taking myself out of here on my own steam." He set the ceramic cup down on the nearest table and walked out of the restaurant in a fair imitation of his usual swagger, though Willow noticed he was still using his cane for balance. Audra, after a quick shared glance with Naomi, slipped out after him.

Naomi shook her head, letting the worry fully cloud her face. "I don't know what's happening; he won't slow down or listen or even call his doctor. I'm afraid there's something seriously wrong, but he absolutely refuses to—" She broke off before finishing the sentence.

Outside the restaurant, people started shouting; an air horn's imperious honk cut through the voices. Naomi and Willow ran out of the café to see Geralt in the driver's seat of his luxury golf cart, peeling out onto the green toward the road away from the village. Audra vainly attempted pursuit but quickly fell behind; before Naomi or Willow could even shout after him, he was halfway across the green, chugging from a plastic water bottle and tossing the empty out onto the grass behind him.

He rounded the corner and out of sight.

Audra limped back and shook her head. "Bloody heels. Turned my ankle. He's gone to the mansion. God knows why." She looked helplessly at Naomi. "He . . . still didn't look good. But he swore if we sent anyone after him, he'll—let's see—" She thought a minute and nodded. "Fire me, divorce you, and sue whoever sets foot on 'his' property."

Oh, for God's sake, Willow thought. She turned to Naomi, who looked ready to burst into tears, and said, "I'll go. The mansion is on my way back to the cabin, and he asked me to come by after the reception, anyway. I can text you and let you know—hang on, my phone battery is dead." She frowned and shook it.

The dark-haired assistant nodded. "Happens to all of us, especially when we are moving around; battery drain is terrible around here. Turn off your Wi-Fi when you're not someplace you'll be using it, or it constantly pings back and forth and runs you down." She jotted down a pair of numbers on a card and handed it to Willow. "Here, you can reach out once you're charged again."

"Great, thank you." Willow reached out and squeezed Naomi's hand. "I'm sure he's fine. And"—she gave a small, sad smile—"thank you for the wine."

Naomi nodded and smiled back, understanding. “Thank you too.” She shifted to include Audra in the circle. “We cast-out women need to stick together, I guess.”

“We do.” Willow looked back into the restaurant, where Rina sat in the corner booth with Diana, Mac, and the red-haired woman gathered around her in solidarity and sympathy. And love—the love was obvious.

Willow remembered that kind of love. But it had been a long time.

CHAPTER NINE

Willow hurried away from the restaurant to the shore path, automatically picking up Geralt's discarded bottle from the grass and shoving it into her pack with her organ shoes and Bach scores. She scanned the path and the seashore along the way, praying she would not see the golf cart on its side in a ditch or a set of tracks veering off into the ocean. She rounded the bend and turned onto the Cameron House front walk, past the pair of stone lions that had stood guard there as long as she could remember.

She was first relieved to see Geralt's cart parked—in a loose definition of the term—beside the front steps. But her heart lurched when she realized he was still seated, unmoving, in the front seat of the cart.

"Mr. Talbot?" she called anxiously, breaking into a run. "Mr. Talbot, please, are you all right?"

After an agonizing moment, his head turned; her heart sighed with relief at the sight of his sharp profile and hawklike nose silhouetted in the late-afternoon light. "For God's sake, Sue's girl, don't tell me you've bought into the 'poor, aging, decrepit old man at death's door' garbage my wife is pushing. I'm fine."

Regaining her calm, at least outwardly, Willow raised an eyebrow. "Your parking job would suggest otherwise."

He scowled. "It'll be my lawn soon enough; I'll drive all over it if I want to." His gaze narrowed. "Are you here because my wife and her slow-moving assistant suckered you into it, or did you come for the tour I promised?"

Willow regarded him carefully. His eyes were as sharp as ever, but the knuckles clutching the steering wheel were white, and his breathing seemed fast and labored. She replied, "I'm here for the tour, of course. If you're up for it." At the very least, she thought, maybe she could get him out of the cart and into the house.

He nodded. "You're lying, but I'll let it pass." He carefully released his fingers from the wheel, climbed out of the cart, and walked with as much steadiness as he could muster to the deeply sunken post at the base of the stairs, from which two weathered wooden signs hung, one above the other. The first, in an old-fashioned flowery font, proclaimed the house to be:

The Cameron Seaside Cottage Historical Site

Beneath the sign was another, smaller:

Home of the North Islands Historical Society

Geralt glared back at Willow. "If you're satisfied that I am not at death's door, perhaps you would help an old man up the stairs?"

Without comment, Willow walked up beside him and offered her arm, which he grudgingly took, and the two stepped into Cameron House.

Geralt hated that the short walk into the entry hall had exhausted him this much, hated the indignity of getting old. Mustering what remained of his strength and composure, he made his way to one of the high-backed foyer chairs and sat. Sunlight from the stained glass scattered fragments of color all around, illuminating his translucent pallor and refracting jittery shards of light from the glass knob of the cane in his trembling hand.

He looked up, irritated, at the solemn young woman watching him. "I presume my wife and her boring little assistant will be waiting for your update that I'm not dead. Satisfied?" he rasped; as hard as he tried to summon his usual curmudgeonly sharpness, his voice came out sounding petulant and weak. And elderly. And sick.

He refused to be elderly. And curse it all, he was not sick.

Willow managed a smile that did not quite hide her worry. He hated the worry too; it told him he did indeed look as bad as he felt, and he felt horrible.

"They were worried, that's all. And they knew you didn't want them coming after you, so I volunteered."

"I'm eighty-three years old; I'm not going to run to the doctor every time I have some little twinge."

"You know what people who live to eighty-five and ninety have in common?" she retorted. "When something's wrong at eighty-three, they go to the doctor. And they get to live longer."

"The young woman makes a sound case, you know," came a mild voice from the top of the stairs.

Willow looked up in surprise at the slim man with his dark suit and neat silvery beard. "It's you," she said awkwardly. "You were in the church, at Aunt Sue's memorial."

Geralt started. He had not expected this. He shot a piercing look at Willow. "You saw him at the church today?" he asked, trying to still the tremors in his hands and legs and failing.

Willow nodded. "He sat in the choir loft. For a little while."

The man said, with a hint of reluctance, "I arrived late and stayed upstairs so as not to draw attention." He descended the stairs and turned to Willow. "Apparently, I was unsuccessful. My name is Joel Drummond; I managed Miss Effie's and Dr. Davis's affairs while they lived, and of course, I worked with them on historical society matters." He paused. "Please accept my condolences for your loss. You are Miss Stone, Susan's . . . niece, are you not?" he said.

Willow managed a small smile. "Honorary niece only. Sue was my godmother."

Joel nodded, a speculative look in his eye. "I see. She mentioned you might be coming to the island soon."

At that moment, Geralt burst into a paroxysm of coughing, and then retching, as he clutched his stomach, face contorting in a rictus of tension and pain.

Joel hurried over to him, feeling for Geralt's thready pulse. "Miss Stone, do you have a telephone?"

Geralt was dimly aware of the voices around him. They were trying to manage him again. Everyone was always trying to manage him.

"The battery died. I was on my way home to charge it. Does the house have a landline?"

"We had it shut off after Miss Effie died; Dr. Davis used her cell phone." Joel turned to Geralt and spoke directly into his face, trying to make the old man understand him. "You are not well, sir. We will help you into the sitting room to lie down, and Miss Stone will go seek medical assistance. And you will let us."

"For God's sake, I'm right here. No need to shout." Jesus, his head hurt. No one had told him high blood pressure would make his head hurt like this. It probably wasn't even his blood pressure—he was dehydrated, that was it. When did he last have water? In a thick, blurry voice, he said, "I'm thirsty. I'm supposed to drink lots of water . . ." He vaguely realized his hand was jerking uncontrollably, and then his whole arm. His cane fell to the floor, the glass knob shattering and throwing sharp fragments around the room.

"Dammit," he slurred. "I liked that cane."

He was dimly aware of words between Willow and Joel, but he couldn't make them make sense, and everything was unraveling. His head throbbed. He couldn't catch his breath. His heart pounded in his chest, thick and uneven. Then he was being lifted between the two of them; he had a few seconds of clarity, able to keep his feet moving under his body as they carefully maneuvered him across the hall. He stopped in the archway, gazing at the wooden rocking chair in the window, sea-blue afghan draped over the back. He remembered his Aunt Effie crocheting that afghan, and he remembered how she used to bake snickerdoodle cookies. The sweet-warm fragrance of cinnamon and fresh butter wafted into his senses as though she were baking them now, as the chair moved slowly back and forth, back and forth.

How could he have forgotten the cookies?

Aunt Effie, from her seat in the rocker, turned her face and smiled at him gently—at the little boy he had been, as though it were his childhood self who stood before her and not the grouchy old sinner he had become.

He blinked, and she was gone.

At least it had been her and not the other one.

Willow's voice. "Please, Mr. Talbot, it's only a little farther; let's get you safely lying down, and then I'll go for help. You need a doctor, you know you do—"

"I'm fine!" he roared, summoning the last of his will and strength to find and assemble, if for the last time, the fiery exterior he was committed to showing the world. "Leave me alone! When it's my time, it's my time. No need to make a fuss over me. Leave me be. Leave me—" He gasped and slid to the floor, Willow and Joel helping to ease him down to a seated position without hurting himself.

Geralt's breath was shallow and fast, his arms and legs shaking uncontrollably now. In a sudden spasm, he groaned and doubled over, curling up in the fetal position and retching. Then he vomited, convulsively expelling most of the food and lemonade he had consumed throughout the afternoon in a flood of foulness.

He realized he was very possibly going to die. If not today, then soon.

Geralt Talbot had never seriously considered the idea of dying before. He did not much like it.

CHAPTER TEN

Willow felt paralyzed, kneeling beside the stricken old man curled in the fetal position at the base of the staircase. Nine years of research and musicology study had prepared her for exactly nothing connected to the lives of the living people around her; she felt more useless than ever before in her life.

The dark-suited man reached across Geralt's gasping body and gently touched her shoulder, then her cheek. His eyes caught hers and held them—dark eyes, so dark the pupils were almost invisible, older than the rest of him, eyes that would notice everything. But they were also, somehow, kind, and his voice was calm and reassuring.

She forced her brain to process what the voice was saying. "There's a linen closet in the kitchen, to the right of the door. You'll find some towels."

Towels. It was something.

Willow burst into action. Among table linens and cleaning supplies were several neatly folded stacks of once-bright terry cloth, now old and faded and reduced to mopping up spills. She grabbed a pile of the towels and came back to where Geralt lay, slipping a couple of them under his head for comfort and spreading out another to sop up his sick. He shifted a little as she gently wiped the corners of his mouth, then he gave a shuddering sigh.

If he had been pale before, now he was positively waxen, his complexion a grayish white, a delicate tracing of veins visible in the translucent skin of his closed eyelids. He was shaking; she could not tell if he was cold or seizing, but on impulse, after removing the soiled towel and tossing it to the side with most of the mess it had soaked up, Willow darted into the sitting room and picked up the sea-blue shawl draped over the back of Effie's rocking chair.

She had a strange sensation of another pair of hands brushing hers, pushing the shawl into her grip; the impulse to weep washed over her.

She hurried back to the foyer, laying the soft sea colors over the old man. He was mumbling now, incomprehensible sounds without words; his breaths were shallow and gasping.

Suddenly, his eyes burst open, his face twisted in terror as he focused on something just behind her. "No," he whispered, fear rising in his face. "No, not you . . . Go away . . ." Willow fought the urge to look over her shoulder; of course there would be nothing there. She tried to comfort Geralt, softly wiping his face again as tears came and he subsided into weak sobs.

"I'm so sorry," he murmured. "Please, I'm sorry . . . Please . . ." Geralt's eyes were bleak. "I can't," he whimpered. "It hurts, and I can't. I—"

Impulsively and against all logic, Willow turned her head to look behind her. A lightning-quick impression, silhouetted in the afternoon sun—a tall man in a suit and fedora—

She blinked, and there was nothing there.

Of course there was nothing there.

Geralt's body convulsed as he vomited again; again, Willow wiped it away.

With a sudden jolt, Geralt's talon-like hand jerked up and grabbed Willow's forearm with a strength that surprised her; her first response, as much as it shamed her, was to jerk away from his grip, but his grasp was hard and implacable.

For a moment, both his face and his speech were utterly clear. "It's you. Sue's girl. Willow. It's you."

For an endless instant, she was frozen in place. Time stopped again, and his gaze bored into her with an intensity that curled her insides. It was as though the will of the whole house were pushing down on her.

Willow . . . It's you . . . It's you . . . Willow . . .

The echo of his words swirled around her like a hushed whisper from countless voices, surrounding her, filling the room.

Panic rose in her, centering in her solar plexus, squeezing hard, holding her immobile.

Geralt pulled her closer, his rheumy eyes boring into hers, and whispered urgently, "The house. It needs to stay in the family. It must." He shuddered and retched again, releasing her wrist and clutching his stomach. She lurched backward, barely noticing that she had put her hand down on a shard of glass from Geralt's broken cane.

Willow . . . the house . . . the family, the whispers spun in a soundless sigh.

She scrambled backward, away from the sick old man; she could think of nothing but getting away—far from this house, from the look of coming death in the old man's face, from the voices. From the almost-visible shadows lurking just outside her vision. From the implacable gaze of the man with the dark suit and silvering beard. And then even thought departed her; there was only the desperate need to flee.

"Willow." Joel's voice, sharp and clear, cut through her terror.

She jerked her gaze to him, then away, unable to bear the judgment she saw reflected there. "I have to go," she forced out in desperation. "I have to get help."

Joel's voice was clipped and tight. "I fear he is beyond that now. What he needs is comfort. He needs to not be alone."

The whispers, again: *Alone . . . Don't leave him alone . . .*

She squeezed her eyes shut as though doing so could squeeze out the impossible sounds or the harsh gasping breaths of the old man. Joel's voice came again, sharper now. "*Willow!*"

But she was too lost in her own panic and fear. She backed away, first scuttling like a crab, then pulling herself to her feet and moving toward the door, her eyes fixed on Geralt. Ashamed to look at Joel, terrified to look around the room for fear of what she might see, all she could think of was her own escape. "Help," she breathed again, her feet crunching on the broken glass of Geralt's cane handle. "I need to get help."

Willow's skin itched with the weight of Joel's stare, with the weight of unnumbered, unseen faces all around, all focused mercilessly on her. The invisible scrutiny had weight, tendrils, twining around her as though to trap her here.

Her hand, groping behind her, touched the doorknob, smooth and cool; she had made it to the door. Joel's eyes were still fixed on her, but the kindness was gone; they were shuttered, distant, even a little cold. At last, he looked away and said quietly, "All right, Willow. Go. Get help. You don't belong here, not for this. Go back. Call for help."

His disappointment pressed down on her even through the fear; she had let him down, though she had no idea how or why it should even matter—this stranger she had met half an hour ago who made her feel like he could tear through her every defense. She nodded numbly; the knob turned beneath her hand, and the heavy door swung inward as though trying to push her back into the foyer; only a step, but it was too much, and she felt the panic rise again.

Geralt shifted again, grasping at the hand of the man kneeling next to him, looking up at Joel with a vague, childlike stare. "You'll stay with me? You won't leave me?"

Joel turned his kind, too-old eyes to Geralt and moved closer to him. "I promise. I will stay with you. I promise."

Willow felt like her insides were shattering as she clawed her way around the door, away from the naked hope and terror on the dying man's face. She thought she could see Geralt's cheeks shiny with tears as he pleaded weakly, "It's going to be all right, isn't it? It doesn't end here, with me? Do we get to go on?"

Joel nodded and gave him a sad smile. "Yes, my friend. We get to go on."

Willow looked back one last time from the doorway, fervently hoping Joel would not notice her again, fervently praying he would. When she tried to inhale, her lungs clogged with the intimacy and emotion that suddenly suffused the room, as though Geralt had become the fulcrum of something rich and incomprehensible.

She turned and ran.

The stone lions watched after her. She could feel them watching her.

She reached up to push her hair out of her face and realized her hand was bleeding.

She kept running.

CHAPTER ELEVEN

By the time Willow got back to the cabin, she was gasping and her stomach hurt. She plugged in her phone, one eye firmly fixed on it so she would know the second it had charged enough to power on. She cleaned the blood from her hand; the cut was deep, but she was fairly sure no shards of glass were still stuck in it. Before she could move for a bandage, her phone's screen came to life; she dialed 911 and breathlessly told the dispatcher to come quickly to the Cameron House, because Mr. Talbot had collapsed. The woman on the other end wanted to keep her talking, seemingly unable to understand that the longer she talked, the longer she was not back with Geralt, whom she prayed would still be alive when she returned. Willow hung up on the dispatcher and, with some reluctance, started running again, back to the house, back to everything she had fled.

When she arrived, she found Geralt Talbot lying on his side where she had left him, white and still. The hands that had clutched his stomach had gone limp, and his eyelids were closed. Joel Drummond was gone.

Oh God, she thought, he was dead, she knew he was dead; she had left him, Joel had left him, and he had died alone. Willow's legs sent a halting message to her brain that they were not going to support her for long; her brain obligingly instructed them to back up to one of the wainscoted walls, where she sank to a seated position on the floor.

A tall police officer burst through the door; in less than a second, he was at the old man's side, feeling for a pulse, shining a flashlight into his eyes. "You made the 911 call?" he asked; it took Willow a beat to realize he was talking to her, but she couldn't make her brain connect to her mouth to reply. She heard him make a call through his two-way radio; the words *pulse thready* and *pupils unresponsive* penetrated her fog of guilt and terror.

Not dead, then.

The officer glanced back over his shoulder at her; he looked familiar, she realized, though she could not place him. Square jaw with a well-trimmed beard, sandy hair, a face that was probably ridiculously handsome when it wasn't fixed in an irritated glare in her direction. "I said, did you make the 911 call?" She nodded weakly. "What happened here?" he persisted. She tried to answer, but the words weren't coming.

Wheels crunched on the gravel road outside and jerked to a stop—an ambulance, one of the few motor vehicles allowed on the island. Two uniformed paramedics rushed into the foyer to the still figure on the floor. A murmured conversation passed between officer and EMTs.

Leaving the paramedics to their work, the officer came over to Willow, squatted in front of her folded-in shape on the floor, and studied her as she stared at the young man and woman working over Geralt, unable to look away. The tall man asked, "Are you okay? Willow?" When she didn't react, he snapped his fingers in front of her face. "Willow!"

It was enough to break through the fog and bring her back to the present. *Rude*, she thought as she jerked her face around to his; then, *He knows my name*. The man was staring at her coolly, as though she had been weighed and considered and deemed unworthy of his time. Her eyes dipped down to the name tag clipped to the dark blue uniform—N. TYLER—and back up to his face.

Her heart shriveled into a tiny lump as she realized why he seemed familiar. The blotches and pocks of a fierce case of teenaged acne were gone, his awkward, lanky build had filled out impressively, and the greasy swath of hair that had always dangled over his forehead appeared to have met up with an actual stylist and been vanquished. But it was definitely him.

Wonderful, she thought grimly. *This day is getting better and better.*

Also: *Nick is hot now? This was unexpected.*

"Are you okay?" he asked. "What happened to your head?"

"My head? Oh—" Willow reached up to her head and realized she had gotten blood in her hair as well. "Nothing. It's fine. I cut my hand on the glass, and I must have touched my hair."

The officer looked puzzled. "What glass?"

Willow looked around the foyer, suddenly realizing that Geralt's cane and the splinters of broken glass it had sent around the entry hall were nowhere to be seen. Had she imagined them? But if she had, how had she cut her hand? She muttered, "Um . . . never mind." Her mind was moving too slowly; nothing connected, nothing made sense.

"Can you get up? Can you walk?" Even after nearly two decades in Maine, a hint of Texas still lingered in his voice.

Her brows came together peevishly. "Of course I can walk," she snapped. The anger and petulance he inspired in her were as familiar as if she had last seen him yesterday, but they were better than the horror, and she held on to them for dear life.

He stood up in one swift move. "Outside, then. Now." He turned on his heel and left the foyer.

Asshat, she thought. *Fifteen years later, he's still an arrogant jerk.*

She took a few more deep breaths, partly from exhaustion but mostly to deny him the satisfaction of her swift obedience. She dragged herself to a standing position, lungs still burning from her unaccustomed sprints. With one last look at Geralt Talbot, she made her way slowly to the front door—then stopped and turned back, realizing the broken glass wasn't the only thing missing.

When she had left, Effie Cameron's shawl had been draped over Geralt's body; Willow had put it there herself. The used towels were still in the foyer, tossed to the side after wiping up Geralt's vomit, but the shawl no longer covered him. She glanced into the front sitting room, and she saw the froth of sea-blue yarn right where it had been when she had arrived at the house, draped over the rocking chair—not in merely the same spot but *exactly* the same, down to the off-center wrinkle across the top and the fringe dangling at the same angle as before. She was sure of it.

The empty chair gave an infinitesimal rocking movement, and a new chill crept up from the base of Willow's spine.

Was she losing her mind?

An annoyed shout from the porch shook her out of her stupor. "Willow? Today, maybe?"

She hurried out after him.

Willow followed Nick out to the corner of the wraparound porch and sat in a wicker chair, pulling her knees up to her chin and hugging them tightly. Nick pulled a clean handkerchief out of his pocket and said impatiently, "Give me your hand." When she did, he carefully wrapped the cloth around her hand, tucking in the ends so it would stay. "Once they're done inside, I'll have one of the techs take a look at this for you."

"It's fine; I don't need it. I'm fine," she said, tension radiating in every word.

"Too bad. They'll look at it for you, anyway," he retorted. "Was Mr. Talbot conscious when you left?"

Willow gave a shaky nod.

"And you left him? By himself?"

"My phone was dead. There were no phones in the house. It was leave and get him help or stay and watch him—" She broke off.

Nick regarded Willow, taking stock of the grown-up version of the girl who'd been such a nightmare when they were kids. He wanted to shout at her, place blame at her feet, accuse her of abandoning the man. But Nick had to admit what she'd said made sense; there wasn't much else she could have done. No way he'd admit it to her, though. He fumbled instinctively for something to criticize.

"You let your phone die?" He looked at her dubiously. Then he shook his head in exasperation. "You left your Wi-Fi on, didn't you? Depletes your battery. On this island, you need to shut it off whenever you're not using it."

"A piece of knowledge I wish I'd had this morning. We didn't have Wi-Fi on the island last time I was here," she said tersely. "Mr. Talbot almost collapsed at the restaurant, then took off in the golf cart on his own for the mansion before his wife could stop him. I told her I'd follow him and make sure he was all right. He was still sitting in the cart, and he looked awful. I got him inside, hoping I could use a landline in the house, but they don't have one. There was another man here—Joel, he said his name was, Joel Drummond, I think—"

Nick looked at her sharply. "Another man? There was someone else here? Where did he go?"

"I don't know," she said. "We were trying to help Mr. Talbot into the sitting room to lie down, but he collapsed right where he is now. He threw up a few times, and he was shaking—" Her voice was starting to shake too. She clenched her fists and took a deep breath before continuing. "Mr. Talbot clearly needed medical attention, so I ran back to the cabin to call, and the man—Joel—stayed here with him." *I thought he was dying,* she did not say. *I was sure he would be dead when I got back. And I ran, anyway.*

"So, this Joel Drummond guy, had you seen him before, or do you know who he is?" Nick frowned. "I've never heard that name around here, and it's kind of my job to know people. It's not that big an island."

"We were a little occupied at the time. Introductions weren't exactly first priority," she said icily, provoking a scowl from him. She threw up her hands in frustration. "I don't know what to tell you. I got here this morning. He was here, and he and Geralt clearly knew each other. I'd seen him earlier at Sue's memorial. He said he would stay with Mr. Talbot, but he didn't, for whatever reason, and he's gone now."

"No phone in the house?"

She shook her head. "He said the landline had been turned off after Miss Cameron died, since Sue used her cell phone. I didn't want to leave Mr. Talbot, but . . . I didn't know what else to do."

Nick let the silence hang in the air before he grudgingly spoke again. "Mr. Talbot is still alive, but barely. My medical training is rudimentary at best, but if I had to guess, I'd say doing what you did may have saved his life."

She looked up at him, a faint glimmer of hope in her eyes. Her eyes had been green when she was a girl, he remembered, but they had darkened to hazel as the years had gone by. She had always had nice eyes. When she wasn't being insufferable.

Which was most of the time. He remembered that too.

One of the EMTs came to the door and gestured for Nick to come back inside. Nick stood and said, "Wait here, please," and went back into the house.

CHAPTER TWELVE

Willow began to wonder why there were so many police officers attending what should have been a simple medical emergency. She was grilled by Nick again, then talked to another officer; she answered questions from one of the EMTs after they brought Geralt out on a stretcher. At some point, they started asking her what Geralt had eaten and drunk at the reception. Someone bandaged her hand. Phone numbers were exchanged. She should please call if she remembered anything new.

Willow did her best, but eventually, her ability to engage faded and gave up; speaking became more and more difficult. Everything felt off, and jagged, like she had taken up residence in a black-and-white Escher print where nothing connected the way it should.

At last, the machines and radios subsided. Emergency vehicles departed; officers pedaled away on their bicycles. Nick returned to Willow's chair and knelt in front of her. The sun had disappeared behind the island's western mountains and the fog had rolled in, depositing a layer of minuscule droplets on Willow's clothing and skin. She didn't mind; the fog muted the hard edges of a painful world, and the chill outside only matched her inner workings.

"Hey. Willow." Nick was squatting in front of her again. She managed to focus on his face—it was surprisingly kind, or at least not angry. She supposed neutral was the best she was going to get from Nick Tyler.

"Willow. It's time to leave."

She found she could not quite form the words to respond. She looked back at the front door of the mansion, surprised to see yellow crime tape across it.

Crime tape. That meant that someone—Nick, the paramedics, the other police—suspected a crime. That this was about more than a sick old man who had neglected his doctor visits. Willow shivered as she recalled the malevolent hiss of the man in the vestibule a few hours ago: *When someone with one foot already in the grave kicks the bucket . . .*

"Willow?" Nick said again, and she jerked her attention back to him. "Can I take you back to the cabin?" The officer's voice was low and soothing, and it pissed her off.

"I'm not a child, and I'll thank you to stop speaking to me like one." The surge of annoyance was good; it was comfortable and a little warm. It made sense. It was the only thing that made sense.

One of Nick's elegant eyebrows went up. "I'm not speaking to you like you're a child; I'm speaking to you like you're a person who's had a terrible shock after a traumatic day, and who seems to need a little help on the self-care front. I don't want to get any calls late tonight because you sat here till after dark and got lost on your way back." His expression gentled again. "Come on, Willow. Let me help." His hand reached up to brush back a stray tangle of hair that had dropped across her face.

A tightness rose in her throat; annoyance fled, replaced by something else—something warm and shaky, something that made much less sense. In an instant, all the emotion of the day threatened to burst through and shatter her, sending her flying in jagged shards in all directions.

She would not shatter. Not now, not yet. She jerked back and stood up too fast, refusing to look at him. "I'm fine. I can make it on my own. I'm fine."

He gave an exasperated sigh. "Willow, you're not fine, and you're not *supposed* to be fine after an experience like this—"

"*I'm fine!*" She heard the hysterical edge in her voice, but she couldn't stop it; escape was her only option. She hurriedly descended the steps, passing between the stone lions with as much dignity as she could muster.

Once away from the house, and from Nick, the fist clutching the inside of Willow's solar plexus began to release its grip. She focused on her breath, exhaling tension and shock, and inhaling the sweet salty fog-mist and balsam fragrance of the softly falling twilight. She wanted to slink back to Sue's cabin, climb up to the second-floor loft where she had slept as a child; there she yearned to crawl under the covers, curl into a ball and go to sleep.

But it wasn't Sue's cabin anymore; Sue had been its heart, its warmth and safety, and now she was gone. The night ahead promised nothing but silence and darkness, no company but terrifying thoughts and unprocessed memories. Willow was alone on Little North.

But as she rounded the last bend, Willow realized the cabin was neither dark nor empty; a warm golden glow shone from the kitchen inside, and someone had turned on the porch light. The furry silhouette of a familiar short-legged dog sat patiently at the top of the stairs, pointed ears on high alert, waiting. A warm scent floated out on the air, mingling with that of the pine trees and the sea: the scent of garlic and tomatoes and herbs.

The dog wagged his tail as she reached the steps; the sound of quiet voices, dishes faintly clattering, and something being stirred on the stove filtered out to her. The knot in her stomach released the rest of the way.

She went inside. The dog followed.

This morning, the cabin had smelled of Maine dampness and benign neglect; now the air was redolent with garlic and herbs and the rich complexity of a perfect marinara sauce. Mac Reyes was sprawled on the couch, tattooed feet dangling over the armrest, typing on her phone. Her mother had changed out of her suit into jeans and a sweater and was working at a bottle of wine with a corkscrew; the red-haired woman who had made eye contact with Willow at the reception was laying out flatware and napkins on the long trestle table. Rina stood at the stove stirring the steaming contents of a cast-iron dutch oven.

Somewhere between a few hours and a lifetime ago, Rina had accused, shouted, and called Willow a liar. Now here she was, making dinner at Sue's stove in Sue's cabin. Rina fleetingly met Willow's eyes, offered a conflicted half smile, and turned her attention back to the sauce.

The corgi sat at Willow's feet and leaned into her calf. She squatted down to pet him; he bobbed his front paws up onto her knee and gazed up intently at her. *You okay?* he seemed to be asking. *You look a little beaten down, like you've had a truly rotten and trauma-filled afternoon. Do you need an emotional support companion, perhaps? And did you happen to bring any more cake?*

"Finn seems ready to adopt you," the redhead said, walking over to Willow. "I'm glad—I hoped he would find someone soon. I'm Catherine Ward, by the way—the village librarian. I don't think we've officially met." She held out a hand, a little awkwardly.

Willow reached up and took it gratefully. Catherine looked to be about Willow's age, with winter-pale skin and thick glasses and a shy smile it was impossible not to return. "Hi. Nice to meet you." She surveyed the room, including all four of them in her question. "You all heard what happened?" Willow asked.

"We heard," Diana replied simply.

Not knowing what to say, Willow turned back to the dog, who leaned in blissfully as she ruffled his neck fur—she had always loved dogs, but her mother had never allowed them into their pristine home. "Finn. It suits him. Whose dog is he?" she asked Catherine.

"Effie took him in when he was a puppy," Catherine replied. "She left him to Sue in her will, along with the house and everything else. When Sue died . . ." She trailed off, then continued. "Rina brought him home, and she's been feeding him. He's been sleeping in the inn's kitchen, but he's a bit of a Houdini; he can get out of any place he doesn't want to be. He keeps running back to Cameron House, probably looking for his people. It's like he hasn't quite accepted they're gone."

Willow was lost in the corgi's big, mismatched eyes as they gazed up into hers. "That's so sad, poor guy." She looked back up at the librarian and asked suspiciously, "Wait a minute—when you say 'adopt' . . . ?" Surely Catherine had not meant it literally.

Finn bounced up and gave Willow's face a long tongue swipe. Then he dropped to the floor and made for the kitchen and source of the fantastic smells.

He turned and looked back at her once, with a decisive tail wag. Willow could swear he grinned at her.

Diana brought a glass of wine over to Willow. "Here you go. More than the average sommelier would offer, but I'm guessing you could use it." She returned to the little kitchen, stepping up beside Rina at the stove and nudging her in Willow's direction, easing the spoon out of Rina's hand.

Rina took a deep breath in and out, willing the hard ball of shame and resentment at her core to dissipate, but knowing Diana's gentle elbow to her ribs would be followed by another less gentle nudge if she didn't move. After a brief hesitation, she relinquished the spoon and crossed the distance to Willow, who stood to meet her, awkwardly brushing away the dog hairs from her black dress and leggings.

A moment ago, Rina had watched Willow relaxing into the corgi's warmth and good spirits, soaking them up like water to a parched plant. Now, as Rina approached, she could see the girl began to shrivel inward again, and her heart broke a little.

The hardest words would be the first, but she knew they were the most important. "I'm sorry," Rina said quietly.

Apologies did not come easily to her. But as she spoke this one, something shifted inside her, transmuting the words from social obligation to truth. "I'm so very sorry. I've been horrible to you since you got here—it never occurred to me you could have been as shut out as Sue was."

Willow shook her head miserably. "No, you were right. I could have pushed; I could have tried harder. I should have trusted her, and I shouldn't have given up so easily—"

"You were a child," Rina said sharply. "You can't blame yourself—I know, I know," she said, her hands up, "that sounds silly for me to say after I lit into you the way I did, but—it *wasn't* you. And I should have seen it or at least considered it. You were a kid, and you trusted and believed in the adults who were supposed to be caring for you. It's not your fault." She paused, giving them both a moment to let it sink in. "You lost as much as she did. I'm so sorry I didn't see it sooner." Sorrier than Willow knew, or hopefully would ever know.

Rina watched as a shaft of hope bloomed in Willow's eyes—deep, steady eyes that reminded her so much of Sue's. She felt the Gordian knot of resentment and self-absorption she had pulled around her heart beginning to loosen, threatening to release the wash of grief its tangled threads had been holding at bay since the morning of the wedding, the perfect day she had dreamed of for so long, that would now never happen.

Rina stepped back, looking away from Willow's conflicted face, knowing if she did not, she would instead step forward and hug the girl. And if she did that, the levees would break and wash her away; she would have to feel things, feel *all* the things, and she was not ready for that.

Besides, with any proper hug came the high likelihood that Willow's wine would spill; Rina did not believe in wasting decent Montepulciano.

Rina cleared her throat. "When we heard what had happened at the mansion today, we thought you might want a dinner you didn't have to think about too much. And maybe that you wouldn't want to be on your own."

Diana added, slipping a foil-wrapped baguette into the oven, "If you want to talk about it, we're here to listen—but only if you want to."

Mac's phone beeped with a received text; she typed a quick response and put it down. She added, "And if you'd rather we go away and leave you in peace—with pasta, of course—we can do that too."

Willow's eyes narrowed as she looked at Mac and the innocent-looking phone on the coffee table. "Who did you text when I got here? Oh God, was it Nick? He's the one who told you about—about all of it?"

Mac shrugged. "He was worried about you. He wanted to make sure you got here okay and had someone to look after you."

Willow scowled. "I do *not* need looking after, and I *definitely* don't need Nick Tyler suddenly deciding he's responsible for me. Besides, he doesn't even like me. And I don't like him. The only thing we agree on, I expect, is how much we mutually dislike each other."

Mac sniffed. "He's a man, and most men are resentful of women who are more complicated than they are."

Diana called in from the stove, "Which is most women."

"Which is most women," Rina agreed. "But he also knew we

would dislocate his exceptionally pretty nose if he let you carry all this alone. He called us hours ago."

Mac continued, "And he texted when you left him at the house so we'd know to watch for you." She looked sideways at Willow. "He's not such a bad guy, you know. For a law-and-order type, he's a decent human."

"Humph." Willow pulled out her own phone. At some point during the afternoon, Nick had given her his number; "Don't hesitate to call or text if you remember anything new or if you think of anything you want to tell me," he'd said. Well, now she had thought of something. She typed, *Seriously? Texting Mac and checking up on me? I am not a child, Nick Tyler. I'm an adult and I'm fine.* She clicked Send and immediately felt like an idiot.

The response came in seconds. *Thank you for the update, I'm glad you're safe, and it's so nice to have you back on the island to be a pain in my tail, Willow Stone. Have a lovely evening.*

Butthead.

Bravado and outrage aside, Willow had to admit—to herself, if to no one else—that they were right, and Nick was right too. She did not want to be alone right now.

Rina hesitantly patted Willow's shoulder. "Sit. Drink your wine." She went back into the kitchen to give the sauce a stir and dropped a package of tagliatelle into a pot of boiling water. "Dinner in about eight minutes."

CHAPTER THIRTEEN

With the first taste of homemade pasta sauce, of crisp-crusted garlic bread paired with a perfect caprese salad, Willow started to feel human again. The wine probably helped; Diana kept innocently topping off everyone's glasses, and Willow could not be sure how much she was drinking. Finn stayed at Willow's side; she couldn't be sure if it was genuine affection or the hope that a bit of pasta or fresh mozzarella might fall to the floor, but she appreciated him nonetheless.

Conversation at dinner remained light and inconsequential, for which Willow was grateful. When everyone had finished eating, they moved back into the main room of the cabin: Willow curled up on the overstuffed chair in the corner with Finn's head resting on her thigh, Catherine perched in the window seat beside the big bow window, and Diana and Mac sat together on the longer couch.

Rina settled into Sue's ancient glider rocker. Seeing a stranger—more or less—in Sue's favorite seat caused an ugly little twinge in Willow's gut, but she forced herself to let it go.

Someone passed around a plate of leftover mini pastries and

cookies from the reception. The women were quiet for a time, listening to the sea outside and the wind in the pines. Mac was the first to speak. "So, Willow . . . what happened? Are you okay to talk about it?"

Rina interrupted gently, "Mac, no. She's had a horrific day; she doesn't need to go through it all—"

"It's okay," Willow said quietly as Finn's tail thumped on the cushion beside her, and he looked up encouragingly. "I think I need to."

Willow told them the story. Most of it. She left out the broken cane, she said nothing of the shawl, and she absolutely remained silent about the thick sense of *presence* in the house, of dozens of invisible eyes watching as she fled.

When she finished, Diana frowned. "Crime tape, you said?"

Catherine murmured, "Told you so."

Mac turned to Willow. "Catherine was convinced, based on what we saw earlier and what Nick told us, that Talbot had been poisoned. We all told her she was nuts."

"I don't think she's nuts," Willow said soberly. It made a frightening kind of sense. Geralt had seemed fine earlier in the day, but from start to finish of the reception, he had gone from bad to worse.

Rina was staring down at her own fingers, which were twisted in her lap. Diana said, "Rina thinks it was her fault from screaming at him."

Rina's lips pursed in conflicted misery. "He's horrible. He deserved it. But I didn't want to give him heart failure or anything."

Mac rolled her eyes. "It would be proof he has a heart, something I'm not sure any of us are fully convinced of. What?" she asked indignantly when they all shot her a look. "You're all thinking it too."

Willow's thoughts tangled in confusion. Should she tell them about what she overheard in the church, about the man in the vestibule and what he'd said about Sue? Geralt had cautioned her against trusting too easily, and now he was in the hospital, barely alive. *And he wasn't the only one who threatened Geralt today*, her mind whispered, remembering the murderous look on Rina's face earlier. Rina had loved Sue.

Oh God, she thought. What if Geralt had been involved, in some way, in Sue's death? And Rina had found out?

No. Willow mentally shook her head. *I can't believe Rina would go that far, no matter how much she hated him.* Sue had loved Rina. That automatically put her in the plus column for Willow.

Still, she thought, *best not say anything. Not just yet.*

"They wouldn't put police tape up if they thought it was a heart attack," Catherine insisted. "I'm betting they think he was poisoned. Or at least that it's a possibility. We all saw him at the reception—he didn't look good."

Mac nodded and snagged another almond cookie. "Right—but we all figured the combination of age and rage, on top of a weak heart and too much heavy food, finally got the better of him."

Rina sighed. "The rage is on me. It was inevitable. Messing with me is one of Talbot's favorite pastimes. And the timing was . . . bad."

Diana reached over and patted Rina's hand. "It's all bad. You lost your fiancée, your best friend, your business partner, and the love of your life. Her memorial was today. You have every right to be way more of a wreck than you are. And I'm sorry I couldn't insulate you from his asshattery. Today should have been about Sue."

Rina squeezed her hand. "I know. And thank you. I still can't quite believe she's gone." She looked around at them, a self-deprecating half smile on her face. "Do you know, I haven't even begun to clear out her things? Everything in the inn is as if she were still around. The book she was reading on the nightstand, her hairbrush on the vanity, her jacket in the hall closet where I see it every time I open the door—for all I know, her keys are still right there in the pocket where she always forgot them. I just can't bring myself . . ." She trailed off. "So yes, I'm a little bit of a wreck, and I guess I am entitled. But my God, that horrible man." She shook her head.

"I was in charge of the lemonade for a while, and he was drinking a lot of it. The guy was seriously thirsty," Catherine said.

"I saw some of the other men slip him God knows how many empanadas during the party," Mac put in, "and those are basically not exactly low on the fat-and-cholesterol scale."

"No criticism of my abuela's empanadas will be tolerated," Diana said.

"Not a criticism, Mom, you know that," Mac said. "They're amazing. But he probably shouldn't have been eating them." She grinned. "I, on the other hand, am young and skinny and athletic, so I would be happy to remove temptation from anyone else and eat the leftovers."

"It wasn't only food, though," Willow said, cautiously entering the conversation, keeping her voice as normal as she could. "A lot of the men were passing flasks around, spiking each other's lemonades like it was a frat party." She took a bite of her brownie. "A few women too. Not to change the subject, but in the name of all that's holy, who made these?"

Rina's smile radiated satisfied superiority. "It's *my* grandmother's recipe, taught to me when I was nine. Diana may be a magician in the bakery, but these are still the best brownies anywhere, period. You're welcome."

"Didn't know brownies were an Italian thing," Mac said idly, snagging one for herself.

"My nonna grew up in Brooklyn, so there," Rina said smugly.

The ability to make perfect brownies doesn't necessarily eliminate her from a suspect list, Willow thought, *but it comes close.*

"Thank you for the pastry praise," Diana said, "but you're

right; I yield the brownie baking championship title to you and your grandmother." She frowned. "Thing is, the list of people who might want Talbot dead is . . . not short," she said. "The man is a homophobic, misogynistic lowlife who owns half the town and has loaned money to the other half, and those were his *legal* business proceedings."

"Like who?" Willow asked.

"Well, most of the island businesses and merchants, for one thing," Diana said. "They—we—make nearly all their annual income in summer, but the bills come all year. He's raised the rent twice on most of the village businesses, and he's made no secret of the fact that he wants to drive the established businesses out and bring in his own corporate cronies. Joe and Frank's bakery, the Dolphin's Tale bookshop, Annie's ice cream place—even old Bill at the Dockside is feeling the squeeze."

"It goes further than the island." Catherine pulled a tablet out of her purse and opened it. "I've been doing research on him—"

Mac laughed. "Hah—of course you were. You can take the librarian out of the library, but—"

"Oh, stuff it," Catherine said good-naturedly. She called up her notes on the screen. "On the business side of things, the man is ruthless. He made his millions in the textile industry, switched to Big Pharma, and eventually sat back and let his money make money. Naomi is his fourth wife—yes, fourth," she said when the others' eyes widened, "and he managed to pay no support or alimony to any of the first three after the divorces. There were lawsuits and settlement battles, and in each case, there was some investigator or smoking-gun witness to testify that the woman had been unfaithful, so none of them ever got a dime."

"Jeez," Mac muttered.

Catherine continued, "So there are a few ex-wives out there with reason to hate him, though I'm not sure they will give us much to work with. Wife number one, Sylvia Talbot Olivera, went on to marry a professional soccer player; they moved to Brazil and seem to be set for life. Wives number two and three also went on to get married and have kids with someone else: number two, Cheryl Talbot Turek, is a retired schoolteacher in Iowa; number three, Nina Talbot Chavez, died of cancer about fifteen years ago, leaving behind five children and seven grandchildren, presumably by her second husband, although . . ." She clicked around a bit. "Her oldest son *may* have been born during the same calendar year as the divorce, so I guess there is some possible question about the timing. I would need to get into some deeper documents to know the actual dates and such, and I doubt he'd be interested in taking a paternity test."

"If he knew he might be heir to this kind of fortune, I bet he might consider it." Mac looked in Catherine's direction, impressed. "You found all this . . . today?"

Catherine shrugged. "About ten years ago, a journalist did a big profile on him; she dug most of this up, citing 'anonymous sources.' I would guess some former HR employee decided she'd had enough and leaked it all." She opened another set of notes. "Ah, here we go. The man received, over the course of his career, sixteen sexual harassment allegations, uncounted tabloid covers with starlets and models, a couple of 'most sought-after bachelor' lists for magazines, at least three paternity suits, and an assault charge. Some of those last few were also picked up by the tabloids, everything from 'Millionaire CEO's secretaries reveal the truth about his secret sex club' to 'Geralt Talbot impregnated me with an alien baby.'"

Mac said, "Seriously? Those are real?"

Catherine nodded. "No joke. This was during that whole shock TV era, where the more over-the-top the story, the more attention people paid to it. And bear in mind that before the #MeToo movement it was incredibly difficult—I mean, more even than it is now—for a woman's accusation to be taken seriously." She clicked over to another page. "He covered his tracks pretty thoroughly and made sure any potential problems were nipped off at the start. Not inconsequential, considering we're talking about an almost sixty-year career here."

Mac shook her head. "But . . . alien babies?"

"That's a sad one," Catherine said, checking her notes again. "This woman in the early nineties apparently accused him of assault at some point—here she is, Marianne Forrest. She seems to have been a little . . . off, and she probably should have been receiving psychiatric care; her story changed every time she told it, and she had a criminal record from when she was young—a single shoplifting charge or something. And of course she didn't get anything from him. I think he smothered her in threats of lawsuits—"

"And possibly an under-the-table payoff," Diana interjected.

"Possibly. She died about twenty years later. Suicide."

"How awful." Willow shuddered. "The poor woman. And the alleged alien offspring?"

Catherine peered at her screen again. "I can't find a record of any baby, alien or otherwise. The woman fell off the grid for a long time, kept a low profile. And I can't find anything on the other harassment or assault charges either; if he was targeted and poisoned by anyone out of his past, my money would be somewhere back there."

Willow shook her head incredulously. "Catherine, you are . . . amazing."

Catherine flushed a little but looked pleased. "I'm a librarian. Research is my jam."

Willow shook her head. "I'm a grad student; research is *my* jam, but you blow me out of the water." She reached for another brownie. "What about the other paternity claims?"

Catherine shook her head. "I couldn't find anything about them. But I'll keep looking."

Diana mused, "We know most of the people who were there today. Rina, did you notice any strangers, folks from off-island?"

Rina looked distracted. "Maybe. I'm honestly not sure. I know some of Sue's old colleagues from the college came for the service, so I would have chalked up unfamiliar faces to that, or to tourists or day-trippers."

"We'll all keep thinking," Diana said. "It was a perfect opportunity. Anyone could have slipped him something at any time. And whether it was a stranger or an islander, like we've said, a lot of people have reason to hate him." *Including me*, she did not say out loud.

Rina cleared her throat awkwardly. "Anyone could have, yes. But as far as I know, only one of those people was passing him a cup of lemonade within thirty seconds of threatening to kill him."

Silence fell again, like a thunderclap, as Rina spoke the words no one else had wanted to say.

"No way. Not your style," Mac said into the awkward pause. "If you were going to kill someone, you'd need a better reason than 'because he was being a garbage human'—and besides, it would be with a meat cleaver and in front of the whole town, not secretly slipping poison into lemonade—way too bloodless for you. What?" she asked indignantly when her mother glared at her. "It's true."

Rina almost smiled. "No, you're absolutely right." She thought for a minute. "Diana, if it comes to it, would you be able to get me off on the meat cleaver defense?"

Diana squeezed her shoulder. "If it comes to it, I'm sure we can do better than that. Yes," she said in response to Willow's startled look, "I am—was—an attorney. I don't practice anymore, but I keep my license up to date. Fifteen years of corporate law was enough for me; now I bake pastries and sell antiques and use my powers for good." She slid the tray across the table to Willow. "Have another scone."

Rina looked up and around at them, the beginnings of fear in her eyes. "If Geralt doesn't come out of this . . ."

Diana came over and patted her shoulder. “He will. I’m sure he’ll be all right.”

“Of course he will,” Mac said encouragingly, and Catherine nodded.

But none of them would meet Rina’s gaze. Willow noticed that too.

CHAPTER FOURTEEN

After the kitchen was cleaned and the leftovers stashed in the refrigerator, the women left. From the porch swing in front of the cabin, Willow sipped the last of her wine, watching their flashlights bob along in the darkness until they disappeared around the curve in the path and were hidden by the mansion.

Willow was, once again, alone.

And yet not alone: Finn had stayed. After slipping down the stairs to pee nonchalantly on a wild rosebush, the corgi came back up and plopped himself on Willow's lap in the swing. When she went inside, he followed.

The little log home, now empty of people, was much as she remembered: cozy, comfortable—and yet it wasn't the same. No magazines cluttered the table; no sweaters were draped over the couch back. There were no size 10 slip-on clogs by the door where Sue had always left them. A laminated card next to the TV set, carefully lettered, offered the Wi-Fi code for the house; a similarly lettered sign on the little door off the kitchen read WASHER/DRYER. The cabin was full of light and warmth, but there was none of the human clutter of a *home*.

Sue's bedroom—or what had been her bedroom—was on the main floor. Willow stepped inside and left immediately. She did not want to sleep here. Instead, she made her way up the steps to the loft and the double bed where her younger self had stayed every summer, where she had sat for hours under the slanted skylight, writing in her journal and hiding from the world. Finn followed, leaping onto the bed and curling into a doughnut shape at its foot.

Willow's mother would never have approved of letting a dog on the bed, but then Willow's mother would never have let a dog in the house to begin with. And frankly, after what she had learned today, emulating anything about her parents was the last thing Willow was interested in. She changed into a T-shirt and sweatpants and joined Finn.

Willow was wrung out. Her brain wanted to keep niggling away at the little pieces of information she'd picked up through the day, looking for connections and patterns, but she found her thoughts unable to move faster than a foggy crawl. She needed to sleep. If her brain would let her.

The loft at least was still familiar, still warm and welcoming and hers. The Tiffany-style bedside lamp Sue had made back when she decided to learn how to work with stained glass, the simple nightstand holding a clock, a CD player, and a beat-up paperback book—Sue loved reading and always made sure Willow never lacked for reading material. The cover of the old novel featured the stereotypical shadowy heroine reaching out across storm-swept seas, like so many of the pulpy thrillers Sue had enjoyed.

There was a padded mailer-type envelope on the bed, with Willow's name written on it in black marker; Rina must have come upstairs at some point and left it for her. Willow opened it and, curious, pulled out a CD and an old hardbound book.

She recognized the CD immediately. Grief and love squeezed her heart; for now, she gently set it aside.

Tucked into the inside cover of the book was another of Rina's notes:

Willow—

I found these with Sue's things the other day; they survived all her Marie Kondo-like purges through the years. I think she held on to them and set them aside for you in the hopes of seeing you again someday soon. I'm sorry she did not get to pass them on to you herself . . . but, again, I know she would want you to have them.

—Rina

Rina, Willow was learning, preferred to express herself not in words but in homemade brownies and pasta, company on lonely evenings, and tokens of the past that connected them in their love of someone they had both lost.

No, Willow thought. *No, Rina wouldn't, couldn't, have poisoned Geralt. I don't believe it.*

She examined the hardcover book, its dusty jacket showing an image of a tall house—like Cameron House, and yet not like—above storm-tossed seas; *Widow's Walk*, it read in large, slanted letters across the top, *by Abel R. Douglas*. At the highest point of the house, the silhouette of a woman stood on the eponymous rooftop walk, gazing out at the sea with a shawl around her shoulders and wind blowing the hair back from her bowed head. She opened the book and read on the inside of the dust jacket, "When her husband perished in the early days of the Second World War, Marie thought her life's journey was over . . . but in truth, it was only beginning."

Willow knew why Sue had saved the CD, but the book was unfamiliar. Why would Sue have saved this for her? She pulled out her computer. A quick internet search showed that Abel R. Douglas had written about a dozen books; *Widow's Walk*, published in 1946, seemed to be the first. All his novels were by now out of print, though some were available from used booksellers or on eBay. She could find nothing else about the author online.

"Hmm," she murmured to Finn. "Maybe I'll stop by the library tomorrow and ask Catherine if she knows anything. What do you think?"

The dog's tail gave a sleepy thump.

Willow nodded. "Agreed. I'm tired too." She scratched his ears, grateful for his company, and together, they curled up on her old bed.

Willow reached for the CD Rina had left her; her hands shook a little as she gently removed it from its case, slipped it into the old player on the nightstand, and pressed Play.

Bach's Passacaglia and Fugue in C Minor exhaled its gentle grounding theme into the loft of the cabin. It was the piece Willow had played at the end of the memorial service—Willow's favorite piece of music in all the world, the one she always kept under her fingers, the one she turned to when she needed steadiness. It had also been Sue's favorite, she suddenly remembered. As often as Willow had played it, how had she forgotten that her love for it probably had grown from Sue's?

She curled up in the bed and let the gentle repetition and variation of the music wash over her, each phrase built on the same foundational footprint, ranging further and further abroad while staying rooted in its home place.

Though she never admitted it consciously even to herself, some part of Willow had always dreamed that one day Sue would wander into a church where she was practicing; she would hear her goddaughter playing Bach, they would recognize each other and reunite, and whatever had driven the yearslong abyss between them could at last be forgotten.

The overlapping phrases curled softly around Willow as she released her hold on the dream that would now never be. The tears finally came, soaking her pillow and racking her body with hard sobs. The corgi crawled up next to her, his solid warmth comforting in the chilly Maine night. She curled her arm around him and held him close. And slept.

Willow didn't know what time she woke in the night or what had awakened her. Nor could she pinpoint the source of the impulse to get out of bed and move to the loft window.

She had forgotten how dark the nights were here. There were no streetlights on Little North Island; the aura of illuminated civilization she hardly noticed in Chicago had no grip here. Even so, the nearly invisible silhouette of the Cameron mansion rose out of the swaying pines and granite shoreline. Its darkness was more than a mere absence of light; it gave weight and mass to the night, wrapping shadow around itself like a cloak.

In a quick flicker, a bright shard broke the darkness, a brief flash of light behind one of the mansion's first-floor windows. It grew and faded, then moved to another room, as though someone was walking around the house with a flashlight. Then it disappeared, and the heavy dark fell again. Willow frowned. Who would be skulking around Cameron House with a flashlight in the middle of the night? Surely no one with any business there.

Willow watched for several minutes, but the light beams did not return. She stepped away from the window, ready to return to bed, then turned back, her eye drawn to a small dormer window on one of the upper floors. There, a golden bloom of light, gentle as a will-o'-the-wisp, ignited and seeped out into the night. This was no flashlight—it looked, if such were possible, like the glow from an old-fashioned gas lamp, filtering through the delicate lace curtain that covered the window. As Willow stared in fascination, a hand reached out and pulled the curtain aside, and a face peeked out. A woman's face, she was sure, despite the distance.

Looking, across the darkness, directly at Willow.

Willow took several impulsive steps back, her heart pounding. When she stepped forward and dared to look again, the little dormer window was dark. But somehow this was worse. Was the face still there? Could it see her?

Had it even been there to begin with, or was she imagining things?

Willow had heard the stories, of course, of the ghosts that supposedly haunted Cameron House, scary tales children told at slumber parties or on campouts, but she had never believed them. Certainly she had never seen a ghost herself. And the intruder with the flashlight had been, she was certain, all too real. Why, then, was she so certain the face in the upper window had been someone else entirely?

She crawled back into bed; Finn writhed irritably at having to make room for her but was snoring again within seconds.

Willow envied him; now that she was back in bed, sleep seemed far away. The burst of adrenaline that had surged when the face appeared in the window still coursed through her, and now her mind was circling again, reviewing the day like a disjointed slideshow, rehearing pieces of conversation. Cameron House. Geralt. Joel. The whispering voices in the foyer. The disappearing cane and shawl. Geralt's claim on the mansion that had been Sue's, and Effie's before her . . .

When someone with one foot already in the grave kicks the bucket, how hard are they going to look for a cause of death? the unidentified man in the church had said. She'd assumed he was referring to Geralt, but . . . *Miss Effie,* Willow thought, and her drooping eyes jerked wide open at the thought. *The ninety-nine-year-old woman who supposedly passed peacefully in her sleep. How deeply,* she wondered, *did anyone investigate* her *death?*

Effie. Then Sue. Now Geralt. One after another, in the space of just a few months.

It was a long time before Willow could relax enough to sleep again, but at last she found herself drifting off. In the timeless moment between wakefulness and sleep, Willow thought she might have heard someone settling down into the glider rocker downstairs. This time, it did not occur to her to be afraid; her mind, shifting into dreams, realized this could only be Aunt Sue, settling into her favorite chair with a cup of tea, gazing out her own big bay window toward the sea.

Feeling safe and warm for the first time in recent, or possibly not-so-recent, memory, Willow at last felt her body begin to release again into sleep.

CHAPTER FIFTEEN

Willow awoke to a bright shaft of sun through the skylight, a wet nose in her face, and a feeling of being fully rested that she had not experienced in a long time. Finn expressed an immediate need to go outside, so she dragged herself out of bed to let him out; after anointing another wild rosebush, he informed Willow in no uncertain terms that it was time for his breakfast. *Oh no,* she thought, *dog food. I don't have dog food.* "Sorry, dude," she said. "I've never had a four-footed roommate before, and I have no idea what you guys eat. And I didn't get to shop properly yesterday. We may be out of luck."

But when she stepped into the little kitchen, Willow realized that, along with last night's dinner makings, Rina had stocked the kitchen with some basic groceries: eggs, milk, yogurt, and juice. A loaf of fresh bread on the counter beside a jar of obviously homemade blueberry jam. Coffee, creamer, and a box of little oatmeal packets.

The small kindness made Willow's heart swell again.

She opened the refrigerator with one hand, searching "what to feed your dog when you run out of dog food" on her phone with the other—but before the first results had time to come up, Finn himself pushed past her to the fridge. Propping himself against the shelf with one paw, he made a beeline for the plastic container of leftover pasta Willow had not realized was there. Delicately maneuvering it into his large corgi jaws, he pulled it out and carried it over to the corner of the kitchen.

Before Willow could react, Finn pried the lid off the container with the technique of one who had done this many times before; within seconds, he had enthusiastically scarfed down the last of Rina's pasta marinara. It wasn't a very big breakfast, even for a medium-size dog like Finn, but he seemed to enjoy it. Willow's shock soon subsided into something like admiration; if she had ever found a man with this much character and resourcefulness, she might not be in her mid-twenties and still completely single. Finn even brought the container back to her when he had finished; his look told her he would have been happy to wash it himself if he could reach the sink, but his legs were too short, and she would need to take care of that part.

Finn, she was coming to realize, was an extremely cool dog.

There was one leftover brownie from the evening before, neatly covered in cling wrap on a plate on the counter. Willow concluded it was as good a breakfast food as any—though she would have gone for the pasta herself if the dog hadn't beaten her to it—and munched away as she waited for her coffee to brew in the small French press from the corner cabinet.

The connection Willow had made before drifting into slumber had stayed with her, as though her brain had gnawed on it as she slept. Sue's death. Geralt's apparent poisoning. Effie Cameron's passing. The clamor of island preservationists, alongside the covert plotting of eager developers with their aspirations for new hotels and luxury B&Bs on the island. And then there was the North Islands Historical Society, whose existence so far Willow had only seen on signs and placards. Cameron House sat at the center of all of it.

Willow pulled on her favorite too-big sweater, remembered to shut off her phone's Wi-Fi, and gathered up her laptop and backpack. She needed information. And as good as her research skills were, she suspected Catherine Ward's might be better. At the last minute, she scurried upstairs to retrieve the Abel R. Douglas novel, slipping it into her backpack; maybe the red-haired librarian would know something about the author.

Before she had opened the front door more than a couple of inches, Finn slipped out and loped down the stairs. He stopped at the coastal path and looked at her expectantly. *Well? Are you coming? Day's not getting any younger.*

Apparently Finn would be coming with her, and who was she to argue?

Willow breathed in the salt-pine-sweet air of a perfect Maine morning, her feet crunching on the pine needles of the coastal path, listening to the raucous calls of the gulls and crows wheeling overhead. An old-fashioned lobstering dory made its way along the shoreline, moving buoy to buoy, pulling up its pots. The battered wooden boat had been dark blue once, but most of the color had worn away, and four or five lobster pots were piled in the stern. The captain looked younger than his boat but fully as weathered; he stood at the helm, a messy tousle of dark hair fighting its way out from beneath a fisherman's hat. It was an unusual sight; every lobsterman Willow had ever seen used much larger flat-bottomed inboard motorboats with power winches. This one looked completely low-tech, with only buoys and oars and pots—the kind of boat lobstermen had used for centuries off the Maine coast.

Willow realized the fisherman had caught her staring. She froze, then awkwardly put up her hand to wave in greeting. He looked puzzled, returned the wave, and went on with his day's work.

My life's encounters with men in a nutshell, Willow thought wryly. Awkwardness, puzzlement, brief acknowledgment, and then they moved on with their lives and promptly forgot about her.

As they rounded the curve in the path that passed near Cameron House, Finn gave a quick, happy bark and ran up the front walk, ducking easily past the yellow police tape across the porch. Willow called him back, but he ignored her, pawing at the outer screen till his paw could slip behind it. Willow watched aghast as he wedged his body into the opening, pushed his nose against the front door, and slipped inside.

Alarmed, Willow followed, but stopped short at the fluttering barricade of yellow tape. She had no business going inside, but how was she going to get Finn otherwise? And why on earth was the door ajar? Didn't anyone close or lock *anything* on this island?

The responsible thing to do would be to call the police, or Nick, to explain that Finn had gone into the house and ask for permission to go after him. She pulled out her phone, and her thumb hovered over the Call button . . . then she muttered, "Nope, not happening," and put her phone away. Willow gingerly grasped the porch railing and swung her leg over the low X formed by the two strips of tape, pulled her long sleeves down over her fingers so at least she would not leave obvious fingerprints, and followed Finn inside.

Stepping through the doorway into Cameron House was like crossing a threshold into another dimension, as though the house held its own distinct reality within its walls. She could hear the rumble of the ocean outside and the faint call of the birds, but the sounds were distant, removed. In here, it was so quiet that Willow imagined she could hear the motes of dust as they flickered in and out of shafts of morning sunlight. She looked up to the second floor; in the chaos of the day before, Willow had barely noticed the giant stained glass panel crowning the landing, but today, its abstract swirls cast shafts of sea colors and sunset hues over floor and staircase and Willow herself.

To Willow's left, Miss Effie's sitting room overlooked the sea; to her right, a pair of glass doors loomed ominously at the entry to the shadowy library. Willow reached out a hand to try the library door, but before she could touch it, a flicker of movement inside the room startled her into backing away.

When her breath had slowed, she stepped back up to the library doors and peered into the room; it was dark and motionless. A waft of sound behind her, like a quiet chuckle, made her whirl around—but the foyer was empty. Just Finn, heading nonchalantly to what was clearly his favorite spot next to Effie's rocking chair in the sitting room.

The dog did not seem to sense anything in the house beyond the two of them—at least, nothing that worried him—so Willow decided she must have been imagining things; it seemed she had Finn's approval to be here, though if Nick or the other cops came back, she didn't think they were likely to consult with the corgi. She knew she should grab the dog, leave the house, and get on with her day.

I should, yes, but . . . as long as I'm inside . . .

She wouldn't explore the whole house; she didn't quite have the nerve, and besides, it would take too long. But she wanted to find the dormer window she had seen last night.

The dog curled up in a rectangle of sunlight; he gave a single thump with his feathered tail and closed his eyes. *You do what you need to do; I'm going to have a little nap, if you don't mind.*

Willow climbed to the second-floor landing and looked both ways down the shadowed hallways. To her right, an unbroken length of corridor led to a pair of double doors inlaid with stained glass; there, the passage angled off to the left toward the rear of the house. The hall to her left was lined with doors—bedrooms, probably, she surmised, imagining the sumptuous decorations and heavy antique furniture that would lie behind them. Willow hesitantly stepped up to one and turned the knob; this wasn't what she was here for, but she couldn't resist a peek. Gently, she pushed the door inward to open it.

With an abrupt jerk, the door wrenched itself out of her grip and slammed shut in her face. She gasped and jumped back, almost losing her balance and falling back down the stairs; she clutched the smooth wood of the newel post, gasping. The jeweled lights of the foyer had dimmed as if a cloud had moved over the sun outside (*But there were no clouds*, she thought desperately), and the spring warmth had been replaced by a bone-chilling cold. *Don't*, the house seemed to be saying. *Just don't.*

Adrenaline still surging, Willow thought in a panic, *Oh my God what is this place I should leave I will leave right now.*

Forcing her hands to release their grip, Willow began her descent to the first floor and back out of the house. She half expected some specter to explode in her face or push her down the grand staircase; instead, she heard a gentle rustling from the landing above; a single sheet of paper floated from the third floor and settled halfway down the staircase, half a flight above her. Willow craned her neck in an unsuccessful attempt to see where it had come from, then cautiously climbed the steps to where it lay.

She picked up the ordinary sheet of white paper, with a single line of type, faintly uneven, as though from a manual typewriter. Willow examined it, squinting at the words on the page.

Fain would I climb, yet fear I to fall

The line of poetry was vaguely familiar, but she could not place it. Willow's eyebrows knitted together in puzzlement. *Coincidence?* she thought. *A little too on the nose for that.* She turned the paper over to look at the back. At the bottom was one more line of text:

If thy heart fails thee, climb not at all

"All right then," she murmured to herself or anyone else who might be listening. "Challenge accepted. Upward it is."

Taking a deep breath, Willow started back up the staircase.

Whoever or whatever had objected to her opening doors on the second floor seemed to have no problem with Willow opening the third-floor doors, a row of modest bedrooms with white cloths draped over what was probably fine antique furniture. But the views of Sue's cabin were not quite right; this was not the part of the house she was looking for.

At the end of the third-floor hallway, in the largest of the house's turrets, she found a small open parlor, its curved walls lined with bookcases all around, one of which had swung open to reveal a narrow hallway.

Willow had read that hidden corridors were often built into houses like this, ostensibly so servants could move around in seeming invisibility to those they served, but she had never seen one herself.

I wonder who moves around Cameron House without being seen these days? Willow thought, and a chill zinged up her spine.

She stepped through the concealed doorway into a dim passage, paneled in the same rich wood as the rest of the house; up ahead, a high window let in light. A small stairway, a sharp turn, and a short stretch along a brick-paved wall; she realized the shadowy journey was taking her around one of the house's massive chimneys. Another turn, another stairway, twisting ever upward.

If thy heart fails thee, climb not at all . . . Willow suddenly wanted to go back, to retrieve Finn from the bright, unthreatening sitting room and head to the safety of the village, where there was sunlight and humanity and no mysterious hands slamming doors or enigmatic typed notes—she did not want to see where this passage went. But before she could turn to head back, she became aware of a rustling behind her, the brush of fabric against walls, near-silent footsteps. The sound of light breathing.

It was her imagination, of course. And all she had to do to prove it was turn around and confront the empty passage behind her. That would settle the question, wouldn't it?

Fain would I climb, yet fear I to fall . . .

She did not turn around.

Soon whatever sounds she might have heard in the passageway were overtaken by the hollow whistling of wind in the eaves; she was certainly up too high by now for the dormer window she sought. The journey was steep now. Willow could feel the stairs swaying slightly beneath her, and she tightened her grip on the handrail, forcing herself to continue.

The staircase at last emptied her onto a small, bright landing and a tiny room. A glass-paned door opened to a broad rooftop deck at the very top of the house.

She hadn't located her lamp-lit dormer window, but she had found the widow's walk.

CHAPTER SIXTEEN

The rooftop deck at the top of Cameron House was larger than she had realized, maybe twenty feet long and half as wide. Its wooden safety railing was battered and pocked, but it looked fairly solid—except for one spot where the railing had split and was awaiting repair.

Out here, the sun was shining again, as though she had stepped out of whatever peculiar microclimate Cameron House held inside itself, back into the normal world. And yet, the rooftop deck filled her with unease. It wasn't a fear of heights—no, it was the distinct sense that she was not alone. And that the house itself had driven her up here for some purpose.

She wasn't sure she wanted to know what that purpose was.

Uneasiness aside, Willow couldn't deny that the view from the roof walk of Cameron House was magical. She felt like she could see forever—the soft pink granite mountains of Acadia National Park to the northeast, the rocky shoals on the mainland, the twin lighthouses on cither side of Little North, marking the passage to the ocean vastness beyond. Nearby in Little North Village, the white belfry of the Congregational church rose above the bluff overlooking the ocean; across the island on St. Andrew's Hill, the steeple of the smaller Catholic church rose out of the sea of evergreens. Closer still, a little boy in an old-fashioned newsboy cap ran happily through the broad lupine field beside Cameron House, a crow circling his head and cawing happily. Beyond the field, a pine-needle-covered footpath led away from Cameron House and disappeared into the edge of the forest. Willow remembered her friends' whispers about the haunted Cameron family graveyard at the end of the path; everyone seemed to have a story about it, but no one would admit to actually seeing the graveyard or its ghosts themselves. *They thought the graveyard was haunted? They should have tried the house,* Willow thought wryly. *As Shakespeare said, "Hell is empty and all the devils are here."*

Not devils, though, she realized. There was no sense of evil or malice in the presences she felt here.

That didn't make the experience any less unnerving.

Willow turned to the side of the roof facing Sue's cabin and gazed down the shingled drop, scanning gables and turrets for the dormer room where she had seen the curious lamplight last night. She found it quickly, a little down and over, sitting just below the ridge jutting off the main wing. The little room had two windows, Willow realized—the dormer facing Sue's cabin, and another that opened onto the roof across from the widow's walk, almost close enough to crawl to from here. The room should have looked awkward, planted there in the asymmetrical roofline, but Willow found it charming and wanted more than ever to find it herself.

Her gaze turned again to the railing opposite her, where the top two boards had splintered violently apart, leaving a gaping space open to the roof and ground below. Willow crossed the widow's walk and crouched down to examine them, brushing a hand carefully over one of the jagged edges. No rot, no weakness, just . . . broken wood.

This was unlike Sue, her brain told her insistently; her godmother had never been one to leave things undone, especially things as dangerous as this. Any railing in a home of Sue's would be all but impossible to break; she would have stood for nothing less.

Willow wondered what had broken this one.

Once outside and back in the world of the ordinary, Willow and Finn continued their walk to the village. The beautiful weather had brought out locals and visitors alike, people wandering the green shopping and eating and enjoying the day. Two little girls in loose skirts and pinafore aprons sat on the grass, playing a clapping game, near where Willow had eaten her tres leches cake. A bored-looking teenager with dyed black hair, nose piercing, and a cropped concert T-shirt pointedly ignored them from where she perched nearby, face buried in a book. Willow could almost believe that the last hour had never happened. Because it couldn't have happened. Could it?

Willow caught a glimpse of the black-bonneted older women from the church, the pair she had come to think of as the Knitting Sisters, gazing out at the sea from an ancient stone bench overlooking the harbor. A trio of lobstermen sat on the granite jetty next to the dock: Two of them, in hoodies and work pants, munched on slices of pizza. The third, a few feet away from the others, she recognized—it was the low-tech lobsterman she had seen out on the water not much more than an hour ago; maybe he'd had a good morning and finished early. As though he had felt her gaze, he turned his head and looked straight at her. His weathered face broke into a hesitant smile, and he nodded in greeting.

It was enough to shake out the cobwebs of her terror, to return her to the world of the living. She smiled back.

The island library had once been a single-story house, renovated years ago to serve its current purpose. Bright windows let in the sunlight, and the air carried the aroma of new carpet, paper between leather covers, and wood oil cleaner, underlaid with the faintest hint of teenager and socks from the kids who stopped by to study or do homework. When the bell at the door sounded lightly, Catherine looked up from her computer and smiled as Willow hesitantly ducked inside, a coffee cup in each hand.

"Hey there," Catherine said. "I'm glad to see you. How are you holding up?"

"I'm good, thanks. I don't know how you take your coffee, but—" Before she could finish, Finn slid past her legs and made a beeline for an old, braided rug in the children's section, where he curled up in the rectangle of sunlight. Willow looked helplessly at Catherine.

Catherine waved away her concern and gave the dog a scratch behind the ears. "Finn goes where Finn wants to go," she said. "I've even thought of making a 'where's Finn?' Instagram account so visitors can try to find where he's hanging out at any given time; add a little local color. Not that Little North isn't already dripping with it."

Willow smiled half-heartedly. "If you're sure it's okay." She looked around at the empty room. "Wait," she said, confused, "you guys are open today, right?"

"We are—but the truth is that on gorgeous days like this, our patron count tends to hover somewhere around zero." Catherine grinned. "And I'm not picky about my coffee as long as it has caffeine, which I'm a little short on today—so thank you!"

"This one is light with sugar, and this one is black," Willow said, holding up the coffee cups. "Take your pick."

As Catherine reached for the cup with the sweetened coffee, Willow said, "I would have brought them, anyway, so the coffee isn't a bribe, but . . . if it's not an imposition, I was wondering, may I ask you some questions—history, research type of stuff?"

Catherine grinned. "The research nerd librarian is ready for you," she said, pushing her glasses up her nose and settling back behind her desk. "It's literally my job. The obscurer the question, the better I like it. Bring it on."

Willow reached into her backpack, rooting around till she found the World War II novel Sue had left for her. She set the book on the desk in front of Catherine. "I was wondering if you knew anything about this author. Or if you had any of his books in the library?"

Catherine's eyebrows went up when she saw it. "*Widow's Walk*?" she asked hesitantly. Willow nodded. Catherine picked up the novel and flipped through the pages. "It looks old, but it's in good shape—did you look online to see if it's available for sale anywhere?" Even as she spoke, she was setting the book down and beginning the search on her own.

"I did," Willow answered, "and it isn't. I was able to find about a dozen other titles by Abel R. Douglas, but none are still in print. Have you ever heard of him?"

"No, I haven't," the librarian answered. She regarded the dust jacket with curiosity. "The mansion on the cover looks a lot like Cameron House—I suppose it could be a coincidence, but I wonder if the author is local." She clicked to another website and started typing a new search while Willow looked over her shoulder.

Willow nodded. "I wondered too. Think he might still be around?"

Catherine's brows drew together as they always did when a search proved trickier than usual. "No information anywhere, no bio. I can't find a website for the publisher, so they may have been a tiny house or one that went out of business before there was even an internet. A couple of volumes pop up on the used book sites and a few on eBay."

"Hey, I know that one," Willow said, pointing at one of the titles on the screen, its cover showing the image of a woman looking out at the ocean. She peered closer. "*Weather the Storm*. Sue had a copy of it; I found it in the loft on the nightstand."

"Hmm," Catherine said distractedly, still searching. "There's *Weather the Storm* again; I think it might have been his last book.

Here's *Will to Live*, and *Sea of Secrets* . . . I don't see *Widow's Walk* anywhere, though." She pulled off her glasses and rubbed her eyes. "Where did this one come from, if you don't mind my asking?"

"Sue saved it for me," Willow said. "Rina left me an envelope last night of things Sue had set aside for me."

Catherine turned away from the computer and gave Willow a troubled look. "Sue left you this particular book? Creepy."

"Why do you say that?" Willow asked, stiffening.

Catherine blinked in surprise. "You don't know? No one told you?"

"Told me what?"

"About Sue," Catherine said hesitantly. "How she died. Where she died."

CHAPTER SEVENTEEN

***Oh no,* Willow thought, *oh no, oh, please, no . . .* Her heart was** racing again and gooseflesh rippled over her skin as she remembered the broken railing on the roof walk of Cameron House. "The news article said she fell, but—" She stopped.

Catherine nodded grimly. "She was up on the widow's walk. No one knows why. Part of the wood railing was weak or damaged; she must have leaned on it wrong, lost her balance, and fell. They found her the next morning—" Catherine shuddered.

"An accident?" Willow asked. "Sue would never have stood for rotten wood in her house, let alone fallen through it."

Catherine's eyes turned sharply to hers. "There was no evidence to indicate otherwise or that there was anyone in the house with her, but . . ." Catherine trailed off, looking uncomfortable.

"But what?"

Catherine fidgeted nervously, shifting papers on her desk. "Well . . . do you believe in ghosts?"

Willow went very still. "Why do you ask?"

The librarian ducked her head, seeming embarrassed. "Everyone says the island is haunted, and especially Cameron House. People . . . see things."

"What do they see?" Willow asked, forcing her voice to remain calm.

"You hear stories, that's all," Catherine said, "especially about that widow's walk. The island workmen hate it and always charged Effie double to go up, and they were thrilled when Sue turned out to be handy enough to take care of most of the repairs herself. People would . . . feel things up there. Folks don't talk about it much, but people who go up there once rarely do again."

Small wonder, Willow thought. She said, "So, people think one of the Cameron House ghosts killed Sue? That's . . ." Willow had been going to say *ridiculous*, but given her recent experience, she couldn't quite get the word out.

"No—no, of course not," Catherine said quickly. "The police did their jobs—they found no sign of anyone else in the house, no break-in, no signs of struggle. But I'm guessing they spent as little time up there as possible. In any case, there was nothing to indicate that anyone had been in that house that night except for Sue."

Be careful who you trust, Geralt had said. Willow may not have been entirely sure about Rina, but every instinct in her wanted to trust Catherine. And she had the feeling she would need the librarian's sharp and organized brain to piece any of this together.

Willow took a deep breath. "Last night, I saw someone prowling around the first floor of Cameron House," she said. "Or rather, I saw a flashlight moving room to room as though someone were going through searching for something." *And then I saw what might have been a ghost peering out a little window in the roofline*, she thought, *but maybe I don't need to say that part right now.*

"Wait, really?" Catherine's eyes widened. "Did you tell Nick?"

Willow winced. "No. Not yet. I honestly . . . forgot. And then this morning when I went over there—"

Catherine's eyebrows went up. "When you what?"

Willow's shoulders hunched, and she looked away, embarrassed. "I know. I didn't mean to, but Finn ran away and ducked into the house, and I went inside to bring him back out, but then I was already there, so . . ." She trailed off.

"So you went exploring," Catherine said, looking completely unsurprised. "What happened?"

Willow reached back into her bag and pulled out the typed sheet of paper she'd found on the stairs. She handed it to Catherine, who frowned. "What's this?"

"I found it on the stairs," Willow said. "Or rather, it floated down the stairs to me."

Catherine took the paper and examined it. "'Fain would I climb, yet fear I to fall'—that's Sir Walter Raleigh, I think? He supposedly carved it into a window for Queen Elizabeth. The story's apocryphal, but it's said that she wrote an answer—"

"Turn it over," Willow said simply. Catherine did.

"'If thy heart fails thee, climb not at all.' That's the one." She looked up curiously at Willow. "This just . . . drifted down the stairs to you?"

Willow nodded.

"And did you take its advice and . . . climb?"

Willow nodded again. "I found the widow's walk. And the broken railing. And—" She looked away. "I don't want to go up there any time soon again either."

She gave her head a single hard shake. "Okay, let's . . . let's put a pin in that one. I have another question, if you don't mind?"

Catherine nodded slowly. "Okay. Does it have to do with more ghosts or weird stuff at the house?"

"No," Willow said. "At least, I don't think so. What can you tell me about the North Islands Historical Society? There's a sign outside Cameron House, but I can't find any proper information about them." She shrugged helplessly. "I'm a research nerd too, but faced with groups that don't have an online presence, I get stymied pretty fast. Who are they?"

Catherine smiled ruefully. "Don't feel bad; the society has been full analog since the beginning, and Effie and Sue were their only official living members as far as I know. There are boxes back in the library's archives I could hook you up with. I can't let you take anything out of the building, but you're welcome to scan or photograph anything you'd find useful."

Willow brightened. "That sounds fantastic; I'll take you up on it, if you don't mind."

"No problem," Catherine said. "Here, I'll show you—there's no one in the library, anyway, and I can get you set up."

Willow followed her to the back of the building, into a small box-filled room with an ARCHIVES AND ISLAND HISTORY sign on the door. "This stuff was stored in the basement for years," Catherine said, gesturing Willow inside, "so I can't vouch for the state it's in. When I took over this job, I moved anything that looked vaguely important out of the damp belowground, but there may be mold in here—aha!" Her gaze lit on a haphazard pile of boxes in the corner. "Here it is; I'm betting most of what you're looking for will be in this stack over here. Effie and Sue were organizing some of this in their efforts to get official historical status for the house. Rina was helping them; she had the idea of adding the house to their vacation rental properties as a luxury inn or B&B, though I don't think Sue was big on the idea."

Willow took the first box from Catherine; she set it on the rickety card table in the best-lit side of the basement. "So that's what Geralt was talking about yesterday morning when he and Rina argued before the funeral. He accused her of trying to get the house for herself after Sue died."

Catherine shook her head. "I don't think that's true, even if it were possible. Sue died before their wedding, and neither of them had made a will yet; they'd planned to do it after they got married. Rina has no claim on the house at all, she's just advocating for what she believes Sue wanted."

"What about that Hank guy?" Willow asked. "He was dropping

hints about wanting to build a resort on the property? It made me wonder if that's what this historical society was trying to prevent."

"Is that what he was going on about?" Catherine rolled her eyes. "I saw he had you cornered for a while there at the reception before everything went off the rails."

"That guy." Willow shook her head wearily. "He was talking about Cameron House, how there are no proper hotels on the island and what a shame it is the old house is sitting on such a beautiful piece of land."

Catherine snorted as she set another box onto the table next to the first. "Hank Ramsey has been angling to get hold of the Cameron property for years. Sue and Rina told me about it; he would show up at Effie's doorstep every so often trying to convince her to sell him the house, but she told him to buzz off." She grimaced. "And it's not like they were the only ones after the property. Like Mr. Ramsey says, it's incredibly valuable land, and for decades now, it's been just the one old woman in that huge house. She's had more developers circling than this island has mosquitoes in July."

Willow frowned. "So . . . Effie left the house to Sue. When Sue died with no spouse or heirs or will, it reverted back to Geralt, Effie's last living relative?"

"That was in Effie's will too: If Sue died without issue or spouse, the house went back to the youngest living member of the Cameron line," Catherine replied.

"What happens if Geralt dies? Who gets the house then?"

Catherine looked up at Willow; the two women's eyes locked as the librarian saw at last where Willow had been going with her questions. "I . . . suppose it would go to Geralt's spouse? Naomi?" Catherine hesitated, speaking carefully. "Look, like I said, there was no evidence anywhere that Sue's death was anything but an accident. No forced entry, no sign of anyone else in the house."

"And Effie?" Willow's voice was carefully neutral.

Catherine said, just as carefully, "There was no indication Effie's death was from anything other than natural causes either. An old woman, passing in her sleep at ninety-nine years of age." She paused. "But."

Willow nodded and gave her a mirthless smile. "But. With Geralt lying in the hospital in a coma, only alive at all due to fast medical intervention, that's three heirs to the most valuable property on the island who've died or almost died over a two-month period."

"Not just three," Catherine said in a hushed voice, "but the only three. The last three."

"The last three," Willow repeated. She looked sharply at Catherine. "You've been thinking about this too, haven't you?" she asked.

The librarian didn't answer, refusing to meet Willow's eyes.

"But you haven't said anything. Not to Diana and Mac, and not to Rina." She hesitated. "Look, I know you care about Rina, but are you absolutely, entirely sure that she couldn't have—"

"Hey, you two!" Mac's voice came brightly from the doorway; Catherine and Willow jumped in surprise, whirling around to face her. "I brought goodies—Mom made way more than we needed for today's morning rush, so—" She stopped, seeing their faces. "What's up? What's going on?"

Willow caught Catherine's eye and shook her head infinitesimally; Catherine understood and said, "Nothing. We were puzzling over some things." She forced a smile. "Got any scones?"

CHAPTER EIGHTEEN

It would take hours, days, Willow realized, to go through all the boxes. The flow of documents seemed endless, mostly scans of articles from old newspapers—local ones from Little North as well as wider-reaching publications from the mainland.

By about three in the afternoon, she found the yellowed sheaf of pages titled "North Islands Historical Society Articles of Incorporation," dated November 2, 1856. *Bingo*, she thought, first photographing the pages, then settling in to read the document. The spiky handwriting, though faded, was tidy and efficient; the text itself was impenetrable legalese. She skimmed through the pages until the end, where the document's signatories were named. The first two were signed in curly feminine handwriting: Miss Delphine Drummond and Miss Dorothy Drummond. Sisters, presumably. Old-fashioned names.

The third name, which looked to be in the same handwriting as the bulk of the document: Joel Drummond. *Interesting*, she thought. *And a little surprising that Nick didn't know his descendant, if the Drummonds have been on the island for this long.*

She kept going. In the next folder, Willow found a reproduction of an old daguerreotype photo. A young couple stood in the center of perhaps a dozen others, all formally posed, she in a heavily bustled white gown and veil, he in a frock coat and top hat.

On the other side of the bride stood a man with a neatly trimmed beard and slicked-back dark hair. The photo was too old and the quality too fuzzy to see the silver threads in his beard—or the kind steadiness of his gaze—but Willow's skin rippled with gooseflesh as her memory filled them in.

This wasn't a photo of a descendant of the Joel Drummond she had met in Cameron House yesterday.

It was the same man.

It couldn't be, and yet it was. He was even wearing the same suit.

She looked again at the photo and saw, among the festively dressed members of the wedding party, a pair of elderly women seated in chairs in front of the group, familiar faces smiling from beneath the unbroken black of their bonnets.

Almost afraid to look, Willow turned the photograph over and read the writing on the back: "Efric Drummond and Andrew Cameron, wedded June 16, 1880." Among the names written below the inscription were Joel, Delphine, and Dorothy Drummond.

"Not possible," Willow murmured, mentally pulling the pieces together. She felt lightheaded, as though there were not enough oxygen in the room; her heart was pounding so hard she was sure Catherine would come in to see what the racket was, and the ceiling lamp above her seemed to grow dimmer. Willow rose, swiftly exiting the archives room and making her way outside the library, where she leaned against the doorjamb and gulped in the fresh air as her mind struggled to process what could not be real, yet somehow . . . was.

The little boy she had seen yesterday morning from the Cameron House roof was running along the beach, the crow flying in circles around him and cawing as the child laughed in delight; curly blond hair tangled in the breeze as he waved his cap in the air.

She knew who this boy was, she realized with a shock; less than an hour ago in a pile of old articles, she had found one announcing the death of Thomas Cameron, age ten, in 1925, an unframed family photo tucked in beside it of a towheaded little boy with curly hair. She went back to the archives room and dug out the photo, confirming it; this was the same boy.

Not possible.

But what if it was?

Her brain was whirling again; it could not accept the pattern the moving puzzle pieces were beginning to form, but it was inescapable. The ancient black-clad sisters with their knitting. The scattering of villagers wearing simple outdated clothing—clothing that, she now realized, was not that of some "plain" religious sect but simply . . . old.

The boy running with the crow, the little girls in their pinafores playing on the green, the broad-shouldered lobsterman in his ancient dory. Joel Drummond, who had held Geralt Talbot's hand and looked into his eyes . . .

(*Yes, my friend, we get to go on.*)

Going on, outside of their time, unchanging. Still living—or whatever one would call it—on the island that had been their home. In fact, Willow realized with a chill as she vaguely recalled her visits to the Quaker meetinghouse when she was a child, they had been here all along.

And then there was the house itself, the glow of a gas lantern in the turret window, the breathing walls and secret passageways, notes typed on old manual typewriters, the widow's walk. Cameron House itself, looming tall and imposing over the village its founding family had built, full of more secrets than she had even dreamed.

* * *

Half an hour later, Willow stood gazing up at the imposing front doors of the mansion. She hesitated for a moment. Did she dare go up to the door? Should she turn the knob? Knock?

A faint click; the door opened gently inward as if in invitation.

All right then.

Willow walked slowly up the stairs to the big porch, pausing at the threshold, then stepping inside the foyer. Nothing had changed, and yet everything felt different; this was how the room had felt when Geralt was lying on the floor gasping, Joel kneeling beside him—thick, rich, full of something inexplicable.

Goose bumps zinged across her skin again as she let the strangeness wash over her, but this time, she felt no impulse to run.

Willow turned her head to the rocking chair in the sitting room, draped with its green-blue shawl, sure she had seen someone sitting there.

The chair was unoccupied. But it was, very faintly, rocking.

Her eye then thought it caught movement at the top of the staircase—perhaps a glimpse of a woman in black and white, wearing a crisply starched apron and a bright cap on her head, like a maid's uniform—but again, when she looked, there was nothing there. A whiff of cooking smell wafting from the old kitchen—garlic, perhaps—and fresh fish, gone as quickly as it came. The sound of a footstep down the hallway where there was no foot to make it, and farther off, the distant clicking of an old typewriter punctuated by the *ding* of the carriage return. A fleeting image of two identical young men seated on either side of the chessboard in the foyer, one reaching over to move a piece . . .

From the glass doors locking away the dark library to her right came the unmistakable *chonk* of a bolt being turned and the click of a latch released. Then only silence, and waiting.

The words of Sue's letter, read over and over until they were memorized, echoed in her mind. *The Willow I remember*, it whispered, *could never resist mystery or adventure.*

Crossing the distance to the shadowed library doors, Willow reached out to the twin brass doorknobs and took hold of them.

I hope life has not crushed that quality out of your spirit.

Willow turned the knobs, pushed the doors open, and stepped inside the headquarters of the North Islands Historical Society.

The first thing she noticed was the library's cavernous size; the second was its smell—the familiar sweet-smoky blend of wood pulp and mustiness and time, with a touch of furniture polish and lemon, common to old libraries everywhere. Willow had spent enough hours in them to know.

Wall sconces gave a little light, but they created more shadows than they banished in the massive room. The library walls rose two full stories, lined with books from floor to impossibly high ceiling, gleaming shelves sharing space with framed paintings and photographs. In one corner, a wrought iron spiral staircase twisted its way up to the second-floor catwalk. A massive freestanding fireplace dominated the center of the room, at the base of an equally massive chimney; the remainder of the room extending beyond it was shrouded in darkness.

The fireplace with its grand granite hearth was flanked by comfortable chairs and a Victorian settee, a perfect place to sit in the warmth and read or perhaps knit. The floor was burnished oak hardwood; side nooks and turret alcoves with deep chairs and jewel-toned rugs created cozy reading spaces.

Willow had never been in such a wonderful room in her life.

She walked around slowly, taking in the generations of paintings and photos. The clothing and hairstyles reflected every decade from the late 1700s through to maybe the 1950s. A photo in an ornate oval frame showed a couple standing arm in arm; another photo contained two lanky young men, like mirror images of one another, grinning rakishly at the camera from opposite sides of a chessboard. Farther down, a small painting caught her eye, of a broad-shouldered man in a dark blue lobster dory with the name *Susannah* painted into the bow—her low-tech lobsterman, when his boat was new.

In one of the larger paintings, she recognized Efric and Andrew Cameron, the couple from the wedding photo she had found in Catherine's library archive. In this image, they were surrounded by children; Willow realized the artist had caught far more than the stiff elegance one might expect of the typical family portrait. The elegantly dressed mother in the high-backed chair showed a hint of frazzled desperation as a pair of identical toddler boys—would they grow up to be the young men at the chessboard?—tried to escape from her lap. Behind the chair, the father figure stood tall and stiff, his hand on his wife's shoulder, looking both paternal and powerful; next to him stood an older boy, perhaps sixteen, equally stiff, as though attempting to look exactly like his father. A small plaque beside the painting read: *Andrew and Efric Cameron, and their children Andrew Jr., Donal, and Dougal. And Annabel. 1897.*

The teenage boy was no doubt Andrew Jr., which meant the babies had to be Donal and Dougal. But—Willow looked at the painting again, puzzled—where was Annabel?

She felt her face break into a smile when she saw, in the background of the painting, a pair of small bare feet peeking out from beneath the window curtains, a set of small fingers at the side of the curtain, and the hint of a face peeking around the edge from the shadows.

A childhood memory slammed hard into Willow's mind: Her parents, hosting some holiday in their home, had demanded that she remain in the big room where everyone talked and clinked their dishes and silverware, conversations layering over one another, tangling and jangling in her brain. Willow hated it, had always hated it; as the minutes dragged on, she had moved slowly backward to the edges of the gathering, then to the wall, then to the curtain, and then behind it. She had stayed there, perched on the windowsill like Jane Eyre, warm and unnoticed and silently swathed in the heavy velvet, until an adult found her and abruptly yanked the curtain back. Everyone had laughed, and the moment, though never repeated, became a joke to retell every year, about Willow and her antisocial nature. She had laughed too, of course; that was what one did, and no one bothered to notice the bleakness in her eyes as she did so.

You and I would get along well, Annabel, she thought. *In fact, I'd very much like to meet you.*

She gave a little pinched shriek as the library door suddenly slammed shut behind her; heart in her throat, she whirled to face it just in time to see the bolt turn—with no hand to turn it—and hear it settle with a hard *thunk* into place.

A familiar voice spoke from the center of the room. "Good afternoon, Miss Stone. Thank you for joining us."

CHAPTER NINETEEN

The fireplace, cold and shadowed but a moment ago, now crackled merrily, sending warm light into the room. Joel Drummond sat calmly on the hearthstone, peering through narrow spectacles at the ledger on his lap and scratching away in it with an ancient fountain pen.

He eyed her over the top of his glasses, then closed the ledger and put it beside him on the hearth, setting the pen precisely in its center. Willow walked slowly across the library, moving, with each step, farther from the safe and rational island outside and closer to . . . she didn't know what.

Joel's dark, implacable eyes followed her as she approached. He did not speak, only waited.

Later, Willow would think, *It would be easier if he were transparent, or had some ectoplasmic aura rising from him, or, I don't know, sparkled.* But the man before her looked so absurdly *normal* that her brain could hardly compute his existence. Normal, except for his old eyes that seemed to see everything.

"Are you . . . real?" she heard herself asking, wincing as her voice cracked a little.

The corner of his mouth quirked, the faint shadow of a smile. "It would seem so."

Her heart was thudding so hard she was sure he could hear it. "I saw a photo. Taken in 1880. Of . . . you."

Joel tilted his head curiously. "Did you? Which one?"

"Efric and Andrew Cameron's wedding."

He nodded. "Ah yes. That was one of the earliest family photos; Andrew was very proud of it."

Another long silence; she struggled for what to say next, and he waited.

Once she found her voice again, the questions tumbled out. "But how . . . how are you here? *Why* are you here?" She paused. "Why am *I* here?"

He nodded as though she had asked him to tell her about the weather. "Three excellent questions. With very different answers." He unfolded himself from his seat on the hearth and began pacing slowly back and forth, his hands behind his back. "The *how* is . . . complicated. We do not fully understand ourselves the mechanics behind our presence here, and no one gave us a guidebook."

"A guidebook *would* have been helpful," said the elderly black-bonneted woman sitting on the divan, fingers swiftly feeding yarn through her knitting needles.

Willow started; the woman had not appeared, exactly; she simply *was*.

"Remember? Like that ghost story film Effie let us watch about the nice young couple who died on the little bridge," she said, eyes flicking up and down from her knitting, to Joel, to Willow, and back down again.

Her sister, sitting next to her on the couch where a second ago there had been no one, picked up the story. "Yes, I remember—but they neglected to read it, and they had so much trouble with that *vulgar* little striped man in the attic—"

"Ladies, please," Joel said, clearly irritated; the women gave each other a knowing look and returned to their knitting with studied innocence.

Willow looked in bewilderment from one woman to the other and then back to Joel. She was either losing it or this was real.

How could this be real?

He gave Willow a pitying look, then gestured to the women. “Delphine and Dorothy Drummond, meet Willow Stone. She is Dr. Davis’s goddaughter.”

“Call me Dellie, please,” the first woman said with a rosy-cheeked smile. “And my sister is Dot. A pleasure.”

Willow cleared her throat awkwardly. “It’s very nice to meet you too,” she said. “I saw you at the church, I think.”

Dot shrugged. “Well, of course we had to pay our respects. Even if Miss Susan was not a proper Cameron, she did her best.”

There was an uncomfortable pause, and then Dellie said brightly, “Do you enjoy ghost stories, Willow dear? Effie loved watching them on her big television. Such a marvel, all those people moving around on the screens as clear as though we were looking through a window at them.” She leaned confidentially in Willow’s direction. “Joel will pretend he was too busy with numbers and ledgers, but he enjoys them as much as we do.” She resumed her knitting. “Remember, Dot, that film about the young woman with the pottery wheel, whose beau was murdered, and his ghost came back to avenge his own death?” she asked.

Dot nodded. “So exciting—and such a handsome young man—improper, of course, sharing a home together before marriage, but oh, Dellie, weren’t they so much in love—”

“*Ladies*,” Joel snapped at the sisters. He turned back to Willow. “Miss Willow Stone, meet the North Islands Historical Society. The original membership, in any case; there are of course many others now.”

Willow’s eyes darted from one to the other of the matter-of-fact trio. “You’re . . . ghosts.”

The little quirk at the corner of his mouth returned. “An archaic word, bearing the baggage of ages." His shrug was nonchalant. "I suppose it is as serviceable as any."

"But . . ." Willow remembered something else. "When I saw you the other day, you helped support Mr. Talbot when we tried to get him to the couch. How could you do that if you aren't . . . real? You had your arm around him. You touched my face when . . ." She shuddered, not wanting to revisit the experience.

"We are very real. Just not tangible in the way you understand reality. And I didn't truly touch you—or him," he said. "I gave the appearance, but your mind filled in the rest. Here," he said, holding his hand out to her—outstretched, as real as her own, every pore and hair and crease, rounded fingernails and ragged cuticles and a smudge of ink on his second finger. Hesitantly, she reached back with her own hand to clasp his; for an instant, she felt his fingers around hers, the warmth and solidity of his steady hand, but as she looked down, she realized they were not touching at all, hands hovering a breath away from each other.

He withdrew his hand from hers and took a step back, resuming his slow pacing. "Suffice it to say that in our state of being, we can only physically interact with things that existed when we lived. Newer objects, and of course humans, we cannot."

"Tell her about the talismans, Joel," Dot said.

Dellie jumped in before he could speak. "You see, dear, most of us have one thing, one tangible object," she said. "An item that was important to us in life, that can interact with both past and present." She waved one of her knitting needles in Willow's direction. "Here, touch it," she said.

Willow did; the needle felt solid and firm and exceedingly . . . ordinary. She looked at Joel, then down at the antique fountain pen on the hearth. "Yours is . . . your pen?"

He nodded. "It is. Even filled with modern ink, on modern paper. These . . . mediate for us." He looked vaguely embarrassed. "Again, I do not understand the mechanics. But these help us accomplish our purpose." He gestured around the library. "Ghosts, spirits, shades—whatever you call us, we are here, and it is our responsibility to see to the house and the rest of the family. Which brings us to your second question: why we are here."

He stopped pacing and looked at her. "Miss Stone, were you aware of what Dr. Davis was attempting to do for us?"

Willow thought again of Sue's letter. *Please come back to Little North—and this is important—come soon . . . you are still part of this place, and it needs you.* She shook her head. "No; she wrote me a letter months ago, but I only received it last week. I came as soon as I could, but it was too late."

"Dr. Davis was working with us, with the historical society," Joel said. "It was Effie's idea; she knew that between herself and Geralt Talbot, the Cameron line was coming to an end. But she believed there were others, descended from previous Cameron generations; if one could be located and brought to Little North, our problem would be solved."

"What problem?" Willow asked.

"The problem of our being," he said heavily. "Our existence here requires a living Cameron on the island, taking responsibility for this house. Once the last is gone, our hold—all of us—will begin to fade until we . . . cease."

"So you can imagine our reaction when Effie left the house to a non-Cameron," Dot said acerbically.

"Indeed," Dellie said. "A questionable decision, *not* discussed with the family."

"I'm sure Miss Effie had her reasons," Joel said, then fixed his eyes on Willow's again. "We believe Dr. Davis, despite not being a Cameron herself, was on the cusp of a discovery—that she had learned something and was pursuing a lead to another Cameron family branch. She brought you back, I suppose, to ask for your help in finding it."

Willow blinked. "Me? Why?"

"Your third question." Joel shook his head. "I haven't the faintest idea, Miss Stone. She wanted you here, and Effie concurred, and neither deigned to share their reasoning with us." He held out his hands in a gesture of resignation. "But here you are. It's not unusual for islanders, especially the old families, to see us from time to time, though they rarely pay us any mind. It's infrequent for someone from Away"—Willow could all but hear the silent capitalization—"to notice us, but not unprecedented, particularly if some aspect of their lives resonates with ours or has a particular connection. We suspect that Susan's bond with Effie, and yours with Susan, are what give you this ability. But that won't be enough to sustain us."

"But Sue wrote to me," Willow said. "She must have known something. She must have had a reason."

Joel's mouth set in a grim line. "Yes, she must have. But she is gone, and whatever she knew seems to be gone with her."

"And why is she gone?" Willow asked. She took a few steps closer to him. "What happened to Sue? How did she die?"

Joel winced and turned away, facing out the window. "Please, Miss Stone."

"Joel, please, *tell me*!" This time, she would not back off, she would not relent. "Someone pushed her, didn't they? Who pushed her?"

"I don't know, Miss Stone," he said tightly.

"And Effie," Willow went on, heedless of Joel's growing tension, "how did Effie die? Did someone kill her too?"

"I don't know!" he cried in frustrated fury.

"But . . . why?" Willow asked, bewildered. "Why don't you know?"

He whirled on her and snapped, "Because I was not there! I wanted to be, I tried, but I could not see, I could not reach them, and then they were . . . gone." He sank dejectedly into one of the wingback chairs.

Dellie said gently, "My dear Willow, you need to understand—when Effie died, everything started to unravel. Without bodies to tether us to time and space, the daily rhythms of sleep, of food, of age, our existences have always been a bit . . . disjointed. Fragmented. And now?" She raised her hands helplessly and let them fall. "With Effie gone and Geralt Talbot slipping away, we are slipping too. Not only the present but also the past; it is all beginning to fade."

Dot reached over and squeezed her sister's hand; their faces were filled with unease. "Most worrisome of all," Dot said, "Effie is not here. She should be here, with the historical society; she took care of this house, and us, longer than any other Cameron. She died. But she is not here."

"Perhaps," said Dellie hopefully, "she is simply taking a little longer to arrive?"

"It's been months," Dot said acerbically. "If she were coming, she would be here by now." Then she looked quizzically at Willow. "It has been months, hasn't it?"

Willow nodded.

Dot sighed. "I thought so," she said with a hint of tears in her voice. "I just . . . I can't remember . . ."

Willow turned back to Joel . . . but he was no longer there. When she turned back to the sisters on the divan, it was empty too. The fire was out, dry wood stacked and ready as though it had never burned; Willow was alone.

Then why did she feel as though the house was still watching her?

She exited the library, pulling the door shut, jumping as the lock slid into place behind her. Glancing into the sitting room, Willow noticed a decorative pillow lying on the floor next to Effie's rocking chair. She was sure it had not been there earlier; maybe Finn had knocked it down this morning. She picked it up and glanced at it idly; it was brightly embroidered all over, in the pattern of a tree whose cascade of trailing branches sheltered a flock of birds—bluebirds mostly, with a single brown one perched off to the side, as though the pillow's creator had run out of blue thread before finishing. There was an indentation in one side, the size of a foot, or perhaps a face; Willow fluffed the depression out and put the pillow back on the couch, unsure why this innocuous object suddenly made her feel so uneasy.

She needed to get out, to get back to the cabin, to normalcy and sunlight and the world of the living.

But the front door would not open. She twisted the knob, tried to turn the bolt, but it was fixed shut. Willow felt panic rise in her throat; now the whispering was back, the soft crescendo of voices, invisible eyes fixed on her. Willow whirled around to greet whatever new strangeness awaited . . .

Silence fell; there was no one there. The room was deserted, as it had been moments ago. Just the rocking chair, and the embroidered pillow, back on the floor again exactly where it had been before Willow picked it up. Like the afghan after Geralt's collapse, like the broken fragments of his cane that had sliced into her hand and yet were gone minutes later, the house had . . . reset.

This time when she turned back to the door and flipped the bolt, it opened. Cameron House let her go.

It knew she would return.

CHAPTER TWENTY

All Willow wanted to do was go back to the cabin and sleep and pray that she would wake in the morning to a world that made sense.

Instead, she found herself meeting Naomi Talbot in a little pub across the bay on Great North. She almost ignored the text when it dinged its alert on her phone, but then she relented, guessing Naomi could use a friendly face. It didn't sound like she had many to call on.

Willow pulled her car into the well-lit parking lot next to a vintage maroon sports coupe and entered the wide shingle-style building whose large wooden sign proclaimed it to be the Raven. It was crowded; the buzz of voices and clattering plates and silverware was partially masked by a small jazz combo in the corner; keyboard, bass, and drums backed up a smooth saxophone riffing on an old Cole Porter tune Willow could not quite place.

Willow watched the little band while she waited for the hostess, blinking in surprise as she recognized the keyboard player. The woman in the casual, white button-down blouse and jeans bore little resemblance to the hostile lavender-clad organist who had frozen Willow out of the organ loft yesterday morning—but it was, without a doubt, Mrs. Patricia MacFarlane Ramsey. Even more surprising, Willow realized the little jazz group was good—really good. Patricia might be heavy-handed on a church organ, but she played effortlessly through the chord changes of the old standard. Most shocking of all, the woman looked relaxed and was almost smiling.

The patrons applauded as the band finished the tune; Willow, hardly aware she was smiling as well, applauded too. As the band looked up briefly to acknowledge the accolades, Patricia's eyes somehow shot straight to Willow, and for a moment, the older woman's smile froze into the cold rictus Willow remembered. Then, unexpectedly, it relaxed. The other woman gave her a regal half nod; Willow, remembering to keep her smile on, nodded back.

This felt like progress.

The hostess led Willow to the corner booth Naomi had secured in a smaller side room off the main space, out of sight of the musicians; given how much Patricia and Naomi detested each other, this was probably a good call, Willow reflected.

Deciding it was best to not even mention the combo or its keyboardist, Willow asked, "How's Mr. Talbot doing? Any improvement?"

Naomi shook her head; faint lines of exhaustion threaded her flawless face, and her eyes were bleak. "Nothing. He hasn't regained consciousness at all. They don't—I suspect they don't think he's going to make it, and no one has the nerve to tell me." She looked up and brushed her hair out of her face. "I needed to get out of there for a few hours, sleep in my own bed. Audra's sitting with him; she and the nurses both said I needed to eat something and get some rest."

"I'm sorry if I'm prying. Maybe it's none of my business, but do they have any idea what—"

"Lithium," Naomi answered shortly. "He's dealing with a massive overdose of lithium; don't ask me where it came from."

Willow blinked in surprise. "Lithium? You mean like the batteries—?"

"I mean like the medication, most likely. Lithium carbonate or something. It's prescribed for people with bipolar disorder. But Geralt's not bipolar—his status as a grumpy old reprobate is consistent and overall monopolar—and it's not a medication he's ever been prescribed."

A server came by, setting down by Naomi a pint of dark beer and two glasses of what looked like bourbon. "What'll you have? It's on me, or rather on Geralt, and they have like a hundred different kinds of beer here." She picked up the menu again. "And what about food? You know what," she said, not waiting for Willow to answer, "I'll have the brownie sundae." She set down the menu emphatically. "My husband's in the hospital, probably dying, I haven't eaten bread or refined sugar in years, so screw my waistline—this has been a horrible day to end all horrible days, and I want a goddamn sundae. Extra whipped cream, please. You want one too?"

The other woman's hands were moving a little too erratically, and something in the hard glitter of her eyes made Willow suspect these were not Naomi's first drinks of the evening.

Willow declined the beer but decided she, too, wanted the goddamn sundae.

Naomi downed one of the bourbons in a single gulp and looked up at Willow, meeting her gaze dead on. "I know what you're thinking. No, I'm not drunk, and I won't get drunk, as much as I'd like to. I just . . ." Her voice trailed off, and she shook her head in grieving puzzlement. "I don't know where he would have gotten the meds from. I keep track of his prescriptions, and his doctors have confirmed I have all the details right. Did he get it from somewhere else, or did someone, like, intentionally—I mean, the cops are asking us so many questions."

She hasn't quite accepted it, Willow realized. *She's still thinking this could have been an accidental overdose or a drug interaction of some kind. She hasn't made the jump to "Who tried to kill my husband?"*

Then again, Willow thought, if Geralt had been deliberately poisoned, the spouse was always the first person the police looked at—Naomi had access, she had opportunity, and, as his sole heir, she had motive. But Naomi's bewilderment looked genuine, her sorrow palpable.

Was she that great an actor? Willow didn't think so.

Impulsively, Willow reached across the table to where Naomi's hand lay and gave it a quick squeeze; Naomi squeezed back, holding for a moment. Then she let go as the server approached with two heaping bowls of ice cream and fudge sauce.

The whipped cream was clearly homemade, and the ice cream, flecked with vanilla bean bits, melted a little where it met the warm brownie beneath it. The women basked in chocolate-laden bliss for a few minutes before Naomi set down her spoon and faced Willow again, looking uncomfortable.

"Okay, so yeah, I guess I did want some company, but that's not the real reason I wanted to meet you tonight."

Willow put down her spoon as well and waited.

"First of all," she said, "the police confiscated Geralt's cup from the party, the one he drank from there. Since that was the last place he ate and drank before he—I just feel like you should know." She leaned in. "I don't know how to tell you this, but you need to be careful who you trust on this island, okay?"

"Your husband said almost the same thing to me, a few hours before he collapsed."

"Did he?" Naomi asked thoughtfully, picking up her spoon for another bite of hot fudge. "Look. I know you're new and all, but the thing your aunt and her bohemian second-career friends probably never told you is that most of the folks on these islands have to live through the year on what they can earn over the summer tourist season. Less than half of the lobstermen are equipped to fish all winter, and there isn't enough work."

Willow protested. "Hang on—first, she's not my aunt, and second, that's not fair. How do you—"

"Where do I get off dissing middle-class business owners who love history and the environment and pitting them against the plight of the underemployed worker, when I'm married to the richest guy on the island and walking around in twelve-hundred-dollar boots?" Naomi's voice took on a slight edge as she jabbed into the sundae. "I didn't start out here, and I sure never expected to be this person. I was a physical therapist, for God's sake, living paycheck to paycheck and paying down my student loan debt, living in a one-bedroom apartment I could barely afford like everyone else I knew. I met Geralt when he came in for rehab after his hip replacement. Trust me, this lifestyle is *not* where I started. Why do you think the blue bloods all hate me so much?"

Because you're young enough to be his granddaughter and they assume you're after his money, Willow thought, but didn't say it out loud. Also, *Twelve-hundred-dollar boots? People actually pay that much for footwear?*

Naomi grimaced. "Sorry, didn't mean to be defensive. It's not you. It's that house. It's Effie Cameron. When she died and left the mansion to a stranger—I know, I know"—she held up a hand before Willow could argue again—"she wasn't a stranger, not really, but around here, if you can't trace your lineage back six generations, you're automatically from Away." There was the silent capitalization again, Willow thought. "So Effie leaves her the house. Then Sue falls in love and is ready to get married—to a woman, yet—and dies suddenly, without a will. If it had been after the wedding, Rina Montalto would have inherited everything, but since Sue died without spouse or children, the house would go to Geralt. Except Rina's got it all up in her bonnet to do the whole historic-landmark-status thing and maintain the house for the Friends of the Historical Society or whatever it is, and it's pissing a lot of people off."

"Not least your husband." Willow's mind shot back to the hushed conversation in the church foyer.

Naomi rolled her eyes. "Geralt was pissed off about everything. And there wasn't much doubt he'd get the house; Effie's will was pretty clear."

"What would he do with it?" Willow refused to refer to Geralt in the past tense, not yet, not one second before she had to. And she noticed, and found it a little off-putting, that Naomi could do it without the slightest flinch.

"He offered to fix it up for us so we could live there, turn it into our dream home and all. But frankly, I wouldn't live there for any amount of money. The place gives me the creeps; it's like the walls are always watching me, like they don't want me there." She shuddered and picked up the second bourbon, taking a sip. "Everyone says it's haunted; maybe they're right. I thought he would sell it off as soon as it was officially his, but he started talking the other day about hanging on to it, so . . ." She shrugged. "I have no idea what he had in mind."

Naomi stood, much more steadily than Willow would have expected, and said, "I have to pee, and then I need to call my ride. Be right back." She walked away from the booth with the studied and too-careful walk of one just sober enough to pretend they are more sober than they are.

Willow sat in thought. Naomi was right about one thing at least—Willow didn't know how island life worked, as islanders seemed bent on reminding her. Naomi's plea rang with passion and sincerity, and it almost made sense.

Still—the rest of the island may not know Cameron House remained occupied, but Willow did. Even if it weren't, there had to be some option besides Hank Ramsey tearing it down and building a hotel as tasteless as his comb-over.

She hadn't told Naomi about hearing the argument in the church vestibule. Was it because she didn't want to burden her further?

Or did some part of her still not quite trust Geralt's very young wife?

Naomi had left her phone face down on the table; Willow was jolted out of thought when it buzzed sharply, vibrating the tabletop. She hesitated, then thought, *What if it's the hospital, and something's happened to Geralt? She'd want to know*, before reaching over and picking it up.

The text message displayed on the screen; Willow's eyes went wide. Naomi had apparently never adjusted the settings to hide messages while the phone was locked. If she were expecting messages like this one, she probably should have.

The text was not from the hospital. It was, instead, from someone with the moniker "Iron Man."

Hey sexy where r u--I only have a couple hours. Jacuzzi's waiting.

As Willow, shocked, sat absorbing what she was seeing, a second message came in. *Bring pizza. Pepperoni. Getting hungry just thinking about you.* Willow held back an eye roll; was this what passed for seduction these days? Then a third, a series of emojis. Willow knew what they meant, though she would not have expected anyone over the age of twenty-one to actually use them in a text to another person.

This is bad. This is very, very bad, she thought, quickly replacing the phone on the table where Naomi had left it and pulling out her own so she could pretend to look busy, wishing she could unsee what she had seen. She was barely in time; within seconds, Naomi stepped back around the corner and slid back into the booth. She picked up the phone, looked at it, and dropped it into her purse.

"I have to go," she said. "Check's taken care of. Look, I'm sorry if I came on too strong before."

"It's okay," Willow said, bringing all her parent-taught social skills on line to hide the shock hovering just beneath her polite mask. "No apology necessary."

Naomi smiled at Willow—a real smile. That smile opened a crack in the smooth, jittery exterior, and for an instant, Willow saw grief and anxiety and a terror that no amount of alcohol or hot fudge could assuage. Naomi reached across and took Willow's hand again. "Thank you. You were with him. He wasn't alone when it all . . . happened. And I know you went with him yesterday partially for me, but you went for him too." Her eyes went a little sad. "He liked you. He'd barely met you, but he told me he liked you. That you reminded him of Susan."

And I liked you better, Willow thought, *when I didn't know you were about to go sleep with another man while your husband lies possibly dying in the hospital.*

Naomi looked down again, as though unsure whether to go on. "Look, I don't know if I should even tell you this, but . . . your letter from your aunt. When did you get it?"

Not my aunt, Willow thought automatically, but wasn't about to say it again. "Three days ago, I think. I just packed the car and came. Why do you ask?"

"Was . . . Did Sue put anything on the letter saying when she'd written it?"

Willow frowned. How had she known? "March. She wrote it in March."

"A long time for a letter to get from Maine to Chicago, don't you think?" Naomi asked, her eyes not leaving Willow's.

Willow nodded. "I did think."

"If it had gotten to you sooner . . ."

She nodded again. It would have gotten to her before Sue died. She would have seen her again. They could have made peace. Sue could have told her about—everything.

Willow realized what Naomi was getting at. "Are you saying someone delayed it on purpose? Sent it too late for me to have gotten here in time for the wedding?"

"I'm saying the person who delayed it never meant for you to receive it at all."

Some irrelevant part of Willow's mind wondered why people talked about the heart as the place emotion sits; for her, it was and always had been her solar plexus. Joy, terror, anxiety, and the ever-popular dread, snaking their way in now. Like a snag in her favorite wool sweater, a thread catching and pulling, tightening in its center and rippling out to her limbs . . .

"Who delayed it?"

Even as she asked, she knew.

Naomi said, almost reluctantly, "The day after Sue died, Geralt and I both went over to pay our respects to Rina. He didn't want to, of course, but I bullied him into it. They had a huge fight, and Rina—well, you've met her, she shouted a lot and stormed out—"

Willow nodded. She was familiar.

"—and then Geralt started rifling through her desk. I tried to stop him, but Sue had apparently told him she'd invited your family to the wedding and written you a letter, and you never answered. He . . . found that letter. In Rina's desk. Unmailed."

Willow was still; her mask had no cracks. Not now. Not yet. "What did he do?"

Naomi said, "He took it, of course. He sent it off to you the same day."

The phone in Naomi's purse buzzed loudly, jarring them both. "Oh, shut up. I'm coming," Naomi grumbled. She stood and looked down at Willow's still face. "I hope it's okay I told you. You had a right to know."

She turned and left the restaurant.

CHAPTER TWENTY-ONE

Willow sat for a few more minutes, poking at the sludgy mix of melted ice cream and disintegrating brownie in the bowl in front of her, numb at Naomi's revelation. By the time she left the booth and stepped out into the main restaurant, the jazz group had finished their set and were packing up; she saw no sign of Patricia. In a daze, she walked out of the restaurant, Naomi's words jumbling around her brain as though in some vain hope that rearranging them somehow could change their meaning.

Invited your family to the wedding and written you a letter . . . Found it in Rina's desk. Unmailed . . . You had a right to know.

Willow thought of the previous night—of Rina's homemade pasta sauce, of the kindness behind the book and CD and the feeling of inclusion by the little group of people who had loved Sue so much—and felt sick to her stomach. She pushed the restaurant door open and hurried out, wanting nothing more than to be anywhere else.

She did not notice the woman standing, talking on her phone, on the shadowed sidewalk outside. With a jolt, Willow bumped into her; the woman whirled around, phone slipping out of her hand and clattering to the pavement. The collision jerked Willow's awareness back to her surroundings; she automatically apologized, "Excuse me, I'm so sorry, I—" She trailed off in shock when she realized whom she had unceremoniously crashed into.

Patricia MacFarlane Ramsey stood in front of her, red-faced and shaking—with rage, Willow at first assumed, and prepared herself to be verbally skewered or worse for the second time in as many days.

But when she looked again, she saw the streaks of wet on the older woman's cheeks, the red eyes, the jaw set in repressed sobs. After a timeless frozen instant, a woman's tinny voice spoke from the phone on the sidewalk, barely audible: "Patty? Patty, are you there?"

Patricia let out an almost feral growl and turned away from Willow, bending to snatch up the phone. "I'll call you back," she said shortly, clicking off the phone and slipping it into her purse. She surreptitiously swiped a hand across her cheek to wipe away the streaks of tears, running a quick finger beneath each eye to catch any telltale smudges of mascara. When she turned back to Willow, Patricia had regained her composure, again radiating her aura of the self-possessed village matriarch, the queen looking down her nose (never mind that Willow was at least five inches taller) at the noxious peasant in her path.

"For God's sake, young woman, why can't you watch where you're going?" She turned to walk back to her car, then whirled back and advanced on Willow again. "In fact," she spat, "what are you doing here at all? You came, you paid your respects to a woman you hadn't seen in more than a decade, the service is over. Why don't you go back home to your big city and leave us in peace?" Her voice was growing higher and thinner with every word, and the red spots high on her cheekbones deepened. "You don't belong here. Just . . . go."

Patricia waited long enough to see Willow's face crumble, then turned and stalked back to her car.

Willow did not move; she felt like one of the rabbits in her parents' front yard, the ones who naively believed utter stillness would make them invisible to predators. In Willow's case, of course, the predator had come and gone, and the rabbit had been well and truly eviscerated—the one acceptable consequence for catching Patricia in a moment of weakness. She waited as Patricia climbed into the dark red vintage sports car parked next to Willow's battered Prius, got in, slammed the door, and pulled out of the lot.

Once she was gone, Willow hurried to her own car. Something had dripped onto the asphalt in the next parking space; she almost slipped but managed to lurch ungracefully into the driver's seat without face-planting on the pavement. She took several deep breaths, turned on the Fauré Requiem—*Lord, have mercy, indeed*, she thought—and forced herself to calmly back out of her own spot and pull out of the lot.

Willow hated this stretch of road; from here to the coast, it was all twists and hills, with too many trucks and not enough streetlights. The drive from the Raven to the sea was downhill all the way; the incline was slight at first but increased steadily, and she never felt like she was fully in control.

Willow shifted her car into low gear. What had upset Patricia so much? Those hadn't looked like ordinary tears of sadness—more like a mixture of shock, fear, and fury. Willow wondered who Patricia had been talking with and what awful news might have been relayed in the seconds before Willow bumped into her. Was it about Hank, their least favorite hotel developer? Or something else entirely?

Willow was so deep in thought, gently nursing her car around the scariest of the curves at the bottom of the hill, that she almost missed it.

But her heart gave a sickening lurch when her headlights flashed over the wine-red hulk of metal buried in the pine trees and undergrowth to the side of the road. Steam poured from under the hood; the one remaining headlight illuminated the pine tree that had stopped its forward motion.

Patricia's car.

Willow pulled onto the shoulder, grabbed the flashlight she always kept in her glove box, and ran back to the place the car had veered off the road; she tried to dial 911, but there was no signal. Her childhood memories recalled the little crosses and flowers so often found at this exact spot in years past, where other motorists had lost control of the curve and crashed into a granite boulder, and she prayed Patricia had not met the same fate.

But Patricia had been unbelievably lucky. The car, about ten feet off the road into the woods, had narrowly missed the huge boulder and plowed into a small tree, crumpling the front of the car and shattering the safety glass of the windshield. The old-model automobile had no airbags, Willow realized; she could see Patricia moving unsteadily inside the car, turning her head from side to side in a terrified haze, cringing away from the bright beam of Willow's flashlight. Blood poured from a gash in her forehead, but she was conscious and moving.

A voice called from behind her, "My God, what happened? Are you all right?" The man got out of his landscaper's truck and ran toward them; he had seen the damaged car and pulled over as well.

"There's no cell service here," Willow called out to him. "I'll see if she's okay. Can you drive up the hill a little and call 911?"

"You got it," he said, hurrying back to his truck and speeding off.

Willow shoved her way through the underbrush to the mangled car. The door was locked; she shouted through the window to a terrified and confused Patricia, "Mrs. Ramsey? I need you to unlock the door." She gestured to the little knob by the window. "Unlock the door, and we'll get you out."

Patricia gaped up at Willow, words finally piercing her panic, and managed to release the lock. As soon as the door opened, Patricia launched herself out of the car, her whole body shuddering; Willow put an arm around the small woman and helped her walk the few yards back to the side of the road.

Patricia's eyes were wide and full of terror; Willow couldn't tell if she even knew whose hands she was clutching so tightly. But she was mumbling something, the same few words over and over again. Willow bent close, listening.

When she realized what Patricia was muttering, a chill came over her.

"The brakes. The brakes were gone."

The man in the landscaping truck came back; soon after, whirling red and blue lights appeared at the top of the hill, and the medics and police took over. Willow stayed as close to Patricia as she could, only stepping aside when the EMTs put her into the ambulance. There were more questions from the police—what had she seen, what did Patricia say, what happened?

It was probably forty-five minutes later when one more police officer pulled up, out of uniform, on a motorcycle.

Nick. Of course it had to be Nick.

CHAPTER TWENTY-TWO

When Diana got back from her deliveries the next morning, Willow and Catherine were already waiting at the café with Mac. Rina had not yet arrived. This worried Diana; her friend should have been there by now.

Rina was not okay. Diana had known her for too long not to be able to see it, though her old friend tried to hide her pain beneath a patina of normalcy. Truth be told, Diana was not okay either; none of them were. The loss of Sue was too fresh and raw, and Rina's grief so huge, that none of them had yet found time to deal with their own.

When Diana Reyes had arrived on Little North twelve years ago, she had not planned to settle there permanently—she only knew she needed to get away from Boston, find somewhere quiet and steady where she could raise her child and heal her heart. But she had fallen in love at first sight with the ramshackle old house with its leaky roof and sagging front porch; Susan Davis, island handywoman and fellow smash-the-patriarchy feminist, had helped her renovate the building and make it beautiful. More than that, Sue was her first friend on Little North, eventually becoming the closest thing to family she and Mac had ever known.

Diana looked around at the quiet group. Catherine sat cross-legged on a cheerful calico cushion on the wide bay window seat, head down, clicking away at the small computer balanced on her lap. Mac sprawled sideways in one of the soft chairs beside the window, one leg dangling over the chair's arm. *For God's sake,* Diana thought indulgently, *she's an adult. Can't she wear shoes inside the shop?*

She took note of Willow as well, curled up in the other chair. Diana hadn't been the best jury selector in her firm for nothing—after years of practice, Diana could read body language as easily as law briefs. The other night at the cabin, Willow had begun to relax and open up; today, the invisible walls were up again, thick and impenetrable and vibrating with energy. Something was up.

Diana's glance skated over to the bakery case and back to the crumb-covered plate in front of Mac. She said in the mixture of exasperation and alarm familiar to all parents, "Please tell me you didn't eat *all* the scones before the lunch rush?"

"Relax, Mom," Mac said lazily, popping the last bite of a cranberry-orange scone into her mouth. "We put a new batch in the oven; there will be plenty." From the kitchen, a timer dinged. "There they are. I'll pull them out to cool."

Before she could move, the bell over the door jingled again, and Rina entered the café, looking agitated. Willow uncurled from the chair and stood up quickly. "It's okay, Mac, I'll get the scones," she said, hurrying into the kitchen without meeting anyone's eyes.

Interesting, Diana thought. *Something's* definitely *up.*

As Willow slipped out, Mac called, "Bring back a plate with a few fresh ones for us—" She caught Diana's glare. "I mean, for Mom and Rina, okay?"

"Got it," Willow called back, already out of sight.

Rina hadn't noticed Willow's precipitous departure. "Did you all hear what happened last night? Have any of you been to the village yet?" she asked.

Diana, on the verge of following Willow into the kitchen to try to talk to her, turned back to Rina. Mac and Catherine looked up blankly.

"No one's told you?" Rina continued. "About Patricia Ramsey?"

They looked at one another blankly.

"Did she finally murder her husband?" Catherine asked.

Diana chimed in from behind the counter, where she filled large mugs of coffee and handed one to Rina, "Or decide at last to pay someone to give her highlights?" It was an open secret on the Island; Patricia was so vain that she wouldn't even let the ladies over at Stacia's salon see her graying roots, so she dyed her hair herself at home, to results only marginally better than her organ playing.

"Drive her car into a tree again?" Mac asked.

"A hundred points to the girl with the tattoos and rainbow hair," Rina said dryly, leaving Mac looking shocked and a little guilty. "She's saying someone cut the brake lines on her car and sent her down Boulder Hill after her gig at the Raven."

Diana and Catherine looked at her dubiously. "Patricia Ramsey?" Catherine said, shaking her head. "Saying someone *cut* her brake lines?"

Diana added, "As in, someone tried to kill her? Where did you hear this?"

"Ask Willow," Rina said, gesturing to Willow as she reentered the room, a plate of miniature scones in one hand and a fresh coffee cup in the other. "Apparently, she was there."

Four sets of eyes swung around to fix on Willow, who awkwardly cleared her throat and brought the plate over to the little table. Resuming her perch on the corner of the couch, she said uncomfortably, "Um . . . yeah." She took a gulp of coffee. "Naomi texted me last night and wanted to talk, so I met her up at the big pub up the hill on Great North. Patricia and her band were playing; I left right after she did and saw her car at the bottom of the hill as I came around the curve. She was . . ." Willow remembered the blood pouring down Patricia's face, the terrified hand gripping hers, the unsteady wobble as Willow helped the shaken woman away from the crash. "She'd bumped her head and was kind of beat up, but she seemed to be mostly okay. Then it was all cops and paramedics and . . . of course . . . Nick." She scowled. "The way he acted, it was like he thought *I'd* done it."

"Isn't it more likely she had one too many glasses of bad rosé and lost control?" Diana asked pragmatically. "I thought cars were designed now to make sure the brakes can't fail precipitously like that."

"Not if she was driving one of Ramsey's old vintage numbers," Catherine said. "Automobiles made after 1967 have dual master cylinders to prevent that kind of complete failure, but older cars don't."

They all stared at her.

"What?" she asked. "I dated someone once who was into vintage cars."

"Because *that's* so totally in character for you," Mac said dryly. She glanced at Willow. "You were at the Raven to meet Naomi?" she asked curiously. "What was that like?"

Willow wasn't sure what to say. *She was lonely and sad and ate a hot fudge sundae and drank too much and wears twelve-hundred-dollar boots and hasn't betrayed or lied to me that I know of, which is more than I can say for all present company, and she may be having an affair and it's possible she poisoned her husband but I don't think so*, she wanted to say but didn't. Instead, she said, "She's . . . nice. Nicer than I expected." She paused. "And she's worried about Mr. Talbot. She said he somehow got a huge overdose of lithium, and that's what's making him so sick."

The room was silent.

"Lithium," Diana said thoughtfully. "I vaguely remember it

from the periodic table, but aside from batteries, I have no idea where it would show up in real life."

Catherine said, "Lithium carbonate. It's prescribed as a mood stabilizer for people with bipolar disorder." She turned to Willow. "I don't suppose he's prescribed it, and maybe he accidentally took too much?"

Willow shook her head. "Naomi says no. She knows all his medications, and lithium isn't one of them."

"If she's telling the truth," Rina said.

"Right. The truth." Willow's voice was tight.

Diana's internal radar pinged again. It wasn't just Willow; her people-sense had picked up two more items of interest during the previous exchange. First, Catherine had not needed to type anything into a search engine to know lithium's primary pharmacological use; as with the peculiarities of brake line construction, she had already known. Second, when Diana had asked about lithium's real-world applications, Rina and Mac had shot a quick look at one another, then looked away and avoided eye contact with each other or anyone else.

"Lithium poisoning." Catherine was typing again. "Let's see what I can find—whoa."

"What?" Willow and Mac demanded.

Catherine read from the site. "Apparently, signs of lithium toxicity include vomiting, confusion, muscle shaking and weakness, slurred speech, diarrhea and frequent urination, and excessive thirstiness, among other things." She looked up at them. "This sounds familiar."

Mac said soberly, "He was shaking, slurring, doing a *lot* of the things on that list right *before* Rina gave him lemonade. We all saw."

Catherine nodded, still scanning the page. "They are differentiating here between chronic toxicity—where you take in a little at a time until you're overloaded—and a onetime 'acute' overdose. It looks like chronic poisoning hits the neurology, and the GI issues are more likely with an all-at-once overdose." She frowned, looking around the room. "The thing is, looking down this list—memory problems, kidney failure, muscle tremors, weakness—an awful lot of them seem to go right hand in hand with, you know, the stereotypical ailments people expect for the elderly."

Catherine looked up from her computer, her face troubled. "All these symptoms—if they happened to a young person, any doctor would be all over it. Maybe they would even with an elderly person, given the chance, but if Geralt himself believed it was nothing more than old age catching up to him, he might not have gone to the doctor to find out. Maybe if he'd seen someone, they would have tested and found it, but . . ."

Curled up on the couch, Willow's thoughts were running in circles, hampered by her efforts to pretend Rina wasn't in the room; the hurt was too raw, the anger too fresh.

Be careful who you trust, Naomi had said.

That's the problem, isn't it? Willow thought bitterly. She couldn't trust Rina, who had, according to Naomi, been responsible for Willow not receiving Sue's letter in time. She couldn't really trust Mac or Diana either, because they were Rina's best friends. She couldn't trust Geralt, even, the person with the best reason to have Sue out of the way—nor, for that matter, Naomi, who had the best reason to have Geralt out of the way.

She was pretty sure she trusted Catherine, who had hinted at her own doubts yesterday at the library . . . but even that might have been a step further than was safe. For that matter, she wasn't sure she could even trust her own mind, which was pretty sure it had spent part of yesterday afternoon talking with ghosts.

But Geralt had been sick before Rina gave him the lemonade. They'd all seen it. Did she honestly believe a complicated string of different people were each individually taking out Cameron heirs, one at a time? No. Occam's razor: The simplest explanation is usually the correct one.

Not that anything about this was simple.

She took a deep breath. "It's not just Geralt," she said in a flat voice. "It's about Cameron House. And who gets to own it."

Still looking down at her lap, Willow related the conversation she had heard in the foyer of the church after the memorial, and her suspicion that not only Effie but also Sue had been murdered by someone who wanted the mansion for themselves. And she told them about Sue's efforts—she carefully did not tell the group that a group of ghosts had told her this part—to find another member of the Cameron line to inherit the property. When she finished, there was a shocked silence.

Mac said, surprised, "Well, *that* changes things, doesn't it?"

Diana shook her head, chagrined. "I feel like an idiot. It seems so obvious, but I don't think any of us even thought to connect Effie's death with Sue's; she was ninety-nine and went, as far as anyone could tell, peacefully, the way she wanted to."

Catherine nodded. "I admit, it crossed my mind to wonder after Sue died, but I had nothing to base it on. And you have no idea who the other man was?" she asked Willow hopefully.

Willow shook her head. "No. I've been going over and over it trying to figure out if I've heard him before, but they were too quiet—I never actually heard the voice itself in normal speaking range."

Catherine was frowning. "'Now that the old lady's gone and the lesbian's out of the way' . . . are you sure that's what he said?"

Willow nodded emphatically. "I'm sure. Exact quote."

Mac's expression was skeptical. "You can remember word-for-word conversations from two days ago?"

"I, um, have a sort of photographic memory for what I hear." Willow looked up. "There must be a word for that, but . . ."

"Echoic memory," Catherine said absently, still clicking from web page to web page, learning all she could about lithium toxicity. "Eidetic memory is for visuals; echoic memory is for sounds."

Mac grinned. "As usual, our librarian, the smartest person in the room."

"Oh, shut up," Catherine said half-heartedly, still studying the screen.

Rina's voice, tight and harsh, shattered their levity. "You're suggesting someone killed Sue. That her fall wasn't an accident. And that you had actual concrete information about it that might have given the police something to go on, and you kept it to yourself."

The room went very still.

Willow forced her voice to stay even. "I'm not suggesting anything; I'm relating what I heard."

Mac spoke hesitantly into the charged silence. "It makes a twisted kind of sense. All three owners of Cameron House, within the space of a few months? How can that be a coincidence?"

Rina wasn't looking at Mac, though. Her eyes were locked on Willow, her face white except for two bright spots of color on her cheeks. "And you didn't think I had the right to know about this? You didn't think it was something you should have told me?"

Willow raised her chin defiantly. "I'm telling you now."

"How *dare* you keep this from me!" Rina said, rising to her feet. "You had no right—"

But Willow was on her feet as well. "How dare *I*? Keep things from *you*? How can you even—" Willow heard her voice rising, could feel her control about to slip away, and stopped mid-sentence.

She turned and fled the café.

CHAPTER TWENTY-THREE

Rina stood frozen, as though carved out of marble.

Diana wanted to move to Rina's side, but she didn't. She could guess now why Willow was upset; Rina had confided in her about the unmailed letter shortly after Sue's death. Diana had been supportive; she would still be supportive. But support was not always gentle.

"Go after her," Diana said firmly to her friend. "Now. No backing down, no putting it off. Follow her." Rina opened her mouth to protest, but Diana cut her off. "You knew it was going to come back and bite you in the rear eventually, and now it has. Deal with it."

Diana knew Rina would continue to argue, would summon back the anger that had always been her way to avoid feeling the more complex emotions of shame and grief and guilt, but Diana did not give her the chance. "Willow deserves better. *Sue* deserves better," she said. "Go."

Rina let out her breath, let her head drop in resignation. Without a word, she exited the café.

In the silence that followed, Mac shook her head. "Geez, Mom, sometimes I forget how tough you can be."

Diana rubbed her temples; she could feel a truly formidable headache in the offing. "She needed it." She looked out the door after Rina. "I hope they can figure it out. Sue would want them to."

Mac looked at her watch and started gathering her things. Her mother frowned. "You're leaving too?"

Mac gave an exaggerated sigh. "Work. I have a shift this afternoon."

"I thought you didn't start for another half hour," Diana said.

"Yeah, but Mike wanted me to come in a little early; he has to take off for some family thing. I told him I would."

Diana nodded absently. "Okay then. See you later."

She looked worriedly after Rina and Willow. She'd done all she could; it was up to them now.

Rina grimaced when she realized Willow had taken the path down to the same beach, the same jetty where she had sat and had her argument with Imaginary Sue the day of the memorial. She picked her way across the round cobbles to where Willow sat on the jetty, knees pulled up to her chest, looking out at the sea.

Rina swallowed the lump in her throat and said hesitantly, "Willow?"

"Go away," was the reply.

Rina fought the urge to do exactly that, stayed put, and tried again. "Willow, I'm sorry."

"You knew about the letter," Willow said in a flat voice. "You knew, didn't you? You knew, because she asked you to mail it for her. And you didn't."

Rina closed her eyes. *You lied to me,* Sue's memory had said to her the other day, on this very jetty. *That's not like you either.*

"It was a horrible thing to do," Rina said finally. "I wanted to tell you, to come clean, but I didn't know how to say it, how to—"

"How to tell me that instead of mailing the letter, you hid it away?" Willow continued, lowering her knees and swiveling her body to face Rina. "How you betrayed me, betrayed your *fiancée*, in the exact same way my parents did?"

She was standing now, facing Rina, her face red, her eyes fierce. "How Sue asked you to do this one thing, and you decided to lie to her, and then me, and pretend I had blown her off? And she died thinking I didn't care enough to come back, didn't love her, didn't want her?" Willow's voice started to shake as tears threatened to well up; she tried and failed to push them back. "How you took away my last chance to see her again, to say goodbye?"

Rina was starting to cry now too, reaching her hands out as though begging Willow to take them, to forgive her. But Willow barely saw. She backed away a few steps, shaking her head wordlessly, and fled up the bank, running as far from Rina as she could.

A slim figure in a gray hooded sweatshirt, overlong sleeves dangling over small hands, watched the pair, unseen, from the dock. Satisfied that Willow had gone in the other direction and Rina was still on the beach, the lurker slipped casually behind the dock and through the back door of the Pottery Shop. A few minutes later, the door opened again; the same figure cautiously peeked out and, seeing no one else on the dock, casually set off toward the village.

Reaching the dumpster at the top of the dock, the figure opened it and dropped something inside—a paper-wrapped package tucked inside a ziplock bag—and kept walking.

Once clear of the dock, she pushed back the enveloping hood and tugged the sweatshirt off, tying it around her waist. After one last surreptitious glance left and right, she ran her fingers through her multicolored hair and gave it a toss. Then Mac Reyes headed for the bike shop.

She arrived only a few minutes late.

Willow ran until her rage and tears burned out and her mind quieted, till there was nothing left but the blood pounding in her ears and the ragged sounds of her breathing. The beautiful morning had faded into an afternoon of chill and damp; the mist in the air was thickening, threatening to blanket the remainder of the day in a heavy, wet fog. Willow didn't care.

At first, she was only running *from*—from Rina, her protestations and pleading. But at some point, she realized she had a destination.

Of course. She was running to Cameron House.

When she got there, she collapsed against the gatepost, eye to eye with one of the stone lions who guarded it. It did not look particularly sympathetic, but she hadn't expected it to.

After catching her breath, she made her way up the stairs to the front door. She reached out a tremulous hand to the heavy knob. Before her hand could touch it, it turned on its own. With a soft creak, the heavy door swung inward.

Willow stepped inside the entry hall.

Without the bright sunlight of the previous day, the interior of the house was bleak and cold. Whatever had made Cameron House feel alive and thrumming with awareness was not here today; it felt hollow and abandoned. Today, it was just a house.

Willow stepped inside a little farther. "Joel?" she called out hesitantly. "Dellie? Dot? Are you here?"

She entered the sitting room, which was as chill and empty as the foyer. The rocking chair was still. She tried the library doors; they were, once again, locked tight.

Her shoulders sagged; she leaned her head against the library door in despair. "Please," she murmured under her breath, without any real expectation of response. "Please, let me come in. Please let me—let me help."

"There is no help left for us," Joel said from behind her. "It's over."

He stood in the front room beside Effie's chair, gazing out the window. His hands were clasped behind his back in what Willow was beginning to consider his characteristic stance, but today, the lightness was gone; replaced by an aura of bitter futility.

Willow said frantically, "Please, there must be something I can do—"

But Joel was shaking his head; his next words hit like a slap of icy water. "There is nothing you can do. Nothing at all." He looked across the room to her, and there it was again, the look of implacable disappointment. "You are young, Miss Stone. Dr. Davis was strong and focused and unafraid. But you?" The pitiless clarity in his eyes pierced like a blade. "You've shaped a whole life around avoiding what you fear, staying away from that which makes you uncomfortable. You have some small amount of spine, but there is no steel in it; when faced with challenges, you buckle and withdraw."

Willow stood frozen, the impeccably aimed words biting into her like tiny missiles and exploding on contact. *Please stop*, her spirit begged. *I know it's true, but please stop.*

She was suddenly aware of Dot and Dellie, sitting on a nearby sofa, knitting calmly. Dot elbowed Dellie gently and murmured, "Hear that, Dellie? He thinks she's weak."

Dellie snorted, somehow managing to remain ladylike as she did so. "Well, that's our Joel. He never understood women in the slightest. We both know it." She gave Joel an irritated glance, then nodded at Willow. "Don't worry, dear. You don't know what you're made of yet, but you will. They all will."

Then Dellie was no longer there, and neither was her sister. Joel closed his eyes for a moment; when he opened them, they had regained a little of their gentleness.

"It's not your fault, Willow," he said quietly. "We needed another Cameron." He looked wistfully, longingly, around the room, out the window at the sea, as though he knew it would be the last time. "Now our time has run out."

And then he, too, was gone.

CHAPTER TWENTY-FOUR

Willow stood alone in the now-vacant house. She wandered out to the foyer and sat on the stairs, miserable and wrung out.

A few minutes later, her phone dinged with an incoming text message. It was from Naomi.

Geralt's gone, the message read. *A few minutes ago. We thought he was improving, but then . . .*

A moment passed, then another text: *I thought you'd want to know. Thank you for being kind, to him and to me.*

Now she understood. *Our time has run out*, Joel had said. Geralt was dead. Murdered. The last of the Cameron heirs. Even if Sue had been onto something, she had died before she could share it, and now there were no Camerons left. *Good job, Rina*, Willow thought. *Your spiteful little gesture really screwed everything up.*

Not long after Naomi's message, Willow's phone dinged again. This time, the text was from Diana, sent to Willow, Mac, and Catherine.

Come to the dock; Geralt has died, and now the police are arresting Rina for his murder. She needs us. Hurry.

Then another text.

You too, Willow. Please come.

For the tiniest fraction of a second, Willow considered ignoring the texts, turning off her phone, and going back to the cabin. But only a fraction.

As she swung the heavy front door open, a whoosh of wind swept the foyer. Willow heard the almost soundless sound of something floating down to the floor behind her.

Another sheet of paper, dusty and a little rough around the edges like the first. A new set of words, in the same irregular typeface:

```
follow up the quest
despite of day and night
and death
and hell
    --AT
```

And at the bottom:

```
Mordre wol out
    --GC
```

Willow stared at the page, then looked up, scanning the hall from the foyer up to the second-floor landing. A quick movement at the top of the staircase caught her eye, but by the time she turned her head, there was nothing to see but the quick flash of a bare foot disappearing out of sight.

Willow smiled. Just a little. It seemed Cameron House was not completely empty, after all.

Diana and Mac were already at the dock when Willow and Catherine approached from opposite directions. "The police found a bag of lithium carbonate in the dumpster outside Rina's shop,"

Diana said. Mac stood behind her, looking ready to burst into tears.

"So?" Catherine asked. "Why would that automatically implicate Rina?"

"Because the bag was from a ceramic supply company," Diana replied. "Apparently, it's also a common glazing agent."

Mac nodded and said in a quavery voice, "It stabilizes the glazes and helps you fire the ceramic at a lower temperature so you can get brighter colors." The tears started coming again. "But she didn't do it. There's no way she did this . . ."

A uniformed and official-looking Nick Tyler stood by the Pottery Shop, scanning the gathering crowd. Willow was unimpressed; compared to the Cameron House ghosts, Nick's patented Intimidating Cop look was less than terrifying. She strode over to him. "What exactly is happening here?" she asked crisply.

He gave her one cold look, then turned away, refusing to speak.

Nice try, she thought, shifting until she was back in his line of sight. "For God's sake, Nick Tyler, when has ignoring me ever worked for you? What exactly is going on?"

Another officer appeared in the shop doorway, escorting a handcuffed Rina. Rina looked on the verge of hysteria; her head darted around, taking in the crowds, strangers and islanders alike, friends of twelve years who suddenly refused to meet her eyes. Her gaze landed on Willow, and her face crumpled. "Willow!" she called as the policewoman quietly guided her toward the boat. "Willow—oh my God, Willow, I'm so sorry. Please, I need to talk to you, and now I—"

Diana moved next to Willow and interrupted sharply. "Rina, best not. Don't say anything. Not now."

With a last desperate glance at Willow, Rina nodded and let herself be led away.

"Rina—Rina, wait!" Willow impulsively called out. A tiny crack was forming in her righteous anger; she didn't want to forgive Rina, but seeing her arrested for murder?

Whatever Rina was guilty of, it wasn't this. It couldn't be this.

Willow took an automatic step forward to follow, but Nick's hard arm caught her in her tracks. "Not now, Willow. Let us do our job."

She whirled on him. "For God's sake, Nick, you *know* she couldn't have done this, you know—*Rina!*" Willow tried to pull away again.

This time, his hand on her forearm was sharp and almost painful. He hissed into her ear, "Stop it. Stop it *now*. You're not helping her. *Let us do our job.*"

His face was resolute, but beneath the Stone-Faced Cop expression she assumed he'd practiced in front of the mirror since he was twelve, Willow thought she detected a flicker of uncertainty. "Nick. Tell me honestly: Do you think she killed him?"

He ran a frustrated hand through his hair. "We have to follow the evidence."

She would not relent. "You've got Geralt, you've got the attempt on Patricia, and Sue's 'accident'—no, don't look at me like that, of course they are related. How could they not be?"

Ignoring her, Nick said to Diana, "Since it's a murder charge, she'll likely stay for forty-eight hours till her first hearing. You'll need to find your way to the precinct for her interview." Diana glared at him and nodded, busily typing on her phone. Turning to Mac, Catherine, and especially Willow, Nick said irritably, "And you three, for God's sake, stay put and stay out of it." He turned and followed the officer and Rina down the gangway.

Rina sat trembling in the stern of the police boat, clutching her hands together, solitary and forlorn. From the dock above, Willow gazed down at this woman Sue had loved, and who had loved her back, feeling the last threads of her rage disintegrate and fade away. When Sue died, Rina's life had shattered irreparably; the happy future she had planned had exploded into loss and emptiness, and now she had to face it on her own, without the one person she had counted on more than anyone else.

Willow didn't want to forgive Rina; she didn't want Rina to matter to her. But it appeared her heart was overriding both wants.

The policewoman started the boat's engine; Nick, his back to Willow, grappled with the bowline of the police boat—he had always been incompetent with knots, she remembered. No one was looking at her. Willow quickly and quietly moved down the ramp to the lower dock. Under the pretense of being helpful, she moved to undo the figure eight hitch securing the stern of the boat. "Rina," she said quietly to the woman sitting shell-shocked in the boat, looking down at her own cuffed wrists. "Rina, it will be okay; we'll work through this. You need to hang on."

The officer at the helm gave Willow a warning look but did not move to stop her. Tears poured down Rina's face, and she begged, "Willow—Willow, can you ever forgive me for keeping you away? I'm so sorry, I wouldn't blame you if you hated me forever. I—"

Willow stopped short. "Rina, *that's* what you're worried about? Good God—" Her own eyes started to fill. "Of course. Of course I forgive you—of course I don't hate you."

Nick, having finally wrestled the line free, turned and saw Willow standing at the dock. His face went dark. "Willow, I told you to stay out of this. Throw me the line. *Now.*"

Willow pressed her hand to her forehead, trying to keep the tears back. "Shut up, Nick. Just shut up." She turned back to Rina. "Rina, look—we know you didn't do this. I promise, we'll put our heads together and find out what happened, find a way to prove your innocence. I promise we won't rest till we do." Rina's tears were beginning to subside, but Willow's were by now flowing freely. She continued hurriedly, "And we'll get you home soon. As soon as we can."

Nick was more furious than she'd ever seen him. "Willow, I swear to God, if you don't step away from the suspect, if you don't give me that line *right now*—"

"Back off, you useless, oversize action figure," she spat fiercely.

"I'm saying goodbye to my aunt." Unbelievably, he did take a step back; she saw the corner of the other cop's mouth twitch from where she stood at the helm. "And I was helping you unmoor the boat, because you suck at knots. You're welcome." She tossed him the stern line and stalked away from the boat—but not before she had seen the surge of joy on Rina's face, along with a new flood of tears, at the words *my aunt*. The eyes of the two women locked, and through their tears they were both—almost—smiling.

Nick boarded the boat, using his foot to shove away from the dock. "You and I are going to have words when I get back, Willow Stone."

"Name the time and place. I'll be waiting," she called back.

Willow stayed on the lower dock, watching them go, her gaze not leaving Rina's until the boat cleared the first marker.

She heard the echo in her mind of an old woman's voice: *You don't know what you're made of yet, but you will. They all will.*

She's got that right, Willow thought. She was done being frozen, and she was done running away. She had a job to do, and apparently a murderer to track down. If the historical society couldn't help her, she would find what she needed somewhere else.

Willow took a deep breath, reveling in the sensation of the sea wind blowing across her face and through her hair.

An old-fashioned sailing lobster dory that might once have been dark blue passed the mouth of the harbor. Its broad-shouldered captain raised a hand in salute.

She raised hers back, then turned and mounted the ramp to join the others.

"No steel, my ass," she muttered.

CHAPTER TWENTY-FIVE

It was after ten that night when the wind slammed the café door open and blew Diana into the room. The fog had deepened, and a thick, roiling cloud cover brought the promise of heavy weather to come.

Catherine, Willow, and Mac were waiting. Finn greeted Diana with a good-natured *woof*, and Mac hurried over to hug her and take her coat. Willow called from behind the counter, "Hey, welcome back. What kind of meeting is this? Coffee or wine?"

Diana gave her a wry grin. "I've been drinking bad vending machine coffee for the past six hours, so let's go with the wine. But I need something to eat first, or it'll go right to my head, and I'll get silly or fall asleep or both."

Willow managed a half-hearted smile in return as she brought over glasses and a bottle.

Mac brought out a tray of panini warming in the oven and set them down in the center of the table. "I borrowed Rina's panini press," she said. "And she has a lot of good stuff in the freezer; we should be able to keep the guests at the inn fed, and we can take turns staying overnight to keep it all covered. Until Rina comes home." They all heard the fierce edge to her voice and nodded; of course Rina would come home. There was no question.

Diana pushed down her own fear and nodded too, watching Willow closely. Rina had told her about the afternoon at the dock, and how Willow had stood up to Nick and tried to comfort Rina; it had, in fact, been difficult for Diana to get Rina focused on her more immediate problem of being accused of murder, so focused was the other woman on Willow's forgiveness. Diana hoped the reconciliation between the two was sincere and lasting.

All four women dived for the sandwiches, and soon Diana felt slightly less like a squeezed-out dishrag. The wine didn't hurt either.

As with their meal at the cabin the other night, by unspoken agreement, the women did not begin serious conversation until everyone had eaten. But Willow could barely wait until Diana had finished her last bite, followed by one more satisfied swallow of Malbec, to ask worriedly, "So . . . is Rina okay? How is she doing?"

Catherine's question followed quickly. "What are they accusing her of, exactly? What do they have on her?"

Diana looked around at them; her face was grim. "I don't want to tell her this, but it doesn't look good." She looked at Willow. "Naomi was right; Geralt died of lithium poisoning, a case so extreme that they couldn't get it out of his system before everything started shutting down; they tried dialysis to filter it out, but they couldn't get ahead of it. Once they pinpointed lithium carbonate as the toxin, the cops went to Naomi and asked for the cup he had been using at the reception and sent it to the lab. It came back with traces of the white powder inside—not medical grade but the kind used for ceramics. Rina was seen giving him the drink, Rina was the potter who made the cups. The icing on the cake was the bag of ceramic-grade lithium carbonate the cops found in the dumpster behind the dock. They're having it fingerprinted, but Rina admitted to her own bag of lithium not being in the shop where it should be, so now it looks like she tried to sneak it out and dispose of it before she was caught, though she swears she didn't—and assuming they can track it back to her, it will look even worse."

Willow blinked, puzzled. "Why didn't she tell us she had her own supply of lithium carbonate yesterday, when we talked about Geralt? She obviously would know it was a common potter's supply item—why did she keep quiet?"

Mac spoke up, her voice low and a little shaky. "Maybe she was afraid of what people would think if she did?"

Catherine looked at Mac curiously. "For that matter, hasn't Rina been teaching you about ceramic art, and glazing, and everything? Wouldn't you have known too?"

Mac would not look up from her lap, and the corner of her mouth twitched slightly. "I didn't . . . I mean, I thought . . ." She trailed off, squeezing her eyes shut to keep the tears from leaking out.

Diana had grown very still. "Mac? Mackenzie Reyes, what did you do?"

Mac burst into tears. Between sobs, she confessed to sneaking into Rina's shop, taking the lithium carbonate off the shelf, and throwing it into the dumpster at the end of the dock. "I'm so sorry. I was so scared. I know she didn't do it, but if they had found it in her shop—"

"Instead of finding it *in* her shop, for which they would have needed a warrant, they found it *outside* her shop, and much more quickly," Diana snapped. "What were you thinking? Why would you do that?" She stopped, aghast. "Did—did *Rina* know about this?"

Mac shook her head hard. "No. No, absolutely not. I didn't want to . . . involve her . . . in . . ." She dissolved into tears again.

"Well, she's involved now, that's for sure," Diana said irritably. Then she sighed; when she spoke again, her voice was gentler.

"Sweetie, why didn't you tell one of us? We would have figured it out, figured something out. You can't go off on your own like this."

Mac sniffled and nodded. "Okay. I know. But—" She looked up at her mother, eyes pleading. "Will this hurt Rina? Did I make things worse for her?" Her voice wavered. "Do we need to tell the police what I did?"

"My advice?" Diana said reluctantly. "Let's give it a day, see if it's necessary. The cops can hold Rina forty-eight hours; then they have to either charge her or let her go. In the meantime, we'll keep piecing things together. If we can find someone else with the motive, means, and opportunity—"

Tucking the last bite into her mouth, Catherine calmly got up and moved an easel out into the room, putting a large pad of paper on it and pulling out a handful of thick markers. Uncapping one, she divided the huge sheet into three columns labeled *Motive*, *Means*, and *Opportunity*. She turned to them expectantly, then looked in surprise at the three women staring at her. "What?" she asked, puzzled.

Mac's tearstained face broke into a wry smile. "Enter the librarian. I'm surprised you don't have a PowerPoint ready to go."

"Easel pads are more flexible and permit greater interaction among participants," Catherine replied primly. "Are we going to do this?"

They got to work.

"We've already talked about how many people on-island and off have a motive to kill Geralt," Catherine said, swiftly adding names to the page. "Then there were all the people we saw giving him food and drinks at the reception. That's opportunity." When the first page was full, she peeled it off and started a second, and then a third, sticking the used pages around the walls and bakery case. Catherine frowned as she looked at the list: island business owners, victims of his harassment and paternity suits, union members and employees. Then she added Naomi's name. "We need to consider his wife as well. Living with him, she has the opportunity, and inheriting everything is a pretty compelling motive. The pool of suspects is huge, unless we can narrow down the means: who might have access to the chemicals."

Diana nodded. "I know. And so far, Rina's the one whose motive, means, *and* opportunity are all advertising themselves like a neon sign. Unless someone else pops up, she's the obvious suspect."

"Except she didn't do it," Mac argued, her eyes welling up again. "Besides, if I could get that lithium carbonate out of her shop without being seen, so could anyone."

"Obviously, she's being framed," Willow put in. "I mean, it's ingenious, when you think about it."

"You mean, poison him with lithium from some other source, and then wait for a slam-dunk opportunity to give the cops a clear connection at the reception?" Diana grimaced. "Unfortunately, it seems to be working." She looked back up at Catherine's easel. "So . . . who was it? What are the other options?"

"And remember, given what Willow heard in the church, it's not just Geralt we have to consider," Catherine said. "I think we have to proceed on the likelihood that all three of the deaths of Cameron heirs—Effie, Sue, and Geralt—are connected. And the motive is possession of Cameron House."

Diana nodded. "If you're right, then we're looking for someone with a reason to break the Cameron House line of succession, who also had the access and opportunity to kill all three potential heirs *and* make the deaths look accidental or natural. And speaking of a slam dunk, whatever we come up with will have to be that as well—the police won't be eager to admit they effed up in wrapping up Effie's and Sue's deaths without proper investigations."

They sat contemplating for a few moments. Catherine said, "A lot of these people disappear off the list then, but Naomi?

She could have gotten rid of Effie to help Geralt get his inheritance sooner, or to guarantee that he would outlive Effie. Then Effie surprised everyone by leaving the house to Sue instead of Geralt, so she could have realized Sue needed to be removed as well, before she married Rina and Rina inherited everything. Spouse gets everything in Maine. Once Geralt's the only heir left, she gets rid of him too and inherits it all."

Diana shook her head doubtfully. "It almost makes sense, right up to Geralt himself, which doesn't. What would be her point in hurrying everything along? I mean, even if we can imagine her killing Effie and Sue, which is a stretch, what would be the point in risking a third death? All she had to do was wait."

Willow swallowed hard, then spoke up. "Okay, there's something else I haven't told you all yet," she said, not meeting any of their eyes. "I think Naomi is having an affair."

CHAPTER TWENTY-SIX

Willow hesitantly told the group about the texts Naomi had received from "Iron Man," with their eggplant emojis and promises of Jacuzzi time and pepperoni pizza. "I don't know who he is, but if she's involved with someone else, that could give her a reason to want to be free of Geralt . . . sooner."

There was stunned silence around the room. At last, Diana asked icily, "And you waited this long to mention it *why?*"

"I would have told you this morning, but then Rina jumped down my throat," Willow shot back defensively. "And it's not like there's been a lot of opportunity since then. Besides, it still doesn't feel right," she said. "I don't see Naomi as some criminal mastermind, and this is a long-term, complicated plan we're talking about here. But it's become something we need to consider."

Diana threw up her hands and glared at Willow. "We're not doing crime-solving-by-vibes here, Willow; we can't unravel any of this if you hold information back." She fixed Willow with her sternest lawyer look. "Is there anything else you're holding back?"

Willow shook her head quickly. She was *not* going to tell this group she was having conversations with the Cameron House ghost population.

Catherine wrote *Iron Man* on the page with a big red question mark beside it.

Mac said doubtfully, "I know Mom just said we shouldn't be making decisions based on vibes, but I kind of agree with Willow about Naomi and the criminal mastermind thing. What about Hank? He totally wanted that land; we should put him up there too."

Catherine nodded and wrote Hank's name on the page beneath Naomi's. "Okay, I guess," she said. "Although, even with Geralt gone, I'm not sure how he could hope to acquire it."

Diana made a note in her file. "We need to check Maine intestacy laws; in some places, if there are literally zero heirs, I suppose it could go to the state to be sold?"

Catherine nodded. "Intestacy laws, I'm on it. I'll check it out."

Then Catherine hesitantly wrote Patricia Ramsey's name under her husband's. "She's an extremely long shot, but by the same logic of Naomi inheriting from Geralt, if Hank got the house and died, it would go to Patricia, right?" Diana and Mac nodded agreement, but Willow frowned.

"But Patricia was attacked too," she said. "Someone tried to kill her and nearly succeeded. Maybe Hank was the actual target, and our saboteur messed up and got Patricia instead—"

Mac interrupted, "Or someone went after her as, I don't know, a warning to Hank to stop whatever he is doing? Like, they weren't even trying to kill her, but wanted him to know they could get to her?"

Diana shook her head decisively. "All right, we're starting to head into the weeds here. Inventing plotlines for *Law & Order* episodes isn't going to help Rina." They lapsed back into thought.

Willow said, "What about the type and amount of poisoning? We talked the other day about how lithium toxicity can come from one big dose or a slow, bit-by-bit overdose, or a combination of the two, and how his symptoms seemed to have aspects of both."

Diana nodded and made a note. "*That* sounds like something a postmortem will tell us." She looked over her red-framed reading glasses at Willow. "And it's probably our best hope—to prove that someone poisoned him incrementally over time, but then found a way to tie Rina and *her* lithium carbonate directly to his final collapse."

Willow nodded. "No one could suspect Rina of poisoning him little by little; they could barely stand to be in the same room together. And he carried that cup around all through the reception, so anyone could have slipped him something to finish him off."

They looked at the pages stuck around the room. "If it comes down to slow poisoning over time," Mac said, "then we are back to Naomi."

Willow shook her head. "I still don't think it's Naomi. It doesn't make sense."

"It does and it doesn't," Catherine said. "The fact is, who else had that kind of access?"

"Anyone on his staff had access," Willow said stubbornly. "I mean, people that rich, they have housekeepers, maids, cooks."

"She's right," Diana admitted. "Housekeepers, secretaries, security guards, Naomi's assistant too, I guess, if we look at it from that perspective. He must have been a real creep to work for. But"—she threw up her hands—"Bill at the Dockside made him his lobster roll every Wednesday. On Saturdays after croquet, he snuck into the ice cream shop like clockwork for his root beer float, and Naomi pretended she didn't know about it. Geralt Talbot was pretty predictable. If someone really wanted to do it, they could have found a way to slip poison into his food slowly over time. But none of those folks have a claim on Cameron House, do they? Just Naomi."

"But why now, after being married to him for eight years?"

Willow shook her head. "I mean, there's the whole affair thing, but—would that be enough to make her do something this risky?"

Mac nodded. "Yeah. Risking that kind of inheritance, not to mention prison, for a guy? He'd have to have, well, one hell of a pepperoni." Mac looked over the array of notes covering the walls of the café. "My brain hurts."

Diana nodded. "There are pieces missing, and without them, this is going to stay a tangled mess. Let's get some rest and try again tomorrow."

It was nearly midnight when Willow and Catherine finally left the shelter of the café to brave the chill winds, each clutching a box of end-of-day pastries—and Willow, some dog biscuits—to take with them, in exchange for a promise to text the rest of the group when they arrived home safely.

Willow was thinking about Patricia's near miss after leaving the Raven. That night, the police and ambulance had come from inland, but so had Nick—out of uniform and on a motorcycle. What had he been doing that night?

Not really your business, an ugly little part of her brain whispered spitefully, *but all the same, I wonder how well* he *knows Naomi Talbot? And if he likes pepperoni pizza?*

Willow unlocked the cabin door and went inside. Finn, after peeing on a stair post, followed quickly; he shivered, gave himself a thorough shake that started with his ears and rippled back to his tail, and trotted upstairs to the loft.

A few minutes later, Willow was sitting cross-legged on her bed with a mug of tea and a lemon bar, which Finn eyed hopefully. Exhausted but not ready to sleep, Willow pulled from her bag the typewritten page that had floated down as she'd left Cameron House earlier in the day. She examined the enigmatic messages, this time with helpful initials to identify the source material. *AT* was Alfred Tennyson, and the quote's instruction to "follow the quest despite of day or night," was drawn from a poem unfamiliar to Willow. The second quote, familiar to anyone who'd studied it in high school, was from Geoffrey Chaucer's *The Canterbury Tales*: translated into modern English, it proclaimed that "murder will out"—that no secret can stay hidden forever, and the guilty will come to justice. Together the quotes left Willow fairly clear about what she was supposed to do: find out who has been killing the Cameron House heirs; bring the truth out into the light.

Rereading the words gave Willow a feeling of satisfaction. Joel might have thought she was useless, but there was someone in the house who clearly did not agree. Even if the task seemed impossible at the moment.

The *Widow's Walk* novel was still in her backpack, all but forgotten; still too wired to rest, Willow pulled it out and opened it. She wrapped Sue's old granny-square afghan around her shoulders and began to read. Between sips of tea and bites of lemon bar, grudgingly shared with Finn, she let herself be drawn into the tale of a young woman whose German family had immigrated to England when she was a child, now struggling to hide her ancestry as the Second World War swept through Europe . . .

Willow woke with a start, still fully dressed and tangled in the afghan. Finn was sound asleep. The overhead light was still on, but even so, she could see that the blackness outside was beginning to yield to the first hints of gray; evidently, she had slept for several hours. She checked her watch; 3:56 AM—still dark out, but a little less impenetrable than the deepest middle-night of the island; she'd forgotten how early dawn came here, especially in spring and summer. Willow sat up and shook herself off. Still groggy, she picked up the book from where it had dropped onto the floor and set it next to the half-drunk mug of tea and empty plate; she gave the still-sleeping Finn a suspicious look, fairly sure there had been at least a couple of bites of lemon bar left the last time she'd been awake.

Oh well. To the victor the spoils, she supposed. She dragged herself out of bed and crossed the room to turn off the light.

As soon as the room was in darkness, she saw it again, across the field by Cameron House: the bobbing and shifting illumination of a flashlight, outside the house this time, approaching the back door. The door opened; the person with the flashlight slipped inside.

Willow's teeth set. This was no ghost—this was a *living* person trespassing on Cameron property, not for the first time. Was it a common thief, hoping to make off with small, valuable family heirlooms and antiques? Or were they searching for something else?

Finn was awake now too. He was still curled up in his habitual doughnut shape, but his ears were pricked up on full alert, and his eyes were fixed on her.

She should call the police, she thought, but abandoned the idea almost immediately. It wasn't that she seriously believed Nick was Naomi's affair partner, but now that the thought had entered her brain, she couldn't seem to shake it. Besides, Nick was furious with her; most likely, he would suspect her of making it up, and maybe even accuse her of being the intruder herself. In any case, walking over to the house herself was absolutely the last thing she should do.

She was still thinking this as she pulled her maroon university hoodie over her head, put on her shoes, grabbed a pocket flashlight, and slipped quietly out of the cabin. Finn, of course, followed.

CHAPTER TWENTY-SEVEN

The wind gusted even harder now; Willow's sweatshirt was far from sufficient to keep the cold at bay, and she was shivering within minutes. She didn't need her flashlight, after all; the gentle lightening of the eastern sky provided enough illumination to find her way. Willow and Finn cut quietly across the Cameron House lawn and around to the back door, where Willow had seen the intruder enter. It was open—not wide but propped ajar, with a junk mail postcard covering the latch, in the usual method of a someone who wants to keep a door from locking behind them. In this instance, were they waiting for another intruder to come in after them? Or ensuring they would be able to get out?

The door gave a little creak as she and Finn slipped inside, sounding gunshot-loud to her ears. Willow froze, Finn motionless and alert by her side; God, she was horrible at this, she thought. Would they be caught before they even got inside?

But nothing happened.

After a few minutes of stillness, Willow's eyes became accustomed to the dark of the big old kitchen, and she was able to make out the shapes of the hulking appliances around the walls and the heavy island in the center. *Keep calm*, she told herself. *Take it slowly.* She carefully made her way through the kitchen, then cautiously stepped through the doorway into the gaping darkness of the entry hall.

After a moment, she realized she could see better here; a dim glow shone down from the second floor. Someone was in one of the rooms upstairs.

After a hair's breadth of hesitation, Willow grasped the banister and put her foot gently onto the first step, and the second, miraculously avoiding noisy creaks or groans from the wood. *What are you doing?* she asked herself. *You've seen this movie; you've scoffed at the nitwit heroine who dives headfirst into situations she is completely ill prepared for. You've always said, "That would never be me"—and yet, here you are . . .*

With agonizing slowness, she carefully ascended, a reluctant Finn one step behind.

The faint light emanated from a partially closed door to the left of the staircase; by the time she was nearly to the top, Willow could hear movement on the other side of the door, footsteps on the floor and drawers opening and closing.

She was at the top step; she was on the landing, the soft rubber soles of her shoes soundless as she quietly moved closer to the door, hoping to catch a glimpse inside. She took two more steps, about to peek through the two-inch crack in the doorway; one more, and . . .

With her last step, her foot landed sharply on exactly the wrong floorboard, emitting a sharp creak the person in the room could not have missed.

She froze; so did the unknown intruder in the room, now still and silent except for quiet breathing. How many seconds did Willow have before she was caught? Two, maybe three? It was the middle of the night, no one knew she was here, and her odds of making it out of the house unharmed or possibly even alive were in a rapid nosedive. She whipped her head around in desperation, quickly calculating her options. Down the stairs and out? Even if she could make it to the first floor without being caught, she had already encountered the sticky front door bolt. The back door through which she'd entered? She cursed inwardly when she realized she'd forgotten to replace the postcard in the door latch; maybe it would open, but she wasn't about to bet her life on it. Upstairs was out of the question; she'd never make it to the next floor unseen, or even down the hallway.

One second gone . . .

Run down the hall or upstairs, try to hide, and risk being trapped? Or dash downstairs, relying on speed and praying the doors would open to let her out before she was captured?

Finn, his eyes not leaving hers, was inching backward down the stairs. *What are you waiting for?* he seemed to be asking. *Let's move!* Okay, she concluded. Slightly better terrible odds than the alternatives. *Two seconds . . .*

Her heart nearly stopped when she saw the shadowy figure—had it been there all along, or had it just appeared?—standing in the hallway on the other side of the bedchamber door, not four feet from Willow, exhaling an icy chill across the space between them. One dark hand, a wraithlike grasp of negative space, reached out to the section of wall and pressed one of the wainscoted squares; a small section of wall shifted, opening inward to reveal a narrow passageway, a pitch-black opening, offering no clue what might be beyond it. Then the figure was gone.

Three seconds . . . She'd waited too long; now it was a choice between certain capture, or a featureless black tunnel to God knew where? *Not much of a choice*, she thought. *But what are the alternatives?* Willow ducked quickly across the doorway into the black hole of the secret passage; she bit back a scream when the same icy hand reached over her shoulder from behind, so cold she could feel the chill emanating off it, to press a spot on the wall to the right of the door.

The panel began its silent slide shut.

Three and a half seconds . . .

In a burst of panic, Willow realized Finn had not followed her—but it was too late to do anything to get to him. As the intruder flung the bedroom door open and burst into the hallway, Finn uttered a single sharp bark and ran down the stairs for the door. With a muttered curse, the black-clad figure followed, just as the wall panel slid shut with a soft *click*.

Finn! Willow thought in panic, listening to the blend of canine and human footsteps descending the stairway; then she remembered to pause. *Keep still*, she told herself again. *Breathe. Breathe until your mind starts working again.*

The corgi knew more about this house than any human, and Diana had mentioned his escape-artist tendencies before; Finn would be fine. She hoped. *Please, Finn, be as smart as I hope you are*, she begged silently.

Willow turned on her flashlight. She was alone again, at least as far as she could tell; in Cameron House, one could never be sure. Another passageway lay before her, narrow and low, warm wood and plastered walls, the flashlight creating more shadows than it dispelled. She haltingly started forward, then paused when she heard the pad of a shoeless footstep behind her, felt a burst of icy air on the back of her neck.

Not alone, after all; Willow might have left the living intruder behind, but someone or something else was in this passageway with her. Her heart thudded violently in her chest; she moved as quickly as she could along the twisting passage, as though by doing so she could escape the unseen presence behind her. Gradually, light seeped into the little corridor from up ahead; the pitch-black dark softened to shadows until Willow found she no longer needed the flashlight. A final turn, a short staircase . . .

She stood inside a bedroom, the smallest she had yet found in the grand old house. Its shape was irregular, tucked into the higher levels of the mansion; it stood neither on the third floor nor in the attic proper, as though someone had decided one day to carve a piece out of the roof of Cameron House and drop this cozy chamber into the space left behind. And it *was* cozy—the chill had left the air, and whatever terrifying presence had prickled the hair on Willow's neck and made her heart beat faster seemed to have left her for now.

A small dormer with a lace-curtained window faced southeast; another, at a ninety-degree angle from the first, faced up the roof to the widow's walk. Together, the two windows formed a nook with a bench-like window seat. Willow walked across to it and saw Sue's cabin framed in the wavy glass. She had found it at last, the room with the glowing gas lamp and the indistinct face behind the curtain. A secret room; a hidden room. A room whose owner had shown Willow the way in and saved her from almost certain catastrophe.

Willow gently drew back the lacy draperies and fastened them on the hooks to either side of the window. She let herself sink onto the window seat, the exhaustion and tension of the past hour—could it have been so short a time?—finally catching up to her. Willow watched as the first brilliant rays of sunrise shot up from forest and sea and the soft quilt of clouds on the horizon.

She took a proper look around the little room, now illuminated by the morning sun. The asymmetrical slant of the ceiling made one feel like a poet in a garret, though perhaps a finer one than the average Victorian starving artist might have managed; the furniture, though spare, was of the same high quality found in the more formal bedrooms on the lower floors. An ornately carved wardrobe stood in one corner; a pair of chairs and a secretary desk, the kind whose writing surface could be folded up and latched to conceal what lay behind it, sat across from one of the dormer windows. The walls, though faded by sunlight and time, had once been painted a soft coral; an antique colonial spool bed was tucked neatly into the larger west gable, covered in a bright patchwork counterpane made of dozens of little circles of cloth sewn together.

Willow sat down cautiously on the heavy walnut chair by the secretary desk, finding the latch that allowed her to carefully lower the lid to its horizontal position. The space it revealed was neatly organized, if smaller than she had expected: a thick stack of slightly yellowed paper to the left, a pile of books to the right. Tilting her head sideways, Willow could see that all six of them were by Abel R. Douglas, author of the novel she'd fallen asleep over the previous night; *Widow's Walk* was not among them, though *Weather the Storm* was. A sheet of paper, the same size and weight as the notes with which Willow was familiar by now, sat neatly in the center of the writing surface:

```
nodding by the fire, take down this book
and slowly read, and dream --WBY
```

and, on the reverse side:

```
a gift of memory, the mother of the
Muses . . . --Pl
```

WBY . . . that's probably Yeats? Willow thought curiously, taking out her phone to search. Yes, the first quote was Yeats. The second . . . Plato.

Curious, Willow thought. After folding the page and tucking it into her pocket, she closed the desk and continued her exploration of the small room.

A little cedar chest sat next to the bed, a small box clearly intended for a child's treasures. One of the hinges had worked most of the way loose and was held precariously in place by a mismatched screw. Willow gently lifted the lid.

A small photo album, exquisitely made and leather-bound, lay just inside; Willow sat on the bed, opened it, and paged through quickly. The first photos were black-and-white, sepia-toned antiques from the early twentieth century; the images moved through time to the drugstore snapshots of later years. Resisting the urge to examine it more closely, Willow gently set it aside. Next, she found an ancient doll wrapped in a baby blanket. The doll's body was sewn from leather so old it threatened to crack or dissolve at the slightest movement, sewn to the smooth bisque head; a few decaying threads attached the fragile porcelain hands and feet to the stiff leather of the limbs. The doll was clothed in a simple white shift, perhaps sewn by the little girl it had belonged to; the blanket, too, had been crocheted by inexpert hands, the labored effort of a young girl wanting to keep her beloved doll warm in winter.

Willow suddenly wondered what the doll's name was.

She gently set it down on the bed beside the photo album, then bent over the chest again. Beneath the doll, she found a small stack of books—old, battered, and much read. *Little Women* sat on the top, with *Wuthering Heights* and *Jane Eyre* beneath it, and *Middlemarch*. At the very bottom, turned 180 degrees so one had to remove all the books to see it, sat a lurid-looking title called *A Phantom Lover* by Vernon Lee.

Willow grinned, recognizing the trick immediately—when she was younger, she, too, had put a row of "appropriate" books in an obvious spot on her bookcase, spines out, while tucked behind them were the Stephen King and V. C. Andrews novels her mother would never have permitted at Willow's age.

In one corner at the very bottom of the chest was a small cardboard box; Willow took it out and carefully lifted the lid. Nestled against faded red velvet sat a gold locket, about an inch high, on a length of pink ribbon. It was engraved with a set of initials, three letters so elaborately interlocked that it was impossible to read them in the still-new morning light. Willow's hand hovered over the locket, as though waiting for some unseen being to object; none did. She cupped it gently in her hands, sliding a careful fingernail into the crack between the two halves of the lock and feeling the little *snick* as it opened.

From one side of the open locket, a young man in uniform looked out at her; on the other, a sad-faced woman held a baby. Willow quietly closed it and laid it back into its box.

Someone had wanted Willow to find this room, to find the locket. Someone shy, someone who loved shadows but disliked shoes. She took a deep breath and spoke hesitantly.

"Annabel?"

The room was silent; nothing moved.

"Annabel? This was—is—your room, isn't it?"

For a split second, Willow thought she saw a girl—no, it was a woman, no longer young, a sea of silver-white hair flowing loose around her face and shoulders—sitting on the window seat, wearing an old-fashioned nightdress. She hugged her knees to her chest, gazing out at the bay as Willow had minutes before. Turning her face to Willow, she smiled, a smile full of tears and years and joy and pain . . . and then there was only the wavy glass of the window and the sun shining into the little room.

Willow swallowed the lump in her throat. "Thank you, Annabel. You might have saved my life tonight. And . . . thank you for showing me your room. It's beautiful."

All was quiet; Annabel did not respond. Maybe she had gone, Willow thought; maybe she had never even been there, was just a figment of Willow's exhausted imagination.

Willow stood, replacing the books and doll in the little cedar chest. She hesitated, photo album in one hand and locket in the other. Not knowing if there was anyone there to listen, Willow said awkwardly, "I hope it's okay; I'd like to take these with me. It will help me—help us—find a solution, and follow the quest . . ."

A faint giggle from the window seat; then a rush of dizziness came over Willow. When her head cleared, she was sitting on the bed again. The locket was no longer in her hand but around her neck.

Annabel's sense of humor was a little unsettling.

Willow swallowed hard. "Okay then . . . thank you. I'll bring them back, I promise." She tucked the pendant inside her hoodie and turned to leave, but paused in the doorway and looked back. "I'm sorry for your loss. For all your losses. If there is anything in my power I can do to help you, I promise I will do it."

The air in the room shimmered, as though in approval, and went quiet again.

CHAPTER TWENTY-EIGHT

Later that morning, Finn lay sprawled in a sunny rectangle on the rug in the cabin. He was unperturbed when Nick tapped lightly on the screen door; this was Nick, after all, and Finn was considered a deputy on the village police force, at least in his own mind.

When Nick's quiet knock got no response beyond a measuring look from the cabin's half-hearted watchdog, the police officer looked deeper into the cabin and saw Willow sound asleep on the couch beneath an old granny-square afghan, an open photo album balanced precariously in her hands. He realized he had never seen Willow's face at rest before; even as a teenager, she had seemed to move through life with an aura of perpetual discomfort—the kind he remembered from Easter Mass as a child, wedged into a pew wishing he could scratch or fidget or loosen his tie but knowing his older sister's elbow in the ribs, or worse, a reproachful glare from his mother, would be his reward if he did. Willow Stone wore that look all the time: desperately uncomfortable, desperately determined not to let it show. But now, in sleep, she looked . . . different. Younger. Uncertain, and a little vulnerable.

He tapped the door again, slightly louder. This time, Finn assisted with a little *woof* under his breath. Willow shifted on the couch; the photo album slid from her fingers and landed with a thump on the floor, jarring her awake. At first, she looked sleepy and confused; then she saw Nick on the other side of the screen door, and her face clicked back into its old defensive expression. "Oh, it's you," she said irritably.

Nick didn't mind. He was more comfortable with antagonistic, pain-in-the-butt Willow than vulnerable, sad Willow, anyway.

"Yeah, happy to see you too. Who were you expecting?"

She dragged herself off the couch and opened the door for him. "I hold out hope that someday one of the Hemsworth brothers will knock on my door, but I'm not holding my breath." She made a face. "I suppose I should offer you coffee or something?" she said somewhat ungraciously.

"Only if you're getting some for yourself. And frankly, you look like you could use it," he said, eyeing her sleep-fuddled expression and drooping face.

"Charming," she muttered, though she knew he was right. The clock over the stove said it was a little after ten. She did not know how long her inadvertent catnap on the couch had been, but it couldn't begin to compensate for the nearly sleepless night before. She headed into the kitchen to put the kettle on, setting the photo album on the counter, and Nick followed, taking a seat on one of the stools by the kitchen island. She got out the battered but serviceable French press, spooned ground coffee into it, and turned back to him. "Well? Why are you here?"

He had picked up the photo album from where she'd set it down. "Where did you get this?" he asked, curiously paging through it.

Willow tensed. "I think it's from Cameron House; Sue must have found it and brought it over." The lie slid out with surprising ease.

Nick paused on a page with two young men standing side by side, arms around each other. He looked closer. "Wait, is this—this is Geralt Talbot, isn't it? When he was, what, in his twenties? Wow."

Willow came around and looked down at the photo. "Yup. That's Geralt."

"Who's the other guy?" he asked curiously, gazing down at the young man in the gray pin-striped suit standing next to Geralt.

Willow had been staring at exactly this photo when she had dozed off; it had caught her, gripped her. The sadness had not yet caught the young man; in this moment of being photographed, he looked vibrant and happy and ready to live forever. "It's Peter Talbot, Geralt's brother," she said. "He died young; I texted Catherine earlier to see if she can find a record of what happened to him." She deftly slipped the album away from him, closed it, and set it on the counter behind her. "So, again, what are you doing here?"

With the bluntness she was coming to expect from him, Nick asked, "What are *you* doing here?"

Willow froze. "Um . . . making you coffee? You'll need to be more specific," she said, feigning lightness.

He was not fooled. "You know that's not what I mean," he said, a tinge of exasperation in his voice. "After fifteen years, you show up on Little North one day. Not only that, you show up exactly on the day of Sue's memorial service. Not for the wedding, which Sue herself could have reasonably invited you to, but the *memorial*. And I have questions."

He started ticking them off on his fingers, his voice rising a little between each item. "One, if you were completely estranged, how did you know she'd died and when her service would be? Two, if you both wanted to rebuild the relationship, why *weren't* you invited to the wedding? Three, on this safe little island where there are essentially no murders ever—why, within a couple of days of your showing up, do I now have a homicide by poisoning and an attempted murder to deal with, and how did you happen to be on the scene for both?" He crossed his arms and glowered at her. "So I'll ask again. What exactly are you up to, Willow Stone?"

What am I supposed to tell him? Willow thought. *"Well, you see, Nick, it turns out Cameron House is haunted, and I'm on a mission from a ghostly historical society."* She could imagine how that would be received.

To buy herself a little more time, she turned back to the counter and pushed the plunger on the coffee press. She poured a cup for each of them. "Take anything in it?" she asked.

"Nope. Just black." He took a swallow. "Quit stalling. I want the truth."

Oh, piss off, she said mentally, but managed to keep the words from escaping her lips as she got the carton of half-and-half from the fridge and splashed a little into her own cup. She turned back to him.

"Okay. Truth. One, I learned she died literally through a well-timed internet search, and I came as quickly as I could so I could attend the service. Two, I never wanted the estrangement; I thought it had been Sue's choice, so I didn't know about the wedding. Three, I don't know what to say about your homicide investigation except to point out you've miscounted by a couple—Effie Cameron's and Sue Davis's deaths ought to be investigated as homicides too, especially now. That's *three* bodies on one little island, and I wasn't here for the first two. You can't blame any of this on me. And frankly, trying to pin it all on Rina of all people is ridiculous."

He rolled his eyes. "Oh, great; now you're trying to do my job for me." He took a swig of coffee. "Look, Rina is being held on *suspicion* of the murder of Geralt Talbot. She has not yet been formally charged. Within forty-eight hours of taking her in, she will either be charged or released. Which means I have about twenty-eight hours left to gather what I need and make a recommendation. Okay?"

"Nick," she persisted, "don't you see? This is about way more than some ongoing feud between Rina and Geralt. It's about Cameron House; it's about every single heir to the property dying within months of each other." Nick shook his head, but she went on. "Naomi told me Geralt had been sick for weeks, with tremors and stomach upset and all of it. Have the doctors been able to pin down whether he died from acute poisoning from one big dose, or could it have been ongoing?"

Nick looked at her sideways. "Someone's been doing their research."

She tilted her head at him. "Diana's a lawyer, Catherine's a librarian, and I'm literally a research scholar. What did you expect?" She paused. "Well?"

His eyes met hers levelly as though he were deciding how to respond. Finally, he said, "I'm afraid I cannot comment on an ongoing investigation."

"Oh, for God's sake!" Willow threw up her hands. "It's a valid question. If he was being poisoned gradually, it couldn't have been Rina, so—"

"Willow, I'll say it again, even though you completely ignored me yesterday: Let us do our jobs. Do you think we sit around eating doughnuts and issuing golf-cart-driving citations all day? Breaking up fights at the bars on Saturday nights?"

Willow set down her mug and faced him. "Nick, Sue died the night before her wedding, literally less than a day before the line of succession to the Cameron fortune would irrevocably pass to Rina and take away anyone else's maneuvers to get hold of it. Doesn't that sound suspicious to you? And then the only other known heir dies weeks later? Is that *less* believable than Rina Montalto crafting some elaborate plan to poison him with pottery supplies? Come on, Nick," she pleaded, "you know Rina. Do you believe she could have done this?"

He shook his head in frustration. "Willow, I'm a cop. It's not my job to follow my beliefs about what someone would or wouldn't do; I need to follow evidence. And the fact that I do know her—that everyone on the force here knows her—makes it twice as important. If we dismiss or overlook evidence, if we fail to follow a lead because the suspect is our neighbor, it will make it almost impossible to prosecute anyone for this or any related crime, ever. So kindly back off."

He set down his cup and took a step closer to her, close enough that she had to crane her neck to look up at him. "That was, by the way, an excellent attempt at distraction. Now you can tell me the part you aren't telling me. About what you're doing here."

She couldn't breathe; he was too close, and she could smell the laundry detergent he'd used to wash his shirt and count the few reddish strands in his mostly blond beard. "I want the truth," he said softly. "No BS. What are you up to?"

Exhale, she thought. *Take a step back.* She forced her lungs and feet into action so she could get a little distance and begin to think again. Mercifully, he did not follow but gave her space.

She took a sip of coffee and then a deep breath, hoping both might steady her. "I can't tell you all of it, Nick. But Sue wrote me a letter. I didn't get it until after she died, but she needs me to take care of something, and I owe her that. After disappearing from her life—no, I know it wasn't technically my fault," she said, waving her hands in front of her face to stop Nick's automatic protest, "but I did go, and I had plenty of time to try to reconnect, and I never did. So I need to do this. For her."

His eyes narrowed. "Is it illegal? Or dangerous?"

She thought of her visits to Cameron House—did it count as trespassing if it had been Sue's home? Sue had invited her, after all—and about her near miss with the nighttime intruder. "It shouldn't be." Far from fully truthful, but what could she do? "But I promise I'll be careful."

He gritted his teeth. "Listen to me, Stone. I'd put you under house arrest if I had the slightest legal excuse, but I can't, and you're going to do what you're going to do, anyway. But the second you give me a reason, be assured I'll take it." She wasn't listening; she had processed his comment from earlier, and—"Wait . . . you said a poisoning *and* an attempted murder. So Patricia Ramsey's brake lines *were* cut, weren't they?"

Nick cursed under his breath, then grimaced and said blandly, "I cannot comment on an ongoing investigation." Then he relented. "Look. I don't know what's going on around here. But if someone is playing a long game, they won't welcome your interference; trust me, I'm not the only one wondering what you're up to. For God's sake, if you find yourself in over your head, call me. Deal?"

She nodded. "Deal."

"Good," he said decisively, draining his cup and heading for the door. "You're enough of a pain in my tail alive; if you wind up dead, you'll still be a pain in my tail because of the crap ton of paperwork you'd cause me."

"God forbid," she said dryly as the door slammed shut behind him.

CHAPTER TWENTY-NINE

Catherine's text came less than an hour later. ***We need to*** *talk; emergency crime-solvers meeting. Can you come back to the café?*

Be there in fifteen, was Willow's response.

God, she was tired. The predawn visit to Cameron House, the intruder, the discovery of Annabel's bedroom, and then having to fence with Nick Bloody Tyler—she didn't know how much she had left in her.

The village looked different today; the anachronistically out-of-place people she had gotten used to seeing were conspicuous in their absence, and the green looked bereft without them. As she walked, she almost thought she caught an occasional flash in her peripheral vision—a white apron, a newsboy cap, a leather boot, a black bonnet—but when she turned her head to see, the elusive flickers were gone.

It was true, then, what Joel had said—the ghosts were fading. Or gone.

She was so intent on searching the green for long-lost Camerons that she didn't notice the lumbering figure of Hank Ramsey until it was too late to escape him. "Miss Stone! Miss Stone," he called out. His comb-over flapped up and down in the breeze in a single sheet as though he had applied hair spray to it.

She turned, putting a polite smile on her face as he hastened over, breathless. "Mr. Ramsey, how nice to see you." The convenient social lie came out smoothly; duplicity, never one of Willow's strong suits, seemed to be getting easier with time.

"Miss Stone—Willow—" Hank reached over and grasped her shoulder; he was panting a little, and she wasn't sure if the physical contact was intended to be friendly or if he needed someone to hold him up so he didn't faint; either way, she wished he would stop.

Hank's grandiose manner was dialed back today, though; something was different, something that went beyond the blotchy face and out-of-breath gasps. *He seems almost human*, Willow thought.

When he regained his breath, he said with uncharacteristic earnestness, "The other night, when my dear bride had her horrible mishap—I wanted to thank you for being there for her, for staying with her and getting her the help she needed." For a moment, Hank looked forlornly out at the bay, toward the mainland and the hospital. "I can't even imagine . . . Thank God she is all right. If anything had happened to her, I don't know what I'd . . ." He trailed off, looking a little embarrassed. Hank cleared his throat gruffly, releasing Willow's shoulder and pulling himself upright.

He cares, Willow thought. *He genuinely cares for her.*

"Do the police know what happened?" she asked, watching his face for his reaction.

He shrugged. "The police are looking into this dreadful attack, though I will insist upon a mechanic's confirmation that the damage was deliberate; as good as our police force is, I'm not sure I have much faith in their automotive knowledge." Hank's voice reclaimed its familiar pompous, rolling tones.

And just like that, the old Hank is back, Willow thought wryly.

"And given what my dear Patricia had been working on," the man continued, "it's clear that some on the island would like to silence or frighten her." At Willow's puzzled expression, he gave a satisfied smile and said, "Ah, you haven't seen today's paper yet, have you?" He pulled a folded newspaper out of a pocket of his sport coat and handed it to her. "Here you go—I'm off to visit my bride at her bedside; they are discharging her this afternoon!" He leaned in and murmured, "Front page below the fold," gave her shoulder another unctuous squeeze, and headed off in the direction of the dock.

Curious, Willow opened the paper. Accounts of Geralt Talbot's death and Rina's arrest filled most of the front page, but at the bottom, an unexpected headline halted her in her tracks.

In large, bold type, it proclaimed, NEW CONNECTION DISCOVERED BETWEEN RAMSEY AND CAMERON FAMILIES.

A photograph of Hank and Patricia Ramsey, below, was captioned "Prominent citizen and amateur genealogist Patricia MacFarlane Ramsey discovers that her husband, Henry Ramsey Jr., is a direct descendant of the Cameron family."

When Willow arrived at the café, two copies of the same newspaper sat in the center of the round table. Mac and Catherine sat glaring at them balefully as Diana got coffee and sandwiches for a couple of visitors. Willow added the paper Hank had given her to the pile.

"So, is this for real?" she asked incredulously.

Mac snorted. "For real? It's from Hank; I have to conclude it's a load of steaming poo."

Willow collapsed into one of the chairs. God, she was tired; she tried to make her exhausted eyes skim the article, but the tiny letters blurred in her vision. "Okay, I don't have the energy. Can someone please tell me what this is all about? What's going on?"

Catherine said, "The Ramseys are claiming Hank's great-grandfather was married to a Cameron. That part's true, by the way; Effie's aunt—her name was Annabel—was married to Bruce Ramsey and had a son with him before he died."

The name pierced Willow's exhaustion. Annabel? *Her* Annabel?

Catherine continued, "The son was killed during the Second World War, no wife or kids. But now Hank and Patricia say they have proof he got married overseas before he was killed, at a military hospital where he was sent after he was wounded."

Willow's eyebrows shot up. "Um . . . wow."

Catherine held up a finger. "It gets better. The hospital where he was treated was apparently destroyed during the fighting, along with all its paperwork. Which means there is no official record certifying the wedding."

Diana murmured, "Convenient," as she set down a giant mug of coffee in front of Willow, who took it gratefully.

Catherine continued, "According to Hank and Patricia, there was a child from their brief marriage, and the baby was Hank's grandfather."

Willow looked up from the article and frowned. "That's . . . Could it be true?"

Mac scoffed, "Please. It reads like a subpar historical novel or a bad movie of the week."

Diana nodded and sat down. "I agree. But they say they have proof."

"Show me the proof, then I'll believe it," Mac retorted.

"I agree," Diana said. "I want to see proof. Especially given the timing of this grand revelation—I'm sure it's not a coincidence that he waited till Geralt was beyond challenging him, which makes me wonder if Hank knows this would fall apart if someone with the resources to do it examined it too hard."

"Yeah," Mac said bitterly. "Someone like Effie or Sue or Geralt, who are now—again we have that word *conveniently*—unable to push back on this."

"It's up to us, then," Willow said. Then, carefully, "What do we know about this Annabel?"

"She's kind of the forgotten Cameron," Catherine said. "No one talks about her on the island much. After her husband died, she seems to have quietly lived out her life in Cameron House as a recluse. She's virtually unmentioned in any news articles, which is strange, given the fascination with the Cameron family around here. I can't find a single public photograph of her, even from her wedding."

Forgotten, she might be, Willow thought, *but definitely not gone.*

Taking a deep breath, she made her decision. "Um . . . guys? I need to tell you something."

The three women turned to her expectantly. Willow cleared her throat and ducked her head in embarrassment. "Okay, before I even start—I know what you'll say, and I know it was a really bad idea, so please let me get through it before you tell me how stupid I was. I don't know if you'll even believe me, but please try to keep an open mind."

Willow hesitantly related her experience in Cameron House the night before, carefully editing out the obviously supernatural elements—shadows opening secret doors, unseen hands putting lockets around her neck, and so on. But it was quite a story even without them.

"I don't know for sure, but I think the little room I found was Annabel's," Willow finished. "It was sort of secluded, hidden away from the rest of the bedrooms, but it was stately and beautiful and just *felt* like a place belonging to family, rather than staff or something like that. And if she really was a recluse, its location makes sense." She reached inside her hoodie and pulled out the locket. She took it off and set it on the table in front of the other three.

Diana gave Willow a searching look. She opened her mouth as though to speak, closed it, then reached over to pick up the locket, cradling it in her hand. "Beautiful," she said almost reluctantly.

Mac lightly brushed the outside of the locket with an envious finger. "It's gorgeous. You're the antiques person, Mom—do you know when this is from?"

Diana pulled her red-framed reading glasses from her pocket and slipped them on her face, bringing the pendant in a little closer. "A monogram locket in the Victorian style. It might date back to the nineteenth century, but it's more likely a newer replica; monogram lockets never really went out of fashion, and sales surged around wartimes. Jewelry isn't my specialty area; I'm better with furniture and textiles." She tilted the locket toward the light, examining the initials on the monogram. "The center initial is an *R*, and it looks like an *A* and a *D* on either side."

Mac nodded and gazed down at the locket. "*R* for Ramsey? And is the *A* for Annabel, then?"

Catherine's expression was doubtful. "Maybe. But the other initial would be a *C* if it was Annabel. Annabel Cameron Ramsey. What does the *D* stand for?"

It was a good question, Willow realized. She was sure it had been Annabel who gave her the locket, but was it actually hers?

Diana carefully opened the locket, revealing the photos of the young man and the sad-faced woman holding her baby. "Oh, how lovely." She gave a little sigh. "I wonder who they are." She looked up at Willow, eyebrows drawn. "You found this in a hidden room in Cameron House? Which you found trying to avoid an intruder—*another* intruder, besides yourself—in the house last night?"

Willow nodded. "I know it wasn't the smartest thing going over there—"

Mac snorted. "Not the smartest? Yeah, you could say that. What were you thinking? You could have at least called us to come too."

"Which would have been equally not smart," Diana said firmly. "What you should have done was call the police the second you saw the person go in. It was incredibly foolish, not to mention illegal. For God's sake, Willow, three people have died; you could have been the fourth. It was *completely* irresponsible."

"I know it was," Willow said. "I'd yell at me too. But I did go in, I wasn't killed, and it's a little late now to say anything to the police. Anyway, I found this too." Willow pulled out the photo album and opened it to a page near the front, sliding it across the table to the other three. The photo showed the uniformed young man from the locket, arm wrapped affectionately around a young woman at his side. Diana looked up at Willow questioningly. "Look on the back of the photo," Willow said.

Diana gave Willow one more stern look. "You realize, on top of everything else, that you've technically stolen both of these items from the house, a house you had no business being in to begin with." Finally she relented and turned her attention back to the album. She delicately removed the photo from its corner pockets and turned it over. The three bent over it.

"Douglas and Effie, May 1942," Mac said, her voice hushed.

Willow nodded. "I'm guessing that's Annabel's son; 1942 was about when the US started sending pilots over. This was probably from the day he left home for the last time."

"The timing fits." Diana gently replaced the photo into the album and looked back up at Willow. "Are there any photos of the woman and baby in here?"

Willow shook her head.

Catherine frowned. "So, we have Douglas—Ramsey or Cameron, we don't really know—who went off to war and never came home. And a locket with a photo of him on one side and an unidentified woman with a baby on the other."

She looked around the room, brows furrowed. "Is it possible? *Could* Hank be telling the truth?"

CHAPTER THIRTY

They looked around at one another, horrified at the possibility Catherine had raised.

Willow took a deep breath. *Trust*, she thought. *These were Susan's friends as well as Rina's. I have to trust them.*

"I think Sue was searching for another living Cameron descendant, and I think she may have found one," Willow said quietly into the silence. "And I'm pretty sure it wasn't Hank. If we can find out who it is, and prove it, that could stop Hank in his tracks." Willow slid the album back to herself and flipped through a few more pages. "There are decades of photos in here—here's Geralt and Peter, his older brother, the one who died young," she said, pausing on another page about two-thirds of the way through the album. "And here they are again, at Peter's wedding. Catherine, when you were researching Geralt, did you come across anything about Peter and his wife?"

"A little," Catherine replied, calling up her notes on her laptop. "His bride was born Marisa Williams. The wedding was a major event on the island, but I went through years of *North Islands Star-Herald* microfilm after that, and there was nothing about her beyond the coverage of their wedding day. She was from Away, you know," she said, rolling her eyes. "It would have been a bit of a scandal." Catherine turned another page; there were Peter and Geralt again, Marisa standing between them, and all three were smiling. "There are a few local accounts of Peter's death in a car accident about three months after the wedding, but not many details. Geralt left the island shortly after his brother died; he didn't start showing up in the news again until he started making his millions over on the mainland. Marisa seems to have left Little North too; I couldn't pick up her trail after that. No offspring we know of from her." She looked up at their disappointed faces. "I'll keep digging."

Diana smiled and patted Catherine's hand. "No, this is fantastic, and if Rina's case does go to trial, I'll hire you as a researcher. You are amazing at this." Her attention shifted back to the photo album as she gently paged through it. She came to a new page and smiled. "Sue," she said softly. "My God, she's so young here."

Willow smiled too. She slid her chair over next to Diana's, and they all gathered around the book. Diana paged through photos of a much younger Susan Davis, maybe in her thirties or forties. Willow had pored over these images that morning, drinking in Sue as a younger woman, sitting at her desk in what must have been her university office in one, walking on the beach in another . . .

Sue wasn't alone in all the photos either. "Is that Effie with her?" Catherine asked, pointing at the other woman posing with her, much older, whom Willow almost recognized. Diana nodded; in this photo, a younger Sue posed with Effie on a tree-lined pedestrian courtyard or avenue with brick buildings on either side. They were smiling amid other wandering tourists or inhabitants—a family pointing at something in the distance, a goth-looking teen sitting on a bench glaring at nothing in particular, a child in a bright pink jacket running by . . . "Where is this, do you know?" Willow asked Diana.

Diana squinted and looked closer. "Looks like Boston to me. Yup—that's the Old North Church in the background. They must have been sightseeing." She looked thoughtful. "I knew they'd been friends forever, but I didn't realize Effie had known Sue this long; this had to have been taken thirty-odd years ago, before she even met Rina."

They thought they had reached the end of the album—until Diana looked closer and discovered something Willow had missed; the last two pages were stuck together. She slipped her nail between the pages and pried them apart, and they all stood looking at the last photo. "Ohh, look," she breathed. "There they are."

This photo, much more recent than the others, showed Sue and Effie standing on the front porch of Cameron House, arms around each other and big grins on both their faces. The three women who had known Sue best sighed, seeing in the photo the Sue and Effie they remembered, standing there so full of life and joy.

For Willow, another puzzle piece clicked into place. The woman standing next to Sue in this photo was wearing a shapeless yellow housedress, a purple sweater, and Bean boots over mismatched knee socks. Her white hair was braided up into a coronet on top of her head. Willow hadn't recognized Effie in her younger photos, but here Willow clearly saw the woman she had seen at Sue's memorial, sharing a pew with the ghost of Peter Talbot.

So Joel and the sisters had not been completely correct about Effie not returning after her death—though it was unsurprising that, if she showed up anywhere, it would be to attend Sue's funeral. It made Willow wonder what else they might not know about.

"So . . . back to Hank," Mac said, drawing their attention away from the photos and locket. "We have the Annabel locket with the baby photo, and maybe he is in possession of something similar, but what kind of proof could he realistically have, especially if the war hospital was destroyed? It's not like the county probate office is going to see his claim and go, 'Yeah, we guess that could have happened; here's the deed to Cameron House.'"

Diana's lip curled. "Oh, no? You haven't asked me who the head county probate judge is."

"Who is it?" Mac asked, but Catherine was clicking away again, navigating to the county probate office website.

When she saw the name, Catherine glowered. "Are you kidding? Robert Ramsey Jr.?"

Diana nodded. "Indeed. Hank Ramsey's younger brother. And spoiler alert: Robert Jr.'s wife is the probate registrar. And *her* younger brother and nephew both work in the office of public records. With even the slightest appearance of propriety, he has a good shot at sliding it right through, since he's got the people in place. They're keeping it all in the family. He must have been laying the groundwork for years."

Catherine frowned. "Plotting to inherit an estate after its already ancient heirs die isn't the same as actually committing three murders."

Willow nodded. "You're right, but think it through. Sue would have been the surprise. He could have had the plan for Geralt's slow poisoning in place even before Effie died, but then Effie left the house to Sue, and he had to act quickly; if Sue and Rina had gotten married, Rina would have inherited everything."

Mac added, "And from what you've said, it sounded like Geralt was already suspicious; that would have sped up his timeline. Rina became a convenient patsy."

Catherine shook her head stubbornly. "None of that explains how he got small quantities of poison into Geralt over all that time. He didn't have the access."

Mac said, "I'm with the smart librarian; I don't think Hank could have done it. My money is still on Naomi. She *did* have the access, and she's the one who would benefit the most from the old guy dying. Hank and Patricia may be trying to take advantage of the situation, but again, that's not the same as murder."

"But," Willow argued, "do we really believe Naomi had it in her to kill Effie and Sue first? It just—it doesn't quite fit. No one quite fits." She picked up the locket and clicked it open again, looking at the images of man, woman, and infant, then set it down and looked around the table. "One thing at a time: Hank's claim that he is a Cameron. What do we do?"

Catherine replied simply, "We find the truth. And go from there."

Willow slept hard that night, but her dreams came in tangled snarls of violence and secrets and mystery; even in sleep, her racing mind kept trying to follow the threads of what she had learned that day. None of her circling thoughts seemed to connect properly to the others; her brain felt like a table on which someone had unceremoniously scattered pieces from five or six jigsaw puzzles and taken the boxes away.

She dragged herself out of bed a little after dawn the next morning, grumpy and still exhausted. Deciding to give her brain a rest, she was reaching for the paperback on the nightstand—the other Abel R. Douglas book—when she remembered the enigmatic note in the typewriter.

Take down this book and slowly read, it had said . . . *a gift of memory* . . .

Reluctantly pulling her hand from the paperback, Willow found the copy of *Widow's Walk* on the floor where she had let it fall the previous night. Was this the book Annabel meant? The one Sue had left for her with Rina?

Willow couldn't quite remember how far into the novel she'd gotten before drifting off the night before, but soon she was back inside Marie's story, a conflicted young woman struggling with her secret German parentage as she served on the side of the Allies, committing herself to serving wounded soldiers in the war as a flight nurse for the Red Cross. It was good writing,

Willow realized, with sharp dialogue and fast pacing, shifting back and forth between Marie's story and brief interludes of a mother standing on the widow's walk of her home reading letters from her soldier son. Willow found herself thoroughly enjoying the fearless Marie as she worked flight after flight evacuating wounded soldiers from the front and patching them up as best she could, while the plane dodged enemy fire and tried not to get shot down. Eventually, Marie was wounded and found herself in a military hospital in England, where she finally met the soldier whose letters made up the other part of the story: Daniel Ramson, a young pilot from the States . . .

Willow looked up with a start, struck by the character's initials and surname. Daniel Ramson.

Annabel's son, whom Hank claimed to be his grandfather, had been named Douglas Ramsey.

Willow turned back to the story. Now that she was paying attention, the parallels between Hank's version of the old family legend and this novel were too obvious to be coincidental—sure enough, as the story continued, Daniel and Marie got married days before his release from the hospital back to active duty, and she discovered she was pregnant the same day she received news that his plane had gone down, hours before the military hospital itself was bombed . . .

Willow was sitting up by now, reading as fast as she could. The hours flew by as she zoomed her way through the narrative—her favorite graduate-student research superpower. Marie went back to the front; as the Allies moved across Germany, and as her pregnancy began to show, she saw places she'd known as a child obliterated by shelling, still struggling with her heritage and hiding the truth of her German birth from those around her.

Even as she zoomed through page after page looking for clues, Willow was moved by the story, feeling Marie's heartbreak and terror as she realized she was carrying Daniel's baby, set against the horrors of the camps and the ill and starving survivors—while Daniel's mother at home waited for letters from her son, letters that would never arrive.

When she had finished, Willow carefully closed the book, lost in thought.

She glanced down at the cover again, and one more thing clicked—an obvious thing, something she could not believe she hadn't noticed yet.

Daniel Ramson. Douglas Ramsey. Abel R. Douglas.

The questions in her mind multiplied, each spawning several more: Was *Widow's Walk* really a work of fiction? Could Hank's story be true? Could the book be an account of an old family secret, clothed in the guise of a novel? What had happened to Douglas Ramsey overseas in the war? And who had been close enough to the family to know the truth, but sensitive enough to only reveal it in this hidden, sideways manner?

Who *was* Abel R. Douglas?

Willow turned back to her computer, searching again for books by their mysterious author on every site she could find. He had written a dozen in total, including the six she had seen on Annabel's desk and the beat-up paperback on Willow's nightstand—*Weather the Storm*, the last book he was known to have written. Willow was able to track down copies of almost every title at online marketplaces and retailers—except one. There was not a single copy of *Widow's Walk* available anywhere.

She picked up her phone and texted Catherine. *Hey, I'm looking for another copy of the Widow's Walk book Sue gave me, but none of the online sellers seem to have it. Any ideas where I could look next?*

Catherine's response: *Actually, the day you brought in that book, I tried to do the same thing. No one has it. Called my librarian friends. The few that own copies have had them borrowed on interlibrary loan within the past year and they weren't returned.*

Willow: *Weird.*

Catherine: *And statistically improbable. Even more when you factor this in: I found a bookseller in Portland who says he had a couple of copies, but someone reached out online and bought them both. Why would this obscure book suddenly be in demand?*

Willow had an idea why. *Can you come over?* she asked.

I'm not on the island, Catherine texted back. *I'm visiting Maine county seats to try to find proof one way or the other about Hank.*

Smart, Willow thought. Catherine was skipping novels and complex plots and going straight to the source of the data. *When are you coming back?* she texted Catherine.

Catherine responded, *Not till evening. And I think someone's following me; I've been from Little North to Ellsworth and Belfast and Machias and even to Augusta, and I keep seeing the same blue Camry.*

Willow refrained from texting *Lots of people drive Camrys* back to Catherine; given what was at stake, she couldn't make light of the librarian's concerns.

Catherine texted again: *Let's meet at the Raven. I'd feel better having this conversation in a public place.*

You found something? Willow texted back excitedly.

Catherine texted back a winking emoji. Then, *Maybe about 7?*

Sounds good. Hey—are you going to be okay? If the Camry person who might or might not be following Catherine intended her harm, there was a lot of highway between Augusta and the Raven.

I'm taking steps. Don't worry about me. I'll be safe. Gotta go!

Willow put down her phone and glared at her computer. Her online searches had long since passed fruitless and arrived at frustrating. She snapped the lid shut with more force than necessary and looked out the loft window across the lupine field to the hulk of the old mansion.

It occurred to her that almost every useful or important piece of knowledge she'd gained since arriving on the island had come from exactly the same place.

Willow jumped up, grabbed her phone, and put on her shoes,

leaving the book on the nightstand. "Finn, let's go!" she called out. Finn's look indicated his lack of interest in traditional dog commands, but he got up and followed her, anyway—out of the cabin, across the field, and to the mansion.

CHAPTER THIRTY-ONE

But Cameron House was closed, locked front and back. Willow stood outside the kitchen door and cursed with frustration. Perhaps Geralt's death had affected the house's ability to decide whom to admit and whom to hold outside—or maybe it simply didn't want to let her in today. Last night's intruder had probably used some more prosaic means, like a lockpick or stolen key, to get in, but Willow wasn't willing to go that far. Not yet, anyway.

As Willow and Finn circled to the back of the house, the dog stopped abruptly and gave a low growl, looking pointedly toward the long footpath leading into the woods. Willow caught the flash of a blond ponytail as it disappeared into the thick stand of pines.

She looked down at Finn, who looked back. Willow was confident she had nothing to fear from the ghosts who made their home here; she wasn't sure the person who had started down the path to the allegedly haunted graveyard could say the same. With a satisfied little smile, she nodded to the dog, and they both took off across the field.

The Cameron family graveyard was bigger than Willow had

expected. A couple dozen mossy gravestones filled the clearing; some were in neat rows, while others were more haphazardly placed. Wild roses dotted the yard with their sharp thorns and flower buds beginning to form, waiting for the sun to reach down to them on bright summer days. But not today; the clouds covered the sky and wind whipped through the trees; swirling branches and creaking wood sounded thunderously loud in this otherwise silent place.

The unexpected visitor stood looking down at a headstone about a third of the way into the graveyard, her back to Willow. When Willow opened the heavy gate with a mournful creak, the trespasser whirled around. Willow found herself face-to-face with Naomi Talbot.

"Jesus Christ," Naomi said, her face sagging in relief as she recognized Willow. "You scared the crap out of me."

"Sorry," Willow said automatically as she stepped into the graveyard and approached Naomi. "Finn and I were out for a walk, and he suddenly wanted to head out here. Probably smelled you or something." Some part of her wondered when she had gotten so good at lying without a second thought. She looked around, realizing the dog was no longer at her side. "Finn?" she asked, puzzled.

Finn sat calmly at the gate. He did not seem perturbed, but neither did he seem inclined to set foot into the graveyard.

Interesting, she thought, and turned back to Naomi. The other woman held a small gardening trowel in her perfectly manicured hand.

Naomi saw her staring and said, in the voice of one not expecting to be believed, "It's . . . it's Geralt. He'll be buried with his parents down in Kennebunkport, once the postmortem is done and they release his body, but—a couple of days ago, he got all weird and maudlin, and he asked if I would make sure to bury something of his out here by his brother's grave." She looked down at the stone beside her; Willow arrived at her side and looked down too. It read:

Peter Talbot
1932–1956
Beloved brother and son

"Brother and son," Willow commented, almost to herself. "Nothing about his wife."

Naomi said distractedly, "He was married? I didn't know." She pulled from her pocket a small wooden box with a simple latch. She opened it and showed it to Willow; inside was a gold pocket watch and a small baggie with—

"Is that a lock of Geralt's hair?" Willow asked dubiously.

Naomi nodded, looking almost embarrassed. "I know, it's bizarre, but he insisted on it. It was the last thing he asked me to do for him, aside from getting off his back about all the empanadas he ended up eating behind *my* back, anyway." She blinked hard and looked away to hide the watery shine in her eyes. "Since I basically did nothing he told me to through his life, I might as well honor this one thing."

Willow let a moment pass before holding out her hand for the trowel. "Can I help?"

Naomi sniffled, then smiled a little in spite of herself. "I guess it spoils the effect if I'm hesitating at fulfilling my husband's last wish because I don't want to spoil my manicure, but thank you." She handed Willow the little shovel.

Less than ten minutes later, they stood, quietly looking down at the tiny mound of dirt beside Peter Talbot's grave. The brothers, in this small way, were reunited at last. The two women departed the graveyard in silence, Finn joining them as they walked along the pine-needle-covered path back toward the house.

After a few moments, Naomi spoke. "So . . . do you think she did it?"

"Who?" Willow asked distractedly.

Naomi shot Willow a sharp sidewise look. "You know who. Rina. Do you think she poisoned my husband?"

Willow took a breath and let it out. "No. No, I don't."

Naomi said, just as calmly, "I don't either." Then she asked, "Do you think *I* did it?"

The silence after this question was a little longer, a little less comfortable.

Do I? Willow asked herself, unsure of what her own answer would be. Finally, she said, "Honestly? I'd be lying if I said I didn't wonder . . . but I don't think you did. You didn't have much of a reason to."

Naomi shrugged. "For the money, of course. It's what they're all saying; it's what they've been saying for years. Even with Rina in custody, they're still saying it. I can all but hear it whenever I walk by."

Careful, Willow thought. *Be very careful.* "Well, are they right? What's the benefit to you from his dying now, rather than, I don't know, letting him live his life out?"

Naomi snorted. "Not a single thing." She stopped walking and turned to Willow. "Here's what none of them know, because my smoke-blower of a husband went to great lengths to keep it quiet: There *isn't* any money. It's all debt and bad investments and lawsuits needing to be settled." A muscle twitched at the corner of her mouth. "If he'd had time, and if he'd been able to legally inherit Cameron House before he died, he could at least have sold it to pay most of the debts and keep our heads above water. But now? I'm left high and dry. I'm the *last* person who wanted him dead. And even after it all comes out, I doubt if anyone will care; it doesn't fit the accepted North Islands narrative about the wealthy Cameron line, or me as a moneygrubbing trophy wife. Once they know I'm broke, it'll be woman overboard in shark-infested waters." She glared in the general direction of the village. "At least Nick believes me. But then, for such a pretty guy, he actually seems to have half a brain. Rare to find both in thc same male specimen, you know."

Something unfamiliar and decidedly uncomfortable roiled in

the pit of Willow's stomach. "I didn't realize you and Nick knew each other," she said with deliberate casualness.

"Oh, of course," the other woman said, not noticing Willow's discomfort. "We've been here every summer and fall for years—we came early this year after Effie died—but Nick has usually been the one to come out and try to talk sense into my husband after he aimed his golf cart at a tourist, or scared a small child on the dock, or any of the various problematic things he used to do for fun." She gave Willow a sly glance. "As embarrassing as it was to have to be on the receiving end of it all, it wasn't *that* much of a hardship. Nick's definitely easy on the eyes. I didn't marry Geralt for his looks."

Naomi gave one last sad look back at the graveyard. "But I miss him. Everything is so quiet now. The house, the town—he was larger than life, you know?"

Willow nodded. "I think he might have been the most alive person I ever met. Even when he was dying."

"Exactly." Naomi nodded. "It's almost impossible to believe even death could stop him."

Willow thought of the little pile of dirt next to Peter's grave. She had an idea about why it was there, why Geralt had asked for it.

But she only said, "It is, isn't it?"

As Naomi and Willow rounded the house to the shore path, they saw Audra DuBois approaching almost at a run. The young widow's frustrated assistant called out, "Naomi, I've been texting you for an hour. Where have you been?"

"I turned my phone off," Naomi said curtly. "I had things to do."

"How am I supposed to find you if you turn your phone off?" Audra asked, clearly frustrated.

"Maybe I didn't want to be found," Naomi snapped. "It looks like you found me, anyway. What's up?"

"I got a call an hour ago from—" Audra faltered mid-sentence and gave Willow a nervous glance.

"It's okay, Audra." Naomi managed an anxious smile in Willow's direction. "Geralt trusted her. I'm inclined to do the same. Willow knows. At least the basics."

"Are you serious?" the other woman exploded. "My God, how can you be so naive?" Audra shook her head in frustration and stepped closer to Naomi. "You know she and her friends are working to get the Montalto woman off the hook—in what universe do you think she won't put you into the hot seat in a fast second if she can? No offense," she added, turning briefly to Willow.

"None taken," Willow murmured, the corner of her mouth twitching.

"Come on, Audra," Naomi said with barely concealed irritation. "Just tell me."

Audra's look flicked back and forth between Willow and Naomi. "*The Times*. *The Globe*. A few more."

Naomi sighed. "Ah. So it's about to hit the fan. When?"

Audra's expression of worry deepened as she glanced at Willow again.

"*When?*" Naomi pressed.

Audra's jaw tightened, then released. "Tomorrow morning's editions."

"The money?" Naomi asked, her voice bleak.

Audra nodded. "And . . . everything else." Her eyes skittered again to Willow, and then away. "How much of the basics? What did you tell her?"

"That the money is gone." She reached out a tentative hand to Willow, who took it. "And no, I don't think she'll throw me under the bus. Besides," Naomi continued, "when the world knows I'm broke and I have nothing to benefit from his death, I basically have no motive to have gotten rid of him."

Willow said, "Believe it or not, none of us are looking for some random person to replace Rina and get her off the hook; I want to know who *really* killed Geralt. And I think you—both of you—do too."

Naomi nodded. "I do." She gave a small smile. "We'll talk later. And—thanks." She started off down the coastal path; when Audra started to follow, Naomi waved her off and said in a voice too brittle to qualify as polite, "Look, I . . . I need a little time to myself, okay? Just let me walk." She turned her back on Audra and Willow and headed toward the village.

Audra flashed Willow a side-eye. "Still like her?" she asked dryly. "Still convinced she's innocent?"

Willow nodded warily. "I . . . do, yes. Both. I mean—" She glanced sympathetically at Audra. "I mean, yeah, that was sort of rude, but she's had an awful week. And it seems like it's just getting worse."

Audra snorted and said bluntly, "You like her because she wanted you to like her. From the start, at the reception after the memorial service, she locked in on the thing you both had in common, which was feeling like the outsider, the one who didn't belong. Bonded with you. A little sisterhood of Little North Island rejected women. Remember?"

Willow remembered and suddenly felt cold.

"That's how she operates, how she is with everyone she meets. She has this instinct for knowing what someone is looking for in her, and she becomes it. With Mr. Talbot, she was ambitious and unfiltered, and she stood up to him in a way no one else dared, and he loved it. With Talbot's business associates, she was always competent and calm, the antithesis of her husband, presenting herself as the ally who could get him to do what they wanted when they couldn't manage it themselves. With me—"

Audra looked away; Willow wasn't sure if those were tears she'd seen in the shine of the other woman's eyes. "At first, she was the perfect best friend," Audra continued. "We went shopping together, got our nails done, shared advice and horror stories about men, talked about our hopes and dreams and ambitions. When she and Talbot got engaged, I became her unofficial wedding planner, helping with vendors and fittings, and keeping her disorganized self on track. She made me feel appreciated and needed, which of course made me feel good about myself, and after the wedding, she begged me to leave my job and be her assistant full-time. By then, it didn't even occur to me to say no; she'd maneuvered me into a place where it felt almost inevitable."

Audra eyed Willow. "You've been here, what, less than a week? Trust me, you do not know the real Naomi Talbot. I'm not sure Naomi herself even knows who she really is."

The shiver that went through Willow had nothing to do with the chill island day or the impending storm. *Be careful who you trust*, Geralt had told her, and Naomi herself had echoed it.

Was Willow putting her trust in the wrong person, after all?

First thing when *all this goes down*, Naomi thought as she strode past the village toward the ugly modern house Geralt had insisted on building, *will be informing my pushy and paranoid assistant that I can no longer afford an assistant.* Then she took a mental step back; she knew she would never have gotten through the past few days, let alone the past eight years, without Audra's near-manic level of organization. Naomi just needed a little space.

The gulls yowled above her; the incessant thundering of the sea was giving her a headache. *Maybe it would be better if I walked away from all of this, found myself a nice, normal life*, Naomi thought. *I never much liked Maine or island life. Maybe I'll go back to Boston—or heck, maybe California or Texas or something.* She thought about Willow's short-legged, loaf-shaped companion. *Maybe I'll get a dog. A dog, and maybe a nice little town house.* She'd saved a little money of her own that wasn't tied to Geralt's; she could do it. She could renew her physical therapist credentials, go back for a couple of classes to update her certifications, be a regular person again if she had to. She'd been one before.

But she'd worked her tail off for this. Being Mrs. Geralt Talbot had taken a lot more maneuvering and strategy than she'd bargained for. She wasn't going to throw it away yet.

She had one more play. One last effort to keep what she had earned.

CHAPTER THIRTY-TWO

There was no band at the Raven tonight—only the speakers blasting '70s classic rock. Catherine had gotten to the restaurant first and, in film-thriller-last-act fashion, sat crouched in a quiet booth in the far corner with a baseball cap on her head, eyeing the front door.

As Willow slid into the booth across from Catherine, she noticed the librarian's eyes were bloodshot and bright, and her smile was brittle. Instead of the amber-filled pint glass most people in the restaurant had in front of them, Catherine was drinking coffee; Willow suspected it was the most recent in a long string of caffeine hits in a long day. Catherine's left arm was curled protectively around a canvas messenger bag on the seat beside her.

Willow took in Catherine's pulled-down hat and gray windbreaker. "Are you okay? You look like you're on the lam."

Catherine nodded. "I'm fine, even if I'm stretched out to my last nerve. I found what I was looking for, and if Hank or any of his goon squad—"

"Hank has a goon squad?" Willow asked dubiously.

"Well, how do I know? He seems like the type to have one, and at least one of them was following me all day, and if he knows what I've got—"

"What have you got?" Willow interrupted.

"For one thing, my own goon squad now, or at least goon, singular." She grinned at Willow's puzzled look. "Later. First—tell me what really happened the other night at Cameron House."

Willow said carefully, "What do you mean? I told you already about the locket and the room—"

"Yeah, but you left stuff out, didn't you?" Catherine's eyes were fixed on Willow, a small, knowing smile on her face. "A lot of stuff."

Clearly, Willow's selective editing of her Cameron House experiences last night had not gotten past Catherine. "You'll think I'm losing it," Willow said.

"Unlikely," Catherine retorted. "I do live on Little North, after all. People see weird stuff all the time on the island, especially in houses and structures built more than a century ago. The library is one of them. I could tell you some stories, and I will someday, but for now, how about if you just tell me yours?"

Willow retrieved the sheaf of mysterious typed literary quotes from her backpack, and set them on the table in front of Catherine. Haltingly, she managed to tell Catherine the story—most of it, anyway. The cryptic typewritten messages. Joel, Dellie, and Dot. Annabel's room with its chest and books.

The librarian frowned. "Let me make sure I have this all clear. You're saying that not only is Cameron House haunted, but the ghosts there . . . talked to you? You've seen them, had face-to-face conversations?"

Willow nodded. *She'll think I'm crazy. This is why I can't have nice friends.*

"And *they* told you Effie and Sue suspected there is another Cameron heir somewhere?"

Willow nodded again.

"When you snuck over in the middle of the night and almost

got caught by an intruder who had *also* snuck into the house in the middle of the night, Annabel herself showed you where her room was, and *she* gave you the locket and photo album?"

One more nod. "I'm convinced she's trying to help me," Willow said. "But since Geralt died, most of the ghosts have . . . faded."

"Wow," Catherine said, sitting back for a moment, shaking her head slowly, trying to take it all in. "That's . . . a lot."

At least she wasn't laughing, Willow noted with relief, nor did she seem to be trying to make up an excuse to get away. "You believe me?" Willow asked.

"I'm reserving judgment," Catherine said. "The rational part of me wants to suspect it's someone's elaborate hoax to convince you the ghosts are real, but I'm not sure why or what the point would be." Catherine's attention was caught by someone at the front of the restaurant. "Okay, let's hold that thought for a bit; my personal goon squad just arrived. Here comes Nick. Maybe don't tell him right away you've been trespassing over there talking to one set of ghosts and receiving enigmatic literary quotes and jewelry from another."

Willow's head shot around as the tall police officer, now in street clothes, approached the table. She stiffened and turned back to Catherine. "Nick? *Nick*, of all people? What makes you think you can trust him with this? Just because he's a cop, you assume he's Officer Friendly?"

Nick slid into the booth next to Catherine and glared back at Willow. "Spoken like someone from Chicago." He glanced sideways at Catherine. "Told you this would piss her off."

"And I agreed," Catherine replied, "but thanks for coming with me, anyway. It was getting creepy, and I needed someone I could count on."

"You're welcome. Happy to do it." He turned on Willow. "And since when have I become untrustworthy? I thought we'd moved past that. What the hell, Stone?"

Willow froze. She remembered the way Naomi had talked about Nick, how Nick had showed up off-island only a couple of hours after Naomi went to meet her "Iron Man."

And she fervently wished she'd voiced her uncomfortable suspicions with Catherine before finding herself in this situation.

Suddenly, a familiar voice called from behind her shoulder. "Willow?" Willow turned to see Naomi coming toward the table, a nearly empty highball glass in her hand. "Fancy seeing you here—we have to stop meeting like this!" Naomi said with a too-bright smile; her eyes had the same sharp glitter they'd had the last time Willow met her here, the one that made Willow sure this was not her first drink of the night. Willow felt her teeth grinding together as Naomi came over and rested a languid hand on Nick's shoulder. "And you too, Nick—as usual, as handsome out of your uniform as you are in it, and—" She broke off and gave a false little giggle. "Oh, no, I didn't mean—I'm sure you're incredibly handsome in whatever you're wearing." She gave him a long sideways look under mascaraed lashes. The unspoken *or not wearing* did not need to be said; it all but hung in the air.

Willow tried not to let Nick catch her attempting to see his reaction, but as it turned out, he wasn't paying the least attention to her. His face had gone an embarrassed shade of crimson, and his hand twitched and nearly knocked over his water glass. He mumbled something unintelligible that might have been, "Nice to see you too, Mrs. Talbot."

Naomi gave his shoulder another squeeze, then wiggled her fingers to Catherine and Willow in a nonchalant farewell. "I'm off to the ladies'—so lovely to see you all!" She turned and walked away.

Willow suspected the extra bounce in her hips was for Nick's benefit, but it was wasted on him; Nick was still staring at the table and rearranging his napkin. Finally, he looked up and glared at her. "What are you smirking at?" he asked.

This was a surprise, Willow thought. Nick Tyler, of the broad shoulders and Central Casting good looks . . . was shy. He had reacted to Naomi's flirting—over the top though it was—like the acne-ridden teen Willow had known fifteen years ago. So yes, it was possible she was smirking. A little. "Nick . . . you have a fan."

He ran his fingers through his hair as he often did—somehow Willow was starting to find the gesture more endearing than annoying—and let his breath whoosh out. "God, that woman—she drives me crazy." He saw Catherine and Willow exchange amused glances and immediately corrected himself. "Not that kind of crazy, for God's sake." He looked away, his face still flushed. "For the past year, every time her husband did some dumbass thing with that golf cart of his, or whenever she was home alone and thought she'd seen someone lurking around the property, she made sure I was the one to come out, and it was so . . ." He shuddered. "Even at the hospital, with her husband lying right there. It was like she thought I was all twelve months of the Hot Cops of the Islands calendar or something."

Catherine grinned. "And which month were you again?" she added, barely keeping a straight face.

Nick glared at her. "Really? I followed you all over Downeast Maine this afternoon and now you're giving me a hard time?" He glanced sheepishly at Willow. "October." He shrugged. "It was a fundraiser. Did well too. Brought our little department into the twenty-first century, by a slim margin."

Rather than imagining that October calendar page, Willow asked the question that had been gnawing at the back of her mind since Patricia's "accident" at the bottom of Boulder Hill. "Nick . . . the other night after Patricia ran one of Hank's old muscle cars off the road after her band gig here, you weren't on duty, but you showed up at the scene, anyway. Except you didn't come from the island side; you were over here on the mainland. Where were you coming from?"

Nick's gaze sharpened as he regarded her across the table. "First of all, that's none of your business. Second, I'll tell you anyway, mostly because I'm curious why you want to know." He sat back and crossed his arms. "I was in Pittsfield all afternoon, talking with some of the union organizers for one of Talbot's factories up there." Nick shot Willow an amused half grin at her look of surprise. "What, you think you're the only one investigating? And you suppose all of it can happen on a computer from your cabin? I was on my way back home when I got a call about the accident. I would have made a stop at the hospital to check on Talbot, but instead, I went straight to the scene. And found, as usual"—he gave Willow a wry sideways glance—"Willow Stone, our newest island visitor, who seems to be in the middle of most of the weirdness happening around here these days."

Willow asked abruptly, "What do you like on your pizza?"

Nick's head jerked around to her. "Seriously? Where did that come from?"

Catherine knew where it had come from; Willow could see from the pained look on her face as the librarian silently pleaded for her to abandon the question.

But she couldn't. "Just tell me," Willow insisted.

He narrowed his eyes. "Fine. Banana peppers with black olives and pineapple." He looked indignant at the expressions of horror on both women's faces. "What?"

Catherine's face twisted in distaste. "Wow, Nick, that's . . . disgusting. A crime against nature."

"Who puts pineapple on their pizza without ham or bacon or something?" Willow asked, looking faintly nauseated.

"I'm a vegetarian. I like it. As an added bonus, it's weird enough that I rarely have to share my pizza with anyone."

A vegetarian, Willow thought. *Okay.* She felt her insides begin to relax a little as she realized how much she did not want Nick to be involved in any of this, how much she wanted him to be on the side of the angels.

Catherine gave Willow an impatient look and jerked her chin

in Nick's direction. "You might as well tell him about the texts. He needs to know," she murmured to Willow.

Willow told him about the texts Naomi had received three nights ago, right there in the Raven. When she got to the part about the pepperoni pizza, Nick exploded at her. "My God, Willow, you thought I was sleeping with the victim's wife? Are you insane?"

"No, I—I didn't really figure it was you, but . . . the way she talked about you, and all the visits you'd paid her, she made it sound like you spent a lot of time together. And when you were off-island the very night she was off with whoever it was . . ."

"Wow," he said, looking hurt. "I mean, totally aside from the fact she's not my type at all—"

"And what *is* your type?" Willow broke in sarcastically.

"None of your business," he retorted. "I can't believe you think I would be that irresponsible, or that bad at my job, or—"

"Cut it out, both of you." Catherine slammed her hand on the table as Nick and Willow broke off in shock. She turned to Nick. "Please. She doesn't think you're having an affair with Naomi Talbot; she's just smart enough to look at things logically, rather than trusting someone automatically because they are a cop, or good-looking, or she likes them."

"Well, one out of three," Willow muttered, chagrined.

Catherine rounded on Willow. "And you. I know you don't know any of us that well, and that whole thing with Rina hiding Sue's letter gave you massive trust issues, but if you'd told us about this particular suspicion, we could have helped set you straight."

"It's none of my business who he sleeps with," Willow said.

"You're spot-on right about that," Nick muttered.

Catherine threw her hands in the air. "You two are ridiculous. Get over it. I did not drag myself all over Maine in a rental car today to listen to you two bickering like a couple in marriage counseling. So do you want to know what I learned or not?" Catherine pulled a sheaf of papers out of the messenger bag and spread them out on the table in front of them.

Nick and Willow froze, avoiding eye contact as they turned to Catherine. Willow cleared her throat. "All right," she said, subdued. "What's all that?"

"It's proof that Hank Ramsey is not the Cameron heir. He made it all up."

CHAPTER THIRTY-THREE

"I spent most of the day in genealogy research rooms in all the county seats," Catherine explained, "with a stop in Augusta too. Definitely got my money's worth from the car rental. Spent a small fortune on photocopies." She handed Willow sheet after sheet of paper: old newspaper items, birth and marriage announcements, a pair of marriage certificates, four years apart, both of which listed Bruce Ramsey as the groom . . .

"Catherine, you're doing that information-fire-hose thing again. What am I supposed to be seeing here? My brain is mush," Willow said.

"You think I'm still firing on all cylinders after the day I've had?" Catherine retorted.

"I got this," Nick said. He turned to Willow. "Bottom line, Hank *is* descended from the same Bruce Ramsey who was married to Annabel Cameron, but he's descended from the guy's *first* wife. No connection to the Cameron family at all." He tugged the papers out of Willow's hand and gave them back to Catherine. "It seems pretty cut-and-dried; I don't know how he thought he could possibly get away with it."

"Because," Willow said bitterly, "the people who could best oppose him were Effie Cameron, Susan, and Geralt, all conveniently out of the way now, and Rina, who's in jail. Then if you factor in that he has family members working in all the right county offices—records, probate—"

"And the state's attorney office too," Catherine broke in. "I found it last night—his sister-in-law's younger brother is the assistant state's attorney. So even if a challenge came up, he's got a legal person in all the right places to help him slide it through."

"But even with all that, his best-case scenario would have been to do it quickly and under the radar," Willow said. "He probably hoped to have everything tied up and in place before anyone did exactly what you did"—she grinned at Catherine—"which was drive around the whole of Downeast Maine and dig up the smoking gun."

Nick was still frowning. "Where did he get that whole song and story about a romantic wartime marriage? I mean, we all know Hank. Creativity is not his strong suit, and that story is way too involved for him to have come up with it."

Willow rooted around in her pack till she found her copy of *Widow's Walk*; she pulled it out of the bag and handed it across the table to Catherine and Nick. "He didn't. Abel Douglas did. The whole story is right there, *literally* a work of fiction."

Catherine straightened. "Wait . . . *that's* what this book is about?"

Willow nodded. "I finished it this afternoon."

Catherine flipped through the book, disappointed. "It's not real, then," she sighed.

Nick, Willow realized, was barely paying attention; he was eyeing the open bag on the seat next to her with a curious expression. "Stone? You drink that enhanced-water stuff?"

Puzzled, Willow followed his gaze to her unzipped backpack and the empty bottle perched on top. "Oh, this," she said. "I keep forgetting to throw it away. This was Geralt Talbot's. He threw it out after—oh!" She frowned. "After the reception. On the way to Cameron House." She looked at Nick, worried. "I'm sorry, it didn't even occur to me it might—I mean, they come from the factory pre-sealed and all, right?"

Nick frowned. "Probably nothing. But I can take it in and have it tested, to be sure." He carefully took the bottle from her bag, napkin around his fingers so he would not touch it, and tucked it into his coat.

His phone went off. "I have to take this," he said, glancing down at the screen. "Don't go anywhere." He slipped out of the booth and into the hallway in the back of the restaurant.

"Well, someone's bossy all of a sudden," Willow grumbled.

Catherine was still paging through the book. "Like I said earlier, every other copy of this novel anywhere in the country has fallen off the market within the past year or two—and there weren't many to begin with. If someone knew they were going to foist this story off onto the world, maybe they wanted to reduce the chances of someone else recognizing the narrative?"

Willow jerked her head around at the loud ring of male laughter from the bar. She turned urgently back to the librarian. "Catherine, I don't know if you knew, but Hank is *here*."

Catherine's eyes grew wide, and she craned her neck around to see. "What? Seriously?"

Willow nodded. "Over at the bar with a bunch of other men—don't look!" It was too late; Hank had seen Catherine staring at him. He put down his beer, excused himself from his friends, and made a beeline for their table. The expression on his face was not the genial bonhomie with which he had always approached Willow in the past; his expression was grim, with one corner of his lip forming the universal curl worn by schoolyard bullies everywhere.

Catherine swiftly gathered her papers into a stack and managed to slip them back into her messenger bag before he got to their table.

"Ladies," he said with false warmth, the hardness in his eyes belying his genial smile. "So nice to see you. Especially you, Miss Ward; you must be exhausted after all your driving around today. I hadn't expected you back on the island till tomorrow."

Catherine smiled sweetly. "I didn't go far—I had some errands to run," she said, trying to sound innocent. "Visiting a friend. But thank you for your concern, Mr. Ramsey."

The easygoing expression fell from Hank's face as he planted his fists on the table and bent over them. "I don't know what you two are playing at, but you're out of your league," he growled. "Whatever you suppose you have, I'd strongly suggest you forget about it, flush it, whatever. This is my town now, these are my islands, and you should be very careful before you think about crossing me." He faced Catherine, his voice full of menace. "Lose it. All of it. Go back to your little library and check out books to children. And you"—his gaze slid to Willow as his mouth twisted in a sneer—"you should get in your car and drive back to your home in the murder capital of the nation. You don't belong here."

He stood up straight, brushed the lapels of his sport coat, and smoothed a hand over his comb-over, which only made the bare patch of scalp underneath more obvious. He smiled again and said brightly, loud enough for other diners to hear, "Have a wonderful evening, ladies. Be careful on that drive home!" And he walked away, slipping out of sight into the hallway in back where the restrooms were located.

Catherine froze. "Oh no," she breathed to Willow. "He knows. He knows everything. He—what?"

Willow's face had gone very still, as though she had barely heard Catherine, had barely heard most of Hank's speech. But now her eyes darted up to Catherine's, and she said, "It *was* Hank."

"What?"

Willow insisted, leaning forward, "The man in the church vestibule. It was Hank. I recognize the voice now—in fact, even the words were the same: 'Be very careful before you think about crossing me.' It was Hank."

The two of them gazed at one another in horror. Then Catherine made a quick survey of the room. "Where's Nick? I'm not budging one step from this booth until he comes back."

Willow stood. "You text him; I'll go look for him. He couldn't have gone far; he went to the back. He may still be on the phone."

Catherine choked something unintelligible to Willow's back as the determined musician strode to the rear of the restaurant, but Willow was out of earshot. Catherine took a deep breath, picked up her phone, and brought up Nick's contact information.

CHAPTER THIRTY-FOUR

The hallway in the back of the Raven had the requisite men's and women's restrooms and an ungendered one in between; entry to the kitchen was at one end, and a door to the parking lot was at the other. Nick was nowhere in sight. Willow loitered for a moment to see if he would reappear.

A sudden thud and a yelp sounded from behind a door marked EMPLOYEES ONLY, as though something heavy had fallen. Thinking someone might have been injured, Willow opened the door to what was apparently a good-size broom closet.

And closed the door immediately.

Immediately wasn't soon enough. Not only had one of the pair inside seen her, but she had seen them as well. And it was a sight she never wanted to see again.

Her feet carried her rapidly out of the hallway and back to the booth where Catherine sat waiting. The librarian took one look at Willow's face and asked, "Willow? What happened? Did you find Nick? Did you run into Hank?"

"Not in the way you're thinking," Willow replied, fighting

back the inappropriate wave of laughter threatening to burst from behind her carefully closed lips. She sat down again opposite Catherine, who waited patiently for her to gather herself.

Finally, Willow said in a voice that was almost tranquil, "I think . . . I think Iron Man is . . . Hank."

In a puzzled voice, Catherine said, "Um . . . that seems unlikely. Why would you say that?"

Willow replied, "Because about two minutes ago, I saw them together in the broom closet across from the ladies' room."

Catherine, stunned, stammered, "When you say, 'together,' you don't mean . . ."

Willow nodded and gulped audibly. "Together. Yeah. I mean." Willow had stepped backward and shut the door as fast as she could, but not before seeing far more of Hank Ramsey Jr. than she could ever forget, however much she wished she could wipe the image from her mind: Naomi, her back to the wall, her legs around Hank's midsection; Hank hadn't seen Willow, since his face was buried in Naomi's neck and his attention was definitely not on the closet door, but Willow had seen the slightly bored expression on Naomi's face turn to panic as she saw Willow standing in the doorway. She shuddered. "Some things you can't unsee."

Catherine put up her hands as if in self-defense. "Please, no visuals. You can keep the details to yourself." Then she winced. "Too late. They're there."

Into the shocked silence, Nick strode back in through the front of the restaurant and slid into the booth again. "What's up?" He looked at their aghast faces. "Hey, what's up? What happened?"

Willow managed a shaky and slightly maniacal smile. "You missed all the fun. Where'd you go?"

"I told you, phone call. I took it outside." He turned to Catherine. "Care to explain? I'd ask Willow, but she looks like she's seen a ghost—"

At that, Willow began to laugh, one of those breathless

teary-eyed fits one prayed would stop before you passed out from lack of oxygen.

Catherine reached across the table to pat her shoulder comfortingly. "Actually," she said matter-of-factly, "she apparently takes ghosts in stride; one of the Cameron House spirits has been passing her notes. This was different. A few minutes ago, she witnessed Hank Ramsey and Naomi Talbot having sex in a broom closet."

Willow managed to squeak out, "Infinitely more terrifying," before the laughter overwhelmed her and she helplessly put her head down on the table.

Nick's face blanched. "She saw *what*?" He looked back at Willow. "Seriously? Please tell me you're both joking before my brain starts—oh no, now I'm imagining it."

"Definitely—not—a visual—" Willow lifted her head briefly from the table and gasped out, "Never—unsee—" She dropped her head back on the table.

By now, Catherine had started giggling too. Nick sat there staring into space. "Okay then," he said. "Hank's the one with the pepperoni."

Catherine and Willow's eyes met, kicking off a new burst of laughter. Nick, looking frustrated, demanded, "What?"

The two women dissolved again. Nick rolled his eyes, trying to keep from laughing. "God, what are you two, twelve? I thought guys were supposed to be the immature ones about this kind of thing." He paused, suddenly serious. "Did they see you?" he asked Willow.

She nodded, and the hilarity faded. "They did. Or at least Naomi did." She reached across and grabbed Nick's wrist. "Hank knows. He knows where Catherine was today. If he doesn't know exactly what she's found, he at least suspects. And he came over and threatened us after you left."

Willow's face hardened as she came to the next, inevitable conclusion. "It's what was missing. The link between someone who wants the property Geralt was determined to acquire, and someone with the kind of access to Geralt that would make poisoning him not only possible but easy. Hank probably reasoned that he could make buckets of money if Naomi were to inherit, all the more if he has even a dubious claim to the lineage himself—and I'd bet you anything she hasn't told him Geralt was broke. Hank sets himself up as the last Cameron heir, while Naomi poisons Geralt."

Catherine's eyes widened. "Which means the last thing left in the way of their happily ever after is . . . Patricia."

The three of them stared at each other.

From the corner of her eye, Willow saw Naomi step out of the back hallway and walk hastily through the restaurant, casting a terrified look in their direction. Nick murmured, "You stall her; I'm heading to the back to see if I can find Hank. He either slipped out the rear door or he's still there."

Willow nodded. She slid from the booth and followed Naomi to the door of the restaurant, catching her elbow before she could open it. Naomi whirled to face her, wrenching her arm away. She jabbed a pointing finger at Willow's face. "Don't. Just don't—not a word. Go ahead, tell all your friends so they can post on their socials about that slut Naomi Talbot, who came from nothing and isn't good enough to occupy space in their precious puritanical polo-shirts-and-boat-shoes island community. But you have no right to judge me, and it's none of your business who I spend my time with—"

Willow swatted her hand away. "Naomi, are you serious? Hank Ramsey?"

Naomi had the grace to look abashed. "All right, so he's no Prince Charming. But he's fun, and he makes me feel gorgeous, and he—"

"He wanted your husband dead so he could have a clearer path to claiming Cameron House and turning the property into a golf course and hotel." Willow's voice was cold and cutting.

Naomi stopped. "What? Please, he's got plenty of hotels already. Besides, he's in the Cameron family line himself; he can do what he wants—"

"He's not. He's not, and he knows it. He made it all up. It looks okay on the surface, but the minute you scratch deeper, it's obviously garbage," Willow said. "Has he shown you any proof? Ask him for proof. He doesn't have any."

Naomi's face clouded. "Geralt wanted the house to stay in the family. I thought—if Hank is family, then . . ."

"Then you can not only honor your late husband's last wishes but more easily move on to the next old rich guy on the island and keep living in the manner you have become accustomed to. And the fact that this old rich guy is married won't stand in your way."

"Oh, please," Naomi scoffed, "I'm not planning to marry Hank. I was just—" She looked, suddenly anxious, at Willow. "He's not a Cameron? It's all a lie?"

Willow nodded. "It's a lie. He lied to you about the Cameron fortune, like I'm guessing you lied to him about coming into millions from your dead husband." Naomi looked abashed, and Willow knew she'd struck home. For an instant, Willow almost felt sorry for her; then she remembered Geralt, his weakness and terror, the bleak despair and confusion as he vomited on the floor, and all pity went away. "But it's over. You guys blew it. I hope you like prison."

Naomi started. "You hope we . . . what?" Understanding hit her. "Oh my God, you think I—we—killed Geralt." Then the next realization came. "And tried to kill Patricia?" She backed away from Willow, shaking her head in terrified denial.

"Didn't you?" Willow spat. "It makes perfect sense. The minute we look at the two of you together, it becomes obvious. Everyone gets what they want. Except Geralt, who is now dead, and his family's house about to be sold to a bloodthirsty developer. But he was old and a creep, so who cares about what he wanted?" Willow's voice was bitter.

Naomi's head was still moving back and forth. "No. No, I would never do that. Hank would never do that. He's a bit of an operator, but he wouldn't . . . I'm sure he wouldn't . . ." Her voice trailed off.

This was unexpected. Willow had anticipated carefully planned denials, proactively offered alibis, and at least some more polished and indignant protestations, but Naomi gave the appearance of being genuinely upset. And Willow didn't think Naomi Talbot was that good an actor. She had shown defensive hostility about being caught banging Hank in the broom closet, but when accused of murder, the woman seemed frightened and shocked.

Was Naomi's only crime her abhorrent taste in men?

Was the young widow beginning to realize the danger she might face, far beyond newspaper headlines and social media cancellation?

A horn honked outside, loudly, aggressively. Naomi recoiled a little at the sound. There was a new resolve on her face as she pulled a thick envelope out of her purse. Her voice was hurried. "Look, my allegiance all along was to Geralt; you know that. So maybe I thought I could have my cake and eat it too—let Hank inherit the house and ride the wake of that for a while until I could get myself set up financially. But if he's—" She stopped; Willow could all but see the wheels turning.

The horn honked again, more insistently.

When Naomi turned back to Willow, there was new resolve in her face. She held out the envelope. "Look. I don't know if this makes any difference at all, but you should have this."

Curiously, Willow took the envelope and looked at the return address: Downeast Investigation Services.

Naomi said, "Geralt hired a private investigator. He was helping your godmother, trying to track down living Cameron descendants.

The guy's preliminary report came this afternoon, and—well, it doesn't change anything about the house or the situation we're in now, but I feel like you have a right to know what he learned." She leaned closer. "Make sure you're alone when you read it. And don't tell anyone you don't absolutely trust." Before Willow could respond, Naomi had slipped out the door.

Willow waited an instant too long before following; she stepped outside in time to see Naomi slip into another vintage car, this one bright blue, with Hank behind the wheel. The man gave Willow a sly, knowing grin, kicked the car into gear, and squealed away just as Nick rounded the corner of the restaurant.

"Son of a—" The tall officer scowled as he joined Willow, panting a little. "He gave me the slip—literally. I almost fell on my face."

Willow was frowning. "How many of those cars does he have?"

Nick did not hesitate. "A '63 split-window Corvette Stingray in Daytona Blue? Only the one. But he has maybe nine of these old muscle cars—a couple of Mustangs, '68 Firebird, a '66 Cyclone, I think he's even got an Olds Toronado too . . . The '69 Camaro Z was totaled when Patricia went down the hill the other day, of course, so he's down one —"

"And what's that?" Willow interrupted, pointing to the asphalt, where a small brownish puddle had formed beneath the car in the few seconds it had stopped to pick up Naomi. Nick walked over and touched it, rubbed the slippery fluid between his fingers, smelled it. His eyes returned to Willow's, aghast.

In the space of two heartbeats, Nick and Willow came to the horrifying realization of what was about to happen.

Before they could spring into motion, they heard the sound rush up the hill to them, the harsh slam of high-speed metal against rock, distant but clear as a bell. And seconds later, the gut-deep thud and boom of a gas tank exploding.

CHAPTER THIRTY-FIVE

Things started happening quickly, too quickly for a stunned Willow to process. A roiling pillar of smoke and soot rose from the base of Boulder Hill, darker than the night sky into which it spiraled. The police found a puddle of brake fluid floating in the space where the Corvette had been parked. Notifications chirped from phone to phone as patrons gathered around in the parking lot in a combination of concern and fascination.

Willow was briefly comforted by the squeeze of Nick's hand on her shoulder. Then Nick looked at her helplessly and said, "I have to go . . . I'm sorry, I have to—"

And he was gone. Her unexpected ally and almost-friend had to go be a cop.

There were more police, more questions, few of which Catherine and Willow were able to answer. Finally, they were allowed to leave. An officer they did not know escorted them back to Rina's inn on Nick's orders; Diana and Mac were already there. "Until we know what's going on," he'd said grimly, "I want all of you together, in one place, as close to the village as possible. Another officer will come by when we're done at the scene and stay overnight."

For a change, Willow was disinclined to argue. Driving past the emergency vehicles lighting up the curve at the base of Boulder Hill, she tried not to look, but she couldn't avoid seeing the hulk of still-smoking metal, black and charred in the circling red and blue lights.

No one could possibly have survived this. Naomi and Hank were gone.

At last, Willow was able to step into a quiet third-floor bedroom in Rina's inn, away from people, and let herself collapse. Her mind had gone all muffled and blurry as though it had safely wrapped itself in a blanket of snow—the first overnight snow of the winter, walking to the chapel for her morning organ practice, when the sounds of footsteps and cars and voices were hushed and deadened beneath the soft layer of blinding white. Safe and alone, she let herself begin to relax into the blurry quiet, into sleep, only to feel the horror punch back into her like a fist to her center, threatening to burst her apart. She squeezed her eyes shut and struggled to remember how to breathe, raggedly at first, easing her breath into a stable rhythm, then slowing it . . . remembering to hear music in her head, music that would ground her and keep her steady. Bach. The C minor passacaglia. Sue's favorite, and hers. The gentle pulse of the pipe organ in her mind's ear brought her back to earth, to the present. It quieted the terrified thing clawing at her insides, gave her space to exist, to release.

At last, she slid into sleep.

Rina was released from custody the next morning. Between the two new deaths for which she could not have been responsible, and medical confirmation that Geralt had far more lithium in his system than he could have gotten in a single dose, Rina had all but dropped off the suspect list. She came back on the morning boat, Diana at her side.

When Rina stepped into the inn's big farmhouse kitchen where Mac, Catherine, and Willow waited, there were hugs, warm and long; there were tears and words of encouragement. And there was worry; Rina was too quiet, too slow-moving. She was clearly exhausted; her eyes were wide and a little wild, and the circles under them were deep. No one talked about crime or death or accusations; they surrounded her with warmth and food and care, in her familiar kitchen and surrounded by the people she loved.

Before too long, though, Diana chased everyone out, proclaiming that Rina needed rest and peace. Mac had to work, Diana needed to get back to her own shop, and Catherine needed to make up for the time she'd missed at the library over the past few days. The inn's guests had gone out on hikes and whale-watch tours, despite the threatening weather.

Willow stayed at the inn to be with Rina.

Rina's first order of business was a long, hot shower, an attempt to scrub off every mote and memory of the past two days of her detention. She came back down to the kitchen, where Willow had prepared mugs of hot cocoa sweetened with maple syrup and sprinkled with cinnamon. For several minutes, the pair sat in silence on the cushioned bench in the big kitchen's breakfast nook, looking out at the rising wind and sea, hot mugs warming their hands.

After a time, Rina said softly, "Do you know, Sue used to sit right there, where you are sitting, in the evenings sometimes? We'd have our tea, or our cocoa, and talk about anything and everything." She looked out the window at the ocean. "Even since she's . . . gone, I sometimes come down here and sit and imagine her sitting there, and we have our little conversations—here, or down by the water, or anyplace we loved being together. Sometimes it feels so real I feel a jolt when I realize she isn't really there." She smiled sadly at Willow. "Real or not, it's like having her back, for a little while at least. Is that unhealthy, do you think?"

Willow had gone still. But she forced herself to smile back. "I don't think it sounds unhealthy at all. In fact, I'm a little envious." She set down her mug on the table and leaned in a little. "If you don't mind me asking, what does she say in those conversations? What do you talk about?"

Rina looked out the window at the sea. "We talk about everything and nothing. I tell her about my guests, I would often rant about Talbot, I—we—" She gave Willow a sad little smile. "We've talked about you. I guess it was my guilty conscience knowing about the letter I never sent, but the Sue in my mind kept bringing you up again and again. We'd argue, and . . . she'd be gone."

Willow asked carefully, "What did she say about me?"

Rina gave a little shrug. "What you'd expect her to say, or more to the point, what I'd expect her to say. To give you a break, to help you, to remember you weren't responsible for your parents' bigotry. And at the jail—" She stopped, looking thoughtful. "Yes, I'd forgotten, I dreamed about her while I was there—dreamed or hallucinated, it's hard to say; I didn't think I'd slept at all, but if I dreamed of Sue, I must have." Rina turned to Willow, her eyes troubled. "She reminded me to tell you the cabin is for you, if you want it. We talked about that before she died too, and the will she never got the chance to write. She always wanted you to have the cabin." She paused. "And then . . . I think she said I should tell you about Robin. Which doesn't make sense, since she hardly ever spoke of her, even to me. I think it hurt too much."

"Who's Robin?"

Rina said with obvious reluctance, "Robin was Sue's daughter."

CHAPTER THIRTY-SIX

Willow's eyes went wide. "Sue . . . had a daughter? Who is she? What happened?"

Rina took another swallow of cocoa and frowned into the mug. "If we're going to have this conversation, we need something a little stronger." She got up and fished a bottle of Jameson out of one of the kitchen cabinets, standing on tiptoe to reach it, and splashed some into each of their mugs before continuing.

When she did, Rina's voice was bleak. "Robin died. Young—she was only a teenager, I believe. She came from Sue's first marriage—yes, Susan was married once, and yes, to a man," Rina said in response to Willow's near gasp. "She was so young herself, barely out of college, and back then, it wasn't easy to simply announce to the world that one wasn't interested in men—getting married was what well-bred girls were expected to do. The marriage was mercifully brief—annulled, I think—with him not even knowing Sue was pregnant. She wanted nothing from him, and he took off."

But Willow had latched on to the first part of the story. "Robin died? Are you sure?"

Rina saw the stab of hope; then, as the young woman thought it through and did the math, she saw Willow's hope wilt, replaced with bewilderment, then disappointment. She reached over and put her hand on Willow's. "I know. You wonder if you could have been . . . her. Sue's daughter. She understood you so much better than your own family, didn't she?"

Willow nodded. "To tell the truth, I don't think my parents ever liked me all that much. I've always felt like this massive disappointment, like they wanted the perfect child and got this peculiar kid who didn't fit into their lives. But with Sue—I fit. Some part of me always wished . . ." She paused. "And then they took her away from me."

"I think part of her wished it too," Rina said. "It was in her face whenever she spoke of you—and she never forgot you, never stopped missing you. But no, Robin would have to be well into her forties now if she'd lived."

Willow looked away, a little embarrassed. "It's silly; of course it couldn't be true. But you're right; Sue was the closest thing to real family I had."

Rina grasped Willow's other hand, turning earnestly to face her. "But don't you see? That's the thing Sue learned, the thing we all learned, Mac and Diana and Catherine too . . . sometimes you're born into your family, and sometimes you go find it for yourself. Family is about *much* more than blood." Her eyes starting to well up, she managed a smile. "Sue was our family. So now you are too."

Willow smiled too. "Can I call you Aunt Rina, then?"

Rina released her hand and took a swig of her whiskey-flavored cocoa. "I'd be offended if you didn't. Aunt Rina I'll be, henceforth."

Willow grinned. Then she asked hesitantly, "Can you tell me what happened? With Sue and the baby? What happened to Robin?"

"Sue wouldn't tell me," Rina said. "Only that she died. They used to travel together—just the two of them, during their school breaks. Sue never said so straight out, but I think something terrible happened on one of those trips, and Robin died. Then Sue found her way to the island and made a new life here; first in the summers and then year-round. She never once left the country, or even Maine, after that, as far as I know."

Willow reached her hand out to Rina again. "Can you tell me about her? About Sue? I know I missed so much, but . . . can you help me know more about who she was?"

Rina took the proffered hand; her heart broke a little at the yearning in the girl's eyes, and she felt the now-familiar stab of guilt at her own role in keeping the two of them away from each other.

"Of course. I'll tell you anything." She grinned mischievously. "Want to hear how we met?"

Willow nodded eagerly.

"It was around twelve years ago, and I had just moved to the island. I was trying to set up the shop and decide where I could put the kiln so it wouldn't burn the dock down."

Outside the window, chill rain and icy gusts presaged the coming storm. Willow listened as Rina spun the memories, loving the stories, knowing the telling of them was likely as healing for Rina as it was for Willow.

It took only one more cup of cocoa and two slugs of Jameson; by midafternoon, Willow could see Rina beginning to sag, the exhaustion of the past three days at last overtaking her. She persuaded Rina to go and rest, maybe try to sleep the night through, promising she would reach out to Diana and Mac about keeping the guests fed and that someone would wake Rina if there was anything at all anyone needed . . .

Willow had no intention of waking her under any circumstances; the poor woman was all but limp with weariness.

Rina went to bed, and Willow climbed back up to her borrowed room. She sat cross-legged on the brass double bed, a well-worn afghan around her shoulders, Finn's head resting on her thigh. She liked this room; with its cozy dormer beneath the sloped roof, it reminded her a little of Annabel's poet-garret room at Cameron House.

Willow found herself staring at her backpack, where she had shoved Naomi's envelope, minutes before hell exploded at the bottom of a hill; she had forgotten it in the chaos that followed. Naomi's final words echoed back to her: *It doesn't change anything . . . but I feel like you have a right to know . . .*

She set her teacup on the nightstand and reached for the bag, pawing through its random contents until she found the envelope at the bottom. A last gift from a dead woman. Willow slipped her thumb under the flap and opened the envelope, pulling out several sheets of dense typing. She read the report. Then she read it again.

It should have been a surprise; instead, the buried truth the PI had uncovered felt almost inevitable. The investigator had tracked down Marisa Talbot, Peter Talbot's widow. After Peter's death, the young woman had departed for her hometown and quickly—too quickly—married her childhood sweetheart. The couple had settled down and bought a house on the shores of Lake Michigan, where she gave birth six months later to a little girl. And eventually, years later, the daughter of Marisa Talbot Davis and Bernard Davis had grown up and found her way back to Little North Island—Effie Cameron's niece, Annabel Cameron's great-niece, Peter Talbot's daughter.

Susan Davis had been the rightful heir to Cameron House all along.

Did Sue even know who she was? Willow wondered. *For that matter, did Joel and the Misses Drummond know?* Willow didn't think they did; Dot's indignance at Effie leaving the house to someone from Away—she realized she was mentally capitalizing the word herself now—had been real, as had Joel's frustration at being kept out of the loop, which had its own implications. Could the ghosts keep secrets from each other as well as from the living? And if Sue had found another Cameron heir, who was it? If her daughter, Robin, had died as a teenager, Sue's line would have ended there . . . but what else had Sue found?

Sue had left *Widow's Walk* for Willow to read. Would she have done that if the novel were truly pure fiction? Hank's lies about his own connection to the family didn't mean that Annabel Cameron Ramsey's son, Douglas, hadn't lived and fought in the war and died there. What if he *had* married overseas and had a child? And if he did, what had happened to the wife and baby? Who was the sad woman pictured in the locket?

Willow needed more information, but with Naomi and Geralt both gone, there was literally no one alive who had the answers she needed, and most of the dead who might know seemed to be beyond her reach. Except, possibly, for Annabel.

Cameron House was locked; she needed to get inside. But how?

She remembered something Rina had said after dinner on Willow's first night at the cabin, the day of Sue's memorial. *Do you know, I haven't even begun to clear out her things? . . . her jacket in the hall closet . . . her keys are still right there in the pocket . . .*

Willow smiled. *Okay then*, she thought. *The quest is still on.*

Sue's coat, hanging in the closet as Rina had predicted, was a dull army green; like Sue herself, it was practical and unglamorous, and Willow would have known whose it was even without the few silvery hairs that still clung to the inside of the fleece-lined hood. In the left-hand inner pocket, she found a small ring of keys.

Willow heard an anxious whine from the hallway behind her.

It was Finn. He was not happy with her; his pointed face made his displeasure abundantly clear. *Where do you think you're going? It's wet and cold outside, and I can smell the rain. You're about to do something irresponsible and ill-advised, aren't you? Be smart; find a nice blanket and curl up underneath it. If you make me a grilled cheese sandwich, I'll share it with you.* The feathery tail gave an encouraging wag.

Willow smiled, walking over to the corgi and scratching behind his pointed ears. "You stay here, boy. I won't be long; I need to check on something. Stay and take care of Rina. She needs the company. Go do your emotional support animal thing. Go to Rina. Rina."

The dog looked at her suspiciously, then made a little chuffing sound and trudged back up the hallway to Rina's room.

You be careful, he seemed to say as he gave her one last look. *I won't be there to rescue you this time, you know.*

"It's okay, boy. I won't need rescuing," she said confidently.

She hoped it was true.

Willow slipped Sue's oversize green coat off the hanger. Promising herself she wouldn't do anything stupid, she shoved her arms into the too-long sleeves, pulled the jacket's warmth around her like a talisman, and stepped out into the whipping wind and rain.

She didn't think Sue would mind.

CHAPTER THIRTY-SEVEN

Nick Tyler sat at his desk in the little mainland police station, his finger clicking on the Refresh button in his email every twenty seconds. What was taking so long?

A few years ago, Nick had gone on a few dates with the pretty brunette who worked in the forensics lab; they had enjoyed each other's company, bonded over their enjoyment of *Doctor Who*, and parted amicably when she realized she was still in love with her ex-boyfriend. Nick had brooded for about forty-one hours, during which time he realized his ego might be bruised but his heart was not particularly broken. They remained friends, and his life went on comfortably without her in its center.

This had not prevented him from taking advantage of Jodie's still-guilty conscience for unceremoniously dumping him; he didn't often beg her to slip his requests through more quickly than her lab would ever admit was humanly possible, but when he did, she usually came through.

A new message appeared at the top of his inbox from Jodie. He clicked it open; there were several attachments and two words:

Call me. He picked up the phone and dialed her number, his fingers drumming impatiently on the desk as he waited for her to pick up.

The coroner's phone call that morning, confirmed by the preliminary written report, had confirmed what he had suspected all along—that Willow and her nosy band of research nerds were correct, and Geralt Talbot's lithium poisoning had been developing for weeks. Considering the extent to which Rina and Geralt had habitually avoided one another, no one could place them together long enough for Rina to have had access. Nor could anyone on the island recall ever seeing Rina in conversation with Naomi—or, for that matter, with anyone working at the Talbots' house on the other side of Little North. Geralt and Naomi had always brought their own people in from Boston when they came to the island, and the staff more or less kept to themselves.

Jodie picked up on the third ring. "Nick?"

"Hey, Jodie; got your email. Thanks for pushing it through."

"No worries. And I know you'll go through the fine print, but I wanted to make sure you got it and that you knew your super-specific question came back with a definite yes. There were traces in the plastic bottle and in the remaining bits of liquid. Fairly high concentration, given lithium carbonate is only partially soluble in water, but I'll tell you what else—whoever put it there clearly knew exactly how much would be able to dissolve in the liquid without leaving a visible sediment. And if they knew that, they would also have known lithium carbonate has a faintly sour taste and that it would be easily disguised by the artificial lemon flavor. Your victim drank a lot of it?"

Nick felt a grin spreading over his face. "By the case, literally. The coroner said he'd been taking the lithium into his system for a while, and guess what one of the side effects of chronic lithium toxicity is?"

Jodie didn't hesitate. "Thirst. It's diabolically perfect, really; give the man something that makes him thirsty so you can put the same poison that makes him thirsty right into his primary drinking source."

"Fingerprints?" Nick asked, moving on to the second page of her report.

"A search for fingerprints on the bottle gave us your victim and one unknown set"—*Probably Willow's*, Nick thought—"and that's it."

Damn. But that would have been too easy, he supposed.

"On the bottle," Jodie said mischievously. "Now ask me about the cap."

Hope bloomed. "Okay, Jodie, tell me about the cap."

"Say please."

"Oh, for God's—please. Please, Jodie, tell me what you found on the cap."

He could hear her on the other end of the line trying not to laugh. "Don't get your hopes up too high; it's not exactly the brass ring. But I don't think they are the original caps. One of my coworkers swills down this stuff on a regular basis—I don't know how, I find it pretty nasty—and has a stash by his desk. I compared the cap on this bottle to his; it fits perfectly, but it doesn't have the company logo stamped on the lid."

His mind was leaping ahead. "You're suggesting that, to get the poison into his sealed bottles of fancy flavored water, someone opened them all, added and dissolved the powder, and *replaced* the original lids with new ones that made the bottles appear to have never been opened?" His email chimed.

"I sent you a link. You can buy 'em on the internet. You can buy anything on the internet," she said a little smugly.

She'd earned a little smugness. "Jodie, you're the best. I can't even—thank you." He paused. "That short guy still treating you okay?" he asked. "If he ever doesn't, I'll arrest him for jaywalking, I'll sit outside his house and look menacing, whatever you need, you know it."

Jodie laughed. "Of course I know. But yeah, David—who's

six feet tall, by the way, which hardly qualifies as *short*—is great. In fact"—he could almost hear her beaming through the phone line—"we have a little David or Jodie coming along in about five months, so I think we're both all in."

"You're—Jodie, that's amazing! Congratulations to both of you." He was glad things had worked out between the two as he pushed down the tiny hollow thread of sentiment that rose unbidden.

"Thanks, Nick. Hey, gotta go—but let me know how this comes out, okay? I'm curious now."

"You bet, Jodie, and—" But she had hung up.

So Jodie was having a baby. He was happy for her. Really. Very, very happy.

Nick brought his crime board file up on his second monitor—he was old-fashioned enough to still call it a crime board, but twenty-first-century enough to use an app rather than a physical piece of cork on the wall—and studied it for the hundredth time that day.

Susan Davis. Geralt Talbot. Naomi Talbot. Hank Ramsey. And, if Willow Stone was right, Effie Cameron. And the attempt on Patricia Ramsey.

This break in Geralt Talbot's murder investigation was running through him like a shot of adrenaline as the noose began to close in. He didn't know yet who it was closing around, but the more people it excluded, the fewer were left inside. It was looking less and less likely that one person could have been responsible for the entire string of violence on the normally peaceful little island. On the other hand, he had a hunch if he could nail down one guilty party, the others—if there were others—would fall into place.

He studied the screen. Every piece of evidence, big and small, still pointed to Naomi Talbot and Hank Ramsey as coconspirators behind Geralt Talbot's death, and likely Effie Cameron's and Susan Davis's as well. She had the access; he had the motive. In this light, even the attempt on Patricia's life made sense: Naomi had been at the bar; Hank owned a long-term parking and car rental facility off the island with its own service department. Maybe, once Patricia had crafted whatever genealogical gymnastics Hank needed, the conspiring pair wanted her out of the way as quickly as possible so they could be together; if Hank's Cameron claims had seemed a little dubious, Naomi's position as spouse of the last Cameron would bolster his, and Hank's station in the town would give Naomi a little more island clout. If this were true, their deaths had probably saved Patricia's life.

But someone had killed them. Which suggested that either there was a third conspirator, or they had not been responsible to begin with.

For some reason, he found himself wanting to tell Willow Stone what he'd found, how the bottle she had absentmindedly picked up might be the break their investigation needed, how they were now that much closer to finding Geralt's killer. But he pulled his hand back when it twitched toward his phone to call her.

He couldn't comment on a continuing investigation. Even if he just wanted to hear her voice.

His email dinged; he clicked on the message and downloaded the deep background check reports on Hank's, Geralt's, and Naomi Talbot's employees and household staff.

It was going to be a long evening. He poured another cup of bad coffee and started reading.

CHAPTER THIRTY-EIGHT

It took three tries to find the key that opened the Cameron House back door; Willow slipped inside out of the rain and wind, through the shabby old kitchen, and into the foyer.

She was beginning to get accustomed to the mansion's shifting moods; today, with no sunlight to filter flickers of magic through the stained glass window above the grand staircase, all was cold and dim, like a sepia photograph. The only sound was the whine of the wind outside and the persistent tapping of raindrops on the roof; within the thick walls, all was still.

Willow hesitantly moved through the rooms on the first floor, looking for any sign of movement or presence. Kitchen, sitting room, dining room . . . all was completely quiet.

In the rear corner of the house, Willow came upon a cozy modern bedroom suite she had not noticed before, completely unlike the rest of the antique-laden house. *This was Sue's room*, she realized in a rush; her godmother had avoided the grand bedrooms of the mansion and instead claimed this simple space for herself.

Willow smiled at how characteristically Sue that choice was.

A layer of dust had settled over the space in the weeks since

Sue's death, but Willow could still appreciate the quiet, contemporary elegance of the space. She suspected from its location that the room might have begun life as part of the food storage and preparation area of the house, but if so, it had been thoroughly remodeled since then. It held a Mission-style bed, with a pair of simple chairs in one corner; a gorgeously carved desk sat against the wall, strewn with books and papers. The contents of the bookshelves lining the walls were varied and eclectic, important-looking leather-bound first editions and historical texts sharing space with the tales of Avonlea and Narnia and Pern that Willow had loved as a child. The novels of Abel R. Douglas were there too, with one conspicuously bare spot where *Widow's Walk* would have gone.

This room feels like Sue, Willow thought.

Reluctantly, she left the comfortable room behind. Finding the key on the first try, she turned the handles to the French doors of the library. The latch gave way with a familiar *thonk*; she stepped in and turned on the light—but this room, too, was deserted. Willow peered into alcoves and corners, giving second and third looks to the chairs and couches to make sure they were as unoccupied as they first appeared.

They were. Today, the once-haunted mansion felt like no more than an empty old house.

Willow climbed the wrought iron spiral staircase in the corner, carefully making her way into the shadowy section above and past the massive fireplace where Willow had first met Joel and the Misses Drummond. There were bookshelves up here too, stretching into the dim recesses of the second floor; on the other side of the library would be the second-floor corridor, Willow remembered—a long stretch of bare wall.

Or maybe not fully bare. On this side, the wall was not flush; the corner bookcase protruded slightly from the others. Willow grinned. Of course the Camerons would have more than one entrance and exit to the library. Once she knew what she was looking for, the little switch was easy to find. The corner bookcase opened inward on silent hinges, releasing Willow into the shadowy corridor behind it.

From the end of the hallway, a faint sound drifted to Willow from the other side of the stained glass double doors—a brief murmur of voices, a whisper of music. Willow hesitantly opened one of the heavy doors and slipped inside.

She stood in a small octagonal chapel. Frescoes of biblical scenes, and more stained glass, lined the walls. To Willow's delight, a tiny tracker-style pipe organ sat nestled in a corner. Her fingers itched to see if the ancient instrument would still play, but she restrained herself—the slightest movement could crack old leather bellows into dust or disrupt families of music-loving rodents that might have made their homes in the depths of the instrument.

For an instant, as though in response to her thought, a current of air seemed to move through the little organ, breathing through the old pipes, wheezing out a few notes of a melody she almost recognized. Out of the corner of her eye, Willow caught a glimpse of a man and woman standing by the altar, smiling at each other as a clergyman wrapped his stole around their joined hands. She whipped her head around, but they were not there. Now she was looking at a casket, too small to be an adult's . . . laid atop it was a single crow-black feather.

Then casket and feather were gone too, and the organ was silent.

Willow slipped out of the chapel and gently closed the doors.

The house, and the ghosts, were still here, at least a little. Joel might have given up on her, but someone—or several someones—had not.

The broad corridor curved around and led her beneath an archway trimmed in vine-carved wood. Willow felt her face break into a smile as she stepped into a high-ceilinged open space with broad windows and gleaming floors. Here was the other side of the sea swirl of stained glass that presided over the foyer, dominating the grandeur of what could only be a ballroom. Eyes shining, Willow slowly moved around the room, admiring the ornate curls of woodwork that drew the eye up from the walls to the starry-painted ceiling. Her imagination filled with images of finely dressed men and women dining or dancing in this room, engaging in sparkling conversation over slim champagne flutes, or slipping out through the row of glass doors to walk arm in arm in the moonlight on the balcony outside. Through the windows Willow could see the balcony opening onto a terrace extending outward. For a moment, she heard fragments of music, the swish of fabric as couples danced and laughed . . . There was the handsome young man from the chapel, in a tuxedo instead of the suit and fedora in which she was used to seeing him, dancing with a young woman in a white gown—Peter and Marisa, gazing at each other with eyes full of love and hope for a long and happy future together . . .

The room was empty again.

Willow went back to the second-floor landing and the stretch of wall where the hidden door to Annabel's garret had been and pressed the subtle switch she had seen Annabel's ghost touch two nights ago.

Nothing happened.

She frowned. Had she missed the spot? No, she was sure she had it right; the lever simply wasn't working.

Evidently, Annabel didn't want company today. Dejected, Willow returned to the grand staircase.

On the floor at the bottom of the stairs—to no great surprise—she found another typed missive, this time Shakespeare:

```
not one now to mock your own grinning?
quite chapfallen? now get you to my lady's
chamber . . . --WS
```

Willow had to give her literary note-leaver points for knowing more than the first line of the "Alas, poor Yorick" scene from

Hamlet. But this was less than helpful. Willow glowered and said to the air, "Well, I tried, but she won't let me in—"

She stopped. Something was niggling at the back of her brain, something she had missed. She turned in a slow circle in the grand foyer, trying to pick up what was different from the last time she had stood there. She scanned the smooth wainscoting, the heavy sideboard, the small table with its chess pieces polished to a bright glow . . . and she had it. Willow grinned and mentally face-palmed; her quote-loving ghost was right to be a little salty—Willow had blown right past the obvious. It wasn't Annabel's chamber the note was sending Willow to—it was Sue's.

Willow hurried back to Sue's bedroom, with its weeks-old layer of dust, and she knew she had been right.

Every room Willow had visited in the whole of Cameron House had been clean, polished, practically gleaming, and it had not occurred to her till now to question why or how. But the memory clicked into place in a brief flash: a glimpse of a young woman in a long black dress with starched white cap and apron.

"A self-cleaning haunted house," Willow murmured to herself. "That's . . . convenient." She wasn't sure how she felt about the ethics of a ghostly cleaning staff condemned to spend the afterlife in service, but she would wrestle with that later. The more immediate follow-up question: Why was Sue's room the only one with a layer of dust?

Willow surveyed Sue's room with new eyes. Joel had said the ghosts could only interact with material things that had existed while they lived, which made the antique-filled rooms of Cameron House perfectly accommodating for even the oldest Cameron spirits. Sue's room, on the other hand, was full of "new" things—abstract area rugs, contemporary furniture, modern window treatments, a coat of paint in a cool shade of cream that Willow knew would not have been original to a Victorian home—even the elaborately carved desk was clearly a newer custom piece, rather than an antique.

Neither deigned to share their reasoning with us, Joel had said acerbically of Sue and Effie when Willow had asked what the pair had been planning for the house.

Effie, and Sue after her, had shared their home with generations of the family's ghosts. To keep certain things private, they would have needed to carve out a place in the house where the rest of the mansion's inhabitants could not enter. That's why they had needed this room, remodeled and decorated for its twenty-first-century inhabitants.

My lady's chamber, the note had said—not Annabel's but Sue's.

Willow turned to her godmother's desk, stacking its piles of books and papers on the floor and carefully moving the computer monitor onto the bed.

Now she could fully see the ornately carved desk. This was no mere piece of furniture, it was a work of art, and it took her breath away. The curved back of the desk had been carved in the shape of a tree, with songbirds peeking from between its limbs; its long vine-like branches twisted and curled sinuously around drawers and shelves all the way down to the elegantly curved legs. Several drawers sat half-open, as though someone had searched them recently. Willow examined the desk, but she found nothing of interest in the papers and books on or around it; whoever had been sneaking into Cameron House was human, not a ghost, and had surely long since removed anything remotely relevant.

But her mysterious typist had sent her here, to this room, today; what was she missing? In the chaos of last night and this morning, Willow had let herself put the question of Sue's and Effie's murders, and Geralt's as well, aside. But now, especially with their only two real suspects dead—themselves also murdered...

Naomi could, in theory, have gradually poisoned Geralt. But could Naomi really have lured Sue up to the widow's walk and pushed her over the edge? Sue had always been strong; surely there would have been a struggle if Hank, Naomi, or frankly anyone had come upon her to push her off the roof, and the police would have investigated it as a potential homicide. And as for Effie—Naomi had told Willow that she and Geralt didn't come to the island full-time till after Effie died. Effie's murder couldn't be attributed to Naomi; but Hank, as a full-time islander, might have been here in March.

But if Hank and Naomi had killed all three Cameron House heirs, then who had killed them? And why?

She closed her eyes, forcing herself to relax, to let her mind shift back into a mental free-association-playback mode, a state that made interesting connections possible and sleeping incredibly difficult . . . Sue and Effie. Hank. Naomi.

Geralt.

Geralt in the hospital. Naomi leaving him there to have a few drinks at the Raven. Hank waiting in the Jacuzzi.

The text from Naomi the day Geralt died: *We thought he was improving, but . . .*

And Diana, that night: *They tried dialysis to filter it out, but they couldn't get ahead of it.*

The investigation into Geralt's poisoning. Poisoning over time, poisoning on the day of his collapse. What if he was still being poisoned *after* he was admitted to the hospital? Was anyone investigating that?

But why? What would Naomi have to gain by it? She was his wife and would inherit everything—which, according to the morning's papers, was mostly a pile of debt, anyway.

Willow's mind kept playing through the past few days, the conversations, the possibilities . . . *paternity suits . . . "Geralt Talbot impregnated me with an alien baby" . . .*

Had they started in exactly the right place that first evening? And then gotten distracted?

Off the grid . . . can't find a record of any baby, alien or otherwise . . . No record didn't necessarily mean no baby. And if Marisa Talbot could go back to the Midwest with no one in Maine the wiser, this poor woman—Marianne Forrest, that was her name—could have too. Changed her identity, had her baby, no one knowing her story. Keeping the child away from Geralt Talbot and Maine altogether, until . . . *she died about twenty years later. Suicide . . .*

And perhaps Marianne *had* given birth to a child, a daughter, who had every reason to hate the man who had sired her. Who, after losing her mother, might also have changed her name and built a whole new identity. Who had, perhaps, found her way back to her birth father, become friends with his wife, staying in their houses, traveling with them. Taking care of odd jobs—like, for example, procuring Geralt's lemon nutrient water. Staying with Naomi in the hospital, and then sitting with him, unattended, so Naomi could slip out for some time of her own.

Willow knew just enough French to know that "from the forest" could translate as *du bois*.

Audra.

"My God," she murmured.

She had to tell Nick. She had to tell all of them. Most importantly, she had to get out of this house right now.

The movement behind her was quick and nearly silent, and Willow was too slow. Before she could turn, a hand grasped her ponytail and yanked her head back; a needle thrust sharply into her neck right by the hairline and someone swept her feet out from under her.

Willow crumpled to the floor. She struggled against the wave of heaviness creeping over her, but soon her body went limp, and her vision blurred into nothingness.

"Go to sleep, Willow," she heard Audra's mocking voice say as though receding into the distance.

"You and I need to have a talk. But for now, you have a nice little rest."

Then everything was darkness.

CHAPTER THIRTY-NINE

It was the throbbing in her head that told Willow she was still alive, a deep ache blooming from her left temple as her consciousness swam to the surface. For a few minutes, she lay still, testing fingers and toes to see if they would move; that was when the pain began stretching its tendrils down to her lower back.

She was lying on her side, hands and feet bound by something thin and tight. Everything hurt—head, back, wrists, and ankles too. She felt woozy and slow, but she wasn't sure if it was from the bump to her head or the needle jab in her neck. She forced crusty eyelids to open, trying to focus on her surroundings. There was not much to see; the wall of gray stone inches from her eyes blocked her vision. Listening hard in the silence, she heard a woman's voice, muffled and indistinct, from what sounded like a room or two away.

Trying not to groan aloud, she forced herself to roll over.

She was in the front room of Cameron House; someone had dragged her to the fireplace and left her there. Through the archway, she could see the foyer and the open library doors. She cursed inwardly; she'd forgotten to relock the library after leaving through the hidden second-floor exit.

Willow wriggled herself into a seated position, wincing every time she moved her head; now she could see the heavy-duty plastic zip ties around her ankles, and she guessed her wrists were similarly bound.

She was weak and exhausted. *Sleep*, she thought. *Maybe I'll go back to sleep, and this will all go away.*

"You mustn't, you know," Peter Talbot said, seated cross-legged on the floor beside her, his gray fedora on the couch next to the brightly embroidered pillow. "You need to get free. You're strong enough. You can do it."

Willow gave her head a little shake, forcing herself to focus. At first, he seemed a little hazy, as though he had wrapped himself in sea mist and carried it into the house with him, but then he stabilized and was fully there, gray pin-striped suit as neat as ever. Handsome as any film star, with the saddest eyes she had ever seen. Sue's father.

She opened her mouth to ask a practical question—something helpful, like how much time there was, or what Audra was planning, but instead, she heard herself asking softly, "What happened? That night, when you—the night of your car accident. What happened?"

She didn't see him move, but now he stood next to Effie's chair, looking out the window at the sea. "That night." He faltered, as though not wanting to push the words out, but continued. "Marisa had told me that afternoon that we were going to have a baby. She hadn't been to the doctor yet, but she knew; all the signs were there. She told Geralt as well; he was like a brother to her, the big brother she never had."

He looked back to Willow. "We went out. To celebrate. My brother and me. We had too much to drink. Geralt was in better shape than I was, so he took the wheel. I remember a bright light and a crashing sound, and I don't . . . I don't remember much after that. I remember Marisa's tears; I remember trying to stop her when she frantically packed her things and left the island."

He shrugged, almost apologetically. “She couldn’t see me, you understand.”

Willow felt her heart breaking along with his. All this time, he was waiting for his Marisa to come back—his bride from Away. She couldn’t see him. And she never returned.

“Geralt could see me,” Peter continued, “and hear me, but he was convinced I was his guilty conscience tormenting him. In the end, I suppose I drove him away as well. He left the island for years, never coming home to this house. I think he still blames himself for what happened.” He shook his head sadly. “I wish I could convince him otherwise.”

You might have the chance sooner than you know, Willow thought.

Peter said, gently but urgently, “Willow, there’s not much time. You have to get out of this. Don’t let her beat you.”

“But . . . she’s his daughter, isn’t she? Your niece? Doesn’t she have as much right—”

“Willow, listen,” he interrupted; he was seated beside her again, his face close to hers. “Understand. Joel explained to you, didn’t he, how the house needs a living Cameron heir to sustain the ongoing life of the family?”

She nodded.

“Here’s what Joel didn’t say,” he continued. “In fact, I’m not sure he even knows himself; it’s not only about genetics and lineage. It’s more than blood. It has to do with responsibility and understanding and acceptance.” He looked at her sadly. “Susan didn’t know, you see,” he said sadly. “Who she was, that she belonged here.”

“Effie never told her?” Willow asked.

Peter glanced to the front of the room, to the rocking chair by the bay window. From it, a woman’s voice, quavery with age and self-recrimination, quietly spoke a single syllable: “No.”

Willow turned her head in surprise. There was Effie Cameron at last, sitting in her chair, rocking gently; the embroidered pillow was somehow back on the floor beside her. “I meant to tell her; I wanted her to know everything, but there wasn't time. I ran out of time," the old woman said forlornly.

Willow looked at the dented pillow and understood at last. *No,* Willow thought fiercely, *someone took away your time.*

Peter said, "Susan didn't know she was my child, my blood, so she never saw herself as anything more than a placeholder, someone whose job it was to look for the next, 'real' Cameron heir. She never—" His voice choked a little; he cleared his throat and went on. "She never let herself truly believe she belonged anywhere. We all hoped getting married would help her settle in and find her place, but . . ." Peter sighed again. He looked back at Willow, his gaze reaching deep inside her. "I wanted to be a proper father to her, but I wasn't there. Just as—"

He broke off as, from the library, the sound of pacing feet and books being hurled to the floor grew closer. "There's no more time," Effie said sharply. She pulled herself to her feet and faced Willow. "We can't help you much, not yet. But remember: You're stronger than she is. You have to fight."

Willow's face clouded. "But I don't know where—"

"Don't you, though?" Effie interrupted. "I imagine you do; you just don't realize it yet. But first, you have to stay alive."

Peter nodded. Taking Willow's shoulders in his strong hands, he said intently, "Aunt Effie is right. Fight for what's yours. Claim it. Claim it, and no one can ever take it away."

A sad smile, a quick nod, and he was gone.

Effie opened her mouth to speak but stopped when she saw the embroidered pillow on the floor, with its face-shaped depression in one side. She shook her head and picked it up, placing it almost absentmindedly back on the sofa where Willow had placed it only days ago.

She doesn't remember, Willow realized. *She doesn't remember how she died.*

Then Effie was gone as well. In the same instant, the pillow was back in its spot on the floor beside the rocking chair.

Effie might not remember, Willow realized, but the house did. She wasn't sure whether that was comforting or not.

But Effie and Peter had been right—the time for thought was past; she needed to act. Willow's eyes darted around the room frantically, looking for anything she could use to break the zip ties; heavy-duty as they were, they were still plastic. "Too bad they couldn't have sent me a ghost whose talisman is a Swiss Army knife," she muttered under her breath.

Her eye caught on the granite hearthstone, its sharp corner showing rough fragments of quartz and feldspar. Not a knife, but it had potential. She shifted as quietly as she could, rubbing the plastic tie back and forth across the stone like a saw, scraping her hands several times in the process. After what seemed like forever, Willow felt the edge of the plastic begin to shred; she continued until it broke, and her hands were freed. She managed the same maneuver on her ankle ties, praying Audra was busy enough wherever she was to leave her a few more minutes.

Willow pulled herself woozily to her feet, bracing herself on the couch as the room spun around her; whatever drug Audra had injected her with—probably the same one she had used to subdue Sue—was still in her system. She managed to make her silent way around to the foyer archway; she looked rapidly into the hall and up the steps, but there was no one there. She tiptoed her way across the foyer to the library door itself. She didn't dare peek around the doorjamb, but she at least could hear better now.

Audra was at the other end of the library, far enough away that Willow could only catch a few words at a time: "What she's doing here? I have no idea, but . . ." followed by several seconds of obscurity. The pattern continued: "—in the library now, but earlier . . . the desk. Yeah, Sue's, and she left it a mess . . . looking for the same thing we . . . I don't know, love, the body count is starting to concern me . . . wait, you think?" The footsteps were coming back in her direction, closer to the door. "On her? How? She's only been here four days."

Who was Audra talking to?

Audra was moving away again, her remaining words even more muffled. "—think she knows . . . Hank . . . revenge for . . . maybe . . ." Then a low laugh, warm and seductive, completely at odds with the mild-mannered persona that was all Willow had ever seen.

But whoever Audra's partner was, he wasn't here. Yet. This might be Willow's only chance to escape. Audra had moved away from the doorway, and Willow took the opportunity to swiftly make her way down the hall, into the kitchen, and out the back door. The wind gusted violently around her; she held up her hand against the nearly horizontal swirls of rain pelting the porch and threatening to blind her, and hurried down the back steps.

Where she ran headlong into a shadowy figure in a hooded raincoat, going the other way.

CHAPTER FORTY

Willow stood in the rain, wind whipping around her, and gaped in shock at Mrs. Patricia MacFarlane Ramsey.

Patricia looked shocked too at first, then irritated, and at last confused, to see Willow standing by the back porch of a house where neither of them belonged, in the middle of the night. "Willow Stone?" Patricia asked. "What are you doing here?"

Willow was all but gasping, the adrenaline surging through her as her abortive run for safety ran into this unexpected obstacle. "Mrs. Ramsey, you have to get out of here. It isn't safe." She threw one desperate look back to the house. "Come with me, please, hurry—it's been Audra DuBois all along; *she* killed Geralt, and Hank and Naomi too, and I'm guessing she's the one who cut your brake lines. Please, we have to get out of here!"

But Patricia held the hood of her raincoat over her head as the wind tore at them both, looking even more confused. "Hank? Audra?"

Willow stepped closer to her, having little option since Patricia was still standing in her way. "Mrs. Ramsey, we have to go—and I hate to ask, but may I borrow your phone? I need to call—"

Patricia's face cleared; she shook her head, not an iota of doubt on her face. "I'm sorry, I never loan anyone my phone under any circumstances. And besides, this is completely illogical; you sound unhinged. Please, Miss Stone, I'm sure you're very much mistaken." She grasped Willow by the arm. "Let's get inside and out of this weather, and we can talk about it."

"But—you don't understand! There's so much more going on than you realize," Willow pleaded.

Now the other woman smiled—and Willow's blood ran cold. The smile was . . . wrong. Lightning flashed again as Willow glanced down at the hand that had come out of Patricia's raincoat pocket and the small handgun the woman had pressed against Willow's midsection.

"No, Willow my dear, you are the one who doesn't understand. And I find that to be a great comfort. You have been a little too diligent in your research—but if *you* were this far off base, I think I can trust that the rest of the town is unlikely to do better." She gestured to Willow with her free hand. "Now. Back inside, please. I have been waiting a long time, and I don't want to catch my death of cold when we are this close. Inside."

Willow went.

The little gun, Willow noticed, was lavender. Of course it was lavender.

"You. That way." Patricia slammed the door shut and gestured with the gun for Willow to move out into the hallway to the grand foyer.

Audra's voice called out, "Patty? Patty, is that you?" It grew closer as it continued, "I've been through drawer after drawer and shelf after shelf in that stupid library *and* the Davis woman's desk, and I still haven't found—"

Audra DuBois stopped abruptly in the kitchen doorway, and her eyes went wide to see Willow there, held at gunpoint by Patricia Ramsey.

Patricia favored the younger woman with a cutting glare. "You had one job. *One.* Make sure the unfortunate little busybody tied up in the sitting room stays tied up in the sitting room. How could you possibly have screwed it up so thoroughly?" She turned to Willow. "All right—move. The library. Now. We need to have a conversation, about what your aunt told you before you got here, and what Talbot told you once you arrived."

Willow's voice was distant as she said, "Sue wasn't my aunt." She walked slowly in the direction Patricia had nudged her, down the hall to the grand foyer, past the wall sconces whose golden light shone warm against the fury of the storm outside. *This is not good*, she thought. *I should have stayed at the inn, listened to Nick—or at least told someone where I was going. No one will even think to look for me till morning, and by then, it will be too late.*

A voice whispered gently in Willow's mind—Peter Talbot's voice, repeating his words from earlier: *Stay strong. Fight.* And quiet Dellie, with her bonnet and knitting needles: *You don't know what you're made of yet, but you will. They all will.*

In that moment, Willow's awareness clicked into high gear, shifting into the mental space she needed when performing a particularly thorny fugue or navigating a new organ's registration on the fly. This was neither fight nor flight; it was clarity, as though a new compartment of her brain had opened, ready for use—not, this time, for following the threads of music but rather for finding a way to stay alive.

Had she not been in this state of hyperalertness, she might not have noticed the umbrella stand to the left of the front door, empty earlier, which now held a familiar wooden cane with a glass-topped handle. Unbroken and whole.

Interesting, she thought.

Once inside the library, Patricia gestured Willow to a chair. "You. Sit. And talk. Who is it?"

Willow stared back at her, puzzled. "Who is what?"

Patricia's lip was starting to twitch in frustration. "Tell me about Annabel Cameron's grandson," she demanded. "What did Susan tell you?"

"Aunt Sue didn't get to tell me anything," Willow said evenly. "She died before I got here. Someone pushed her off the roof walk." She glanced sideways at Audra before continuing, "I'm guessing she was injected with something, like I was, some drug that made it possible to get her up there without a struggle—probably the same person who slipped a steady stream of lithium carbonate into Geralt Talbot over weeks or months, slapped him with one big dose at the memorial, and then found a way to give him even more under the noses of the hospital staff."

Audra smiled. "Patient care isn't what it used to be," she said smugly. "Neither is law enforcement. They were so busy investigating how he was poisoned before he got there that it never occurred to them to suspect he was getting more right there in his hospital room."

"Let alone that you were the one doing it."

Audra looked pleased with herself. "Keeping a low profile was part of my job. I knew they would figure out it wasn't the Montalto woman eventually, but also that once they did, everyone would look to Naomi."

Patricia said dryly, "Too bad she and my late spouse blew up in the car about four days earlier than planned, before Hank could get the house declared in his name. We could have pinned it on them *and* had a solid claim on the house."

Audra shook her head. "Nope, we had to move. I heard Naomi and Geralt talking; Hank was coming to his own conclusions about what happened to Effie, but he thought it had been Geralt. Once the old man was gone, we had to move fast before he figured out the rest. Besides, admit it—you liked seeing her get what was coming to her. She was screwing your husband, after all."

"I didn't care who my husband screwed, as long as I got what was coming to me. This wasn't the plan," Patricia said, her voice tightening into shrillness. "Remember? The plan? Where Hank inherits Cameron House? And then dies and leaves it to me?"

Oh, this is so very bad, Willow thought. *They don't have the slightest intention of letting me live, or they wouldn't be talking like this.*

The sharp, clear compartment of her mind answered, *Then keep them talking.* Willow said to Patricia, only partially feigning puzzlement, "But . . . what about your crash? If you two were behind cutting the brake lines on Hank's car, who cut yours?"

Patricia answered primly, "Every good plan needs research and rehearsal. Causing a car accident by cutting the brake lines may work all the time on TV, but in real life, it's much more difficult. Did you know cars are manufactured now with—"

"—dual brake lines, yes, I'm aware," Willow broke in.

Patricia's lips compressed in irritation. *Bull's-eye,* Willow thought. *Patricia MacFarlane Ramsey doesn't like being interrupted while she's monologuing.*

Patricia continued, "Then you know the only way it could work is in an older car, and even that . . . needed testing."

"So, you tested it first yourself," Willow nodded, realizing. "Audra cut the lines, and you drove the car out of the Raven, knowing a successful dry run would send you hurtling down that awful hill without brakes." She remembered something else. "That's why you were on the phone; that's why you were crying. You were talking to Audra, and she had to talk you into doing it."

But Audra was gazing at Patricia, almost tenderly. "No, actually. I was trying to talk her out of it," Audra said, "trying to persuade her to find a safer way. It was still risky, even going as slow as she could manage and knowing where to safely steer the car." She walked over to the older woman and gently touched her cheek. "I was so afraid for you, afraid it would happen like last time—or worse, that you wouldn't make it through."

Patricia's expression softened; the hand holding the gun did not waver, but with the other she reached up and ran a tender hand over Audra's hair. "Last time, *you* got me through," she said softly. The pair leaned forward until their foreheads touched and their lips brushed together in a kiss.

Audra glanced at Willow and laughed. "Oh, sweetie, you look so confused, it's precious," she said. "The short version is that Patty had an accident in one of her husband's stupid cars twelve years ago when she drove away from him in a rage. She hurt her back."

"He gave me a watch," Patricia said, her teeth clenched. "He asked me to forgive him and gave me a gold watch."

Audra nodded. "I know, darling. He was the worst." She turned back to Willow. "That's when we met; she ran into some trouble getting the pain meds she needed, and I . . . helped her. Got her what she needed."

"Got her what she needed?" Willow asked, still bewildered. "What were you, a drug dealer?"

"A pharmacy technician," Audra said. "Okay, *and* drug dealer. They go together surprisingly well." She turned back to Patricia and kissed her again.

And there it was. The missing piece. Audra had been preparing for this for her entire life; God knew what kind of pharmacopeia she had managed to slide out of her employers' inventories over the years.

Willow felt like a fool. They had been so focused on Hank and Naomi that it had never occurred to them that the people closest to each might have as much access and motivation to claim the Cameron fortune, nor that they would have an alliance of more than convenience. It had been Patricia and Audra all along.

Audra murmured into Patricia's hair, "And now you're free. We're both free. Geralt is gone. Hank is gone. We don't need them. It's just us now."

Patricia's lips pursed again, and she pulled away. "Yes, just us. But Cameron House—"

"Hank's claim is bull, you know," Willow interrupted, keeping her voice even and conversational. *Keep them distracted. Keep them off-balance. Piss her off a little, but try not to get shot.*

Patricia snapped back, "Prove it. I'm a genealogist; I traced the family back—"

"No, you read a novel," Willow said, allowing scorn into her voice for the first time. "*Widow's Walk*, a novel about a field nurse who married a soldier and had his baby after he died. And you bought up every single copy of this obscure book you could find, relying on favorable odds that no one would ever make the connection. And fed the whole romantic tale to the world as Hank's backstory."

Willow paused, realization dawning. "That's why we're here. *You* think the story might be true, and you need to know whether another Cameron heir is going to come out of the woodwork." Willow knew by the twitch of Patricia's jaw that she had been right.

Willow turned to Audra. "But here's what I don't understand . . . why all the business with Hank and getting him into the succession? When all you need is—" She caught the quick expression of puzzlement on Patricia's face, the narrowing of Audra's eyes.

"Oh," Willow said softly to Audra. "You haven't told her, have you?"

"Told me what?" Patricia said, an edge of anxiety in her voice.

Willow waited.

Audra's measuring gaze rested on Willow for a moment; she took a step back and smiled at Patricia. "All right then. This house should have gone to Geralt Talbot, and after his death, to his descendants. Regardless of how they got here. And that's me. Geralt Talbot was my father."

CHAPTER FORTY-ONE

Patricia stared at Audra, stunned.

Audra stared back, her cool exterior beginning to crack open, revealing something dark and frightening and full of a lifetime of deeply suppressed rage. "It's true," she said. "She may have lost the paternity suit, but my mother kept all the files, the paperwork, everything."

"But our plan," Patricia said in disbelief. "Everything we've been working for—the inheritance, the house . . ."

"Poor Patricia," Audra said to her lover in a low, dangerous voice. "You assumed *you* would be mistress of the manor, the village matriarch, everyone kowtowing to you the way they have for years. They might even pretend to accept your little lesbian girlfriend, at least in your presence; behind your back, they'd still exclude her the way they do anyone not in their generations-old circle." She shook her head. "No. No way, Patty. That's not why I'm here. I'm through being invisible, done being on the outside. I'm here for what's mine."

The mask was off, Willow realized. This was Audra, the real Audra—not the unobtrusive assistant who had served quietly on the sidelines, ignored in years of fatal miscalculation. She could see the horror begin to bloom on Patricia's face as understanding grew.

But Willow managed to keep her voice even, conversational, almost admiring. "How did you find your way to England? Is that where you picked up the accent? And how did you manage to become his fourth wife's assistant?"

Audra was still smiling, clearly enjoying this. She said, the accent dropping off like a discarded scarf, "Oh, the Brit thing was totally fake; that was backstory. I'm good at accents. After my mom died, I disappeared for a little while, changed my name . . . Once Patty and I worked out our plan, I shadowed old Talbot like a hawk; when he got his hip replaced, I found out where he was getting his physical therapy. Naomi was his therapist."

Audra walked as she spoke, looking acquisitively at the photos and art lining the library walls, as though wondering what they might be worth. "It was easy to become friends with her—at first, I just meant to use her to get information about him, but then she started dating him. When he proposed, she knew she was in over her head, the first kid in her trashy Jersey family to make it through college marrying this rich upper-crust guy. So I helped her plan the wedding, and then she hired me as her assistant." She straightened out a photo on one of the shelves, an image of the Misses Drummond at a younger age.

Patricia's aristocratic face was beginning to crumble as she began to understand she was not in charge of things; she had never been. This had been Audra's game from the start. Patricia was another of her pawns, maneuvered into place to get Audra what she wanted. Willow almost felt sorry for her.

Almost. Because something else had clicked. The Talbots and their staff hadn't come to Little North this spring until *after* Effie had died; Audra couldn't have been responsible for all the murders.

From where she sat, Willow could see into the sitting room.

She saw Effie's chair, rocking again, one veined and wrinkled hand closing over the armrest. She saw the now-familiar couch pillow in its place on the floor.

Effie stood slowly and bent to pick it up, as she had earlier, but this time she stopped, holding it, staring at the pillow as though she had never seen it before.

Willow damped down a quick surge of hope; Effie was back.

Patricia is the weak link, a voice in Willow's mind whispered. *And you're beginning to understand.* She said to Patricia, "So your job was to clear the way, to out-research Effie and Sue and make sure there were no other Camerons ready to come out of the woodwork. And you bought up all the copies of *Widow's Walk* so no one would recognize the story. But then there was Effie. Maybe she got suspicious; maybe she was taking too long to die on her own. Maybe you got impatient."

Patricia was as still as marble; beyond her, in the front room, Effie's face first reflected puzzlement, then memory, as though rereading a passage of an old story she had forgotten. The old woman's face turned toward Patricia.

Willow saw Effie's expression change, darken, and knew she remembered. How she'd died. And who had done it.

"What happened that day?" Willow asked in the same level voice, feeling anger rising as she witnessed Effie's shock at revisiting the horrific memory of how her long life had ended. "Was it as easy as you thought it would be to press that pillow down on her face, feel her struggling, hold her down till she stopped?"

Patricia's face had grown paler as Willow spoke, and something like regret—remorse, even—began to grow there. Her head jerked back and forth in choppy denial. "No, it wasn't like that. I never meant to—I didn't want anything like that, I only wanted to talk to her, but . . ."

"Wonderful," Willow said with a sarcastic twist of her lip. "That makes all the difference, of course, and I'm sure that's a great comfort to her now." She studied Patricia, noting her jerky movements and the shrill tinge to her voice. This memory was about more than guilt; this was terror. Willow continued, "And I can't help wondering—they say the house is haunted, you know. I imagine it wasn't too happy about what you'd done. What happened next? Did it just . . . let you go?"

Patricia was trembling hard now, practically vibrating in her fear as Effie walked slowly into the library and came to a stop right behind her. This version of Effie was dark, misty, as though incompletely drawn by a slow-working sketch artist, pulling what little light there was in the foyer into itself and setting the wall sconces flickering.

Audra stood several yards away as Willow spoke; she had been watching the front room as well, and her expression had shifted to one of growing trepidation. Willow smiled at Audra—a bitter smile, full of dark anticipation. "Ah. You can see her too, can't you?"

Patricia's voice was rising in panic. "See who? What are you talking about?" Her head whipped back and forth in panic from one to the other. "Tell me, tell me *right now this minute*—what are you looking at?"

In a careful voice, Audra said, "Patty . . . I think you should stay right where you are. Don't move. Don't turn around. Stay there."

"That's probably for the best," Willow said calmly, nodding. She turned her gaze back to Patricia. "I'm told the ghosts of Cameron House often manifest to those with whom they have a particular bond or link. And, Mrs. Ramsey, I would definitely say you fall into that category."

Patricia's lips trembled, as though ready to burst into tears. But she clenched her teeth and said with a firmness she clearly did not feel, "I don't believe in ghosts. It's not real. None of it is real. Besides, she knows I didn't want to hurt her; she knows—" And she defiantly turned to face what was behind her.

A flash of lightning hit so close that all three of them felt the surge of pressure and a tingling in their extremities. One of the sconce bulbs exploded outward as a violent whip of thunder shook the house; the power died, and the foyer was left in near darkness.

Except for Effie Cameron, suddenly large and luminous and terrifying, inches from Patricia's face. This was not the kindly old woman Willow had seen in photos or watched holding her nephew's hand at Sue's memorial. This was Effie as she would have appeared after death, face slack and eyes staring—and worse. In the space of a few seconds, the old woman's face fell into an image of decay and decomposition, a corpse months under the ground.

Patricia screamed. Frozen in place, face-to-face with the horror she had created, she could only scream.

Close to Willow's ear, a familiar voice, Effie's voice, whispered, "*Now! Go find what you need; we'll hold things here as long as we can. Run!*"

Willow understood; she eased backward into the darkness of the library, past the portraits, past the fireplace, found her way to the little wrought iron stairway in the corner, and sprinted up to the second level.

Patricia Ramsey stood face-to-face with the specter of the woman she had killed—a furiously swirling glow, indistinct except for the eyes, Effie's eyes, sharp and bright. Patricia could see her own reflection in them, unable to move or think, frozen in terror. She felt the gun slip out of nerveless fingers and heard it thud to the floor. She realized she was still screaming.

Patricia was dimly aware of Audra standing next to her, murmuring into one ear, "Patty, Patty, please, it's okay—I'm here. Turn away, stop screaming, for the love of God, please stop; it's only a ghost, it can't hurt you . . ."

But it was the voice in her other ear that held her fast, fed her fear and her shame and guilt. *You pretended to be her friend*, it whispered. *You visited her in her old age, brought her meals, gained her trust . . .*

She tried to turn her head toward it but found herself still paralyzed, her eyes focused on the shadow of Effie's decaying body before her.

Another voice, from a little behind: *President of the Ladies' Club. Head of the church board of directors. Prominent citizen. You pretended to love this island, its people. But it was a lie, all of it a lie.*

She was still screaming; she tried to scream louder, but the voices cut right through, every word clear as a bell, slicing into her mind, shredding her hold on sanity. *The islanders will know. They will know what you are. They will know what you did . . .*

Finally, Effie's voice, slack and slurred, coming from the half-destroyed mouth in front of her, exhaling the dust of the graveyard onto Patricia: *You killed me. You held me while I struggled, till I stopped breathing. You did it with your own hands. Murderer. Murderer.*

The other voices took up the chant, the same chant she had heard the day she had taken up the pillow and held it down over the ancient and peaceful face. *Murderer. Murderer. Murderer.* She could almost see the misty figures around her, feel them pushing her, crowding her in, taking her oxygen, taking her breath. *Murderer. Murderer.* Some part of her welcomed the pressing sense of suffocation, as though she knew she would never stop screaming as long as there was air in her lungs . . .

"Patty!" Audra grabbed Patricia's arm and jerked the terrified woman around to face her.

Patricia's scream cut off, subsiding into harsh whimpers, and she stood facing Audra.

The Effie ghost was gone. But Patricia was still gasping, sobbing, her body shaking hard enough to hurt her teeth.

Audra tried to calm Patricia, to take her in her arms, but with the first touch of the young woman's hand to her face, Patricia

make it a little gentler for you." She raised the gun and aimed for Patricia's heart; one more shot, just to be sure.

Before she could fire, the heavy door slammed shut, seemingly of its own accord.

Audra told herself it had been the wind.

She knew it hadn't been.

CHAPTER FORTY-TWO

Willow had made it to the top of the spiral staircase and to the hidden door in the corner of the library by the time Patricia stopped screaming; she was out into the hallway before the first gunshot sounded.

She could not escape through the front door; Audra and Patricia were there, and she would be seen before she set foot on the staircase. Had one of them shot the other? Was she dealing with one or two killers now? There was no safe way to know. And besides, she wasn't here to escape; she needed to find what Sue knew. *Get you to my lady's chamber*, the note had said, and she still hadn't found what it wanted her to learn. *The servant passageways*, Willow realized. *There will be a set of stairs somewhere else, if I can find them.*

As quickly and quietly as she could, she made her way down the hall to the ballroom. Surely there would be a way down to the kitchen from there.

She heard the slam of the door. And moved faster.

* * *

The bolt had slid back into place, Audra realized, and it was not going to yield this time. "I'll have to find some WD-40 when I move in," she muttered. "This is bloody inconvenient." After struggling for a few moments, she took a breath. Patricia wasn't going anywhere; Audra had seen the blood pooling beneath her, heard the gasping before she lost consciousness, seen the pallor on her face. If she wasn't dead already, she would be soon; even if she survived the next half hour, she wasn't going to be getting up and going anywhere. Audra could finish the job as soon as she took care of the little interloper from Chicago.

She stepped back into the library. "Yoo-hoo, Willow," she called out softly, mockingly, as though she knew she had no reason to rush or panic. "I know you're in here. At least I hope you are, because you'll want to hear what I have to say."

Audra listened intently but heard only silence. Willow couldn't hide forever, Audra thought, but it would be easier to draw her out than to chase her down.

"If you'd asked me yesterday," Audra continued almost conversationally, "I would have said I didn't believe in ghosts, but after tonight—yeah, I'd say Cameron House is most definitely, fully, *abundantly* haunted. And I think you knew that. More, I think you like the spooky little bastards, with their slamming doors and mind games and all." She made a quick move around a bookcase to shine her light into another corner. Nothing there.

"And it makes me wonder . . . when a haunted house burns down, where do the ghosts go?"

She stealthily moved along the floor to the next alcove, shining her light into the little space, shifting the curtains to make sure no one was hiding. Nothing.

"No answer to that one? Unless you'd like to find out the hard way, I suggest you step out and we can have a little conversation."

She whirled back to face the room; she'd find the little coward and—

Audra stopped. There was now a fire in the fireplace, crackling merrily, sending its warm light around the far end of the room. A man sat calmly on the hearthstone, silver-threaded dark hair smoothly combed back, a neat beard and old-fashioned spectacles on his face. He was calmly writing in a ledger.

Audra frowned. "What the—?" she murmured, and hesitantly walked in the direction of the firelight, the lavender pistol pointed at the man by the fire.

He looked up at her, ignoring the firearm. "Miss Audra DuBois, I believe?" he said politely.

She did not answer. The man set his book and spectacles down on the hearth and stood. "My name is Joel Drummond; I manage the affairs of the Cameron family." He smiled politely. "I represent the North Islands Historical Society."

Patricia's first awareness as she drifted back to consciousness was cold, a cold that had nothing to do with the predawn chill or the storm that had preceded it. Cold all over, except for the hot ball of pain somewhere in her midsection. And wet—from the blowing rain above and the growing sticky puddle beneath her. Every time she tried to inhale, a sharp, stabbing pain in her chest cut her short.

Unconsciousness was better. But a voice had called her name, she thought. Was someone here with her?

She managed to turn her head, just a little, but the small movement brought on a cresting wave of dizziness and more pain.

She was alone on the porch.

Everything went dark again. And she welcomed it. The dark didn't hurt so much.

Willow had guessed right; she quickly found the subtly placed staircase on the other side of the ballroom and let herself down to the kitchen, and from there to Sue's room.

The electricity was still out, but some helpful soul had lit a gas lamp and set it on the little table just inside Sue's room, someone who could open and close doors but who perhaps couldn't enter the room themselves.

Willow stepped inside, then shut the door and shoved pillows across the crack at the bottom of the door to block the light, hoping Audra would not find her here. She studied Sue's elaborate desk, realizing Effie had been right; she *did* know where to look. She just hadn't looked hard enough. Like Cameron House itself, with its concealed doors and covert passages, this desk all but announced a proclivity for false drawer bottoms and secret compartments. Audra, too, had been through this desk already, but had she thought to look beyond the obvious?

Willow started her search, methodically moving from drawer to cubby, feeling for sliders or levers or false bottoms. She found several, but all were empty.

As she searched, Willow could feel the house gathering itself; she could feel the now-familiar sense of breathing in the walls, of eyes on her . . . The house was awake.

She didn't know how much time she had, but it wouldn't be enough. In frustration, she sat back, glaring at the desk.

The tree in the center of the carving caught her eye, casting its long and loose branches flowing around every part of the desk, little birds nestled here and there in its branches. She started in surprise as she recognized the pattern. *It's like the pillow*, she realized with a jolt. *Or pretty close to it.* Willow realized something else as well: The loose, draping curves of the branches belonged to one particular kind of tree, and one she knew well. "It's a willow tree," she breathed. She bent closer to the carving of the tree, looking between the branches . . . and then she saw it. Of all the birds carved on the desk, only one was singing. Only then did she remember the single brown bird that had been embroidered into Effie's pillow.

A robin.

Willow reached forward and pressed on the little carved bird, smiling as she heard the quiet *snick* of a panel opening.

The little drawer the robin had revealed held a small stack of photos and an envelope—Sue's most hidden treasures, the story she had kept secret: a story of a robin, a story held in safety until a willow could come and discover it.

Willow carefully retrieved the contents of the drawer, moving quickly, looking at each photo one at a time before setting it down on the desk in front of her in a single long row. A young Sue playing patty-cake with a toddler in dark pigtails. Sue and the girl standing by the ocean, throwing rocks into the water. A few more as the girl aged, first with a bowl haircut, then one in valiant imitation of Farrah Fawcett's elaborate feathered style. In each photo, the pair posed in a different distinctive location: one by the Golden Gate Bridge, another by the Grand Canyon.

By the photo with the Eiffel Tower in the background, the girl had hit her teen years, and with a thud to the pit of her stomach, Willow realized she was indeed looking at the sullen teenager from the Boston photograph with Effie, whom she had assumed to be a random bystander. It hadn't been a bystander at all—it had been Robin, Sue's lost daughter. Had Effie known who she was? The photos continued as Robin grew and Sue got older, threads of gray emerging in her hair, a chronicle of the many places mother and daughter had visited—the Trevi Fountain in Rome, a picturesque village with the pair framed against what looked like the Alps, the deck of a ship too rustic to be a luxury cruise, and, to Willow's awe and amazement, the Taj Mahal. There was never anyone else with the two of them—only mother and daughter, traveling the globe together.

Willow came to the last three pictures. And stopped.

And finally understood.

The envelope in the little compartment held two documents; Willow took them out and read them, knowing before she did what they would say. She carefully replaced the photos and the birth certificates in the hidden drawer and slid it shut again.

Willow stood unsteadily, feeling as though her world, her whole existence, was part of some cosmic kaleidoscope, and someone had given it a big turn and changed everything; the same pieces were there, but the picture was completely new.

She knew what she had to do.

She did not, however, know if she could manage it successfully without being killed.

CHAPTER FORTY-THREE

Joel Drummond, in his old-fashioned dark suit and neat silver-threaded beard, faced Audra calmly. Audra felt like she had stepped from the last scene of a horror movie into an episode of *Downton Abbey*. How on earth had he gotten here? Where had he come from? Her head felt a little strange. Had she passed out? Was she dreaming?

Joel Drummond waited a moment as though to give her the opportunity to speak, then continued, "It has come to our attention that you believe yourself to be part of the Cameron family line by blood, and you intend to claim this house and its legacy as your own. Is that correct?"

Audra blinked. Was he for real? "Yes. Yes, I am, and I do. Geralt Talbot was my father, and since his little trophy wife is dead, everything he has will come to me. I'll contest any part of the will that tries to shut me out, I'll do DNA tests, whatever it takes."

Joel nodded. "I see. I'm afraid that will not be necessary, however."

Audra blinked and brought the gun up again. "Who are you, anyway? How did you get in here?"

The man did not react to the firearm but remained utterly calm. "I told you. I'm Joel Drummond; I provide legal and financial representation for the Cameron family, and I head the North Islands Historical Society," he said. "Miss DuBois, upon conferring with other interested parties, we have concluded you are not a suitable heir for the Cameron home and estate. Your lack of regard for its historical importance, not to mention your clear disregard for human life"—he pointedly looked past her to the heavy front door, and the porch where Patricia had fallen in a puddle of blood—"make you ill-suited to represent us in the future." He drew up his thin shoulders and faced her squarely. "Even if that means our futures end here."

Audra's face had grown dark as he spoke. "Who the *hell* do you think you are, telling me what I'm suitable for or not? And as for disregard for human life, you supercilious bastard—" She pointed the gun at him and fired three shots, point-blank, into his face.

Even as she did so, she remembered how Patricia always chided her poor impulse control. *Sorry, Patty*, she mentally apologized. *He pissed me off.*

The bullet ricocheted off the stones of the fireplace behind him, and she ducked; when she stood, he was still there. And he had company.

"Oh, dearie," the ancient black-clad woman suddenly present on the couch beside the fireplace said. "That won't work on him. Though it's incredibly rude of you to have tried."

"Incredibly rude, indeed," the second woman said, shaking her bonneted head.

"What the—?" Audra fired once more at Joel, and then at the two old women, shot after shot, until the hammer clicked on an empty chamber. *Stupid little lady gun with its tiny magazine.* She hurled it across the room and turned back to them.

She smiled again, a thick, ugly smile full of a lifetime of hate. "Now I get it," she said. "You're not half as scary as the last ghost;

you should maybe take lessons from Effie. So you'd rather I burn down your home than let me have what I'm entitled to by birth?"

From the library doorway, Willow spoke. "You're not entitled to anything here, Audra." She crossed the room and stepped into the firelight to stand next to the thin man. "Hi, Joel," she said quietly, a little smile on her face.

"Miss Stone," he answered, his face placid.

Willow turned back to Audra. "I want to be clear about one thing. I could have run, I could be halfway back to Rina's by now, but I'm not. Not because I'm afraid of you but because I found something Sue needed me to find. And because someone needs to set you straight on what's going on here." Willow stared straight into Audra's face and said, "This is not, and will never be, your house."

Now Audra smiled. "Oh yes, I believe it will. The property, anyway. I don't care what your crazy old dead people friends think about it; it's not up to them, and you'll be joining them shortly, anyway. The house itself will tragically be lost in a fire, but I can build on the remains. Or sell. I haven't decided." She looked around the shadowed library. "The more time I spend in here, the creepier it gets."

She sneered at Willow. "Besides, I don't know who you think would get it if I don't. You think Rina Montalto is going to have her way now that everyone else is gone, give it to the Park Service or something? Not gonna happen. It's mine. Susan Davis wasn't a Cameron to begin with, and you weren't even related to her, as you keep saying."

"But Sue *was* a Cameron," Willow said simply.

Joel's eyebrows shot up; Dellie's and Dot's faces wore matching expressions of astonished delight.

Willow continued, "Sue was Peter Talbot's daughter by his wife, Marisa, who walked away from the family and the island after he died. But Sue came back and made her home here on Little North, where she was Effie's best friend and caregiver for years.

Effie intended to tell Sue about her Cameron identity—but then Patricia killed Effie, so Sue had no idea of her blood connection to the family."

Audra looked surprised. "Wow. Who knew?"

"I didn't," Dot murmured to Dellie, shaking her head.

"I hoped," Dellie said. "But no, we didn't know."

Willow glanced sideways at Joel. "I . . . wondered," he said. "But I was not sure until now."

Willow took a step closer to Audra. "Your problem is you neglected to do any actual research; all you cared about was what you convinced yourself you're entitled to. But Cameron House needs more than Cameron blood, and it definitely needs more than you. You never bothered to learn anything about Sue Davis, did you? For example, that once long ago she was married? That she had her own child?" Willow saw Audra's eyes widen. "Or that her child died young? And if you didn't know that . . ."

Willow saw in her mind the images in those last three photographs from the hidden drawer in Sue's elaborately carved desk: The first, Sue standing next to a young and very pregnant Robin, outside an ancient brick hospital; the second, Sue and Robin in the hospital, holding a newborn. Robin looked tired, but she was smiling; it was the only smile Willow had seen on the young woman's face in any of the photographs.

Willow continued, working hard to keep her voice from shaking. "If you didn't know that, you wouldn't know Sue's daughter had a baby too."

Robin was not in the third picture, taken somewhere else far away from Little North, perhaps Michigan. This one showed Sue, a Sue who looked like all the joy had been sucked out of her world, standing next to a man and woman, who were holding the baby.

The man and woman were Willow's own parents.

The final two documents in the drawer were copies of two birth certificates—both for the same child, one before and one after adoption—and they merely confirmed what she had already guessed. In the first, the baby, the daughter of Robin Davis, no father listed, was named Willow Cameron Davis. After adoption, she had legally become Willow Stone—with no idea of her parentage, never asking herself who the kind professor she stayed with every summer really was, or how she had come to know Willow's parents in the first place. Because the kind professor was not only her godmother but her grandmother.

Joel's face was a study in shocked surprise; the sisters by now were grinning at each other. Audra rolled her eyes. "What? Please, now you're just fantasizing to stay alive."

"I don't need to make it up." Willow gathered herself and took a slow step forward. "Sue Davis was my maternal grandmother by blood, which makes Peter Talbot my great-grandfather."

The house was ready; she could feel it, feel the inhabitants gathering around her, a few more with every breath, filling the library. Audra took an unconscious step back, from Willow and from the gathering energy surrounding the young woman like a vortex.

In a soft voice, Willow said, "This is my home."

And then, with more steel, "Get out of my house."

CHAPTER FORTY-FOUR

The voice—voices? She couldn't tell—called Patricia's name again, dragging her reluctantly back into a woozy consciousness. The storm was letting up, she realized; the air felt lighter, softer, gentle on her tormented and pain-racked body. From the corner of her eye, Patricia could see her right arm, her hand, covered in her own blood. Her brain told her fingers to wiggle; her eyes told her they did, though with a strange sense of dislocation, as though they weren't really hers at all. Her brain sent another message; the fingers moved once more, this time closing into a fist and reopening.

Her mind moved sluggishly. Her fingers were obeying her brain; she was not paralyzed. She was not dead, which meant the bullet had probably not hit a major artery, or she would already be gone. But there was still blood, a lot of it, everywhere, soaking into her clothes and pooling around her. And pain—lots and lots of pain. Audra's bullet might not have immediately killed Patricia as she intended, but it would probably do its job, anyway; Patricia had no illusions about that. And even if it didn't, the once-alluring woman she should never have trusted would doubtless be back shortly to finish the job.

She could tell herself as many times as she wanted that Audra had been the one to persuade her that Effie had to be eliminated, had opened her mind to the possibility of murder, something she would never have contemplated in her wildest ambitions—but Patricia had gone along with it; she couldn't escape that truth, not here, not now. Then Audra had killed Susan and Geralt, and then Hank and Naomi, secure in the belief that her accomplice would stay in line, would never oppose her, since Patricia had killed too. When Patricia finally did attempt to resist, Audra had not hesitated to take her out of the equation. *But I am still a murderer*, Patricia's mind said to her quietly, the same dispassionate voice that told her fingers to move. No emotion, no excuses, simply a statement of fact. *I murdered Effie Cameron. Not Audra. I did. I set all this into motion. Maybe this is justice. My death, here, at sunrise. Beside the ocean, my ocean. On my island.*

But now Audra was going to kill Willow.

No, Patricia thought with a hint of her old fierceness. *No.*

She could barely move. But her eyes watched her hand twitching, saw it feebly drag itself along the blood-soaked boards of the porch until it reached her side. The elbow did not want to bend at first—the hand at the end of the limb was too heavy—but with another breath, another burst of pain, it obeyed her and successfully positioned the hand at the opening to her skirt pocket. The hand found the phone inside and clumsily slipped it out.

Another wave of pain swept over her, a paroxysm of coughing seized her; the blackness crept back, threatening to swamp her again . . .

No.

Audra's laugh was a cocktail of steel and malice. "Are you serious? '*Get out of my house*,'" she mocked. "Do you honestly believe

I'll let a melodramatic story and a few jump scares stop me now?" At that moment, another bolt of lightning lit up the room.

For a split second, the warm firelight was overtaken by that cold blue flash. The cheery old women were replaced by skeletal figures whose gray skin stretched over their skulls, the black dresses torn and shifting as though uncounted tiny grave creatures swarmed beneath them. Joel, too, in that instant, was an emaciated corpse, decades longer in the grave than Effie, his long fingers little more than bones as they delicately balanced the antique pen that, Audra noticed, had a sharp metal tip.

Then the rush of thunder; it rattled Audra, which made her furious—but when it receded, she was back in the calm firelit room with the impeccably neat trio, all three staring unblinking at her.

Except now it was a quartet. Effie now sat in the tall wingback chair opposite the elderly twins, also staring at Audra.

And . . . there was another man leaning against the fireplace, in a gray pin-striped suit and hat, dressed like a character from an old Cary Grant movie; he was staring at her as well.

In fact, Audra realized, there were eyes all over the room, aimed at her with unsettling intensity. The dark library, growing ever lighter as the storm dissipated and the day began, had filled with people. They were of all ages, from child to elderly adult; some wore more modern dress; others looked like extras from a Gilded Age streaming series. All staring at her. And they were not happy.

Joel spoke, his voice gentle but firm. "Miss DuBois, it is time for you to leave. I suggest you depart this house and this island forever and that you do not return."

For half an instant, Audra considered it. She had Naomi's jewelry, plenty of money, and a stash of convincing fake IDs; she could leave this godforsaken island and make a new life, an ordinary life, for herself and never have to see this place again.

But I'm not ordinary, she told herself fiercely. *I won't be cowed or sent away or dismissed. Especially since I haven't accomplished what I came here for.*

First, Willow Stone would die. And then Audra would crawl over her body and claim for herself everything Geralt Talbot had owned.

Patricia's gun might be useless to her now, but it wasn't like she'd come unprepared. She pulled her large folding knife from her pocket and opened it, enjoying the heft of the handle, and smiled at Willow. "Once you're dead, we're still back to me as heir. And even if I would have considered leaving this place standing"—she turned her gaze to the ghosts all around her, her lip curling in contempt—"now that I've met you, I have to say I have no interest in protecting your precious homestead."

At that, the ghosts shifted, murmuring to one another, and stepped in a little closer. Audra tried not to shiver. She wasn't afraid of them, she told herself.

She looked back at Joel; he was whispering into Willow's ear. A burst of fury went through her. "What?" she demanded. "What are you saying to her?"

Joel and Willow ignored her.

"Are you ready?" Joel asked.

Willow nodded.

His gaze raked the room, taking in each of the ghostly inhabitants of Cameron House. Audra saw each of them meet his eyes; some stood a little taller, some nodded almost imperceptibly, and she saw on a few of their faces faint smiles of fierce anticipation.

For the first time, Audra DuBois felt a stab of real fear, felt control of the situation slipping away from her. "*What?*" she demanded, her voice rising to a shriek. "Stop it, all of you, stop it! This house is mine by right, and I deserve it, so to hell with all of you—and *especially* you, Willow Stone!"

As she shrieked the other woman's name, Audra raised her arm and lunged forward with the blade, intent on burying it in Willow's heart.

"Now," she heard Joel murmur to Willow as he stepped forward and jabbed his fountain pen into Audra's knife hand. Willow did not hesitate but turned and ran to the rear of the library. *Stupid*, Audra thought, wincing at the pain in her hand; it hurt, a lot, but the ghost creep with the fountain pen hadn't done anything but slow her down a little. And get her good and mad. *Where exactly does she think she's going to hide? I'm faster and stronger and—*

Suddenly, Audra realized she didn't know exactly where she was or what direction she was facing. A sea of faintly glowing spirits surrounded her like a thick mist full of faces; she could no longer see the fireplace or Willow or anything but the surrounding press of bodies—

Then she remembered they had no bodies.

"Get away from me!" she screamed, slashing around ineffectually with her knife.

For a fragment of a moment, they fell back; Audra heard the faint sound of a door closing—upstairs? In the corner of the library?

She realized what had happened, both now and earlier; there was a second exit from the library through a hidden door upstairs; Willow knew about it, and Audra had not. Audra's target had taken that way out, doubtless planning to run downstairs and out of the house while the ghosts held Audra up in the library. *The hell you will*, Audra thought. *You think you've beaten me, but I know where you are, and I'll get you.*

She sprinted for the foyer, past the empty umbrella stand, and up the front stairs, shouldering through the sea of people who both were and were not there.

In the library, the Cameron family exchanged glances and were gone.

Willow cracked open the hidden library door and peeked out into the second-floor hallway. No sign of Audra yet, but the young woman in the maid's uniform was there, busily dusting the stair rails with a feather duster. She saw Willow, held up her finger for her to wait, and snuck a few steps down to listen into the library; a second later, she returned, nodding furiously and gesturing Willow to hurry.

Willow hesitated at the stairway, every fiber of her being yearning to run downstairs and out of the house. Instead, she headed for the third floor, up, higher.

"It has to end," Joel had whispered into her ear. "You know that. And you know where."

She knew. She dreaded it, but she knew.

When Willow heard the first footfall on the grand staircase by the front door, she deliberately looked over the railing so Audra would see where she had gone; their plan would only work if Audra followed her. Sure enough, the other woman locked eyes with her and, with a snarl on her face, leaped up the stairs two at a time.

She's quick, Willow thought in dismay, running as fast as she could, pushing through aching knees and the tightness in her chest. The drugs from the night before were mostly worn off, but her head still hurt. Audra had gained the second-floor landing before Willow even reached the top of the third.

Willow gave an extra lunge forward to reach the top—and kept running. Down the hall, into the little parlor at the end, and through the door that kept her going up, up, farther, till there was no place left to go.

Willow stepped onto the widow's walk into the gray-cast light of a clouded dawn, with Audra seconds behind.

What was Joel thinking?

She pressed her body to the outside of the doorway, the only spot not visible to someone running up the stairs. But what then? Should she hope Audra slipped on the post-storm wet of the deck as she burst through the door? Take advantage of her disorientation to run back onto the staircase, slamming the door behind her and praying the ghosts could lock it long enough for her to get out, find a phone, and call Nick?

Or did they expect her to push Audra off the roof the way Audra had Sue?

Even if she were physically capable, Willow didn't think she could bring herself to do that. Besides, if Audra got hands on her, she knew she didn't have a chance. *I'm a doughy grad student,* she thought, *and she is a go-for-a-run-and-do-actual-workouts kind of woman; she'll kick my butt . . .*

Willow had only one advantage, and it was meager at best. She had seen Audra in the library, and hers were no longer the eyes of the dispassionate predator of a couple of hours ago. Patricia had been the planner, the calculator. Without her, Audra was rudderless. Then she had been forced to face down a roomful of dead people, feel the pressure and the weight of almost-heard voices closing around her. She had come face-to-face with the impossible; it suffused the very air around her, and she had no choice but to inhale it, to take it in.

Willow still had her wits about her, but Audra, Willow suspected, was beginning to lose hers.

Audra burst through the doorway onto the widow's walk, her feet sliding a little on the wet boards, windmilling her arms to stay upright. Willow lunged at her, hands outstretched, hoping to knock her down long enough to escape through the door back downstairs, but Audra was too fast. She wheeled her arm around as she fell, grabbing a handful of Willow's hair and pulling her down with her; Willow yelped as the knife sliced through Sue's coat into her shoulder. Within seconds, Audra was on top, pinning Willow down to the deck, holding her wrists with one hand while the other brought the knife up for its fatal blow.

See? Willow thought inappropriately. *I knew this was a terrible idea.* The knife began its inexorable journey down toward her chest . . .

It never made it. A long and solid object swung in an arc into

Audra's forearm with a sickening thud, sending the knife skittering across the widow's walk, out of reach. Willow heard Dot's—or was it Dellie's?—voice in her memory: *We can only touch things that existed when we were alive . . . and we each have our own little talismans . . .*

As it swept by, Willow caught a glimpse of the long wooden stick with its faceted glass handle and understood what it meant.

Geralt Talbot was back.

CHAPTER FORTY-FIVE

Willow lurched upward and threw off her attacker, clawing her way back toward the stairs. She stopped when she saw Geralt Talbot standing in the doorway, tall and craggy and looking every bit as irritated as he always had in life. He peered down his hawk nose at her, shook his head, and said, "See, Sue's girl, this is why I never wanted children. They are invariably a disappointment." He glared down at Audra, who was lying on her back, looking up at him in shock. "And you—you are more of a disappointment than most."

Though he had on the sweater and dreadful plaid pants he'd worn on the day she met him, and he still held his now-unbroken glass-topped cane, this was a version of Geralt that Willow had not seen before. Gone was the frail curmudgeon who had barked ineffectually at everyone around him. Geralt's hair and eyebrows were still white and wild, his face still carved with the deep lines of years, but this man stood straight and tall and strong; this was the version of Geralt Talbot who had taken over companies, reigned as CEO over multimillion-dollar businesses, and cemented his dominance by crushing even the smallest insurgency.

By the look in his eye as he scowled down at Audra, he would not tolerate insurgency here either.

Audra pulled herself to her feet, her face twisting with rage. "You! You disgusting—horrible—evil—" She lunged at the old man, but he stepped easily out of her path, while Willow inched as far away from the pair as she could, trying to avoid Audra's notice.

She need not have worried; Audra only had eyes for the old man, the father who had abandoned her, the reason for all her troubles. She lunged for him again; again, he stepped aside.

Audra was panting now, terror and hatred warring in her. "I killed you!" she spat. "I killed you once, I'll keep doing it over and over if I have to. I promise I'll never stop. You ruined my life; you ruined my mother's life. You destroy everything you've ever touched—"

"For God's sake, don't be so dramatic." He sneered back at her. "You killed me because you wanted my money. You killed my wife because you hated that someone might get even a little of what you thought you were entitled to." His eyes narrowed as he moved to the railing directly opposite and stood facing her. "Your mother was one of the worst mistakes I ever made in my life, and I have made many. Thanks to you, I will not have the opportunity to make another. But know this: You will never take ownership of this property or anything of mine." He smiled at her, the smile of a crocodile watching its prey through the reeds. "The choice is yours. You can walk downstairs, walk out the door, climb over the body of your easily deceived lover, and accept the consequences for what you have done. Or—"

Audra did not let him finish. The growl started deep in her throat and escalated to a scream; she lunged wildly across the platform to where the old man stood.

Willow rose sluggishly and moved forward, trying to stop her, but the enraged woman's leap was too committed. Geralt was suddenly not there; now Audra could see the broken rail his spectral body had concealed, the boards Audra had broken to stage Sue Davis's death. Terror bloomed through the rage; Audra tried to shift her balance before she went over, to grab for something solid. For a moment, Willow thought she might succeed.

Just as Audra looked as though she might be about to right herself, Geralt swept his cane around and caught her by the ankles, jerking them out from under her and propelling her over the edge. Willow crawled forward in a vain attempt to stop her from going over, but Audra had disappeared from view.

As Willow watched, a hand came up and grasped the railing; the other released its hold on the roof edge to swing around and grasp one of the spindles.

A police siren sounded from the causeway bridge, getting closer.

Willow, spent and dizzy, crawled her way to the edge. Inches below her, Audra dangled, struggling to pull herself up, feet kicking for purchase on the steep roof.

"Oh, for God's sake, Sue's girl," came Geralt's voice from behind her. "Leave her be; you know she'll try to kill you again if you drag her back up here."

Willow looked over the edge to where Audra hung. "Help me—please—" Audra's eyes were bleak and pleading.

This is a terrible idea, Willow thought. *I seem to be full of them lately.*

She reached down. "Give me your hand!" she called out.

Audra swung her arm around and grasped Willow's outstretched hand; Willow braced herself against the railing so Audra could pull herself up.

For a moment, it seemed everything would be all right, that an exhausted Audra would safely make it back up to the widow's walk, that the police would arrive and take her into custody . . .

But as she dragged her knee over the edge and back onto the decking, Audra saw Geralt, standing there with his smirk and his scorn. The fury and hatred returned to her face.

In a single move, Audra threw herself at Willow, grasping

Willow's arm with both of hers. Willow had but a split second to understand what was happening; then Audra launched herself backward off the platform, intent on pulling them both down.

The force of Audra's lunge propelled an unstable Willow over the edge of the widow's walk; only the crook of her elbow around an ancient piece of railing prevented them both from sliding off the roof and to the rocky ground far below. Willow struggled to free her arm from Audra's grip, but the other woman held on like a vise, her body a deadweight pulling them both down, her eyes shining with dark glee.

The police cruiser pulled up below; dimly, Willow saw Nick leap out of the driver's seat, while Rina and Finn jumped out the other side. Her arm was beginning to slip; worse, she could feel the wood of the railing beginning to give way beneath her unstable grip . . .

A piercing *Caw!* sounded from above; a large crow dive-bombed Audra, beating around her head and shoulders with its wings. Audra instinctively tried to bat it away, her grip loosening enough for Willow to wrench her arm free.

Willow's world went into slow motion, the next few seconds feeling somehow inevitable and eternal all at once. Audra slid backward down the steep pitch of the roof; she vainly scrabbled for purchase on the uneven surface, but she was moving too fast. Her shout of fury devolved into a wail and then a terrified scream as she slid over the edge and out of view.

Audra's scream below blended with the creak of too-old wood as the railing Willow clung to began to give way; she whipped her head around to see the wooden spindle bend and then shatter beneath the weight of her crooked elbow, and she felt herself begin to fall. In a last attempt to save her life, she swung her other arm up—

It closed around a smooth stick of wood with a rounded ball of glass at one end.

With a single powerful yank, Geralt used the cane to pull Willow back onto the widow's walk, where she collapsed, panting.

There was shouting far below and the sound of a barking dog.

Geralt folded his arms and scowled down at her. "I told you. Didn't I tell you? Idiot."

Willow nodded. "You did. But I had to try." She looked down the roof to the place where Audra had disappeared from view, glad she couldn't see the broken body on the ground below. "It's just that she—we started in the same place, you know? If I'd had the kind of life she did, who knows who I'd have turned out to be? I had Sue; I had this place. She had nothing . . ."

Geralt rolled his eyes. "Great, so she had a rotten childhood." He glared at Willow. "That's not what made her a killer."

Willow smiled weakly, pulling herself to a sitting position. "Well, maybe. I guess."

"And a pathological liar. And a homicidal maniac."

"Oh, shut up," Willow said half-heartedly.

Geralt crouched beside her, for a moment looking almost kind. "You'll be all right, Sue's girl."

"Willow!" Rina's voice called from the ground. "Willow, please, are you all right?"

Willow looked down at her and waved weakly. "I'm okay, Aunt Rina. I'm okay."

When she turned her head back, Geralt was gone.

CHAPTER FORTY-SIX

Three days later, Willow slipped Sue's old key in the Cameron House front lock—Willow's key now—and turned it easily. She stepped inside. The entry hall shone in the early-morning sunshine, and the stained glass sent bright specks of colored light dancing through the room.

A crow flapped its way down the stairs and out the front door; Willow ducked, but the movement brought a twinge to her bandaged shoulder.

"Master Thomas, if I've told ye once, I've told ye a hundred times—that creature does nae belong in the house, and if I see it again, I'll be tellin' yer mam, and she'll have sommat to say—Oh, good mornin', miss." From the second-floor landing, the maid in her black dress and starched white apron broke off her scolding and smiled down at Willow. "Ye look a fair sight better than ye did a few days ago."

"Sorry, Peggy!" the boy said, scampering down the front stairs past the exasperated maid and out the door. His face brightened when he saw Willow. "Going out now—Oh, and hi, Miss Willow!" he called back before disappearing off into the lupine field after the crow. The good-humored Peggy shook her head indulgently, and then she was gone as well.

In the three days since her showdown with Audra DuBois on the widow's walk, Willow had done little more than sleep and binge-watch detective shows. Rina had brought enough lasagna and red sauce to keep both her and Finn fed for weeks, Joe and Frank stopped by with fresh bread from their bakery, and Mac and Diana were keeping her stocked with pastries (even if Mac ate half of them).

Her memory of what had happened after Audra fell from the roof walk was hazy. She had made her way back downstairs somehow. Sometimes in her memory, the tall lobsterman had been beside her, supporting her; in other foggy moments, she thought it had been Nick's arm helping her down the four flights to the bottom.

An ambulance had arrived as well, and the pair of EMTs worked frantically over Patricia before transferring her to a stretcher and driving away. There had been statements to the police, the same story over and over like on the day Geralt had collapsed. Rina sat beside her the whole time, holding her hand.

Effie sat on Willow's other side, though no one else could see her. Willow had no idea what to say to the police, but Joel, sitting on the porch swing a few feet away, helped her abridge the truth into a believable and ghost-free version of events until the police were satisfied.

Willow remembered retrieving the photos and birth certificates from Sue's desk and showing them to Nick and Rina, who were as shocked as she had been. She remembered the island's EMTs checking her and urgent care on Great North treating the gash in her shoulder. The doctors had assured her that her wound, thanks to Sue's coat, had been shallow enough to avoid permanent damage to her muscles but would hurt like crazy for a while. She should rest, drink lots of fluids, and not lift anything heavier than two pounds for the next couple of weeks.

But this morning, Willow had awakened feeling almost herself again. She'd showered, dressed, and walked—as fast as her recovering body would allow—back to the big old house that had changed her life: first by almost ending it and then by saving it. There was one big question still unanswered, and one Cameron who had remained scarce over the past few days.

Willow climbed the staircase to the second floor, moving slowly and nursing her lingering aches and bruises. The last time she had looked here, she had been sure she had found the lever that should have opened the hidden hallway, but it had not worked. Her suspicion that Annabel simply hadn't wanted her there that day was borne out when today it opened easily, revealing the passage to the little garret bedroom.

She made her way to the sunny chamber and sat down at the heavy secretary desk.

Sue's desk had been full of secrets, and those secrets had changed Willow's life. Now she wanted a look at Annabel's.

"Okay, Annabel," she said. "Anything else you can show me?" She began her search.

The lever was tucked under the desk; when she found it and shifted it, a whole section flipped and clicked into place, revealing a heavy manual typewriter.

There was a single sheet of paper in it with three typed lines of text:

```
at last words of truth are drawn from the
depths of the heart and the mask torn off
reality remains --Lucretius
```

And then, a little farther down the page:

```
took you long enough
```

Willow grinned. Of course. Who else could it have been? "So, there you are. Nice to meet you, Abel R. Douglas. Novelist and note writer." Then her eye was caught by something tucked beside the typewriter.

A bundle of yellowing envelopes, tied with a string of faded green yarn.

A few hours later, Catherine and Willow sat together at a sunny front table in the village library. Catherine untied the yarn and gazed down at the pile of letters. She looked up at Willow, who nodded.

"These were Annabel's? From her son?" Catherine asked in a hushed voice.

Willow nodded.

"And she wrote the novels? All of them?"

Willow nodded again.

Catherine opened one of the letters and skimmed it, then another. "I figured. I suspected Annabel had to be our mysterious author as soon as you told me about the books hidden in her chest."

Willow looked surprised. "What about them?"

"She had books by both Brontë sisters, Louisa May Alcott, and George Eliot in there?" Catherine gently laid down the first two letters and retrieved a third.

Willow nodded. "Yes, and one other I can't quite remember, something with a phantom."

"I'd bet it was *A Phantom Lover* by Vernon Lee." A satisfied smile spread across Catherine's face. "A veritable who's who of women writers who first published under male pseudonyms."

Willow blinked, and then burst out laughing. "I didn't even think of that, but it seems very like her."

Catherine nodded, still reading the letters. "These are . . . beautiful. And so sad."

"I found them in Annabel's desk with her typewriter, in a concealed compartment—not even very concealed; I just didn't know to look for it. They're Douglas's letters from the front, the ones he wrote while he was at war."

Catherine looked up, her eyes shining. "Like the novel," she said, a little breathless.

"Except for this one." Willow extricated the final envelope from the bottom of the pile, pulled out a letter, and handed it to Catherine.

Catherine scanned the letter. "It's from her. From his wife. The nurse." She looked back up at Willow in wonder. "It's real. The story." She ran her finger over the stack of letters. "You've read these? It happened in life the way it did in the book?"

"It's real," Willow said. "Douglas *did* get married to an army nurse he met overseas, and the hospital *was* destroyed within a few days of his departure."

"The baby," Catherine murmured. "It was a girl." Then she scanned down to the signature at the bottom of the page. "The mother signs her name as Annemarie. No last name." She looked up at Willow. "Do we have any idea where she settled?"

Willow shook her head. "No return address. She could be anywhere."

"She could be anywhere," Catherine echoed, then lifted her chin defiantly. "But we'll find her. Somehow."

"Find who?" Neither woman had heard Nick enter the library; they turned in surprise at the sound of his voice.

"The mysterious unidentified widow of Douglas Ramsey, Annabel Cameron's son, who was killed in the Second World War," Willow said.

Nick's face brightened. "Nice. You were able to find information on her?"

"Of course," Willow said dryly. "We have a first name. Which may or may not be her real name. And that she gave birth to a daughter."

Nick blinked. "And? That's it?"

"That's it." Willow winked at Catherine. "But given our

librarian's research superpowers, I doubt it will slow her down for long."

Catherine frowned. "It's not much to go on."

"No, it isn't," Nick agreed, "but if anyone can pull it off, I suspect it's you."

Willow swiveled her chair around to face him. "So what brings you off the mainland on a workday?"

He grinned. "I had been thinking, given we finally have a nice day, and you two were a huge amount of help in solving this whole mess—"

"Even if I nearly got killed in the process," Willow put in.

"Which you wouldn't have if you'd listened to me and stayed at the inn—we were working it out and would have gotten there." He grabbed a chair, swung his leg around, and sat down on it backward. "Turned out, that bottle you picked up was the clincher piece of evidence, after all. And then the background check told us Audra wasn't who she said she was, but by the time it came through, we had no idea where to look for her. Then Finn woke Rina, and she realized you'd sneaked out at some point, and we didn't know where *you* were either." He pinned her with a good-natured—mostly good-natured—glare. "It was a given that if something was up, you were probably in the middle of it. If Mrs. Ramsey hadn't managed to make an emergency call, sort of miraculous given her condition, who knows what might have—" He stopped and rolled his eyes. "God, woman, you can turn anything into an argument."

Willow held up her hands in mock helplessness. "Who's arguing? I didn't say anything." She paused. "How is Patricia doing?" she asked hesitantly.

"Alive," he said. "Pretty messed up; she's got a lot of surgeries and rehab ahead of her before she can even stand trial." He shrugged. "She admitted to everything—it was like she wanted to get it off her chest in case she didn't make it. She won't be a free member of society anytime soon."

Willow was silent. Patricia had stood up to Audra, had made the call that got Nick out to the house—but she had also killed Effie and been a party to all the recent murders on the island . . . including Sue's.

Nick got up and righted the chair. "But I'm not here to talk about her. I'm inviting the two of you to lunch. At the Dockside. On me. Diana and Mac are already there, and Rina's coming." He grinned. "Best lobster rolls on this or any island. What do you say?"

Willow nodded emphatically. "You're on."

CHAPTER FORTY-SEVEN

As the trio walked along the coastal path toward the village, Nick asked Willow, "So now that you're the heir to everything Cameron around here, are you going to live in the house, do you think?"

Willow looked almost wistfully up at the massive house, then back at Nick. "I'm not sure I want to. It's too big, too"—she shared a quick glance with Catherine—"haunted to live in." She looked around her, bright greens and blues of the ocean, the murmur of the wind in the trees and the soft roar of the sea beneath, breathed in the salt and pine, and smiled. "But I'll stay on in the cabin for a while. I still have to finish my dissertation, and I can do it here as easily as anywhere else. Our fantastic local librarian can get me books"—she flashed Catherine a quick smile—"and most of what I need I can find on the internet, anyway."

Willow looked across the green toward the row of boulders where she had eaten Diana's tres leches cake after Sue's memorial. She said, "Hey, guys—I'm a little more winded than I thought; I'm going to hang out for a sec, but I'll be there in a few minutes, okay?"

The other two paused. "You sure? We can wait with you," Catherine said.

She shook her head. "No, I'm fine, go ahead. Order me a lobster roll. I'll only be a sec."

Nick shrugged. "Suit yourself. See you in a bit."

As the two walked off toward the dock, Willow eased herself down on the large rock. Nearby sat the dark-haired teenaged girl Willow had seen there on the day of Sue's memorial reception, reading a book. No phone, no earbuds, just a book.

That should have been Willow's first clue.

"Hi," Willow said softly.

The girl looked up in surprise. Without the sullen glare and goth makeup she'd had in the Boston photos, Willow might have recognized her sooner and put it together, but she knew her now. "Hi," the girl said back.

Willow suddenly had no idea what to say. She cleared her throat and asked, "What are you reading?"

The girl held the book up. It was *Weather the Storm*, the same paperback that had sat untouched on Willow's nightstand in the cabin since she arrived. Abel R. Douglas's last novel.

"What's it about?" Willow asked cautiously.

The girl looked vague. "It's about a woman who travels the world with her daughter. Even though they love each other, they don't get along, but they keep on going."

Willow went very still.

Take down this book and slowly read, and dream, Annabel had typed for Willow, and left the note atop a pile of her own novels, including this one. And Willow had missed it completely. She, along with Patricia and Audra, had focused their attention on the wrong book.

Willow asked gently, "What about your mother? Do you get along with her?"

The girl looked down at the book in her lap, and Willow thought she might not answer. But she said, "Not really. I mean, we should have, but I was sort of awful. Now I just miss her."

Me too, Willow thought. *So much.*

The girl went on, "We used to come here sometimes in the summers. I thought she might come back here, so I guess I'm . . . waiting for her." Her expression went vague again.

Willow's hand trembled, but she reached out and took the girl's hand. At first, nothing happened, as though it was not there; then she felt the young fingers close around hers. Willow swallowed hard. "I guess I'm waiting for her too."

The girl nodded; then she turned to Willow as though seeing her for the first time. Which, in a way, she was. "Do I know you? I feel like I should know you."

Willow nodded, a hard lump rising in her throat. "I think so. It's been a long time, though."

"I guess it has." The girl's face clouded. "Everything seems like a long time ago."

They sat in comfortable silence for a minute, listening to the dance of the sea. At last, Willow said, "She loved you incredibly, you know. All her life, it was there on her face. She would have done anything for you." Her voice shook a little. "And your baby. Anything."

The girl's sad eyes shifted to Willow, holding doubt at first, then the dawning of hope. Then she glimpsed someone behind Willow, and her face went incandescent with joy. "Mom?" she asked, her voice quivering.

Willow swiveled on her boulder; she knew who it would be, but her heart leaped, anyway.

"Hi, Robin." Sue sat cross-legged on the ground, the way she often had when Willow was young, oblivious to bugs or grass stains. She wore a stretched-out blue sweater and a green sun hat over her shaggy gray hair, her luminous smile turned on her daughter. Sue stood up, brushed pine needles off the rear of her jeans, and turned that smile to Willow. "Hi, Willow."

After a breath-held moment of stillness, Robin launched herself from the boulder and flung herself into Sue's arms, holding tight. Sue, ever tall and strong, lifted her off the ground and whirled her around before setting her down again.

Sue gave Robin's hand a squeeze, then released it. She walked with open arms to Willow, who stood to meet her; if Willow closed her eyes, she could feel Sue's arms around her, slim and angular and familiar. She pulled back, tears running down her face, and faced the woman she had not known was her grandmother.

Sue smiled, her face full of love and pride. "I'm sorry, my dear Willow, you amazing girl. Woman," she amended. "So much stronger and braver than I ever was. I should have told you long ago. I thought I would have time . . ." She trailed off. "But you came back. You came back, and I could see you, see you struggling and in danger, but I couldn't break through . . ."

"It's okay," Willow reassured her. "You're here now." She did not tell Sue, any more than she had told Nick and Catherine, about her brief visit to the Cameron House graveyard yesterday at dawn; that would be her secret. Even Rina, who had gone with her, hadn't understood, not really. To Rina, it had been a loving ritual of closure, as together they buried the little box containing the simple gold ring Rina would have given Sue on their wedding day. Rina had not noticed as Willow slipped a single gray hair, retrieved from the lining of Sue's old green coat, into the little hole in the earth with the ring. Rina and Willow had hugged and cried and, after refilling the hole with dirt, had walked back to the inn together, leaving a little piece of Sue—literally—behind in the Cameron family resting place.

Rina had not seen the dozen or so Camerons who walked with them, but Willow had.

As though she sensed the direction of Willow's thoughts, Sue asked softly, "And Rina? How is she holding up?"

"She's . . . holding up," Willow said. "I mean, she's grieving, like, a lot, but . . ." She thought a moment. "She's carrying you with her, you know? All the way. Like she can feel you here with her even though she can't see you."

Sue smiled. "That's not because I'm still here; that's just . . . love." She looked toward the dock, and Willow turned to follow her gaze. Rina was stepping out of the Pottery Shop, heading down to the Dockside, where the remainder of her Little North family waited. Before stepping into the restaurant, Rina paused and looked out at the bay; the wind caught her hair as she lifted her face to the sky. For an instant, Willow saw Rina as though through Sue's eyes: glowing with life and strength, passionate and powerful, as beautiful as the island that was her home.

Willow turned back to Sue, who nodded. "Rina will heal," Sue said softly. Then her eyes shifted from Willow's toward the rocky beach beside the dock. "Is that . . . ? Willow, who is that?" she asked in a low voice.

A tall man in a gray pin-striped suit and fedora, handsome as any film star, stood on the shore beside a simple dinghy; behind him, a few yards out into the water, a gleaming single-masted sailboat waited. Peter Talbot looked, for the first time since Willow had encountered him, happy.

"That's Peter," Willow said. Then, haltingly: "Your father."

Sue was already walking toward the man in the boat, her steps slow and dreamlike. Willow and Robin remained where they were, watching as father and daughter met one another and embraced.

From the ocean path, a dog barked; Finn had, of course, gotten out of the cabin and decided to join the lunch party, perhaps realizing his former human had stopped by the village. He launched himself across the green, a short-legged fuzzy blur, and headed straight for Sue. She crouched down to greet him; from across the green, Willow heard her say, "Hey, Finn—good boy. You take care of my Willow now, okay?" He barked in response. Finn trotted obligingly toward Willow, though not without looking back over his shoulder several times.

With one more brilliant smile for Willow, Robin turned and ran to Peter and Sue as well. Peter Talbot gallantly helped his daughter and granddaughter into the dinghy. He gave Willow a little bow and tipped his hat to her, then pushed the dinghy off the shore and rowed away.

Finn bounded around Willow, pawing at her legs and whining, till she crouched down and let him frantically attempt to lick her running nose and tearstained face and any part of her he could reach. *You left me home*, he seemed to say, *but I was able to correct your error and come out to see how you're doing. Plus lobster rolls.*

Willow gave the dog a watery grin—it was hard to stay sad under this onslaught of energy. "Okay, fur face. Lobster rolls. Best on this or any island."

Willow wasn't sure exactly when the three spirits faded from view; when she looked up again, she and Finn were alone on the point.

She turned and looked back at Cameron House. A woman stood on the widow's walk, long white hair blowing in the wind. She raised a hand to Willow and waved enthusiastically.

Willow waved back.

She and Finn turned and made for the dock. Nick was standing in the doorway to the restaurant, watching for her. "Got us a table on the patio," he said. He looked again. "Hey, you okay, Stone?"

She nodded. "I'm fine."

His eyes were kind, and he didn't press. "Then hurry up and get in here. You gonna make us wait all day?"

She elbowed him in the ribs. "It's not like the lobsters are going to swim away, you know. Have a little restraint. People might think you come from Texas or something."

"Be nice to me, or I'll give Mac your fries."

Bickering good-naturedly, they took their seats with the others—Rina, Catherine, Diana, and Mac—on the deck of the restaurant. Willow gazed out at the water, feeling relaxed and at home for the first time in more than fifteen years.

Out in the bay, a familiar lobstering dory sailed by. Its captain gave her an approving nod.

ACKNOWLEDGMENTS

***Murder Will Out* would not have been possible without the** support of many individuals—starting with those involved in the Minotaur Books/Mystery Writers of America First Crime Novel Award, whose confidence in my novel set it, and me, on this journey. Thank you for this amazing opportunity; I will never take it lightly.

Two people in particular have walked with me through every step of the road to publication: My agent, Alice Speilburg, has been a font of strength and wisdom, and I look forward to many more years (and books!) together. Deep thanks also go to Madeline Houpt, my editor—the book owes *so* much to Maddie's impeccable taste and eye for what makes a mystery work. Between them, Alice and Maddie have been incredibly patient with this newbie author, teaching me what I needed to know and weathering my various existential crises: I'm grateful to both for their expertise, and for their faith in this book and in me as an author.

My thanks also go to the rest of the team at Minotaur who worked on *Murder Will Out*: designers David Rotstein and Meryl Levavi; editorial and production staff Alisa Trager, Ken Silver, and

Cathy Turiano; publicity and marketing team Kayla Janas, Ana Couto, Maria Snelling, and Drew Kilman; the copyediting team at ScriptAcuity; and of course Kelley Ragland and Catherine Richards for putting their—and Minotaur's—trust behind this little fictional corner of Downeast Maine.

Please assume any factual errors in the book are my fault—but everything I got right comes from a support system of wonderful folks who know their stuff. My mother, Christine Breedlove, retired chemistry professor and ceramic artist, came up with the core idea of trying to murder someone with pottery supplies; she has advised me extensively on ceramics, poisons, and Downeast Maine island life. My father C. H. Breedlove's stories and writings for the Somesville Historical Society and Friends of Acadia were also invaluable to shaping the novel. My former student Dinah Arafeh drew on her knowledge as an EMT to help me realistically describe the painful bodily harm I've inflicted on my characters, and Southwest Harbor Police Chief John Hall and department dispatcher Megan Kelley—along with Chief Hall's dog Telos—were kind enough to sit down with me on a random weekday morning to talk about their work on the quiet side of Mount Desert Island.

I am blessed to be part of not one but two writer groups, and this book would have fizzled before the first draft without them. In November of 2020, editor Anne Hawley of Pages and Platforms (with the remarkable Sue Campbell and Rachelle Ramirez) began a daily Zoom writing sprint; it was intended to run only a month, but those of us who remained to the end were enjoying it so much that Anne extended it. That group is still meeting every day, nearly five years later. Anne, Drew, Kim, Don, Irene, Linnie, Pamela, Nancye, Virlana, Emmanuella, Sara, Catherine, Alexandra, and Stephanie—your steadfast presence kept me going even when I felt wrung out and without any words left. May the muse keep our writing fresh and our butts in the chair!

Out of Anne's larger group, a smaller subgroup formed: Oona, Carolyn, Janet, Rivkah, and I gather twice a month to read and guide each other's work on questions of structure and narrative; we have become not just colleagues but trusted friends, turning to each other for strength through some of life's awful moments and rejoicing in one another's victories. The fingerprints of these extraordinary authors are all over *Murder Will Out*, and they were the first to read and help shape it; I cannot *wait* to read their books.

The Sisters in Crime organization, and my Chicago chapter siblings, have been a great source of mentorship and growth; writing can be a lonely endeavor, and it is a joy to know that we are not on our own. And Claire, Jenny, Kate, my first "real author" friends, you stomped through the snow before me and tamped down a path to the possible, whether you knew I was following you or not.

Finally, I am beyond grateful for the support of my family: My husband, Allen, my son, Josh, and my daughter, Analise (my toughest editor and a wonderful writer in their own right), have been unwavering in their belief in me, never doubting me or humoring my cycling certainties that I wouldn't be able to pull this off. No thanks will ever be enough.

ABOUT THE AUTHOR

Allen Budziak

Jennifer K. Breedlove is a Chicago-area composer, conductor, author, editor, and educator. A frequent visitor to Downeast Maine since childhood, she has an enduring affection for the wild beauty of the coastal islands and the warmth of the people who make their homes there. Her debut novel, *Murder Will Out,* won the Minotaur Books/Mystery Writers of America First Crime Novel Award, and was also a finalist for the Killer Nashville Claymore Award.